BROKEN PROMISES

Jerval de Vernon had promised Chandra when they were wed that he would respect her virginity until she herself asked him to possess her.

Never, she vowed, would that ever happen.

But never was a long, long time. And now as Chandra sat on the edge of their bed, her legs locked tightly together, she stared at her husband as he swept off his clothes.

"I will not hurt you," he promised, and then stretched out his full length against her, his hands sweeping over her body, fondling her until she was languid and easy in his arms. And when he bent down to capture her mouth, Chandra parted her lips and felt a stunning shock of desire. Suddenly she was returning his demanding kisses with an ardor that matched his.

So this is what passion is, Chandra thought. . . .

CHANDRA

Great Reading from SIGNET

CHANDRA
CATHERINE COULTER

A SIGNET BOOK
NEW AMERICAN LIBRARY

NAL BOOKS ARE AVAILABLE AT QUANTITY DISCOUNTS WHEN USED
TO PROMOTE PRODUCTS OR SERVICES. FOR INFORMATION PLEASE
WRITE TO PREMIUM MARKETING DIVISION, THE NEW AMERICAN
LIBRARY, INC., 1633 BROADWAY, NEW YORK, NEW YORK 10019.

SIGNET TRADEMARK REG. U.S. PAT. OFF. AND FOREIGN COUNTRIES
REGISTERED TRADEMARK—MARCA REGISTRADA
HECHO EN CHICAGO, U.S.A.

SIGNET, SIGNET CLASSIC, MENTOR, PLUME, MERIDIAN AND NAL BOOKS
are published by The New American Library, Inc.,
1633 Broadway, New York, New York 10019

First Printing, January, 1984

1 2 3 4 5 6 7 8 9

PRINTED IN THE UNITED STATES OF AMERICA

TO HENRIK

AUTHOR'S NOTE

Eleanor became the first English queen to be crowned with her husband shortly after she and Prince Edward returned from the Holy Land. The legend of Eleanor sucking the poison from Edward's wound was first told by Ptolemy of Lucca a century later, and has been debated since.

The treaty Edward achieved in 1272 at Caesarea guaranteed the Kingdom of Jerusalem and its possessions for a period of ten years, ten months, ten days, and ten minutes. Acre was taken by the Saracens in 1291, and the remaining Frankish cities soon shared its fate.

I have taken the liberty of shortening the time the English spent in the Holy Land, and ordering the events of the Eighth Crusade for dramatic effect, for which I beg pardon.

Castle Croyland, Cheshire

Marvel not, lady, if I take
Such joy in you, but give me leave
To love you. . . .

—Bernard de Ventadorn, *Canso*

1

"GOD'S BONES, AVERY! WHAT HAVE you got there—more swine for my dinner?"

Lord Richard de Avenell tossed the remains of a roasted pork rib over his shoulder to his favorite boarhound, Graynard, and rose from his great carved chair. There was a sudden silence in the great hall.

"My lord," Avery said, striding forward, "we found this whoreson skulking about the exercise field."

"Bring him to me," Lord Richard boomed, stepping down from the dais.

One of Lord Richard's squires, Ponce, dragged a slight, cowering man forward and sent him sprawling to the rushes on his stomach at Lord Richard's feet. His coarse tunic was shredded across his back and matted by his blood to welts raised by a thonged whip.

"He is Welsh, my lord, and a spy." A wide grin split Avery's mouth. "He had nothing to say to me. Kept whining about seeing the master of Croyland."

Lord Richard nudged the toe of his leather boot against the man's ribs. "Stand up, fellow, and look well."

The man struggled to his feet and stood trembling. He raised a soiled hand and pushed disheveled black hair back from his eyes.

"I am innocent, my lord," the man muttered finally, his thin voice thick with the Welsh tongue. "I was but journeying to see my sister in Wales."

"Lying bastard!" Avery shouted.

Chandra rose gracefully from her chair, ignoring her mother's white face, and stepped quietly to her father's side. She said in a thoughtful voice, "He does not appear to be much of a spy, to be caught so easily."

Lord Richard frowned a moment at her words. "We will

11

know soon enough, daughter." He looked toward Avery and said in a soft, bland voice, "A Welsh spy who lies to me has no need of two hands. Bring me my axe, Ponce."

The man let out a high wailing cry and fell to his knees before Lord Richard, his fingers clutching at the hem of his robe.

"It is not cowardice, but the truth that will save your hands, man."

The man raised his face toward them, his dark eyes wide with terror. "I will tell you, my lord," he whimpered. "I will tell you the truth, I swear!"

Lord Richard turned away from him and eased his large frame back into his chair. "If you lie, you will lose more than your hands."

"Cadwallon forced me to come to Croyland. He rides even now with his men to the west. If he does not hear from me, he will know that you are here at Croyland, and no threat to him. He fears you, my lord."

Chandra felt gooseflesh rise on her arms. Cadwallon. He was an old man now, but only last year he had showed he could still ride from his Welsh castle in the Brecon mountains into England to devastate the village of Sudeford, and a marcher baron's keep. Lord Richard rose suddenly from his chair and gazed from his great height upon the groveling Welshman, his lips curled in anger.

Chandra found herself frowning as ready answers to Lord Richard's questions passed eagerly from the man's mouth. It somehow seemed incongruous that such a pitiful scrap would know the plans of the great Cadwallon. She wondered if her father shared her doubts when he suddenly strode toward Avery, his voice taut with anticipation. "We will ride at dawn, and surprise Cadwallon and his Welsh pigs at Rydnor's Pass. He will have no chance to escape us. Prepare the men for battle."

A great roar of approval filled the hall, and the rhythmic hammering of knife butts on the wooden tables echoed from the smoke-blackened beams. Avery's eyes held the memory of his younger brother slain on his freehold farm but the year before, and then the fierce gleam of bloodlust.

"The traitor, my lord?" Ponce asked, his young, beardless face alight with excitement.

"Throw the oaf into the dungeon." Lord Richard turned to

Chandra. "Hold him for my return, daughter. I have a fancy to bring Cadwallon here to see what manner of fool brought him to me." He rubbed his large hands together and said almost as an afterthought, "You will protect Croyland in my absence."

Chandra remained silent, her tug of disappointment that he would not let her ride with him tempered with pride, for he had placed the safety of Croyland in her hands.

"I go with you, Father?"

Richard lowered his amber eyes to his son, slight for his ten years, and dark like his French mother. His jaw tightened at the interruption. "Nay, John. You will stay and do as your sister bids you."

John's pointed chin trembled, his lips thinned into a sullen line, but his father's eyes had long since left him.

Lord Richard threw back his lion's head and raised his wine goblet. "Drink up, men! To the blood of the filthy Welsh that will soon sweeten the soil of England!"

Chandra gazed toward the jagged hills to the west that lay melancholy under a blanket of early-morning fog. Giant oak trees poked through the thick shroud, their naked branches like mendicants' arms reaching heavenward. She drew her thick wool cloak more closely about her and rubbed the soft fur collar against her throat, smiling at her fancifulness.

She closed her eyes a moment, recalling her father, proudly tall astride his mighty destrier as he urged his men southwest along the narrow strip of land between the barren cliffs and the sea. His thoughts, she knew, were even now upon seeing the Welsh raider, Cadwallon, spitted on his huge lance like one of the strawmen from the tiltyard. Lord Richard and his men would have ridden hard all the day before, and by early tomorrow morning, they would circle Cadwallon to the east, giving the wily old robber no choice but to fight. She felt no great fear for her father, for he had the strength of a bull and was a seasoned warrior. She wished only that she were riding at his side, rather than held by his order at Croyland, passing the days until his return listening to John's shrill-voiced carping and her mother's pious prayers to the Virgin.

The chill early-morning air cut through Chandra's thick cloak, and she strode briskly along the narrow walkway atop the outer wall of Croyland to the stark, crenellated south tower. She stopped a moment to gaze toward the thick south forest. The villagers had spotted a wild boar rutting through the tangled undergrowth, and she fancied she could hear him grunting through the trees, rooting and digging for worms.

"Lady Chandra."

She looked down from the wall into the courtyard and waved her hand in greeting toward Ellis, a grizzled old soldier, one-armed now from a battle several years before with a greedy lord from the south who had thought to extend his lands. It had been Ellis who had taught her how to wield a broadsword, and how to dig her knees just so against her horse's belly to free her hands for battle.

"Aye, Ellis?"

"The sun is breaking through," he called up to her. "The men are eager, and if it pleases you, we shall mount a hunt."

Chandra's eyes sparkled. She loved to hunt. "However did you guess what was in my mind, Ellis! I was just thinking of the boar in the forest." She strode down the rough wooden stairs to the mud-clotted court below.

"Gather the men. We leave within the hour."

Chandra drew up the furred hem of her cloak to protect it from the rain puddles and made her way though the throng of people already gathered in the vast outer courtyard, their day's work begun. She paused a moment to speak to her father's master armorer, who was repairing the mail links of her hauberk, raising her voice to be heard over the squawking chickens, the moos of cows being led from the courtyard to the grassy field outside the castle walls, and the shouts of barefoot children. She walked to the stables, sidestepping the buckets of slops outside, and listened patiently as the smithy complained about how he had had his head nearly crushed two days before when he had reshod her destrier, Wicket. She splayed her hands before her in rueful apology for her destrier, assuring the smithy that she would be present to calm Wicket the next time he needed a new shoe, then turned to walk beneath the raised portcullis into the bailey, nodding to the porter, Anselm. There were fewer people in the inner bailey and the racket of the morning's activity was muted by the thick stone walls that separated it from the vast outer courtyard. She walked quickly over the cobblestones and nodded respectfully toward Father Tolbert, who stood in low conversation near the stone chapel with her mother. Chandra

had already done her morning devotions and had no wish to
be drawn into one of Father Tolbert's gentle reproaches about
piety, particularly with her mother present. She turned and
climbed the stone stairway that curved upward some fifty feet
to the great hall of the keep. She walked through the hall and
up the narrow stairs to the apartments above without interruption from the servants, who knew well that she did not like to
be bothered with household concerns.

John stopped her outside her chamber as she was fastening
her leather quiver strap over her shoulder, his voice at once
sullen and demanding. "I want to go," he announced, plant-
ing himself in front of her.

"Nay, John," she said as gently as she could manage, for
she was impatient to be gone. "You will stay here, with
Mother. I promised Father I would keep you safe."

"But Henry told me about the hunt. It's only a stupid boar,
and I'm old enough. Even Henry thinks so!" Chandra considered whether Henry, a new man, would actually say such a
thing to John, and decided that he would not do anything so
ill-judged. She found that John would not be mollified, and
he fretted and complained of ill-usage as they walked to the
bailey. A dozen men-at-arms waited there astride their horses,
and her white stallion, Wicket, danced about, tossing his
head, as a terrified stable boy tried to hold his reins.

"You are afraid that I will kill the boar for Father!" John
shouted.

"You may watch from the wall, John," she said calmly.
She mounted Wicket easily, and the stallion quieted instantly.
She knew that there was magic in her hands, at least with
him.

"Wait, just wait, sister, until I am older," she heard her
brother growl under his breath. Chandra saw some of the men
look pointedly away at John's outburst. John already strutted
among the men like a little coxcomb, trying to ape Lord
Richard. Soon, she thought, her father would have to send
John to another great lord to become a page, then a squire in
the accepted manner of things. It would doubtless improve
his character. She tried to chide herself against such thoughts,
but she was coming to realize that eventually John would
become a man. She closed her eyes a moment against a stab
of anxiety. She was only a girl, and in a few years even the
sullen John would be of more importance to Lord Richard

and Croyland. What would become of her then? She pulled
Wicket about and shouted the order to Anselm the porter to
lower the drawbridge.

Chandra flicked Wicket's reins and took her place at the
fore of her small troop. The winches had been freshly oiled,
and the drawbridge flattened itself noiselessly over the wide
ditch, swollen with early-spring rainwater. The sound of the
horses' hooves pounding over the thick wooden drawbridge
dinned in her ears, and she smiled, relishing her sense of
freedom. Her father's greyhounds and boarhounds barked
wildly behind the men, their necks straining against the thick
hemp ropes held by their keepers.

They rode slowly so as not to outdistance the houndkeepers
past the exercise field and tiltyard to the well-worn dirt road
that led southward from Croyland. They skirted the village of
Croyland, nestled at the base of a barren hill, like a small
weed in the crevice of a wall, its thatched huts nearly touching the mouth of the harbor.

When they reached the edge of the forest, she ordered the
men to spread out, then held them back until the hounds were
unleashed. Graynard led the hounds yelping wildly through
the thicket, their heads held low in search of the boar's scent.

The horsemen followed slowly, listening for the frenzied
din of barks that would lead them to the boar. Chandra smiled
when suddenly the hounds raised a great racket some two
hundred yards ahead of them. "We are lucky," she said to
Ellis. "The dogs have found him quickly."

Ellis grinned. "You say that, lady, because we are closest,
and there is a chance you yourself will bring the brute down."

Chandra smiled and motioned Ponce to stay at her right
side. They plowed deeper into the forest, spears and arrows at
ready, listening intently for the dogs' howling over the snapping of leaves and twigs beneath the horses' hooves, until
only slender shafts of sunlight, like bright silver daggers,
pierced through the thick trees.

Chandra heard a yelp of pain and spurred Wicket forward.
The boar had gored one of the hounds.

"There he is, my lady!" Ponce yelled.

"Blow the horn, Ellis. The men can cut him off if he
doesn't want to fight."

Chandra whipped her horse toward Ponce as Ellis raised
the great hunting horn to his lips and blew three sharp notes.

She drew up beside him when she saw the boar pressed like a shadow against the rough bark of an ivy-covered tree trunk, its coat matted and filthy, its small eyes vicious and filled with rage.

"He is yours, Ponce," she called softly to him. She slid quietly off Wicket's back. She could see beads of perspiration on Ponce's forehead as he dismounted. He balanced his boar spear and stiffened his arm, his muscles knotting in readiness. Chandra kept her eyes steadily on the boar, for she knew he would charge with incredible speed. She quietly drew an arrow from her quiver and slipped it into her notched bow.

The boar sniffed the air and bared his tusks. One of her father's greyhounds lay ripped open beside him, and the other hounds circled him, yelping.

Ponce felt beads of sweat roll down his forehead and sting at his eyes. He saw Chandra nod toward him, and he stepped slowly forward, shouting curses at the boar. The boar slewed his massive head about at his cries. Ignoring the baying hounds, he leaped straight toward Ponce through the thick underbrush.

Ponce felt his every muscle tense, but he held his ground, his boar spear braced straight before him. The boar lunged upward, impaling his shoulder on the spear, and threw Ponce backward. It was not a deathblow. Enraged, the boar lurched sideways, ripping the spear from Ponce's hands, and plowed it against the ground until his mighty strength splintered it. Ponce hurled himself back, clutching at a tree trunk.

Chandra stepped forward and smoothly drew back the cord of her bow until her fisted fingers touched her cheek. The boar was grunting in fury and pain, his small eyes fastened upon Ponce.

She gave a loud yell, bringing the boar's head toward her, and released the arrow. It struck the boar in the head with a dead thud, its tip buried in the beast's brain. The boar leaped upward, then dropped heavily upon its side.

"God's bones," Ponce breathed, stumbling toward her.

Chandra laughed, with relief and pleasure. "You slowed him, Ponce. Now we must keep the hounds from ripping him apart."

Ellis, who had seen the young man's spear miss its mark, resolved to have him on the practice field until his arms dropped from his shoulders. If Lady Chandra had been hurt because of one of his men's blunders, he would have offered his head to Lord Richard. He smiled toward her, his chest swelling with pride. Trust her not to let Ponce believe himself a clumsy knave.

They kicked the hounds away until their keepers came running into the small clearing to leash them. They waited for the other men to find their way, then tied the boar with thick rope to a heavy tree limb and heaved it to their shoulders to carry it back through the forest. The men's brows glistened with sweat, and their woolen cloaks were hung with fallen leaves and twigs, but they worked with good-natured laughter.

"Aye, lady," Dobbe said in his deep gruff voice, as he heartily pounded Chandra between her shoulder blades, " 'tis a fine kill you made."

Simon raised his sandy eyebrows. "You've the right of it there, Dobbe. Since she killed the bloody boar, she needn't get sweaty and bent carrying the beast back!"

"Since you were off watching the flowers grow," Chandra laughed, shaking her fist at him, "the both of you must now earn your dinner."

When they reached the rutted road to Croyland Castle, Chandra pulled the leather cap off her head and let her long, wheat-colored braid, thick as a man's forearm, fall down her back. The sun was free of the low-lying fog, and she raised her face, letting its warmth touch her face. She pictured her father's amber eyes deepening with pleasure at her gift to him. And it had been she who had killed the beast.

"By all the martyrs' bones!" Ellis whipped about, his horse dancing sideways. "Lady, look!"

Chandra followed his flailing arm, and Wicket reared back at the sudden tension on his reins. Between them and the castle, fanned out across the horizon, stood a large troop of men, several of them in full armor. At their head was a man astride a huge black stallion, his armor shining like bright silver in the sun. His surcoat was black velvet, and even from their distance, Chandra could see its richness. A scarf of black silk trailed from his helmet in the breeze.

Chandra raised her arm and shouted for her men to halt. "Who are they, Ellis?" she asked. She weighed their chance of escape back through the forest, for they were cut off from the safety of the keep. The man at their head held his destrier quiet, and the massed soldiers stood motionless behind him. "Why do they not come forward?"

Ellis' voice caught in his fury. "The man in the silver and black—it is Graelam de Moreton. See the three wolves on his banner? God, lady, Lord Richard was tricked!"

Chandra forced her eyes away from the man. Graelam de Moreton—the name was vaguely familiar to her. "If I remember aright, he is a mighty lord from Cornwall." At his nod, she understood even as she asked, "What do you mean, a trick?"

"The man we captured, he must have lied! By the fires of hell, Cadwallon and his Welsh bandits are nowhere about! Lord Richard was lured away." He whipped his horse about, his hand shooting out to grab Wicket's reins. "We must flee, lady! There is no time to lose!"

Chandra backed Wicket away and shook her head for silence. She remembered the Welshman's ready answers, answers that had nagged at her. "What could he want, Ellis? Surely he knows that he could not hold Croyland for long. My father's vassals would be gathered within the week. He would be killed and all his men with him."

Ellis frowned at himself, for what she said was true. "I will talk to him, lady. You will remain here with the men. Hide yourself—he must not see that you are a woman."

A booming voice broke the silence across the expanse of open ground. "Lady Chandra!" Graelam de Moreton's black stallion pranced forward, another man in armor at his side.

"I think, Ellis," Chandra said quietly, "that this lord knows precisely who we are. Stay here with the men." When he tried to remonstrate with her, she added sharply, "That is an order, Ellis! I'll have no one killed when there is no chance!"

Chandra loosened Wicket's reins and dug her heels into his sides. He bounded forward over a small grassy rise. She drew him up some fifty feet from Graelam de Moreton.

The deep voice boomed again. "You are Lady Chandra, daughter of Richard de Avenell?"

She held herself perfectly still. She shouted back at him, matching his commanding tone. "Aye. And you, I am told, are Graelam de Moreton. Your treachery has served you well, my lord. Why have you come to Croyland as an enemy?"

"I have come for what is mine, Chandra."

"There is nothing here for you to rightfully claim. Return to whence you came, Graelam de Moreton, and there will be no battle between us."

She heard an ill-muted laugh from the stocky man beside him. The man yelled toward her in a mocking voice, "Brave words from a girl who plays at being a man! Battle, lady, with twelve ragtag men at your back?"

She felt anger knot in her belly. Her fingers touched the steel sheath of her sword, strapped to her waist beneath her woolen cloak. She saw Lord Graelam turn to the man beside him and speak in a low, fierce whisper. She could not hear his words, but the man shrugged and drew his horse some feet back.

"Can you not speak for yourself, Graelam de Moreton? Must your coarse bully hurl your insults?"

Graelam de Moreton held his powerful destrier still and seemed to draw himself up to a greater height. "I do not come to insult you, Chandra." He did not shout, but his voice carried to each of the twelve men behind her.

"I will ask you but once more. Why are you here?"

"I have come for you, Chandra. You will be the mistress of my holdings and the mother of my sons. There will be no killing, no looting, if you will agree."

She reeled at his words, her tongue frozen. She heard snarls of fury swelling behind her from her men. Was the man insane? Did he believe he could calmly take her like an ancient barbarian? She forced herself to swallow her fear and block his words from her mind. She studied him as she had been taught, searching for a weakness. But he was fully armored, and she could tell nothing about him, save that he appeared to be a huge man. The visor on his helmet was drawn back, but she could not make out his face or his age. She looked back at her men and saw that Ellis was kicking his horse forward, his gnarled hands trembling on the reins. He drew up his horse, and before she could stop him, he roared at Graelam, "Bastard son of a witch! Get yourself a servant wench, insolent knave! Our lady is not for the likes of you!"

Ellis drew his sword and jabbed the heels of his boots into his horse's belly. He flailed his sword above his head, shouting, "*A Avenell!*" and galloped like a wild man toward Graelam de Moreton.

Chandra shouted over her shoulder to her men, "Hold! All of you, stay here!" She whipped Wicket forward, her cloak flying out behind her as her stallion closed on Ellis. "Fool!" she grated toward his back. Without armor, he would be cut down before he drew a breath.

She saw Graelam de Moreton turn and shout at his press of men. The few that had started forward stopped where they stood. She drew alongside Ellis and stretched out her arm to him. "Do not be a fool!" she yelled at him. "My father would flay me alive if you were hurt!" It was an untruth, but it slowed him.

"I don't want to kill an old man," Graelam shouted. "Keep him back, lady!" His destrier was dancing forward, eager for combat, its eyes flaming.

"Old man am I, you miserable whoreson!" Ellis roared, jerking his horse away from Chandra. "We shall see how an old man fights!"

Chandra charged Wicket toward Ellis and flung herself out of her saddle. She crashed against Ellis, and they hurtled together to the rocky ground. Ellis took the brunt of the shock and lay gasping for breath, Chandra beside him.

She heard a roar of laughter and saw de Moreton riding slowly toward them. She rolled away from Ellis, grasped his sword, and flung it away from him.

She rose to her feet, her hand on her sword. Graelam drew his destrier up, dismounted, and strode confidently toward her. He was a giant of a man, as she had thought, his strength likely twice hers. She saw that his face was swarthy, his eyes nearly black, assessing as they rested upon her.

She swallowed a lump of fear. She did not disbelieve that he intended to do just what he claimed. He took it as a man's right to seize a woman, as if she were naught but a prized mare to add to his possessions. God help her, if she did nothing, he would doubtless slay all her men and overrun Croyland. There were not men enough within the walls to prevent its being taken.

She forced herself to calm. His size would make him slow, it had to be so, and the full weight of his armor. He held his sword in his right hand, his left hand empty. He had tossed his shield heedlessly to the ground beside his destrier, confident that she was naught but a vain girl. She gazed at him coolly, knowing that he had no wish to kill her. She forced a smile of contempt to her lips, praying that his man's weakness would give her a chance.

"It is between us, Graelam de Moreton," she hissed at him. "You have no choice but to fight me!" She lunged forward toward his left side and struck her sword against his. It was as if she had slammed with all her strength against a rock, and the impact rattled her teeth. She stepped quickly aside and again hammered her sword against his, high, near his mailed hand. He leaped back, releasing, and she saw that he was laughing, his white teeth flashing in his dark face.

"You stinking pig!" she yelled at him, furious that he thought her only a silly amusement. She calmed her anger and slipped her left hand to the belt at her waist, clutching the slender handle of her hunting knife. She pressed him, turned to her left to hide her hand from him, and forced herself to keep her eyes steady on her attacking sword as she readied her knife. She saw Ellis from the corner of her eye, struggling to rise. He was clutching at his right leg, screaming curses at de Moreton.

She felt the muscles in her arm cramp with each harsh ring of the swords, but she kept her eyes fixed on him and slowly raised her knife behind her. With a graceful leap, she bounded forward and struck her knife with all her strength at his throat.

It was as if he knew what she would do, for he stepped neatly aside and let the sharp blade graze off the steel mail of his arm. He tossed his sword easily into his left hand and clutched her wrist, his grip tightening until she hissed with pain. The knife whirled from her fingers and fell with a thud to the ground.

"A boy's trick, Chandra. It will not fool a man."

She growled in fury and wrenched her hand free of him. She dashed her hand across her forehead, droplets of sweat cloying her fingers.

"Have you more surprises, my gentle lady?"

She said nothing, for all she had left was the strength of her arm. She rushed at him, both hands gripping her sword, crashing the finely honed blade against his.

She heard a grunt of pain. It was Ellis. "Nay!" she yelled at him as the old man bent to retrieve his sword.

Graelam's arm closed about hers in an instant, binding them against her body. The steel mail of his hauberk cut into her. She tried to jerk free of him, to hook her leg behind him, but he only tightened his hold until she could not move and forced her sword from her hand.

"Hold, old man! I have your lady now!"

Chandra saw the stout soldier who had insulted her ride toward Ellis, his sword raised. She screamed at Graelam, "If he dies, I swear I will kill you!"

"Hold, Abaric!" Graelam shouted again. The man slowly drew in his mount.

"It is over, Chandra. You have fought and lost, and now you will surrender to your lord."

She did not feel the tip of his sword against her breast, but her men saw it, and held their horses back. She heard Ellis moaning and cursing his leg. At least she had saved him from certain death.

"Release me."

"No, not as yet, Chandra. Not until you swear by your honor that you surrender."

She had never before been in battle or known defeat, and it burned raw in her throat. If she did not surrender, her few men would die, and for nothing.

She felt the coiled excitement in him, and she nodded. When he released her, she took a quick step back and hissed at him, "Damn you, my lord! You have the luck of the devil! It was only by a twist of chance that I and my men were without the walls." He was silent for some moments, staring over her head toward the gray stone walls and massive towers of Croyland. She saw him turn and nod toward her men.

The young man, Henry, new to her father's service, dug his heels into his horse's belly and rode toward them.

"No, Chandra," he said, "chance had nothing to do with it. When I planned to take you, I knew well what to do. The last thing I wanted was to lay siege against Croyland. Time would have been on your side, for the keep is strong, and your father, my lady, is renowned for his stubbornness."

For a long moment, she did not understand him. Henry stopped his horse a few paces away. "I am sorry, lady," he said, not meeting her eyes. "I am Lord Graelam's man, not yours."

Chandra closed her eyes, unwilling for a moment to believe that she had been betrayed. It must have been Henry who had pressed to go hunting, and she, blithely unsuspecting, had willingly agreed.

"You devil's spawn!" Ellis screamed at him. "Miserable sow's offal!"

Chandra took a furious step toward him, but Graelam grabbed her arm and pulled her back against him.

"I choose my men carefully, Chandra," he said, "as it appears your father does not."

"Release me," she said.

When he loosed her, she turned to face him. "Do not think you will hold me long. My father will return and cut your miserable heart from your breast." She turned to Ellis. "When Lord Richard returns, you will tell him that I am Graelam de Moreton's prisoner."

He laughed. "Nay, never that, Chandra. Did you not hear me? You will be my wife."

She shook her head at him, her voice drowned in a well of fear.

He stared down at her for a long moment. "You are more beautiful than I expected," he said softly, "even dressed as a man, and covered with sweat and the smell of the boar. Did you know that our minstrels sing about you? The golden virgin warrior of the north who belongs to no man."

She held herself rigidly stiff. "Do not believe, noble lord, that my father will disregard what you have done. I am not chattel to be taken at a man's whim and used for a man's pleasure. If I ever take a man, he will be of my choice. Your victory is but a single dark cloud on the horizon. It will pass and you with it."

"There is much you do not know, my lady, much that your father has not told you. You will speak to the dwarf, Crecy. He will tell you that I have sought an honorable marriage alliance with Lord Richard for two years. I was at first refused, your father's reason, I was told, that you were too young for a husband. Since that time he has sent me vacillating words, through Crecy, to keep me at bay. I grew tired of waiting, and now have taken what is mine. Your father will not come after you, Chandra, for I will wed you this evening in the great hall of Croyland, by your priest, with all honor that is due you. And this night, you will share your chamber, and our marriage bed."

She stared at him open-mouthed. Her father had never

spoken to her about Graelam de Moreton, or about any other man he wished her to wed. She remembered hearing her mother remarking to her on her last birthday that she was becoming a woman and old enough to be wed. She had held herself stiff and apprehensive until Lord Richard had said curtly that the matter was for him to decide, and he wanted to hear nothing more about it. She had breathed a sigh of relief, for Croyland was her home, and her life was just as she wanted it to be. Did this ruthless man believe he could force her to do anything against her will? She threw back her head and scoffed at him. "You are a fool, my lord, and you have failed. All your treachery is for naught. I will never wed you and you cannot force me. And if you believe that my men will let you into Croyland, you are a greater fool."

Graelam smiled, and she felt herself stiffen, for there was pity in his dark eyes.

He stretched out his mailed arm. "Come, Chandra. I would now see Croyland. I thank you for providing fresh meat for our wedding feast. You may mount your horse, but on your honor, you will not break your oath of surrender."

He turned away from her and spoke to Abaric. Within a few moments, Graelam's men had surrounded hers and tossed aside their weapons. Two of his men helped Ellis onto his horse.

Graelam rode beside her to the walls of Croyland and drew his men to a halt before the stark towers. Before he could bellow his orders to the few men clustered at the outer wall, she shouted at them, "Do not lower the drawbridge! I order you!"

He only smiled at her again. He drew his sword and laid its sharp edge against her throat.

"I am Graelam de Moreton. My name is known to you. Lower the drawbridge and raise the portcullis, else the Lady Chandra dies and her men with her."

Chandra gnawed at her lower lip. Her father's men could not know that he would not kill her. She saw Anselm the porter in furious conversation with the men, his hands waving wildly. She watched numbly as the great drawbridge was lowered and the iron portcullis raised.

"Do you swear that your men will not loot or kill my people?"

"Of course. I want no ill will."

"You will allow me to tell my people."

She rode beside him over the drawbridge and into the outer courtyard. Never, she thought bitterly, was a keep taken so easily. She saw the servants cowering away from the oncoming men, their voices lowered in fear. She slid off Wicket's back and tossed his reins to a waiting groom. Oddly enough, Wicket went docilely, nickering softly back to her.

"Croyland is surrendered to Lord Graelam de Moreton," she shouted. "Lay down your arms. He has promised there will be no killing."

She turned stiffly, vaguely aware that horses were still neighing in their stalls and chickens were clucking and strutting about as if nothing untoward had happened. She watched Graelam disperse his men to take the guards prisoner. He turned back to her, and she led him silently to the stairway that rose to the great hall. As she climbed the stairs, Graelam and a dozen of his men close behind her, she turned to see his soldiers take positions along the outer walls. Even if one of her men could escape the keep and reach Lord Richard, he would have to lay siege to his own keep.

The hall was eerily silent, for the servants had scurried away to hide. Crecy, the dwarf, stood next to her father's great chair, alone. His eyes flickered up at her, and suddenly she smiled. How could she have been so stupid as to have forgotten her father's long-standing order! If ever the keep was threatened, her mother and brother were to be placed in a hidden chamber above the dungeon until all was safe again.

"Well, Crecy," Graelam said, drawing off his helmet. "I have come and now have what is mine."

The dwarf bowed low. "It would appear so, my lord. Lord Richard will not be . . . pleased."

"He should not have played me false," Graelam said in an abrupt voice. "Now he pays for his stubbornness."

"I will not wed you," Chandra said. "My father said nay to you. Believe me, Graelam de Moreton, I cannot be forced!"

Graelam turned to Abaric. "Fetch Lady Dorothy and the young lord, John."

Chandra felt his hand upon her arm, and he said, as if speaking to a half-wit, "Listen to me, Chandra. If you refuse to wed me, I shall take both you and the boy back to Wolffeton. Then your proud father will negotiate a marriage alliance to get back his precious heir. Surely Lord Richard must prize his son more than you.''

"You will not find him, my lord,'' she said, forcing her voice to be steady. Graelam regarded her calmly, his dark eyes sweeping her face. She thought suddenly of him touching her, as a man touched a woman. She felt a knot of fear in her belly, but forced herself to close her mind to it when he spoke again, his voice indifferent.

"He is hidden, then. No matter; he will be found soon enough.'' He called to another man, a fresh-faced youth whose hair was flaming red. He spoke in a low voice, but she could make out his orders. "Do not let the men kill any of Lord Richard's soldiers, unless they are forced to. As to the servants, use whatever means necessary to serve up a fine wedding feast this evening. I will speak to the priest, Father Tolbert.''

Graelam turned back to her and took her arm. "You will come with me, Chandra. Crecy, you will take note of all that happens and give Lord Richard an honest accounting.''

Chandra fell into step beside him, her shoulders squared disdainfully, her eyes set ahead. He nodded toward two of his men, and they followed a short distance behind them.

"Where are we going?''

"To the women's quarters, to your chamber. Perhaps the boy is there.''

She said nothing, her thoughts on the hidden room that lay deep in the castle, behind a panel in the guardroom above the dungeons. They would not find John or her mother. Graelam would be forced to abduct her. It was not much of a victory, but at least she would not be bound to him by the laws of the Church.

She preceded him up the winding staircase that led to the women's quarters, and stopped in front of the oak door of her chamber. One of Graelam's men stepped forward and flung it open, and they passed through the antechamber into her room. The shutters were drawn over the narrow windows, leaving the room dim and chill.

Mary stood in the center of the bedchamber, a pale hand pressed against her breast. Chandra heard a man draw his breath behind her.

"One of your servants, Chandra?''

"Nay, my lord,'' she said flatly, drawing away from him.

"She is one of my ladies, Mary, daughter of Sir Stephen, a vassal to my father."

She strode forward to stand beside her friend. "She is a maid, and not sport for your men." Chandra could feel Mary's fear as her slender fingers clutched at her arm.

Graelam smiled, and held his men in place with a nod. He walked to Mary and took her trembling chin in his large hand.

"Tell me, Mary, where is the boy, John? I wish him to be present at his sister's wedding."

Mary tightened her fingers about Chandra's arm.

"I do not know, my lord," she whispered. She stared away from the huge man whose dark eyes seemed to bore into her. She gazed at Chandra's face, stained with sweat, tendrils of her hair falling damp over her forehead. She tried to draw herself up, to show this man the contempt she saw in Chandra's eyes.

His eyes dropped from her face.

"You are a lovely maid, Mary," Graelam murmured. He reached out and touched his hand to her breast.

Chandra lunged at him, reaching for his throat. He turned smoothly, grabbed her hands, and bore them to her sides. "Does the virgin warrior wish to protect her lover?"

Chandra stared up at him and ceased to struggle. Her look of puzzlement was not lost to him. "You will not touch her, Graelam. She has done nothing to harm you, and she is my friend."

"I am pleased that my wife, though she apes the ways of men, does not desire women. I will ask you again, Mary," he said, turning back to the trembling girl, "where is the boy, John?"

Mary shook her head, beyond words. She did not understand what was happening, but knew from the fierce look in Chandra's eyes that she must keep silent.

Graelam stared at her thoughtfully, then turned to his men. "Hold the Lady Chandra."

The men dragged her away from Mary and pinioned her arms to her sides.

"What are you going to do? Damn you, answer me!"

Graelam said easily, "Nothing, if you will tell me where your brother is hidden."

Chandra kicked out at him, and her foot struck his thigh.

The men jerked her backward, twisting her arms, and she closed her eyes in pain.

"Do not hurt her," Graelam said sharply. He turned slowly back to Mary. "Take off your gown, maid. The first man to have you will be Graelam de Moreton. It is only just that your lady see the man who will be her husband."

Mary stood still. She looked with unspoken fear at the huge man who spoke to her in a soft, compelling voice.

"Where is the boy?"

"I do not know." Her voice sounded faded and vague, like the gentle whisper of a lyre.

Graelam clasped her slender shoulders roughly in his hands. He spoke in the same soft voice. "I will not rape you, girl. You will accept me, else it will be your lady in your place."

"No, you bastard!" Chandra yelled at him.

Mary shook her head, her brown eyes holding a desperate calm. "I do what I must, Chandra. The heir to Croyland must be protected. Do not, I beg of you, plead for me." She stepped back and began to unfasten the soft leather belt at her waist.

Chandra heard the quickening of Graelam's men's breath and felt their fingers dig into her arms as Mary slipped off her gown and her linen shift. She stood motionless, her eyes cast to the floor in her shame. Her body was white, newly matured, her small breasts rounded and thrust high. The soft matting of brown hair between her thighs formed a gentle wedge below her narrow hips, and her flanks were straight and long. A girl's body, not a woman's.

Graelam stood back from Mary, his eyes deliberately studying her young body, waiting for Chandra to speak. But she said nothing, her eyes held tightly closed.

He undressed slowly, his eyes on Chandra's face. It took him some time to remove his armor without the assistance of his squire. When he leaned over to unfasten his cross garters, he saw Chandra's eyes upon him, and he raised his dark brows upward in silent question. He rolled down his chausses and stepped out of them, naked.

"You will not shame her, Graelam!" Chandra shrieked, struggling furiously against the men who held her. "I swear to you that if you harm her, you will die for it!"

"You have but to swallow your pride and tell me where your brother is hidden," he said. "I have no wish for this."

"Damn you, no!"

"Then watch well, my lady." He turned from her and motioned Mary to the soft featherbed.

Mary walked to the bed like a dazed child, her steps hesitant and short. She gazed toward Chandra, and then at the huge man who stood over her. His back and chest rippled with muscle, and raised scars of battle showed white beneath the black hair that covered his chest. Her eyes fell to his swelled organ, and she drew in her breath.

Chandra watched him bend over Mary and saw his back tighten as he grasped her slender thighs and pulled them toward him. His body was like her father's, graceful and hard, but he was a blackamoor, not a golden warrior.

"Stop it!" she cried. "I will wed with you, I swear it! Leave her alone!"

Graelam stared at her for a long moment. "You will tell me then where your brother is hidden."

She shook her head. "I cannot give you Croyland's heir. What difference does it make?" she shouted at him. "I give you my word."

His dark eyes swept over her and he said in a voice of harsh finality, "If you are to be my wife, Chandra, you will do my bidding, in all things. You will obey me in this, as well. Where is he?"

She chewed furiously at her lower lip, knowing that she could not endanger John, no matter the consequences. She shook her head and lowered her eyes, unable to look at Mary.

"Very well, my proud lady." Graelam turned to Mary and said softly, "I do not wish to hurt you, child." He grasped her hips and pulled her upward. Mary's body went slack with fear. Her mind was blank until a sharp pain brought a harsh cry from her throat. Then she felt him drive inside her, his hands molding her hips against him.

Chandra could not look away. She saw Mary shudder as Graelam moved over her, and a yawning darkness closed over her mind. It was not Graelam she saw, but a long-buried child's memory of Richard, her father, his powerful thighs locked, his golden hair covering his face as his mouth suckled at a serving maid's breast. The woman was thrashing beneath him, her legs inching upward to close about his hips. Her body was open to him, deep and mysterious. Her father reared back and rammed into her, and she moaned, tearing cries that sounded like death. His body was taut, and he threw his head back, his teeth flashing in triumph. He cried out with the woman, like an animal on the kill, in a final howl of victory.

Chandra's hair whipped into her face. She was sobbing, swallowing in deep rasping gulps, and bile rose in her throat. She could not help herself, and lurched down to her knees.

Graelam heard a whimpering cry and jerked his head about to see Chandra hurling herself forward. Her face was white, her eyes blank. He heard her retching, and watched her wrap her arms about her shuddering body. His men leaned toward her, afraid to touch her. He pulled himself from Mary's body, finished with her, and rose from the bed.

"Dress yourself, girl," he said to Mary, then gazed toward Chandra. He had expected her to scream at him, to curse him, perhaps even to give in and tell him where her brother was hidden. But she had done none of these things, and he watched her silently, the virgin warrior who would have thrust her dagger into his throat, rocking on her knees before him, a small wounded girl. He did not want to break her, merely show her that she could not fight him, that he, as a man, had the power to do as he pleased with her. Without her weapons, and held by his man's powerful arms, she was as any other woman. Her fierce pride would exist only if it pleased him to allow it.

"Chandra."

She felt a hand upon her shoulder. She looked up into her father's golden face. He paled, a shadow darkening in the sunlight, and it was Graelam's dark face she saw. She brushed the back of her hand across her mouth, tasting the bitter bile. She lurched to her feet and staggered to the basin. From the corner of her eye, she saw Mary standing by the bed, pulling her gown over her head. Graelam ordered his men from the chamber and began to dress himself.

When Chandra turned from the basin, the blank look was gone from her eyes. She moved like a panther toward his sword, and the hilt was in her hands before he wrenched it from her. She hooked his legs in a wrestler's grip and drove her fist into his groin.

His legs buckled and he lurched backward, closing his hand about her thick braid of hair, and jerked her forward on top of him. He felt pain build in his groin and growled deep in his throat. He rolled on top of her, pinning her under his body.

He knew that he must be crushing her ribs, but she still continued to fight him. He lay heavily, not moving, until she could not draw a breath.

"Your promise, Chandra. It was surrender. Have you forgotten your man's honor?"

His great weight cleared the fury from her mind, and she quieted. He rolled slowly off her and rose. He did not look at her, for he did not want her to know she had hurt him. He finished dressing himself, strapped on his sword, and said to Mary, "See to your lady. Bathe her and dress her in her wedding clothes."

Chandra pulled herself to her feet. There was hatred in her eyes, a fierce, blinding hatred for him for what he had done. "There will be no wedding, Graelam."

There was a sudden, loud commotion in the antechamber, Graelam strode to the door and flung it open.

Lady Dorothy stood trembling between two soldiers. Her thin face was pale, and her gray-streaked black hair hung in disarray, freed from her wimple. She clutched her rosary in her hands, her fingers frantically clacking the beads. She saw her daughter and stumbled forward.

"Chandra!"

Graelam let her pass, smiling in triumph over her head. Lady Dorothy gasped and threw herself with hoarse cries against her daughter.

"You were found," Chandra said flatly, closing her arms about her mother.

Lady Dorothy drew back, shaking her head wildly until her wimple fell unheeded to the floor. "I was frightened, Chandra. I could hear the strange armor clanging, the shouts of unknown men, and John would not be still."

Graelam looked over Lady Dorothy's head at Chandra's face. A look of confusion, and then anger, filled her eyes.

"You revealed yourself? You disobeyed Father's order?"

Lady Dorothy shrank back from the icy contempt in her daughter's voice. "I was frightened, I told you! It was so cold and dark and I could hear rats! John kept crying that it was not fair, that you were only a girl and needed his protection."

Chandra saw John struggling with two soldiers who held him. His boy's voice squeaked high and loud. "I will kill this

Graelam de Moreton, Chandra! But show me this coward and I will kill him!''

Chandra ignored her brother and looked coldly down into her mother's blanched face. "You are a fool, Mother. By God, I will never forgive you this.'' She met Graelam's eyes. When she finally spoke again, her voice was controlled and flat.

"You will make your greeting to Lord Graelam de Moreton. He is to be my husband.''

Lady Dorothy looked bewildered and fluttered a thin hand toward Graelam. "You cannot wed this man, Chandra. Your father has not given his consent. Your father is not even here.''

Chandra clenched her hands at her sides. She heard a soft, defeated whimper, and turned to see Mary crumple quietly to the floor.

2

ALICE STOOD BEHIND CHANDRA, DRAWING her heavy mane of damp hair over the length of her arm and muttering to herself about devil's demons within Croyland's keep as she pulled a tortoiseshell comb through the tangles.

Chandra turned slightly in her chair as her chamber door opened. "Are you all right, Mary?"

"Aye," she said, not raising her eyes.

Chandra said no more. Mary's life would be a misery if it became known that she had lost her maidenhead, and even Alice could not be trusted to keep such a juicy tidbit behind her remaining teeth. Only Graelam and his men knew, for Mary had been clothed when Lady Dorothy had come into Chandra's chamber. She watched Mary walk quietly to her bed and smooth abstracted fingers over the pale-blue silk gown that lay there.

Aye, Mary thought, she was all right, save for the soreness between her thighs, and her shame. She sat on the oak chest at the foot of Chandra's bed and watched her friend in silence. Chandra appeared so calm, as if she were preparing herself to greet Lord Richard's guests, not to wed Lord Graelam de Moreton. But Chandra's thoughts were clearly written on her face when she turned to Mary, her eyes, usually the color of a clear sky in spring, hooded and troubled. Mary felt her helplessness, and a tremor of pity passed through her.

"I am sorry, Chandra," she said. "If only Lady Dorothy . . ."

"Aye," Chandra said, "if only my mother had . . ." She broke off, aware that Alice had become all attention. "What is happening, Mary?"

"Lord Graelam holds your brother with him. He is now in your father's chamber, readying himself."

"Is Ellis all right? Graelam de Moreton's men have harmed no one?"

"One of your mother's serving maids set Ellis's leg." She smiled wryly. "I could hear him cursing. There has been no violence, save that one of the servants was kicked because he did not move quickly enough." Mary rose abruptly, her hands fluttering in front of her. "What will you do, Chandra?"

"I must wed de Moreton," she said. "Please fetch me Crecy, Mary. I must know what manner of man he is."

The dwarf, Crecy, Lord Richard's scribe and steward, soon bowed himself into the room. He was an ugly man, his nose jutting out like a bumpy rock, his thick bushy brows grown together over his eyes, now dimmed with pity. But his mind was as powerful as his body was twisted, his words always soft and skilled, and he was treated by her father with the respect he deserved.

"My lady," Crecy said. "I have spoken with Lord Graelam. He is set upon this madness, and I cannot sway him."

The antechamber door was open, and Chandra could hear the servants moving about belowstairs, preparing for her wedding feast.

She said to Crecy, "Lord Graelam wanted a marriage alliance two years ago. He told me that Lord Richard refused him because of my youth. I ask you, Crecy, why does he do this? My father is certainly no threat to him, nor can I credit his motive to revenge. I have never heard my father speak of Graelam de Moreton as friend, enemy, or suitor."

Crecy rubbed a thick finger along his bearded chin. Lord Graelam had treated him with kindness, both two years ago and today. Crecy had not understood Lord Richard's harsh refusal of the mighty overlord, for Lord Graelam, like Lord Richard, was a favorite of King Henry's. An alliance between the two great houses would only increase their power with the king. Still more important was Lord Graelam's friendship with Henry's son and heir, Edward. Lord Graelam had continued with written proposals for Chandra's hand, but Crecy had guessed that Lord Richard would never agree. At least now he knew of his master's reasons, but he could not speak of it to Chandra. Even he, Crecy, could no longer prevent Lord Graelam from seeing the futility of his continued goodwill. He had come for what he wanted.

"My lady," he said, "Lord Graelam has made it clear

during the past two years that he seeks no dowry from your father. It is you he wants. In return, he swears aid to your father against the Welsh and any other lords moved by greed against Croyland.''

"It makes no sense, Crecy," Chandra said. She pulled away a circlet of twisted gold Alice had set upon her forehead to hold back her thick hair, a trapping of highborn ladies that was an annoyance to her. "Graelam never saw me until today. A mighty lord does not choose a wife for no gainful reason, particularly a wife who would most willingly slay him, a wife who holds nothing but hatred for him.''

Crecy raised his black eyes to her face. "You have just stated one of his reasons, my lady. That you, a girl, would have the skill and courage to fight him in battle, to slay him if you were the more skilled, the more wily, fascinates him. He first heard of you two years ago when you were but fifteen from your mother's French minstrel, Henri, who, before he returned to France, stayed for a time at de Moreton's keep in Cornwall. Henri fancied you an enigma, a descendant of the Viking princesses. He sang of you in vivid verse to Lord Graelam as the virgin warrior of great beauty who rode and hunted like a man, a woman who was above men, be they commoner or king. His words wove the portrait of a woman more desirable than any lady in the king's court, a woman without a woman's wiles. Graelam's wife, a whining lady from the French court, had just died in birthing a stillborn child. He had wed her to please his father, and to fill his father's coffers. Graelam became his own man again and he determined to have a wife who was like none other in the kingdom.''

"If Graelam wants a warrior, then let him enjoy the boys of his own house!''

Crecy's eyes widened, but he only shook his head. For a lady to speak with the vulgarity of a man-at-arms made him wince. He sought to prepare her, for he saw no choice for her now. Lord Richard could not return to Croyland before Graelam left with Chandra, even if they managed to send a message to him. "Lady, I do not believe Lord Graelam to be an evil man, and he is comely and not a callow youth. His holdings in Cornwall are vast, and he wields great power. I have heard it said that the Earl of Cornwall, the king's brother, has offered him several heiresses, but he has refused them. He

has given his oath that he will not harm you, even if you—''
He swallowed, his eyes darting away from her face.

"Even if I what, Crecy?" she said harshly.

"Even if you refuse him."

"Refuse him! By all the saints, I have done naught save refuse him!"

Crecy nervously fingered the leather belt at his waist and said finally in a quiet voice, "He believes you will yield to him . . . eventually, as a woman must to a man."

Chandra strode away from the dwarf, her step shortened by the clinging soft silk robe. She picked up a slender dagger, a gift from her father, and fingered its razor-sharp blade. She saw Graelam thrusting himself into Mary, his eyes triumphant with his victory of man over woman. She saw herself bowed, retching like a madwoman, shame and fear blinding her eyes.

"Lady, you have cut your finger."

Chandra dropped the dagger to the floor and sucked the drop of blood from her fingertip. She pulled herself up rigidly straight as the sound of Graelam de Moreton's voice came to her through the antechamber. He entered her bedchamber, John at his side, three of his men flanking them.

Graelam was clothed in one of her father's rich wool robes. He was larger even than her father, for its red-bordered edge did not reach the floor.

"Chandra." John's young voice shook. He stared at his sister, tall and slender as a young sapling. She was dressed as richly as was Graelam, her golden mane of hair flowing loose to her waist. She looked proud and controlled, as a lady should, and he straightened himself to match her.

"It is time, lady," Graelam said, stepping toward her. She suffered the touch of his hand on her arm, not moving.

"I have seen you as the warrior and now as the proud lady of Croyland. I am not disappointed, Chandra." He dropped his voice, his dark eyes amused. "Our sons will ride beside England's king. You will nurture them, and I will teach them honor and glory."

"You want a brood mare, Graelam, a dumb creature that is content to be possessed, to be owned and used at your whim."

"I shall possess you, lady, because it is my right as your conqueror and your lord. You will learn my strength and bend to it."

Crecy heard his quiet words and saw Chandra go taut as a bowstring. He regretted now that he had not had time to tell her more clearly that Graelam de Moreton admired her strength in the same degree that he wished her to recognize his. But Graelam was a man of few words, and he believed she would understand and respect his power. When Crecy had visited Wolffeton, Graelam's stronghold in Cornwall, Graelam had plied him with questions, never tiring of hearing the tales he told of her. Crecy had thought it an excellent match, and was surprised that Lord Richard had ranted of Graelam's impertinence, and his age, though Graelam was several years younger than Richard.

He heard Chandra say in a distant voice, "Your strength, Graelam, is nothing more than the bully's coarse bragging, hollow as a reed flute. I do not have to bend my will to any man, save my father, and I am possessed only by myself."

Crecy saw a gleam of challenge light Graelam's dark eyes. Did he not realize that his intemperate words would make her wild to fight him?

"We shall see, lady, beginning this night," Graelam said, his eyes falling to the curve of her breast. "It is time to show ourselves in the great hall." He pressed his hand into the small of her back and pushed her forward.

Sir Jerval de Vernon swung off his horse's back and stretched his cramped legs. "I tell you, Mark," he said, striding stiffly to his friend, who stood staring into the distance toward the great stone towers of Croyland, "Lambert had better return soon with a welcome from Lord Richard. I grow tired of my own stink." He grinned as Mark turned to him and added, "As I do of yours."

Mark shrugged. "If you hadn't insisted upon ensuring our welcome first, you would likely now be soaking off your horsely scent."

Jerval grinned and slapped his friend's back. "Father always preaches the wisdom of announcing oneself, instead of riding up like a pack of Welsh raiders."

Jerval was bored, and his muscles ached from three days astride his destrier. He disliked the idea of presenting himself to Lord Richard de Avenell like a horse for inspection, though he knew that he had more choice in the matter than did Lord Richard's self-willed daughter. Although his father,

Lord Hugh, was hot for the match he had arranged some four years ago with Lord Richard, when Jerval had won his spurs in the service of the Earl of Chester, he had at least agreed to allow his son the opportunity to see if the Croyland heiress was pleasing to him. If what Jerval had been told about the Lady Chandra was true, she was likely a coarse, hawk-faced wench with no manners. Lord Hugh had told no one the reason for Jerval's visit to Croyland, giving his son at least that measure of choice.

He gazed down at the rugged coastline, where the late-afternoon sun bathed the waves in red as they crashed against the rocks. The twenty men sent with him as a guard by his father were sprawled about on the rocky ground in small groups, secure in the knowledge that the bandits who preyed on unwary travelers through the hilly passes from Camberley to Croyland would never dare to challenge twenty armed men. Jerval turned to see a cloud of dust rising in the distance, heralding Lambert's return from Croyland. His horse nearly stumbled when he finally raced down the steep rutted path toward the promontory where they waited.

"Damnation," Jerval growled. "Lambert must take care. I have no wish to haul him back to Camberley in a litter."

"My lord!" Lambert shouted as he drew his horse to a panting halt in front of his master. "Croyland has been taken!" He kicked his feet free of the stirrups and jumped to the ground, his sunbaked face red with excitement. The men gathered about him, clutching at their swords.

Jerval raised his hand for quiet. "What has happened, Lambert?"

"I met an old man on the road near the village of Croyland. He told me that Lord Richard has left with his men in search of Welsh raiders and that Graelam de Moreton has captured Croyland and now holds Lady Chandra. The villagers believe Graelam will force Lady Chandra to wed him this night in the keep."

There was a great rumble of angry voices from Jerval's men.

"Good God," Mark said.

Jerval rubbed his thumb over the stubble on his jaw. "Lord Richard left Croyland unguarded? The man must be a fool."

Lambert shook his head. "No, the old man said he left the Lady Chandra to guard the keep."

"A woman?" One of Jerval's men guffawed loudly. "The man is a fool!"

"Evidently Lord Richard believed that there would be no danger, for he left only a dozen or so of men with his daughter." Lambert paused, his brows arching in disbelief as he said, "It is said that she fought Graelam by herself, even tried to thrust her dagger in his throat."

Mark saw the powerful muscles flex in Jerval's arm. "What? She took him on by herself?"

Lambert shrugged. "So the villagers say."

"What are we to do, Jerval?" Mark asked.

A smile spread slowly over Jerval's face. "I think it might prove interesting to rescue this proud lady from the foolishness of her father and her own vanity." He looked momentarily thoughtful. "Lord Graelam is holding a wedding feast?"

At Lambert's nod, he said, "There will likely be much wine flowing. A drunken soldier is not worth much." He turned to his men. "I think we would make a handsome lot of merchants and servants!"

Mark cocked his thin face to one side. "Merchants?"

"Aye," Jerval said, smiling, "and servants."

Chandra sat stiffly in a massive wooden chair, clutching an untouched goblet of wine. She looked out over the great hall, at the scores of Graelam's men who lounged on the hard benches, sated with drink and food. Her mother sat on Graelam's left, in a seat of honor, her face pale but composed, lowered to her trencher. Chandra thought she saw a small smile play about her mother's lips and shook her head, knowing she must be mistaken. John was seated between two of Graelam's soldiers. He looked frightened, his dark almond eyes darting about the hall, and squirmed nervously on his bench.

Graelam sprawled in her father's great carved chair beside her, laughing loudly at a joke from one of his men. She knew that at any minute he would call for silence, and that Father Tolbert would enter to hear her vows. She thought of the night ahead, and quickly swallowed a gulp of wine.

"You are silent, Chandra."

She raised her eyes to Graelam's dark face, harshly rugged from years of battle. Confident triumph lit his eyes and sounded in his words. She wished she could smash her heavy goblet into his proud face.

He laughed, guessing the violence of her thoughts. He leaned close to her, and she smelled sweet wine on his breath. "You can fight me, Chandra, but not here, not now. There will be time for that tonight. I will not take you as I did the girl, Mary. I had not time to give her pleasure. You will learn that women are soft and yielding creatures in bed, Chandra, and you will be no different."

He saw that her face had paled and her pupils were wide. He saw her again, huddled and retching on her knees, and frowned. "You are not a man, Chandra," he said. "You were not meant to remain a chaste virgin."

He saw her lips move, but there was no sound. He wondered what was in her mind, behind her wide-eyed stare. Her beauty had surprised him. Minstrels were forever painting women in the most perfect of images. But the minstrel, Henri, hadn't lied. The thought of finally possessing her after two years made his loins tighten under his full-cut robe. He forced himself to turn away from her and watched the servants pour wine into the outstretched cups of his men. He felt quite pleased that all had gone as he had planned. The picture before him was as settled as any at his keep on a day of feasting, even to the small group of merchants who had arrived bearing bolts of fine cloth, hopeful that he would be generous to his new bride.

He thought of the impotent rage Lord Richard would feel when he returned, empty-handed, to Croyland, and he smiled. He would lose his golden daughter. The man who had deceived Lord Richard into riding after the Welsh raider had been well rewarded. He sat now at the end of the long table, his laughter louder than most, his winecup never empty.

A servant appeared at Chandra's elbow with a jug of wine, but she paid him no heed.

"Lady Chandra."

She started at the low whisper and turned her head slowly to face the servant. She did not know him. She saw a warning in his gray eyes, and her pulse suddenly pounded in her temples.

"Pour me more wine," she said, and held up her goblet.

"Listen carefully, my lady," Mark whispered. "Look about you. The servants you see are the soldiers of Jerval de

Vernon. You must be ready when Graelam calls for the priest. That will be the signal.'' He eased out a slender dagger from the long sleeve of his coarse woolen robe and slowly straightened. ''You must protect your brother.'' He nodded, his brown hair tousled and shaggy over his smooth brow, and walked away from her, his step shuffling.

Chandra slid the dagger down beside her and covered it with her robe. She stared with new eyes about the hall, searching out the soldiers from among her father's servants, and spotted them easily now. She had never heard of Jerval de Vernon, but it was of little importance. She waited, her muscles tensed, fierce hope filling her.

''Chandra, it is time.''

She turned to Graelam, and he saw that she was smiling. He raised his arm toward the cowled priest who stood in the corner of the hall, his face shadowed by a thick brown wool hood, his scribe standing beside him.

The priest moved with grave dignity toward the dais, his scribe trailing behind him, carrying a thick roll of parchment. He raised his face as he neared her. She felt a shock of recognition. It was as if she were looking at a young Lord Richard, a golden lion with blue eyes, flecked with amber lights.

Jerval whipped off the heavy wool robe. He threw back his head and shouted, *''A Vernon! A Vernon!''*

Graelam flung himself toward Chandra even as the battle cry swelled in Jerval's throat. She lurched out of her chair away from him, the dagger clutched tightly in her hand. She was at John's side in an instant, arching her dagger toward the soldier who struggled up from his chair, gaping at her. She grabbed her brother's hand and jerked him toward her.

''Hide yourself, John, under Father's chair!''

The boy obeyed her. Even as the soldier on John's other side pulled himself drunkenly up, Chandra whirled away from him, shouting to her mother to hide with her brother.

The hall was a pandemonium. Over Graelam's shouted orders, goblets of wine and trenchers of food were hurled to the floor, and benches crashed as his men flung themselves into action, dazed with wine and surprise. A new battle cry filled the hall—*''A Avenell!''*—as a score of Lord Richard's men burst through a small door from the solarium and rushed into the fighting.

She saw Graelam hacking his way toward her, his face grim, his eyes set with fury. She leaned down and grabbed the sword of a fallen soldier.

Mark caught her eye and yelled, "Lady, run! Get to safety!"

She stared at him for an instant in surprise, then whipped about to face one of Graelam's soldiers.

"Son of a pig!" she roared at him. He backed away from her, his eyes wide with drunken fright. She felt a man's heavy hand upon her arm and heard a death gurgle in his throat. She was knocked forward, her sword spinning from her hand, and pinned under him.

The man was kicked off her and she was grasped by her arms and pulled upright. "Are you all right, lady?" Mark shielded her behind him. "For God's sake, hide yourself!"

She shook herself free of him. She saw Graelam at the head of a knot of his men, fighting his way backward toward the huge oak doors to the hall. The man who had disguised himself as Father Tolbert, the man golden as Lord Richard, was pressing toward them, kicking aside strewn benches and tables. He shouted to Graelam over the din, "You have lost, my lord! I am Jerval de Vernon! Fight me, Graelam!"

Graelam was escaping, drawing back, his men in a circle about him. She knew a deep, galling anger. The overlord would leave Croyland free, untouched. She ran forward, oblivious of the fallen men at her feet.

"I will have your blood, Graelam!" she yelled at him.

Graelam could not reach her, for Jerval de Vernon blocked his way. He sized up the young giant and knew he faced a man of his own strength. Their swords locked, then released. They hacked at each other, the clash of steel on steel ringing above the cries of the soldiers.

The great oak doors were flung wide. Graelam's men streamed through them and down the narrow outside stairs. Graelam drew Jerval with him, his teeth gritted in fierce concentration. With a sudden cry of rage, he plunged his sword downward with all his strength, shearing away Jerval's shield.

They were both panting, sweat blinding their eyes. Graelam saw Owen, his father's man, bold and coarse, weakening under the onslaught of a younger man. He swung his sword in great arcs, pushing Jerval back, but he was too late. Owen fell on a roar of pain. Graelam lunged at Jerval, fury at Owen's death burning in his eyes.

Jerval slipped on the treacherous footing. He saw Graelam's sword above him as his shield hand clutched at the empty air for balance.

Suddenly, he heard a soft, hissing sound. Graelam staggered back, his hand clutching at his shoulder. Chandra's dagger lay deep in his flesh. She was beside Jerval, her hand upon his arm, steadying him.

"Give me your sword," she cried.

He hesitated, staring at her blankly.

"There will be another time, Jerval de Vernon!" Graelam shouted. "I will have you, lady!" He grunted in pain as he jerked the dagger from his shoulder and flung it to the floor. It slid toward Chandra, nearly to her feet, its blade wet with his blood.

"Your aim is that of a woman, Chandra, not a warrior! I shall have to teach you!" He laughed through his pain, taunting her.

Chandra growled deep in her throat and grabbed Jerval's sword. Jerval lunged at her, gripping her arm. "Hold, lady. Even with your men, we cannot defeat him. Let him go."

The men of Croyland and Camberley were pressing about them, streaming down the outside stairs into the bailey. They gave a shout of victory as Graelam's men leaped onto their wildly rearing horses and rode out of the courtyard over the lowered drawbridge.

There was silence in the great hall, save for the wailing of women and the moans of wounded men.

"Are you hurt, lady?" Mark said.

She shook her head, straining to hear the retreating horses. "Raise the drawbridge, Ponce," she shouted, "before Graelam changes his mind!"

"You are Lady Chandra, daughter of Lord Richard de Avenell?"

She turned and stared up at the man who had saved her. "I am," she said.

Jerval smiled. "Your aim was that of a warrior's. It was your anger that blinded you." He said to Mark, "Send some men to the walls. We must be certain that Graelam takes his leave."

Jerval looked again at Chandra. Her flowing hair, the color

of ripening wheat, fell in tangled tresses over her shoulder. The gold circle on her forehead sat askew, her robe torn and spattered with blood. If he had not seen her fight with his own eyes, he would have believed he was in the presence of a helpless young girl, beautiful as the lyric of a song.

"Who are you, Jerval de Vernon? How came you here?"

He was startled. Lord Richard had not told her of his coming. He said slowly, "I am here to visit your father, an ambassador from my own, Hugh de Vernon."

Chandra jerked the gold circlet from her forehead. "You are welcome, Jerval de Vernon, as a priest or a warrior."

3

LORD RICHARD SPRAWLED OUT IN his carved, high-backed chair and stretched his long legs out before him, toying with his wine goblet. The roast boar had settled comfortably in his belly, and the wavering light from the cavernous fireplace, orange ember light now in the late evening, reminded him how weary he was from the hard ride back to Croyland.

He gazed from beneath his heavy lids toward Jerval de Vernon, who sat on a low stool near the fireplace in seemingly pleasant conversation with Chandra. He heard her laugh in the rich tones that always made him smile, but tonight the sound of her voice safe beside him rekindled his annoyance at his own stupidity. It had taken him two and a half days to realize he had been lured into Wales, and that Cadwallon and his Welsh raiders were probably ensconced in their fortresses deep in the mountains. Thank the lord that Jerval had arrived in time! Jerval de Vernon, Hugh's son. The young knight appeared to be all that Chandra could wish: a bronzed, handsome face saved from being too comely by a strong, square jaw, intelligent eyes, nearly as blue as Chandra's own, and a powerful lean body, healthy and banded with hard, sinewy muscle. Lord Richard was both surprised and relieved that Jerval did not appear to be at all nonplussed or disapproving of Chandra's ways. If what Crecy had told him of the melee three nights ago was true, Jerval had seen her at her most unwomanly, brandishing a sword dressed in her wedding gown, had even seen her most unfeminine rage, because her dagger had not struck Graelam's black heart.

"Crecy," Lord Richard called to the dwarf, who had pulled a stool up next to Jerval.

"Aye, my lord," Crecy said, scurrying to his master's side.

He motioned to Crecy to come closer. "You are certain

that Graelam did not touch her?'' he asked again in a low voice, his eyes flickering toward Jerval.

"As I told you, my lord, de Moreton wanted her honorably, as his wife."

"The gall of that bastard!" Richard growled, allowing his rage again to the fore. "When the men are rested, I've a mind to mount them and hang the arrogant lout!" His hound, Graynard, until now quiet at Lord Richard's feet, raised his huge head and growled his agreement at his master's harsh voice.

Chandra heard her father's words and turned excited eyes toward him. "I agree with you, Father, and I want to ride with you this time. The brute does not deserve to live, after what he did!" She was not thinking of herself as she spoke, but of Mary, and of the secret only they two shared.

"He humbled you last time, girl," Ellis said, hobbling forward on his crutch. "And you broke my damned leg in the bargain!"

Chandra quirked a thick eyebrow at Ellis. "Next time," she said, "we will choose how to fight. If you, my friend, had not been so intent on slaughtering his whole troop single-handed, I would not have had to send you tumbling!"

"I doubt it is worth the cost, my lord," Crecy said quietly. He added in a muted whisper to Lord Richard, "I think it more prudent to assure that before too much time passes, the prize he sought will already be claimed."

"He lost, Lady Chandra," Jerval said. "Crecy is right. To mount a siege against Wolffeton would be costly and bloody for all our houses, and there would be no guarantee of victory. I know that the king would not be pleased."

"Graelam nearly killed you," Chandra said stiffly to Jerval.

He smiled. "True, but he did not succeed. You made certain of that, Chandra."

"But surely King Henry would not approve of such a barbaric act!"

Lord Richard waved his hand for silence. "How many of Graelam's men are still alive, Ellis?"

"Three of the bastards, my lord," Ellis said, and spit into the rushes.

"Excellent," Richard said. "See that they are well kept."

"Why, Father?" Chandra asked, her head cocked to one side.

He shrugged. "Because I wish it," he said, closing the topic.

Richard rose from his chair and stretched. He saw that Chandra would join him and waved her away. Before he left the great hall, he heard her already arguing in a whisper with Jerval about Graelam de Moreton. Their two golden heads were close together, and he realized that it pleased him to take a son-in-law who so closely resembled him in his youth. Lord, the children they would sire—golden and bronze, all of them.

His contented thoughts lasted until he reached Lady Dorothy's chamber. She had assiduously avoided him since his return during the afternoon, and he had soon understood why after he had talked to Crecy. Weak, sniveling woman! He paused, unable to keep a scowl from his face, and shoved the door open. Her small room had always reminded him of a nun's cell with its narrow, hard bed, its one backless chair, and its ornately carved prie-dieu she had brought with her from her father's home in Normandy.

She was standing in her brown woolen bedrobe, looking as severe and uninviting as her stark bedchamber.

"My lord?" Lady Dorothy said uncertainly, drawing back from her huge husband, who seemed to fill her small chamber.

He continued to gaze negligently about him. "Nothing ever changes, I see," he said finally. He remembered her screaming at him once in fear and loathing in this room long ago when he had first made love to her in his house. He had not taken her to his bed in two years, for it gave him no pleasure to pry her thin legs apart and listen to her whimpering. This was the first time since that he had stepped into her bedchamber.

He saw her cowering from him and said with deep sarcasm, "You have no need to worry, wife. I have not come to enjoy your winsome favors."

"Then what do you wish, my lord?" she asked hopefully, her shoulders straightening slightly.

"I want to know, lady, why you betrayed your hiding place, why you disobeyed me, and nearly cost my heir his life and Chandra her freedom."

"I—I was frightened, Richard. It was so dark and cold, and there were rats—"

He looked at the coarse gray strands of hair that threaded

through her once rich raven tresses. He felt an unwonted surge of pity for her. There was no gray in his golden hair.

"Did you know what was at stake?" he asked, trying to keep contempt from his voice.

"Nay, not at first." Her pale-gray eyes suddenly met his, and he felt himself start at her next words. "When I did understand what Lord Graelam wanted, I felt glad that I had disobeyed your order."

"What do you mean?" He started to walk toward her, but her oddly defiant look disconcerted him and held him still.

"I mean, my lord, that our daughter is a woman grown. Lord Graelam is a powerful lord and sought an honorable alliance. It is time that she wed, time that she become a wife, a mother, and a lady. You have allowed her to be as wild as a boy, encouraged her to ignore me, her mother, and all that is expected of a lady."

"Stupid sow!" he roared at her. "God's bones, had I left her in your saintly hands, you would have broken her spirit, robbed her of her courage, made her into a sniveling, pious nun!"

"Better for her than what you have made her!" Lady Dorothy shouted back. "She is oblivious of her womanhood, uncaring of anything save earning your approval. And you, all you do is encourage her! She fought Lord Graelam, as would a man!"

"I would expect nothing less from my daughter," Richard said, more calm now. "Undoubtedly it would have pleased you if she had fallen to her knees and wept." He turned away from her. "You cannot seriously think I would forget she is a woman, and approaching marriageable age. Her upbringing will serve her well, and the man I have chosen for her will treat her with the respect she is due." He saw that she was staring at him, not understanding. "Can you not even guess why Jerval de Vernon is here?"

Lady Dorothy drew a startled breath. "You said nothing to me. How should I have guessed?" She added, her voice wary, "Have you told Chandra?"

"Nay, there is no need, at least for the present. I wish to be certain that Hugh's son is indeed worthy of her. And you, my dear wife, will keep your tongue between your teeth."

"Aye, my lord." Lady Dorothy nodded. "I will pray to the blessed Virgin that it will come to pass as you wish."

*   *   *

Chandra tightened her leather sling strap and smoothed the figured buckle over her shoulder. She pulled an arrow from her quiver, set it into its notch against the bow, and drew it back until her bunched fingers touched her cheek. She watched the arrow as it arced smoothly upward, crested, and embedded itself with a thud in the center of the target.

A shout of approval went up from Lord Richard's men, a murmur of surprise from Jerval's.

Mark said to Jerval, his voice low with laughter, "I lose my wager if you cannot split Lady Chandra's arrow. The pride of Camberley rests on your shoulders, Jerval, as well as my money."

Jerval smiled, flexed his arm, and stepped forward to stand beside Chandra. She stood quietly, as if used to the accolades of the men, but her face was bright with pleasure. Her skill had amazed him, just as had the sight of her striding into the exercise yard dressed in a man's tunic and a man's wool trousers. He had had the presence of mind to turn a dark, warning eye toward his men, and luckily they had held their tongues.

Jerval gave Chandra a long, appraising look, wondering if he should let her win. He dismissed the notion, guessing that such a victory would give her no pleasure.

He said in a bland voice, "The distance is too short, lady, but I will declare you winner of this beginner's competition, if it is your wish."

The corners of Chandra's mouth turned down, but he saw that her eyes were soon twinkling. "Beginners, Jerval?"

"Aye. Let us have a greater test of skill and strength." He wondered if she would protest, for she was, after all, but a girl.

Instead, she shrugged, cocked one of her thick fair brows, and waved to Cecil. "Go to the target," she called to her loose-limbed page. "Tell him the distance you wish, Sir Jerval. We beginners do not wish to carry away a prize that you warriors would scorn." She swept him a mock curtsy in her trousers.

Jerval returned her curtsy with a mock bow, then shouted to Cecil, "Back it to the base of the hill!"

Chandra chewed on her lip and flexed her arm. He was doubling the distance, and she had her limits. She stared toward the target and wished for a moment that she hadn't been so cocky.

"Would you care to choose a champion, Lady Chandra?"

"Champion, indeed! I have eyes like an eagle, Sir Jerval, and you have likely done yourself in with all your bragging!" She saw Lord Richard from the corner of her eye, standing beside Ellis, watching the match. She smiled toward him and stepped forward, stretching straight and tall with her side to the target, measuring the distance. She released her arrow and stood motionless, watching it soar upward.

The arrow missed the center and embedded itself into the dark-blue outer rim of the target. She felt pleased with herself, though she knew it was a lucky shot at this distance. She grinned broadly at the cheers from her father's men and the astonished rumbling from Jerval's. Had they expected her to miss it altogether?

"It is a great distance," Jerval heard Avery say in his deep voice to Lord Richard. "Few of the men could do better."

It wasn't precisely true, Chandra thought, but trust Avery, Croyland's master with the bow, and her teacher, to praise her to her father.

John, who was on his haunches chewing on a blade of grass near his father, raised his head and said in his petulant child's voice, "I will do better someday, Father! Avery has said that I have your eye." He added proudly, almost as an afterthought, "And I will be strong when I am a man."

"Aye, John," Lord Richard said, grinning down at his son. "You will indeed someday be a man, and I have never known Avery to be wrong. You can learn much from your sister. 'Twas a difficult shot."

Ellis shouted to Chandra, "So, my girl, you have finally learned to keep your eyes on the target, not on the toes of your boots!"

"You old fake!" Chandra shouted back. "I'd like to see you do better! All you could do is beat the target with your crutch!" She turned to Jerval. "Now, Sir Warrior, let us see this skill and strength you talk so much about."

Jerval met Mark's eyes, and he winked. He drew an arrow from his quiver and set it against the bow. He took his time, aware of Chandra tapping her foot with an air of impatient anticipation.

His arrow shot straight toward the target, its speed so great it was a blur. It slammed into the packed straw with a loud thud.

A smile played about Lord Richard's mouth as Ponce ran to the target and dropped to his knees in front of it. When he rose, he cupped his hand to his mouth and shouted, "Sir Jerval's arrow split Lady Chandra's! Hers is closer to the center!"

Jerval smiled down at her from his great height. "I salute you, Lady Chandra. You have won. Even staring at your toes, your skill is unequaled."

Chandra was silent for a moment, torn between amusement at his cleverness and a kind of awed disappointment that his skill was so much greater than hers. "It is brute strength that has carried the day!" she shouted in an equally loud voice. "But pay off your wager, Sir Mark, for you have indeed lost your money!"

"There is always hope," Jerval said, his eyes warm upon her face, "when you grow up and become more skilled. Perhaps I can be persuaded to give you lessons."

"Conceited braggart," she said, in high good humor. "Just because you have an arm the width of an oak tree!"

Jerval watched Chandra walk to her father. Lord Richard thwacked her companionably on the shoulder and called out to Jerval, "You have taken her at her own game! Next time she won't be so careless!"

"I knew Sir Jerval would win," John said in a prim voice, throwing back his head.

Lord Richard looked for a moment at his son's upturned face. He had his mother's pointed chin and his mother's querulous voice. John was spoiled, and, Richard thought, it was his fault. "Perhaps Sir Jerval will give both you and your sister lessons," he said. "But allow me to wager on Chandra, at least until you are older."

Jerval said kindly, seeing the young boy's crestfallen look, "Fetch your bow and arrows, John, and we'll soon see if Avery is right about your excellent eyesight."

Lord Richard said to Crecy as he strode back toward the keep, "Sir Jerval controls her well. Hugh's son pleases me."

"He appears to please Lady Chandra, but of course she doesn't realize why he is here. She thinks him merely your guest, an ambassador of his father."

"I want it that way, Crecy. If Sir Jerval wishes to wed her,

he will make her understand soon enough. He does not seem
to be a fool, or an overeager buck. Chandra is, after all, a
girl, and not above being wooed, I'll wager.''

"I am sure you are right, my lord," Crecy said, rubbing
his thick thumb over his new beard. He agreed with Lord
Richard that the match was an excellent one, certainly as
brilliant as a marriage alliance with Graelam de Moreton
would have been, and the vast de Vernon lands were closer
than de Moreton's lands in distant Cornwall. He wondered
when Lord Richard would want him to write a formal request
to the king to approve the marriage.

He was pulled from his thoughts when Lord Richard said,
"I think it wise that John cease spending so much time in the
women's quarters. He's too old to whine like his mother."

"And too old to be jealous of his sister," Crecy added. It
was a good sign, Crecy thought as he took a double step to
keep up with his master. The boy wasn't bad, only undisci-
plined, and uncertain of himself, for he had lived all his ten
years in his sister's shadow.

"Aye," Lord Richard said, then shrugged. "John will stop
mewling like a child soon enough. I think Arundel just the
man to take him as a page."

Jerval rode silently beside Chandra away from the tiltyard
toward the sea. Her face was streaked with sweat, and her
thick wheat braids were plaited tightly about her head, dulled
with dirt.

In the tiltyard, her lance held firmly against her side,
urging her beast of a destrier at full gallop, she had showed
nearly his own skill when he had been her age. He had no
particular wish to turn their every encounter into a competition,
but oddly enough, it was she who seemed to relish it, and in
the most natural way imaginable. She seemed to like her new
companion, and though he could and did outdo her, she never
took offense at being beaten, merely laughed and made light
of it.

Although he had heard much about Chandra from his
father, he had hardly believed him that she was a beauty, and
it still surprised him that she cared so little about being a
woman. He thought of Julianna, his young cousin, soft,
fragile, and white-fleshed, fluttering her slender hands
helplessly, sighs of praise on her lips for his bravery and his

man's strength. Looking at Chandra riding tall and graceful on her huge destrier beside him made Julianna's image seem pallid by comparison.

Lord Richard had made it quite clear to Jerval that he would not tell Chandra the purpose of his visit. This he found equally surprising, but after turning the matter over in his mind, he decided it was probably just as well. It would give him ample time to decide if he wanted her as his wife.

"Lady," he called to her.

Chandra swiveled in her saddle to face him, rubbing a smudge of dirt from her brow. "I know what you have in mind, Sir Jerval," she said in a mocking voice. "You wish to gloat, no doubt, about how well you handle your lance. Very well, Sir Knight, I concede defeat, but recognize that you are older, and have won your spurs."

He laughed easily and said, "Am I as filthy as you, Chandra?"

She looked at his powerful arms, dampened with sweat. His tunic was open and the golden tufts of hair on his chest were matted with dirt.

"More so," she said in a judicious voice. "It is because you are so large, I think, and you sweat so."

"Your appraisal warms me."

She grinned at him, revealing even white teeth. Was there nothing about her that was not inviting? "You know," she said, "that father is holding a banquet tonight, in your honor. Two of his vassals, Sir Andrew and Sir Malcolm, will attend." But not Sir Stephen, Mary's father, she thought thankfully. She needed more time to persuade Mary not to tell anyone that she was no longer a maid, least of all her father. Chandra knew Sir Stephen to be a rigid man, and even Mary could not guess his reaction if he was told. Damn men anyway, she thought, that they would see it as Mary's fault that she was no longer a virgin.

Jerval saw her frown and wondered what she was thinking. "You will be present, will you not?"

"Of course. I assure you I like my share of wine as much as anyone!"

Chandra drew in Wicket's reins and carefully guided his descent to the rocky stretch of beach below, cut off from the harbor at Croyland by an outjutting cliff. Jerval followed her,

resting his eyes on the soft lapping waves collapsing gently
on the coarse black sand.

When they reached flat ground, Chandra dismounted, pulled
off Wicket's bridle, and shooed him away. Jerval did the
same, and when he turned to face her, he saw that she was
eyeing him oddly.

"I have not really thanked you properly, Jerval," she said
quietly. "Allow me to do so now. You saved me when I
thought all was lost to Graelam de Moreton." She smiled at
him openly, with no feminine wiles. "Your timing could not
have been better, and your plan of rescue was magnificent."
She looked down at her toes and added, "Of course, beating
off a pack of drunkards who could hardly hold their swords
was not much of a challenge."

"You praise me, then make me out to be a lucky fool in
the next breath," he complained with a grin.

"I do not wish you to become too conceited." She touched
her hand to her thick braid as if it offended her. "Filthy as
usual," she said, and sighed. "Father will not let me crop it
off. It takes hours for my women to comb it dry."

"I am glad," Jerval said.

"Ah," she said, "it pleases you that I must be held in my
chamber while you, undoubtedly, are swapping coarse jokes
with the men."

"That is not what I meant."

She had a habit of cocking her head to one side, and he
smiled at the question in her eyes.

"I think you would look like a ragamuffin with your hair
cropped off."

"You are ever kind, Sir Knight."

Jerval looked down and kicked the coarse sand with the toe
of his boot. She was so damned direct and honest, and
exceedingly obtuse. He found himself somewhat irritated.

"Do you wrestle, Jerval?"

"Wrestle." He looked at her for a moment blankly. "Aye,"
he said slowly, "I do."

She laughed brightly.

Lord Richard heard the sound of voices from the beach
below and dismounted from his palfrey. He walked to the
edge and looked down. He saw Chandra, crouched, circling
around Jerval. Wrestling! Good God, could she never remem-

ber that she was a girl? He saw that Jerval was smiling, and he shook his head, bemused.

Chandra charged at Jerval and pulled at his arm as she kicked her legs out to lock his. Jerval quickly turned to his side, jerked his arm free, and grabbed her about her outstretched thigh. He tossed her easily off her feet onto her back, dropped to his knees, and straddled her, pressing his chest against her, his hands locked about her shoulders.

Lord Richard's smile deepened. He knew what Chandra would do, for he had taught her himself. She twisted sharply to her side, squirming out from beneath him, and caught his shoulder between her legs, pulling him off balance. Jerval gave a shout of laughter as he rolled onto his side.

"By all the saints, Chandra," he said as he rose to his feet, "I will not underestimate you again!"

" 'Twill do you no good, Jerval! You are slow as an unshorn sheep!"

They circled each other again, Chandra panting in her heavy woolen tunic and trousers. Jerval watched her eyes and saw that she would lunge for his legs. He decided he would let her. She lunged swiftly, locking her hands behind his knees, and jerked upward, hurtling him backward. Jerval caught her waist and pushed her forward upon her belly, letting himself fall on top of her. He felt a moment of fear that he had hurt her, for she lay still. He eased his hold on her arms. She gave a yell and twisted onto her back, arching upward to throw him backward. She was almost free of him when he grasped her thighs and jerked her upward. This time he took no chances. He covered her with his body, his legs heavy upon hers to keep her from kicking him, and pinioned her arms above her head. He felt her belly and her breasts heaving in gasping breaths against him. He heard a rip of material and saw that her tunic had pulled open and her shift had torn.

She grew still. "You tricked me, Jerval," she gasped, trying to catch her breath. "You are not so slow as a sheep after all."

He found that he could not answer her. He looked down into her dirt-streaked face. Her eyes were rueful and laughing. He felt her breast pressing bare against his chest.

"My father has often held me pinned like this," she said.

He had beaten her fairly and she took no offense. She wondered at his sudden silence and his sudden tense expression.

Her body moved slightly beneath him, and quickly, Jerval released her and rose unsteadily to his feet. He turned away from her, cursing his body, and wondering how the devil she could not realize what was happening.

Chandra felt cool air on her breast and hastened to draw her tunic together. "Clumsy oaf," she muttered to herself.

Lord Richard realized Jerval's problem when he saw the young man turn away, while Chandra pulled her tunic together over her. He sighed. Chandra did not even have the sense to know that pressing against her lovely body had made Jerval taut with desire.

Richard remounted his palfrey and rode back toward Croyland, wondering if he should, perhaps, suggest to her that she was too grown up now to expect a man to wrestle with her without overly enjoying himself.

The great hall was bright with rushlight torches of mutton fat, and the air was heavy with laughter and conversation. Sir Andrew, Sir Malcolm, and their men lounged about the long tables, waiting for the servants to serve up the thick slabs of roasted beef and the casks of wine.

Jerval sat to Lord Richard's left, impatient that Chandra had not yet come into the hall. He knew that he was being studied, his worth to Croyland weighed and discussed. Lady Dorothy sat at the far end of the dais, her face pale and pinched, her thin hands fretting at the pleats in her gown. Never, Jerval thought, had he seen a mother and daughter more dissimilar. He raised his goblet, and a serving wench hastened to fill it.

"You bested my daughter in wrestling."

Jerval turned to Lord Richard. "Not at first. She said I was slow as an unshorn sheep. I assume you taught her." How very normal it sounded to speak of a lady wrestling with a man. Jerval shook his head at himself.

Richard said, "I have told her that her eyes give her away. They tell her opponent what is in her mind."

"Perhaps," Jerval said. "Did Chandra tell you of our match?"

Richard shook his head, his eyes upon the deep-red wine in

his goblet. "No, I was watching you from the cliff above the beach."

Jerval felt himself redden. Chandra had not questioned his abrupt release, nor had she noticed that his body had responded to her. She had merely laughed and fetched her horse.

He said, "If she were a man, with a man's strength, few could best her." He added carefully, "My father told me that she was unlike other women. I did not know whether to really believe him."

"He spoke the truth," Richard said, "though I doubt that Lord Hugh would be quite so diplomatic. My daughter is strong-willed and proud, and I suspect that you have already discovered she does not yet realize she is becoming a woman, though a more graceful girl I have yet to see."

"Aye, I have realized it," Jerval said quietly. "She sees me as an oversized friend."

"She does not give her friendship lightly, Jerval. If you have gained her trust, you have made remarkable progress."

There was a sudden hush, and Jerval looked up to see Chandra walk into the hall, one of Lord Richard's pages, Cecil, at her side. When last he had seen her, she had been covered with sweat and coarse sand from the beach. He drew in his breath, disregarding Richard's eyes upon him. To honor him, she had attired herself in a light woven gown of pale pink. A gold filigree belt was about her slender waist. Her long hair flowed to her waist, held from her forehead by a thin golden band. She has but to gaze into a mirror, Jerval thought, to see that she has grown into a woman.

As she approached her father, she nodded to Jerval, her slight smile spontaneous and serene. She seemed to belong here, with the men, even in her woman's garb. He chanced to catch Mark's eyes, and his friend smiled widely at him and gave him a mocking nod.

A servant pulled back her chair and seated her next to Jerval, much to his delight. Her hair smelled of wild lavender, and his fingers itched to touch it.

Lord Richard, in high good humor, asked her about her defeat at the hands of a rascal from the north. Chandra laughed and wagged her finger at Jerval.

"He crushed me, Father," she said, "just as you have done. There is little skill in that, I think."

"Do not boast too loudly, lady," Jerval said, pulling his eyes from her thick golden hair. "I crushed you so that I would not have to twist your arm and cause you pain."

"Ha!" Chandra said.

Contrarily, Richard said, "Are you saying, Jerval, that you did not afford Chandra the courtesy of wrestling with her as you would any other opponent? She thinks no more of pain than would you."

Jerval eyed Lord Richard warily. Of course he had not treated her as roughly as he would a man.

"My lord," he said, "I treated your daughter no more roughly than she treated me. It was not a combat to the death, merely a game. I trust that she will remember at our next match that I do not care for pain when it is unnecessary."

Sir Andrew, hearing his words, nodded his approval. "Well said, Sir Jerval. Crecy," he shouted down the table, "take care, de Vernon has a tongue as smooth as yours!"

"It appears that your father raised you well," Richard said. He waved his hand for silence. "Make your speech, daughter."

Chandra rose and gazed calmly over the crowded hall. "We are here to honor Jerval de Vernon. Without his cunning and bravery, the ruthless overlord Graelam de Moreton would now be allied to my father's house. We must take care never again to allow Croyland to be so vulnerable. I salute you, Jerval de Vernon!"

The men cheered, and one of them sent a wine jug crashing ceremoniously to the floor. A servant hastened to mop up the wine and the broken shards.

Jerval rose slowly from his chair to stand beside her. "I accept your honor. Let it also be said that Lady Chandra saved my life during the fighting. When your minstrels write of that night, let her name be sung as loudly as mine."

Chandra felt a warm glow of pleasure at his unexpected praise. It was not her experience that men shared their glory with women, and his generosity pleased her. She saw that her father was gazing toward Jerval, a bemused smile on his face.

Richard rose to stand beside Jerval. He grasped his arms in a salute of friendship. "May the great houses of Vernon and Avenell always stand as allies."

Chandra did not cheer. Her eyes were drawn first to her father, then to Jerval. Jerval could be his son, so close was their physical resemblance. Both were golden, men of stature, strong and intelligent. She wondered if she would have looked like Jerval if she had been born her father's son. She felt an unwanted twinge of envy, then shook it off. She liked Jerval de Vernon and would miss him when he took his leave of Croyland.

Chandra shared Jerval's trencher. When he tried to give her the choicest bites of beef, she waved her knife at his hand. "Gallantry is stupid, Jerval, when one is hungry. Here." She neatly divided the meat in half. "If you cross this line, sir, expect to find your hand pinned to the table!"

"But you have given me all the tough pieces of meat, anyway," Jerval complained, smiling at her.

"You have not told me about your years with the Earl of Chester," she said, chewing on a chunk of warm bread. "My father tells me that he is a hard man, with little humor."

"Hard but fair."

"I also hear that Chester has a very lovely daughter."

He wished for a moment that he had heard jealousy in her voice, but there was none, only gentle teasing.

"Eileen is her name, and if you would know the truth, she is squat, with no neck at all, and has rabbit teeth."

."Poor Jerval! No wonder you became so skilled in Chester's service. There was no dalliance to ease your nights."

"On the contrary," Jerval said coolly, "there was a younger daughter, Joan. She much admired me." Indeed, he thought, Joan had trailed after him like a puppy, much to his chagrin. "Of course, there were the local girls," he added, arching an eyebrow at her.

He saw her stiffen and was pleased.

Chandra gazed toward Mary, reminded by Jerval's show of lechery of what men could do with women if they wished. Though Mark was trying to make amiable conversation with her friend, Mary looked silent and withdrawn.

"Men are sometimes . . . rotten," she said.

"And women are always angelic and virtuous?"

His sarcastic tone pulled her eyes away from Mary, and she jabbed him lightly with her dinner knife. "Since this is your banquet, Jerval, I shall try to be nice to you, though it is difficult."

"If your idea of honoring me is to skewer me with your knife, I beg you to find other ways."

The evening was far advanced when Richard motioned to Cecil to bring Chandra her lyre. She set the wooden instrument lightly on her lap and gently caressed the strings, testing their pitch. She tried several chords, and their haunting echoes filled the hall.

Jerval sat back, the rich sweet wine lulling his senses, his eyes on the fall of thick hair that cascaded over Chandra's shoulder as she leaned over the instrument.

Chandra lightly flicked the high strings again, then turned to face the company. "This is an old Breton legend," she said in a clear voice. "Behold the faithfulness of the lady as she laments her dead lover." She began to sing, her voice sweet and throaty.

> *"Hath any loved you well down there,*
> *Summer or winter through?*
> *Down there have you found any fair*
> *Laid in the grave with you?"*

Jerval was pleased at the selection. He moved his chair slightly to see her face better, and watched her eyes darken as she sang.

> *"Is death's long kiss a richer kiss*
> *Than mine was wont to be*
> *Or have you gone to some far bliss*
> *And quite forgotten me?"*

The strings sounded a rippling crescendo. Jerval heard suppressed passion in her sad, clear tones. He stared at her, at her smooth skin and her soft, parted lips. He felt his loins tighten as he watched her slender fingers caress the lyre strings, as they would a lover. He pictured Chandra trembling in his arms, her lithe body alive with passion, whispering his name in her need for him. As she neared the climax, she shuddered slightly, as if she were sharing his thoughts of coupling, and let the ringing high notes cascade downward until they bellied into bass chords, muted and soft.

> *"Hold me no longer for a word*
> *I used to say or sing;*
> *Ah, long ago you must have heard*

So many a sweeter thing.
For rich earth must have reached your heart
And turned the faith to flowers;
And warm wind stolen, part by part,
Your soul through faithless hours.''

Jerval watched her eyes clear and a small smile play about her mouth. In that moment he knew he wanted her as he had never wanted another woman. She rose, bowed slightly at the waist, and handed the lyre again to Cecil. Jerval remained still in his chair, not heeding the boisterous clapping from the company.

His eyes met Lord Richard's.

"She was taught by our minstrel, Henri. She sings more sweetly than did he, poor fellow." Richard added in a gently mocking voice, "Were you surprised that she sang of love?"

Jerval shook his head, clearing his mind. Had he looked like a mindless fool? "She is a woman," he said in a thick voice.

"Aye, that she is."

Chandra tugged at Jerval's sleeve. "It is not kind to insult my poor efforts. Did you like my song?" she asked shyly.

"I trust you will never ask me to compete with you," Jerval said, relieved that he had regained control of his voice.

Chandra chuckled. "Finally I have put him in his place, Father! He is not crowing like a cock on a dung heap!"

Jerval smiled at her jest, but he felt a strange tightness in his throat. He knew now why Chandra had played. Her father had wanted him to see the passion in her.

When Chandra's attention was drawn to John, he turned to Lord Richard. "I believe, my lord," he said slowly, "that my father's house and yours must be joined together."

Richard smiled and nodded. He but hoped that his daughter would be as pleased as was his future son-in-law.

4

THE MORNING WAS OVERCAST, THE air cool and damp. Chandra drew her short mantle about her shoulders and walked briskly from the outer courtyard to the exercise field. She had slept later than was her usual habit and had not managed to escape the keep until she completed her morning devotions. She frowned as she thought about them. Father Tolbert had had the gall to reproach her in his gentle tones about staying with the men the previous evening instead of excusing herself and retiring to the women's quarters, as a lady should. Obviously her mother had dropped that hint in Father Tolbert's waxy ear. She had listened impatiently as he droned on about a lady's duties, and her dear saintly mother's wisdom. She had learned long ago not to argue with Father Tolbert, for his mind and training prevented him from comprehending anyone who disagreed with him, especially a lady. It was much easier to keep quiet, if she could, until she could make her escape.

She waved to Anselm and he shouted a happy good morning down to her from his post on the west tower. The hall had been empty when she had broken her fast on a savory chunk of cheese, fresh-baked bread, and a mug of ale, save for a few dithering serving wenches taking advantage of her mother's gentle manners. The wenches who were comely enough to gain Lord Richard's attention smirked behind their hands at her pious mother. Chandra frowned, disliking this thought, and took a deep breath of the cool morning air. She hoped it wouldn't rain, for she chaffed at being mewed up indoors. Since Sir Malcolm and Sir Andrew were still at Croyland with their retainers, and bad weather would mean inevitable scuffles among the men. Sir Malcolm, in particular, was a testy man who seemed to enjoy bickering. He had been particularly fluent about the ineptitude of the king the previ-

63

ous evening, gesticulating so wildly with his stick above his gray grizzled head that Chandra feared he might drop from his ire.

"Henry has done naught for the past thirty years save extort money from us!" Sir Malcolm snarled, wiping red wine from his mouth with the back of his hand. "Simon de Montfort, now there was a man to lead England."

"He unlawfully imprisoned the king," Chandra said tartly, "and usurped power that was not his."

"You don't know, girl, what it was like in those days," Sir Andrew said solemnly. Like Sir Malcolm, Sir Andrew was used to Chandra's being with the men, and did not gaze at her as if she had sprouted wings when she spoke her mind. It was Jerval, Chandra noticed, who looked at her oddly.

"It is said," Jerval mused, smoothing over the troubled waters, "that even though Edward came to hate de Montfort and eventually killed him, Edward learned more about his responsibilities as England's future king from him than he ever did from his doting father."

"That is true," Sir Andrew agreed. "Simon had a genius for organization, and he meant well. He could have killed Henry, you know, but he was too honorable."

"It does not seem so honorable to me," Chandra persisted, puckering her brow, "that de Montfort married the king's sister without his permission. That was a calculated act, as if he was already plotting to usurp Henry's power."

"It was said to be a love match," Lord Richard said, amused sarcasm in his voice.

"I think I could be convinced to love a king's sister," Sir Andrew laughed, "even if she was squint-eyed and had the pox!"

Sir Malcolm scratched his head. "Henry grows old, thank the saints. Tell us something, Sir Jerval, about young Edward. You have passed some time with him, I'm told."

Jerval smiled wryly. "Edward is thirty, Sir Malcolm, not so young anymore, and has been wed for the bulk of his years. I met him when I was in the Earl of Chester's service, and the Princess Eleanor also. He is a Plantagenet through and through, but he seems to have avoided the worst of their excesses."

"It is said that Edward bends this way and that, and his

friends of one day must take care the next," Sir Andrew said, forever the pessimist.

"Perhaps when he was younger that was true, Sir Andrew," Jerval said calmly, for Edward had indeed been unpredictable in his youth. "But I count him as a friend, and a man whom I would gladly serve. England's barons will not suffer shifting policies when he becomes king, of that you may be certain. And he has chosen his lady well, for the lovely Princess Eleanor is anything but barren."

Chandra drew up short as she approached the exercise field. Some of the men were about, as usual, but Jerval caught her eye, engaged with wooden swords with her brother, John. Mark was standing near, shouting encouragement to the panting boy.

"Keep your eyes up, John!"

John lunged at Jerval, who neatly sidestepped him.

"Nearly skewered!" Jerval shouted.

"It is kind of Sir Jerval to practice with my brother," Chandra said to Mark. She added ruefully, "Especially since John does not care to be with me lately."

Mark smiled at her kindly. "I would be surprised if he forever accepted being thrashed by his sister. As for Jerval, he is teaching your brother because he enjoys it. He is fond of children."

"I wonder that he has not yet married," Chandra said, watching Jerval feint once again to avoid John's wooden sword.

Mark blinked. There was only curiosity in her voice, nothing to betray that she had more than a passing interest in his answer. "He likely will before long," was all he said. He was surprised to see the girl Mary walking timidly toward them, her mantle held delicately in her small hands to keep it from the muddy ground. He wondered at the friendship between the two girls. They seemed so different to him, yet they appeared genuinely fond of each other.

Mark waved at her. "Over here, Mary," he called. "Lady Chandra and I were just discussing the merits of wooden swords."

Mary met his eyes for an instant, then quickly lowered her face, as if embarrassed. "Good morning, Sir Mark," she said shyly.

"Circle to your left, John!" Chandra shouted to her brother.

"Chandra," Mary began apologetically, "I'm sorry to bother you, but . . ."

Chandra groaned at the look on her friend's face. "Don't tell me," she said, sighing.

"I fear your mother has taken a chill. She wishes that you prepare a draught for her."

"You know herbs and medicines, Lady Chandra?" Mark asked.

"My old nurse had time to teach me but one concoction before she died. I'll come in a moment, Mary, I promise."

"I will tell Lady Dorothy," Mary said softly. She gave Mark a tentative nod, then walked carefully from the exercise field.

"Such a timid little creature," Mark said, his eyes following Mary's retreating figure.

"She has a right to be," Chandra said in a clipped voice.

Mark looked at her with some surprise, but she did not explain.

Their attention was drawn back to Jerval when he gave a sudden loud cry and toppled backward, John following him, his sword pressed against Jerval's chest.

"Sir Jerval is kind," Chandra said. "I have not seen John so excited and . . . uncomplaining in months. Excuse me, Mark, but duty calls. Tell Jerval that I will take him on next, and no wooden swords!"

Chandra, much to Jerval's disappointment, was kept with her mother for the entire morning. When she did not appear for the midday meal, he could scarcely contain his impatience and kept glancing toward the stairs that led to the upper chambers.

Lord Richard observed him with a benign smile. "Lady Dorothy is not often ill, but when she is, she uses it as an excuse to keep Chandra indoors and away from the men," he said finally. "It is likely that Chandra will escape her soon."

Jerval flushed. "It seems that I am being quite obvious."

"I gather you find my daughter to your liking," Richard said dryly.

"Would you not believe me a fool if I said nay?"

Lord Richard grinned. "Aye, a giant of a fool!" He paused for a moment, tearing a chunk of black bread from the round loaf. "Have you thought about how Chandra will deal with your mother?"

Jerval started in surprise. In all truth, he hadn't given his parents a thought since he had arrived at Croyland. "Actually, sir," he said ruefully, knowing Lord Richard was acquainted with his sharp-tongued mother, "I haven't." He shrugged hopefully. "I can but hope she will appreciate Chandra for what she is." He swirled the ale about in his mug and was silent for a long moment. "Chandra does not yet realize that I wish to take her to wife."

"It is my fault if she does not," Richard said. At the younger man's questioning look, he continued, "Let me speak bluntly, Sir Jerval. When Chandra was but a child, I saw much of myself in her, for better or worse. Not just in our physical resemblance, which was marked even then, but in our characters. Even as a scamp, she was forever hanging about the men, artfully dodging her mother whenever she could. Perhaps I have allowed her too much freedom. She is proud and stubborn at times, and cocky as a young buck. But she admires you, I have seen it in her eyes. And she is loving."

"I would not wish her to be any other way. I will teach her what it means to be a woman." He broke off, not wishing to speak sexually of Chandra in her father's presence.

"Since I have taught her the ways of men, it is right that her husband teach her the ways of a woman." Although Richard spoke the words easily, it was an effort for him to say them. He remembered clearly the day some four years ago when she had run to him, ashen-faced, crying that she was bleeding. She had always come to him, not to her mother, and he had tried, carefully and tactfully, to explain what was happening in her body. She had shuddered, not liking what she heard. And when her full breasts first sprouted, she had bound herself tightly, as if ashamed of them, and hunched her shoulders forward to hide them. It was his wife's minstrel, Henri, he supposed, who had achieved the impossible. He had enticed Chandra when she was fifteen finally to wear gowns. Her hunched shoulders suddenly straightened, and to Richard's profound relief, she seemed to come to enjoy dressing up for their guests and having her incredible hair brushed to her waist until it gleamed. Now she made the transition from hoyden to lady gracefully. He knew that he had kept her with him overlong, and that Jerval de Vernon understood her as well as he could hope.

Richard swallowed a last bite of roasted lamb, then rose. "It appears that my daughter will not soon escape her mother," he said.

Jerval's eyes went one last time to the stairwell before he nodded agreement.

Richard gave him a commiserating wink and said in a hearty voice, "Avery tells me that a ship from France has just put into the harbor. Why don't you join me and see the wares the captain has to offer?"

Chandra was sitting cross-legged on a grassy patch above the promontory looking out over the sea, chewing on a blade of grass. It was early afternoon and the sun, finally, was bright overhead. She turned her head at Wicket's whinny and saw Jerval atop Pith, riding at a gallop toward her up the rocky slope. She felt a rush of pleasure that he had sought her out, for she liked his company. He wasn't coarse in the manner of her father's men, and he never boasted on the exercise field, except of course with her, and that was merely good-natured jesting. There was much joke-telling and laughter among the men when he was about. She smiled toward him, admiring the lines of his simple white woolen tunic, draped softly over the bronzed muscles of his powerful chest, and the gentle strength of his hands on his destrier's reins. His golden hair, thick and curling at his neck, looked burnished in the bright sunlight.

He dismounted gracefully from Pith's broad back, and when he saw her gazing up at him, his eyes held a tender look. She started at the odd feeling it gave her and turned her head away in confusion.

"Mark said you had ridden up here."

Chandra patted the grassy ground next to her, and he dropped to his knees beside her. "I was just thinking about you," she said. "How much longer will you stay at Croyland?"

A thick bronze brow lifted, and he looked away from her, toward the sea. "My father set no limit. Why? Do you wish me to leave?"

"Sometimes."

He was startled. "Why?"

A dimple deepened near her mouth. "When you make me look like a mewling cat in front of the men, and my father."

"You mewl nicely," he said, and shrugged elaborately. "I doubt that Camberley keep will collapse without me."

"I have never known a man," she said, turning to gaze at him full face, "so like my father."

"Should I be flattered, my lady?"

"Nay, it is your due. I sometimes wish I were like you."

A stiff breeze was blowing up from the sea, pressing her woolen tunic flat against her full breasts. He said on a grin, "If you were, I would likely find myself continually embarrassed. I am glad that you are not a man, Chandra."

She was toying with the thick braid of hair that fell over her shoulder, but at his words, her fingers dropped away from it, and she sighed. "God must have been angry with Lord Richard at my birth, and thus I am a girl. Have you any other truths, Jerval de Vernon?"

"Aye," he said. "You are beautiful."

"A man who is a flatterer! It ill befits you, Jerval. You should heed my father. His tongue is never smooth with guile."

"You liken me so much to your father, Chandra?"

"You look much like him, and he is above all men I know. And you are kind, as he is."

Jerval had seen one of the maids emerge from Lord Richard's chamber early that morning, when he had risen to relieve himself. She had looked tousled, and when she saw him, she had lowered her eyes and hastily smoothed out her kirtle. In matters of sexual appetite, he thought, Lord Richard was very much like other men.

"I used to think of my father that way," he said, "until I became a man and saw that he was as I. When I was your age, I was still under his spell."

"You are now an old sage, humbled with your knowledge?"

He laughed. She was clever at turning his words into nonsense. He knew he no longer questioned that he loved her. But he still could not be sure she felt anything more for him than simple friendship. Even his men did not quite know what to make of her. Mark had told him of a fight in the men's barracks. Hubert, one of his seasoned warriors, a man who had no use for women, had flung out an insult about the soldiers of Croyland being a flock of sheep, content to be led about by a girl. He had nearly had his skull bashed by Avery, Lord Richard's master-at-arms.

"Nay, I am not humble," he said, trying to remember her words, "save before God. I do not think humility in men a sign of wisdom."

She nodded with great seriousness, her eyes mocking him. "And what is wisdom, Sir Philosopher?"

"I think," he said, "that if a man understands and accepts what God has intended him to be, that is true wisdom."

"And you accept what you are, Jerval? You are lucky, and blessed."

"It does no good if one does not listen, Chandra. To struggle against the inevitable, to cloak oneself from what one is, is blind weakness. I remember some three years ago I was entered in a tourney near York. It was held quietly, for King Henry, as you know, forbade them. My friends praised me, told me that there was no one to beat me. A lord's son from Scotland, a fellow with squinting eyes, defeated me. I was at first disbelieving and then angry. I saw finally that if a man believes himself above other men, he dooms himself to misery. A man must accept what he is, and what he isn't."

"Does your lesson also apply to women, Jerval? Or are they too insignificant for your concern?"

"Only a fool is insignificant, Chandra."

"Lord Richard believes most women to be fools, I think."

"Your father could treat you with no greater respect and affection, and you are a woman."

"Lord Richard does not see me precisely as a woman."

"You are wrong, Chandra."

She was silent a long moment, then said in a flat voice, "I know little of Camberley. Is it like Croyland?"

He accepted the rebuff. "In its defenses, aye, it is, but it has not the ancient heritage of Croyland, nor its dampness."

"Dampness? I have never thought Croyland to be damp."

"I am not criticizing your home, Chandra. Croyland Castle is a century older than Camberley. My grandfather, Lord Guillaume de Vernon, built Camberley during the reign of King John. He added comforts that were scorned or unheard of when Croyland was built. There are many windows to let in the sun and keep the stone dry."

"He does not sound like much of a warrior to be so concerned about such trifles."

"Actually, he had a wife from Aquitaine whom he loved dearly, my grandmother. She was not well in our northern

climate and yearned for the warmth of the southern sun.
Guillaume did his best for her.''

"What happened to her?"

Jerval grinned. "She lived to a ripe old age, still craving
her native land. My mother, Lady Avicia, is like her in some
ways. She will not have rushes in the keep to breed fleas and
filth. When Prince Edward married Eleanor of Castile, I
remember her joy and my father's grumbling, for King Henry
furnished his new daughter-in-law's chambers at Windsor
with thick Spanish hangings and carpets from her homeland.
In all the bedchambers at Camberley, the stone floors are
warm with soft woven wool underfoot. I hope that you
will—" He broke off abruptly, but Chandra was still regarding him with polite interest. For a moment, he felt put off
with her. Then he smiled, pleased with her innocence.

"You have no brothers?"

"Nay, one sister only, Matilda, now dead."

Chandra's eyes shadowed. "I am sorry."

"It has been a long time and I knew her only as a child.
And there is my cousin, Julianna. She is my uncle's daughter.
He, unfortunately, had the bad judgment to be aligned with
Simon de Montfort, and lost his life as well as most of his
holdings. Julianna is near your age."

"Oh?" Chandra asked, wondering at herself. "Is she
pretty?"

"Extremely," he said. "Julianna is a very feminine girl,
with huge soft brown eyes."

"Rather in the nature of a cow?"

He grinned at her acid retort and continued in a bland
voice, "There is nothing bovine about Julianna, I assure you.
She is gentle, and soft-spoken." It was not exactly true, but
Jerval would have called Julianna an angel if he thought
Chandra would show him jealous claws.

Chandra forced an indifferent shrug. "You must pine to
return to Camberley."

"Perhaps," Jerval said easily. *With you as my wife, little
one*. He raised his face to the sun. "It is hot, an unexpected
blessing."

Chandra untangled her legs and rose to her feet. "Would
you like to swim? Not in the sea, for the water is still too
cold. I know of a small lake in the forest."

He nodded, no longer surprised that she, a lady, would ask him to swim with her alone.

When they mounted their horses, Jerval decided to be perverse. "A race, Chandra. Let us see if that beast you ride has any speed, and you any skill as a rider."

He gazed at her destrier. Wicket was a huge, long-necked animal, a full fifteen hands high. The horse should have been too strong for her, as he was for the grooms, but whenever she stroked his silky neck and whispered to him as to a confidant, it seemed that she and the mighty destrier had long since come to an understanding.

Jerval gave a shout and they were off. The horses jostled each other until they veered off to the rutted road that led south to the forest. Chandra pressed her face close to Wicket's neck and hugged her thighs to his belly, as she had been taught. Wicket lengthened his stride, and Pith fell back. She saw his shadow disappear behind her and gave a shout of victory.

A flock of birds rose from the trees in front of them, squawking loudly. Wicket lurched sideways, startled by the sudden commotion. He ripped the reins from her hands and snorted angrily. Chandra flattened herself against his neck and stretched her full length to reach for them. She felt annoyed when Jerval swerved toward her, his hand outstretched.

"See to yourself, my lord!" she shouted, grabbed the loose reins, and dug in her heels.

They were fast closing on the forest ahead, and Chandra heard Jerval's stallion panting behind her as he struggled to close with Wicket. She touched her hand lightly against the straining muscles of Wicket's neck.

"But a little farther," she whispered.

Wicket bounded forward in a last effort. Chandra gave a cry of sheer joy. She had won, by a horse's length. She whipped Wicket about and he reared, dancing on his hind legs.

She saw that Jerval was smiling as he reined his destrier in beside her. Although he had felt a moment of fear when Wicket had pulled the reins from her hands, he did not voice his concern.

"A fine race, Chandra. There are only a few hearty wild flowers for a victory crown."

"I will take your words, Sir Knight. It is enough, at least this time."

They dismounted, and she led them into the forest along a narrow, serpentine path. The sunlight fell in a checkered pattern through the thick trees, casting the moist, lush foliage in a misty blur. They soon reached a clearing and the small lake, and left the horses to gorge themselves on the thick grass at the edge of the water.

"This is one of my favorite spots," Chandra said, drawing a satisfied breath. "My father first brought me here when I was but five years old." She gave him an impish grin. "The water is deep in the middle, but you need have no worry, Jerval. I will save you if you flounder."

He gave her a vacant smile, for he was wondering what the devil she was going to wear into the water.

Chandra turned and quickly stripped down to her shift, paying him no more attention. She seemed to have no thought about stripping to her undergarments in front of him, though he could not seem to take his eyes off her. Her shift was, he supposed, a reasonably modest garment, though it reached only to her knees. He rubbed his hand across the back of his neck. Did she really not realize that what she was doing was a clear invitation?

"Come on, Jerval," she called. "The water will not get any warmer!" She ran gracefully toward an outjutting rock and shinnied up it like a boy. She stood poised for a moment before she dove into the water.

Jerval watched her until her golden head cleared the surface. He looked ruefully down at his own clothes, knew that he couldn't swim nude as was his habit, and stripped to his brown wool chausses. He walked to the edge of the water, the heat of the sun soothing and warm on his back, watching her as she swam across the small lake, her movements graceful and sure. He cursed softly to himself as he slipped into the water, his skin tingling from the cold, thankful at least that it eased his desire. He flipped onto his back and floated free, closing his eyes against the brilliant sunlight.

He was pulled from his revery by the touch of her hands upon his shoulders, pushing him downward. He held his breath and smiled as his head went under, until the water reeds weaved about his legs near the bottom. He twisted about, locked his hands about her waist and legs to prevent her from kicking him, and pulled her down to him. When she ceased to struggle, he carried her to the surface.

Chandra was gasping for air and laughing at the same time, her vivid eyes alight with mischief. Her braid had come loose and her thick wet hair fell into her face. He held her about the waist, treading water, while she pushed her hair back from her forehead.

She broke away from him, still laughing, and showed the soles of her bare feet as she slithered underwater. He watched the ripples pass, then swiveled about and swam back toward shore. Just as his feet touched bottom, he felt her hands lock about his ankles, throwing him forward.

She rose to the surface some feet behind him, wagging a teasing finger. "How trusting you are, Jerval de Vernon!"

He realized that she was still in water beyond her depth. He dove toward her under the surface and saw her legs pumping fast away from him. He closed his hands about her hips and pulled her against him. He felt her smooth belly taut against his face through the wet linen shift. His hands dropped lower until they were cupping her buttocks. He felt her struggling, flailing at his back and tugging at his hair.

He released her and swam to the surface, trembling from the feel of her.

"I did not think you would be so fast," she gasped. "I will know better next time."

"I doubt that that will help you," he said. He held out his hand to her, his loins knotted with desire. He had to get out of the water and away from her. "Come, I am hungry. Enough exercise."

Chandra cocked her head at him, but took his hand for support until she felt the bottom. They walked slowly forward until the surface fell to her waist and Jerval turned to face her, a remark about the water on his lips. But his eyes dropped to her breasts, and her nipples pushing stiff against the clinging wet linen.

She looked at him as the water lapped about his belly, her eyes squinted against the sun. His body was more finely honed than her father's, she saw, for he was younger. His bronzed chest was splendid, and only lightly furred with fair hair that narrowed at his waist.

He mistook her studied glance. "Chandra," he said, his

voice husky. He grasped her shoulders and pulled her against him, seeking her soft lips.

Chandra felt his mouth pressing against hers, his tongue probing her lips, and the hard demanding strength of his muscled body. For a moment, she did not move, held still with surprise, and then for an instant, she shuddered. Suddenly she cried out against his mouth and pounded her fists against his chest.

Jerval was so stunned that he dropped his arms.

"How dare you!" she screamed at him, dashing her hand across her mouth. "Damn you to hell, Jerval de Vernon, I am not some serving wench for your pleasure!"

"I know that," he said, still stunned. He held out his hand to her. "Chandra, you don't understand. You must listen to me."

"I believed you my friend," she gritted in a fierce voice. "I thought you were different, but you are like other men, concerned only with your next rutting!"

"Dammit, I am your friend! Wait!"

But she didn't wait. She thrashed through the water, away from him, ignoring his call, and did not turn to him until she had gained the shore. He followed her, furious with himself for losing his control, and furious with her for being so blindly innocent.

As she grabbed for her clothes, she saw him step out of the water, silhouetted by the sun. He stood motionless, staring at her, his hugeness suddenly frightening. Her eyes fell down his body to his swelled organ, bulging and taut against his wet chausses. She whirled about, clutching her clothes against her chest, and ran to Wicket. She grasped his mane and hurled herself onto his back, forgetting his bridle, and whipped him into the forest, not looking back when Jerval shouted her name.

She managed to pull her tunic over her head, but she had lost the low belt, and the sleeves dangled open about her wrists. She whipped Wicket into a frenzied gallop toward the welcoming walls and towers of Croyland. The drawbridge was down, and she barely slowed until they reached the inner bailey. She ignored Ellis, though he waved his crutch at her to gain her attention, and rushed into the great hall.

She found her father there alone with Crecy. "Leave us," she said, her voice high and shrill.

Crecy frowned under his bushy brows toward Lord Richard. Richard slowly rolled up the parchment he was studying and nodded toward him. The time of reckoning had come, he knew it in his belly, and she was as upset as he had guessed she would be.

Chandra rushed forward and clutched at his sleeve. "Father," she gasped, "Jerval must leave! He can stay here no longer!"

Richard gently disengaged her fingers, praying for some kind of inspiration. "Why, Chandra?" he asked her gently, knowing that he was postponing the inevitable. "I had thought you liked Jerval."

As she shook her head wildly, droplets of water fell onto his velvet surcoat from her wet hair. "He tried to dishonor me!" Her voice sounded taut and bewildered. "We were swimming in the lake, and he forced me against him and kissed me, like a . . . like a village wench!"

Richard imagined her in her wet shift, her woman's body molded against the clinging linen. He was not surprised that Jerval had finally succumbed, for the temptation must have been overpowering. He only wished that Chandra had herself felt a tug of desire for her future husband. He laid his hands on her shoulders and said gently, "Surely you cannot blame him. You are a woman, daughter, and he a man. I assume it was you who invited him to swim with you."

Chandra stared at him. "I don't understand, Father. It is you who must blame him. It is you who must demand that he leave Croyland. I can no longer welcome him as your guest. He has broken faith, Father, and lost his honor."

Richard closed his eyes for a moment. He had created her, and he had let her become blind to what she was. He forced himself to continue calmly. "Jerval de Vernon came at my request."

"I know. He is here for his father."

"He is that and more. Chandra, you are a beautiful woman, the pride of my body. I have held you overlong with me."

"But I belong with you, Father," she said, her mind locked against his words. "I belong at Croyland. It is my home!"

"Croyland cannot be your home forever. You must have realized that. Do you still not understand? Graelam wanted you, as have others. I turned them away." He paused a moment, wincing at the stunned look in her eyes. "Listen to me, Chandra. Four years ago, I met with Jerval's father, Lord Hugh de Vernon, and saw his son. Even then, Jerval was a fine man, a man worthy of you. Lord Hugh and I decided that our two houses should be bound together. Jerval should have come two years ago, but I held him off. You were too young, then.''

She drew back from him as if he had struck her. "You wish me to wed him?" she whispered. "That is why you brought him here?"

"Aye, he will be your husband. He and his father wish it, and so do I.''

"You cannot mean it," she cried. "You would not send me away." She saw her mother, in her fine clothes, surrounded by her women, and her tapestries, and her endless devotions. A woman who was a great lady, a useless prisoner, of no more use than a stone.

"By God, Father, I'll not wed that rutting stud! Do you hear me? I will not do it! I am the flesh of your flesh, you have said it many times. I will not be some man's chattel, some man's brood mare!''

He said softly, "You are a woman, daughter. You will be whatever your husband wishes you to be.''

"But I am not like . . . other women!''

"What you are," he repeated patiently, "and what you will be, Jerval will decide.''

"How can you simply give me to a man who will have control over what I am to do and how I am to act?" She whirled away from him, her hands clutched into fists.

"There are few choices for any of us. Do you believe I wed your mother because I was enamored of her? I wed her to enrich Croyland's coffers, as you well know. There was no choice for me . . . a man. At least Jerval de Vernon is besotted with you, and if you are possessed of any woman's wiles, he will treat you just as you wish.''

"But a woman must obey her husband—it is her vow before God. You wish me to dismiss what I am and become a soft, devious creature, a woman who can control her own destiny only to the degree that she can play men for the fools they may be?''

He pulled her against him, cutting off her furious spate of words, and buried his face in her damp hair. He felt her holding herself stiff and unyielding, and he stroked her until she eased and nuzzled her cheek against his neck. He remembered the pain he had suffered the year before when he had been gored by a rampaging boar. Chandra had been distraught with fear for him, and had nursed him herself, ministering to his every need as if he had been her beloved child. He felt the pain again, gnawing at him. "I have taught you to be strong, Chandra. You will do what you must, just as I have done. Do you not wish to have children, be mistress of great holdings?" He felt her shaking her head against his shoulder, and he continued more quickly, "You cannot remain at Croyland, child. You were not fated to spend your life as a woman who does not know womanhood. Perhaps I should not have encouraged you to ignore what God intends. You must trust me, Chandra, trust me that I do what is best for you."

"But I love you," she whispered, raising her face from his neck. "I want nothing more than to remain at Croyland. My life is here, not with a . . . stranger, a man whom I must obey, a man I do not even know."

"I have given you time with Jerval. You know him, better, in fact, than most girls know their future husbands. I have watched you with him, watched you smile and laugh, watched you enjoy his company."

"He is no longer a friend, Father. I wish never to see him again." She drew up, pushing away from him, and flung her head back.

"It is my wish, daughter." He lingered on the last word. "You will wed Jerval de Vernon. Your loyalty to me will become his. You will trust him as you now trust me, and obey him as you obey me."

Her eyes became hard, but her voice caught on a muffled sob. "You are forcing me to leave because I was not born your son."

"You are wrong, Chandra. I would not lie to you. You must not blame Jerval. He loves you well, I know it. I trust him always to stand with you, to care for you, and to protect you."

"Protect me!" she cried. "I need no man to protect me! Please, Father, do not do this! Please, you must give me more time."

"Cease pleading with me like a willful child!" Aye, he

thought, he must show her anger, show her that his decision
was final. "It will be done."

Words lay leaden in her throat. She felt hollow, empty,
like a reed flute that a minstrel had tossed heedlessly away.

She turned away from her father and walked, shoulders
squared, to the door.

"You will wed Jerval, and very soon, daughter," he called
after her. He suddenly feared that she would spew her hurt
and wrath on Jerval, and forced his voice to deadly calm, a
tone he had never before used with her. "You will behave
with the greatest respect toward Jerval, Chandra. You will
endeavor to remember that before an hour ago, you held him
as a good friend."

She turned and held his gaze, her eyes filled with bitter
sadness. "Respect, Father? If you had not agreed to wed me
to him four years ago, would you just as easily have given me
to Graelam de Moreton? I cannot see that one is much
different from the other."

"Once you become Jerval's wife, you will come to
understand," Richard said steadily.

She bowed her head, as would a chastened child, and
walked awkwardly away from him.

5

CHANDRA GRABBED HER FUR-LINED CLOAK and ran without looking back at Jerval, cursing her woman's long, narrow-skirted gown. She wasn't ready to see him, not yet. Not ever.

She felt a strong hand close over her arm, steadying her, as she stumbled in her haste on a sharp-edged cobblestone.

"Slow down," she heard Jerval say in an amused voice behind her. "You can't be a mountain goat in your gown."

He turned her slowly about to face him. Chandra kept her head down, refusing to meet his eyes.

"Chandra," he said, the amusement gone from his voice, "we must talk, you and I."

A raindrop fell on the tip of her nose, and she dashed it away.

"Come," he said gently, "before we get soaked." He led her inside the stable. It was dim within, and warm, and the smell of fresh-cut hay was sweet in the air.

Jerval nodded dismissal toward a stable boy who was busy forking hay into one of the horse's stalls.

"I have spoken with Lord Richard," Jerval said, gazing down into her shadowed face. He clasped her shoulders in his large hands and felt her stiffen at his words.

"As have I," she said in a flat voice, trying to pull free of him.

"Nay, I shan't let you go, Chandra. Come, sit down with me."

His hand slid down her arm until his fingers laced through hers. He pulled her down beside him on a thick bale of hay and released her hand.

"What is it you have to say, Jerval de Vernon?" she asked in the same flat voice.

She was not making it particularly easy for him, he thought, studying her averted face. How mature she seemed when

80

confronted with what she knew and understood, and how bewildered and vulnerable now, despite the coldness in her voice.

He cleared his throat and said, "I want to apologize to you, Chandra, for losing control of myself at the lake. I frightened you, and I am most sorry for it."

"You are a man," she said stiffly.

"Aye, I cannot deny it, and seeing you, a beautiful woman dressed only in a wet shift, made me forget myself. I promise that I will not touch you again until—"

"Until we are wed?" She meant to show him her anger, but her voice broke on the words.

"If that is your wish."

"Damn you, Jerval!" she hissed at him, hating the gentleness in his voice, for she knew all too well that he could afford to be generous. "And damn my father! If you would know my wishes, my lord, it is never to have to suffer your presence again!" She drew a deep breath, her father's warning words in her mind. She said coldly, "You duped me— you lied to me, all the while pretending to be my friend—"

"I am your friend, Chandra. There was no pretense there." He pulled an unwilling hand from her lap and held it tightly. "And you became my friend too. It should not cost you so very much to admit it."

"Do you deny, most noble knight," she continued, disregarding his words, "that you came to Croyland to look me over, to appraise me like some mare up for auction?"

"I found you quite up to my weight," he said, amused for a moment. He felt her fingernails dig into the palm of his hand, and realized this was not the time for jests.

"It is true," he continued in a more careful voice, "that your father did not wish you to know the reason for my visit to Croyland. He knew that you were innocent in the ways of women, that you had not yet awakened to a woman's feelings and needs. He, like I, hoped that our friendship would lead to something more . . . lasting. I believe that it will, if you will but let it."

"It will not," she said flatly, "and I don't have any of these ridiculous feelings and needs you speak so arrogantly about!"

"You will, once you are wed to me."

He saw her expressive eyes widen, and cursed himself

silently for frightening her. He knew in his own mind that he had spoken but the truth, though his words had seemed to hold masculine arrogance. He would caress her, tame her wild spirit, until she wanted him. He said gently, releasing her hand, "We are friends, Chandra, and friends talk to each other and work out their problems together."

"I had not thought about wedding anyone," she said finally, plucking a straw casually from her skirt, "until Graelam came with his demands. But then he was gone so quickly."

"I am truly sorry that he frightened you."

"He did not frighten me, Jerval," she said quickly, unwilling to show him any weakness. She shrugged her shoulders elaborately. "He merely angered me with his presumption."

He smiled at her, a thick brow raised mockingly. "Ah, I beg forgiveness yet again, my lady, for presuming to understand you."

She rose suddenly, whirled about to face him, and blurted out, "It is too soon! Marriage was supposed to come later, much later, when I was ready!"

"You are ready."

"Nay!" she cried, shaking her head. "I will never be ready to become a man's possession, a man's chattel! I do not want to be under your thumb, forced to obey you as I do my father! I do not want to leave Croyland, and give up—" She splayed her hands before her. "To give up everything!"

"Who said aught about your giving up anything?" he said, smiling into her flushed face. "As to being under my thumb, you'll find that I have a gentle touch." It was his turn to shrug. "And as to your obeying me, it is quite natural and God's commandment that a wife yield to her husband."

"It is natural only to you, not to me! I do not want to be owned, like a dog."

"Listen to me, Chandra. I love you. I have come to admire your courage, your spirit. I assure you that I would never feel such things about a dog. I vow it is more to your advantage to wed me than, say, a man who would want you only for the wealth you would bring him. I really do not see myself as your master, and quite frankly, you would make a dreadful slave."

"You are mocking me, and I do not think this is at all funny!"

"Nay, nor do I. I ask that you think about what I have

said, after, of course, you forget this nonsense about being auctioned off like a mare. You are seventeen, and a woman grown. It is time that you saw yourself in that light."

He rose and clasped her arms gently in his hands. He felt her tremble, and stroked her arms gently to soothe her and quiet her.

"Tapestries and devotions," she muttered, her eyes on the soft velvet of his surcoat. "There is aught else expected or allowed."

"And making beer," he teased her gently, "and raising children."

"I . . ." The thought of her belly round with child, her body clumsy and slow, made her shudder. "I . . . it is too soon. Nay, I do not wish it."

"It is too soon," Jerval said. "Everything will be all right, Chandra, I promise you. You must trust me, just as you trust your father, and believe that I will try never to hurt you or to demand things of you that you would dislike." He cupped her chin in his hand and forced her face upward. "Do not fret, little one," he said gently, "and do not curse me while I am gone—"

"You are leaving?" she asked hopefully.

He grinned down at her. "To fetch my family. I will return in two weeks for our wedding. Your life will change, Chandra, I cannot deny that. I think eventually you will prefer being a wife to being a daughter. There are many pleasant benefits, you know, over being one and not the other." Before she could disagree with him, he quickly leaned down and lightly touched his mouth to hers. He would have liked to stroke and caress her until she yielded, but he knew he must go slowly with her, and gain her trust again. He felt confident when he released her, for she simply stood before him, staring vaguely up at him.

"I must tell the men," he said. "We will leave at dawn on the morrow. Contrive, my love, to miss me whilst I am gone."

He left her, his step jaunty, and smiled upward into the rain.

"I will never miss you!" she cried, but he did not hear her.

*   *   *

Lord Richard pulled up his destrier and dismounted. "You are jousting like a blind man!" he called to Chandra. "Come here, and let me look at your arm."

Chandra slid off Wicket's broad back, tossed her broken lance to Ponce, and walked toward her father.

"You must be more careful," he said, his voice sharp with worry. "You have gashed your arm." He saw the red stain spreading outward through the rent in her hauberk. The banded mail of her armor was formed by rows of flat rings, slightly overlapping, sewn to leather. The rings were fastened farther apart than on a man's armor to make it lighter; it was not dense enough to deflect a blow. He pushed up the heavy sleeve to look at the wound, then drew a relieved breath, for it was not a deep cut. But it hurt him nonetheless that he had been the one to break her guard.

"It shouldn't scar," he said, wiping away the blood with his mailed hand.

She shrugged. "It doesn't matter." She pulled off her helmet and shoved back the meshed mail hood from her head. Her hair was matted and damp with sweat.

His eyes narrowed at her seeming indifference, but he said nothing more. In all fairness, she had behaved well the past two weeks, although she had been quieter than usual. When he had complimented her on her wedding gown several days before, she had merely nodded, her eyes on her blue leather slippers. Now she stood before him like a young squire, her armor shining in the bright afternoon sun. He wished she would be more the cocky lad, but she had not even yelled her victory when she had unseated Ponce in the practice field.

"You must pay more attention," he said finally. "You know well that it is dangerous not to concentrate on your opponent."

"I will endeavor to do your bidding, Father," she said ironically, "in all things."

"I know. You are a good girl, and obedient." He watched her wipe the sweat from her brow and shook his head at himself. She was his pride and joy when she took the field in her armor, her lance tucked under her arm, her back straight, her eyes unyielding on her approaching opponent. When he had seen Jerval off two weeks before in the foggy dawn, the young knight had been in high spirits, and confident that she would bend to him. It had been Jerval who had reassured him that all would be well.

He raised his head at Avery's shout. "My lord! Sir Jerval has returned!"

Richard shaded his eyes and followed Avery's pointing finger toward a large contingent of horses approaching from the north. He gazed over at Chandra, standing tall and proud in her armor, and knew a moment of uncertainty. Lord Hugh would not take her appearance too much amiss, he was certain, but Lady Avicia was another matter. He cursed softly, imagining well what that lady's reaction would be.

Chandra chewed on her lower lip as she watched the troop near. The two weeks seemed to have disappeared as quickly as the confection of honeyed nuts on John's plate the previous evening.

She drew a resigned breath. There was nothing for it. Her father's bidding was law.

"Come, Chandra, mount Wicket. It is polite to greet your new family."

She fell behind Lord Richard, trying, she supposed, to hide herself in the midst of the men.

Lord Hugh de Vernon was stiff and weary to his bones. Jerval had set a pace that had made his mother shriek in dismay, although she, he thought sourly, was riding comfortably in a damned litter! He saw Lord Richard riding toward him and felt a twinge of envy. Richard hadn't grown soft in the intervening years, as had he, but then, Richard wasn't cursed with the damned gout. The man would probably still make Avicia sigh in admiration. He looked for the girl, Chandra, aware that his son was tense with anticipation.

"Well, Richard," Lord Hugh said, as the two men pulled to a halt beside each other, "it is good to see you again. Four years! God's bones, 'tis a long time!" He heaved himself off his palfrey's back.

"And you, Hugh,' Richard said, joining him. They embraced formally.

"I see Jerval wasted no time," Richard continued, smiling toward his future son-in-law.

"It appears our chicks have a great liking for each other. I am pleased. Jerval has talked of nothing save your daughter since his return to Camberley."

"Where is Chandra, sir?"

"You have but to look for the prettiest boy to find her!"

"Hugh!"

"Aye, Avicia," Hugh called. "Leave Jerval with his lady, Richard, at least until you have paid due deference to mine!"

"Some things never change, do they, Hugh?" Richard grinned.

"Nay. I swear she wears me down more by the year!"

Lady Avicia pulled back the curtain from the litter, quickly patted her hair into place, and placed a brilliant smile on her lips.

"My lord," she said in a demure voice that made Hugh start. "It has been too long a time since I have seen you."

"My lady, 'tis my pleasure," Richard said. "The years have but added to your remarkable beauty." She was in truth still a handsome woman despite her age, Richard thought, with her flashing black eyes and the thick raven hair, now only slightly peppered with gray.

"I await the pleasure of meeting your lady wife and my new daughter."

Jerval said gaily, "You will meet her in just a moment, Mother. Let me fetch her."

Lady Avicia raised a thick brow as her eyes followed her son. "Jerval has told me, my lord," she said carefully, "that my new daughter is not precisely what I should expect."

"He has told you much more than that, Avicia," Hugh said.

A younger voice said, "Aye, Aunt, Jerval says that she is a warrior of sorts . . . as if a girl could be such a thing!"

"My niece, Julianna, my lord."

Richard noticed the young girl for the first time. She was lovely, her soft chestnut hair framing her face, her eyes large, a deep brown. He reckoned her to be about Chandra's age.

"Welcome, Julianna," Lord Richard said.

"St. Peter's eyes!" Lord Hugh boomed in an incredulous voice. "By the Almighty, Avicia, you've a rare treat in store for you!"

Richard turned to see Chandra dismount from her great destrier. Her armor glistened silver in the sunlight, and her surcoat of blue wool, flat over her chest, gave her the look of a young squire.

"My daughter, Lady Chandra de Avenell," Richard said, his pride sounding through in his voice.

Lady Avicia stared at Chandra. Both Hugh and Jerval had told her that the girl had been raised by Richard to play at men's sports, but armor!

"My lady," Chandra said in a tight voice. "Forgive me, but I have no skirts to curtsy with." She bowed at the waist, like a boy.

"Dear me," Julianna tittered, covering her mouth with her hand.

Lord Hugh eyed his future daughter with great interest. It did not take him long to recognize her beauty beneath the sweat and dirt on her face, and to understand why his son was besotted with her. "My lady," he laughed, saluting her as he would a man, his belly shaking, "you have provided us with quite a surprise."

"My lord," Chandra said seriously, turning to Jerval's father. "We were in the tiltyard. There was no surprise intended."

"There is blood on your arm," Lady Avicia said in a loud voice.

"I was clumsy," Chandra said, dismissing the matter. She saw her future mother-in-law stiffen, and said in a more conciliating voice, "Welcome to Croyland, my lady." Her eyes flickered toward Julianna and rested upon her face.

"I am Julianna, Jerval's cousin," Julianna said, staring at her closely.

Richard clapped Hugh on the back. "If you will accompany me, we will make you comfortable within."

As Chandra moved away from the litter, Jerval beside her, she heard Julianna hiss in a whisper to Lady Avicia, "She is a man, Aunt! But look at her! Jerval must be bewitched!"

Jerval touched his hand to Chandra's mailed arm. "Ignore Julianna," he said, smiling down at her. "Her mouth moves more quickly than her mind."

"She is quite pretty, just as you said."

"Aye, but she looks terrible in armor. I have missed you, Chandra. If I had been away from you much longer, I vow that my parents would have had a gag stuffed into my mouth. I fear they have grown weary hearing me sing your praises."

As she pursed her lips and did not reply, he said gently, "I hope you have thought about our last conversation, Chandra. I meant all that I said."

"Aye, I have thought about it. I have no choice but to obey my father."

"A commendable decision, and said with such longing!" He cupped his hand for her, but she ignored him, and jumped unassisted onto Wicket's back.

They rode side by side toward the keep. "The gash is not deep?" he asked, unable to keep concern from his voice.

"It is nothing."

"You must point out your opponent, poor fellow," he said, grinning.

She gave him an elusive answering smile, then bit down on her lip. He chuckled. "So you have forgiven me, though you are loath to admit it! The smile is much nicer, Chandra. It makes me forget the dirt on your face."

"You smell like a sweaty horse yourself, Jerval!"

"Perhaps I can persuade you to join me in my bath."

To her mortification, she flushed.

"Do not take it amiss that my mother was not more welcoming to you. She is a rather conventional lady, and seeing her future daughter-in-law in armor was a bit of a shock to her."

Chandra raised a disdainful brow. "I have taken nothing amiss, Jerval. Your mother may be just as she wishes."

"I have no doubt that both of you will do just as you wish."

They reached the inner bailey, and Chandra dismounted clumsily from Wicket's back. "See that the stable boys give him a good rubbing, Peter," she said, ignoring Jerval behind her. "He has earned his dinner."

She dropped Jerval a ridiculous mock of a curtsy. "I assume that I have no choice but to see you at dinner."

"I look forward to it, Chandra. It seems to me—but of course I can't be certain with all that chain mail—that you have grown thinner, pining for me. At dinner I will begin to fatten you up."

She glared at him in frustrated silence. There seemed to be no end to his hearty good humor. She turned on her heel and strode away from him.

Jerval stood silently for a moment, smiling after her.

Avery said from behind him, "I am glad you have returned so speedily, Sir Jerval. The men are pleased." He was silent a moment, following Chandra's progress up the stairs to the hall. "It is hard for her, sir," he said quietly, "to leave her home and all that she has known."

"Aye," Jerval sighed, "I know it well. Has she been a . . . problem since I left?"

Avery chuckled, stroking his graying beard. "Nay, my lady is never a problem, but she has seemed a bit less full of fun lately. Though," he amended judiciously, "she did yell at poor Ponce the other day when he chanced to recall your skill with the bow."

"Poor Ponce! I trust she didn't bash his head in."

"Nay, he hid behind the target to escape her wrath. She wants taming, I suppose, but one forgets that she is a girl, and not a cocky lad."

"She can be just as she likes," Jerval said, "just so long as she doesn't take a knife to me!"

In the small guest chamber next to Lord Richard's room, Lady Avicia paced back and forth, her wimple flapping about her flushed face like raven's wings.

"It is no wonder the girl is so wild," Avicia said. "Lady Dorothy is such a weak little mouse, of no influence over her daughter!"

Lord Hugh tossed down the rest of his sweet mulled wine and sat back against the back of his chair, waiting patiently for her tirade to run its course.

"She is a remarkably beautiful girl."

"However could you tell?" Avicia said acidly. "Armor! By the Virgin, the girl was in armor!" She paused a moment, and groaned. "Jerval has lost his mind! And you, Hugh, you agreed to this match four years ago—without telling me—knowing that the girl was being raised like a boy!"

"It is a brilliant match," Hugh said, wishing he had more wine.

"That's all you think about—land and more land! The girl will be his wife, and living at Camberley. What in heaven's name am I to do with her?"

"Regardless of her ways, my love, Chandra is a lady. It will be up to Jerval to decide how she will behave once they are wed."

"Your son seems totally blind to her man's arrogance!"

Hugh raised a beefy hand. "Nonetheless, Jerval is not a fool."

"And Julianna is none too pleased, I can tell you! She has been in a continual snit ever since Jerval returned home, every other word he spoke of that girl!"

"Julianna had best learn to keep her ire behind her tongue, else Chandra might well spit her on her lance."

"Stop making light of it, Hugh! However will I make a lady out of that . . . sow's ear? To think that she will be mistress of Camberley one day after I am dead!"

"You die, my love? Impossible!"

When Chandra entered the great hall, she saw Jerval talking to his cousin, Julianna. The girl's soft white hand tugged gently at the sleeve of his velvet surcoat. Worthless little flirt, Chandra thought, unaccountably peeved.

Lady Avicia turned away from a depressingly religious conversation with Lady Dorothy, wondering fleetingly if Lord Richard beat his wife, thus her religious fervor and her timidity. She dismissed the notion, seeing in the man who held an amazing resemblance to her son a virile force that could bend almost anyone to the strength of his will and personality. That his daughter had inherited all his male beauty and turned it to extraordinary account brought her little pleasure at the moment.

She could scarce believe that Chandra was the girl she had seen but three hours earlier suited in armor. Even to her critical eye, the girl was beautiful, her thick wheat-colored hair loose to her slender waist, confined from her forehead by a thin band of gold. Her eyes were a brilliant blue, and bright with intelligence. Her figure, set off now in a soft silk gown of pale yellow, was exquisite. She found it amazing that Chandra could be so much like her father, and resemble her mother not at all. Strong-willed she likely was, just like Richard. Chandra would learn quickly enough that Avicia was not a weak-kneed copy of Lady Dorothy, and that it was she who held sway at Camberley. She watched balefully as her son turned away from Julianna, as if she did not exist, and strode to Chandra, his eyes alight with pleasure. She knew that Julianna had hoped Jerval's marriage to the Croyland heiress was simply a matter of convenience and gain for the de Vernons, and when she had first seen Chandra sweaty and filthy as an urchin, her jealousy had seemed to still. But now as she watched the creature who stood in Jerval's giant shadow, she would know her hope to be foolish.

Lord Hugh smiled broadly as he watched his son with Chandra. "What a beauty," he said to Richard. "Your girl did not disappoint me in her man's garb. In her woman's trappings, there is no lady to compare to her. My son will know much enjoyment with her."

Aye, Richard thought, if Jerval could ever get her into his bed. He had tried once before Jerval returned to speak to her frankly about her duties as a wife, but she had stared up at him, her face paling. He had seen fear and distaste in her eyes. "There is pleasure in coupling," he had said. "Aye," she had muttered, "but not between men and their wives!" He had flushed, momentarily angry with her at her insult, and said stiffly, "I hope it will be different for you, Chandra."

Chandra stopped by Mark's place at the long trestle table and greeted him more warmly than she had Jerval. Jerval, who was standing at her elbow, merely smiled, watching Mark stutter uncomfortably at her attention.

"You have not the knack, Chandra, to make me jealous," he whispered in her ear as he led her to the dais. "And I beg you to have pity on poor Mark! You left his tongue tied in knots with your attempt at flirtation."

"I find your male presumptions ridiculous, Jerval!"

"My, but your tongue is sharp tonight, my lady," he said softly, his fingers caressing up her arm. "I wonder how I can gentle it."

"You are incredibly thick-skinned," she hissed at him.

"You, my love, are incredibly soft-skinned, and you smell of lavender. It is my favorite scent."

She growled her frustration, saw her father was eyeing her, and forced a smile to her lips. "I am hungry," she said.

"Excellent. You have indeed grown thinner, I see, but we shall put an end to that. No man wants a skinny wife."

"The pork is tasty," Lady Avicia said some moments later to Lady Dorothy, as she gazed with disapproval at Lord Richard, who had tossed a meaty bone to Graynard.

"Aye, Lady Dorothy," Lord Hugh agreed, "a splendid meal. The wine, in particular, Richard, is most remarkable."

"Thank the French captain who anchored in Croyland harbor some weeks ago. 'Tis from Bordeaux, red as blood and sweet-tasting as a woman."

Richard said the last words in Lady Avicia's direction, and she blushed, like an untried girl. She wasn't skinny, like his wife, and he wondered if Hugh still enjoyed her bed. Hugh, he thought, gazing toward his longtime friend, seemed to find enjoyment only in his food.

Jerval grinned toward Chandra at Lord Richard's provocative words, and pressed his thigh against her, as if by accident. She flushed and pulled away from him. "Let me cut your meat," he said softly, leaning his side against her.

"I would that you keep to your place, Jerval!" she whispered furiously.

"Our chicks do not seem to be paying much attention to their food," Lord Hugh said, copying Lord Richard and tossing a bone to Graynard.

"I ask you, Father, if you were seated next to Chandra, could you concentrate on a meal?"

"Ask me that question again after you have been wed for thirty years!"

"Hold your tongue, Hugh," Avicia said acidly, poking his expanding stomach.

"How will you look in thirty years, I wonder?" Jerval mused aloud to Chandra.

"If I have to live with you all that time, I'll likely be a withered old crone."

"Crone?" Lord Hugh said.

"Nay, Father, never that," Jerval laughed. "Indeed, you will soon see that she is an angel, and under my careful protection, she will remain such for at least thirty years." He smiled at her mutinous expression. "You will play for us, will you not?"

"Of course she will," Lord Richard said quickly, before she could refuse.

"Ah," Avicia said brightly, one black brow raised. "A lady's accomplishment."

"My daughter has many accomplishments," Lady Dorothy said, "and she has all the pious modesty of a young lady. She has had religious instruction from Father Tolbert all her life."

"Poor Chandra," Jerval said. "And I thought you were ever trying to escape him."

"What will you sing?" Julianna said, praying that she would hear a stiff, wooden voice.

"Something joyful, to fit the occasion," Jerval answered.

"It will be something . . . appropriate," she said.

Ponce fetched Chandra's lyre for her when the meal was over, and she seated herself calmly, with a flickering look toward Jerval. "My song will be of Tristan . . . and his tragic fate."

She realized only when she reached the middle verses that she had not chosen wisely, for Tristan's love for Isolde transcended even death. It was a tribute to eternal love, and she flushed furiously at the amused look on Jerval's face.

When she finished, Jerval leaned over to her and said under the cover of the applause, "You were right, my love. Your choice pleased me greatly."

"Clod!" she grated. "I did not mean it!"

He arched a fair brow and grinned at her. "Perhaps it was your heart speaking." At her glowering look, he added, "You do have a heart, Chandra. It lies yon, beneath your beautiful breast."

"You know nothing of my—of anything!"

"How soon you forget our memorable wrestling match, my lady."

She turned red, for the memory of the two of them wrestling on the beach was now clouded with the image of her torn shift, and Jerval turning abruptly away from her.

"Nay," she snapped, "I forget nothing!"

"Well sung, daughter," Lord Richard said when the hall was again quiet.

"Aye, it was," Avicia agreed, frowning.

"If the weather holds," Lord Richard said, "I think we should hold the wedding in the orchard. The trees are beginning to blossom and 'twill make a pleasant setting."

"Father Tolbert will conduct the ceremony," Lady Dorothy said. "I have, of course, invited all Lord Richard's vassals and their retinues. 'Twill be a vast company."

"When do your vassals arrive, Richard?" Lord Hugh asked.

"If all goes smoothly, our wedding guests should begin arriving day after tomorrow."

"There is so much to be done," Lady Dorothy said, her hands dithering in her lap. Lady Avicia wondered if she should offer to help, for she doubted Lady Dorothy could handle even the servants.

"I trust you will stay out of your armor, Chandra," Avicia

said in a loud voice. "It would be most unsightly for a bride to be covered with bandages on her wedding day."

"Never fear, Mother," Jerval said. "I will see that she comes to no harm." He added in a caressing voice, so close that Chandra could smell the sweet wine on his breath, "You are mine, now, my love, and I have every intention of faring better than did poor Tristan."

Just after dawn on the morning of her wedding, Chandra slipped from the keep and made her way in the chill low-lying fog to the east tower on the outer wall. It was a favorite haunt since childhood, a quiet, isolated spot.

A tired guard stood silent vigil some twenty feet away, leaning forward on the crenellated wall, and did not hear her approach. She had passed but one of the guests outside the keep, a man in Sir Stephen's service, on his way to the jakes. Soon, she knew, the servants would be up and about and the guests who had had to spend the night wrapped in blankets in the great hall would be jostled awake by the racket. The barracks were packed and even the wall chambers overflowed with guests.

She sighed and crouched down against the damp stone wall, pulling her fur-lined cloak close about her. She ran her finger slowly over the rough surface, tracing the chipped crannies that had been deep in the stone before her birth. She rested her head against the stones and felt tears sting her eyes. She could not imagine leaving Croyland.

It was there that Mary found her, curled up fast asleep, her head leaning against the hard stone.

"Chandra," she said softly, touching her hand lightly to her friend's shoulder.

"It cannot yet be time!" Chandra gasped, jerking awake.

"Nay, 'tis still early. I am sorry to disturb you, Chandra, but I wished to speak to you. I could not find you, and guessed that perhaps you would be here."

"It's the only private place left," she said in a bitter voice. She looked closely at her friend and seemed to catch herself. "I'm sorry, Mary. Come, sit beside me. No one will see us." She had had little time to think about Mary in the past two days.

"You have said nothing to your father, have you?"

"Nay, I have not told him, just as you wished." She drew

a deep breath. "I cannot remain at Croyland, Chandra, once you leave." Mary turned away her face. "Please," she whispered, "take me with you to Camberley. I could not bear to return to my father's keep, knowing that he would give me eventually to someone in marriage, and that I would have to tell him I am no longer a maid. I could not bear the shame of it. I do not know what he would do."

Chandra felt ashamed that she had not thought to ask Mary to accompany her herself. "Of course you will come with me. Do you think you could bear Jerval's mother, and that malicious snit Julianna?"

"Oh, Julianna is just jealous of you, that is all. She will doubtless bide her tongue once you are wed. As for Lady Avicia, she is a bit overpowering, I'll admit, but not a mean person."

"Ah, Mary," Chandra sighed, "you always see the best in people, perhaps even when it is not there."

She rose to her feet and gave her hand to Mary. A frown puckered her brow. "Damn," she muttered. "I must ask Jerval's permission, for Camberley is his home."

"Do you think he will permit it?" Mary asked, suddenly apprehensive.

"Of course he will," Chandra said sharply.

"You are right. Jerval would deny you nothing." She paused a moment, looking out toward the fog-veiled harbor. "How very lucky you are."

"He denies me my freedom," Chandra gritted. "How can you say I'm lucky when I must leave Croyland?"

"I hardly think you would wish to spend the rest of your life here," Mary said tartly, "particularly after John grows up and becomes master. Can you imagine the kind of girl he will marry?"

Chandra could not help but grin. "You sometimes see things too clearly, Mary. It is an appalling thought! Now, let me go see Jerval."

Mary started to remind her that the bride was not supposed to see the groom before the wedding ceremony, but she knew that Chandra would just scoff and do what she wished.

Chandra pinned a smile to her lips as she made her way through the hall, where at least fifty people were eating their morning meal, amid boisterous joking. When she reached Jerval's chamber, one that he shared with Sir Mark, she paused a moment, hearing several serving maids giggling within.

"Good God!" Mark exclaimed when he opened the door and saw Chandra. "I have just got Jerval into his bath."

"I would speak to Jerval, Mark. Please remove the serving maids."

Mark gave her a questioning look, but merely nodded and left her. Two young girls emerged, wet and laughing. They shot her a smug, knowing look at they passed, herded out by Mark.

"By your leave, lady," he said and bowed.

Chandra walked into the small chamber. Jerval was sitting in a sturdy wooden tub, water swirling about his waist. His golden hair was plastered wet about his head.

"I must speak to you, Jerval," she said without preamble, keeping her eyes firmly on his face.

Jerval wiped the astonished look from his face. He was delighted to see her, and pleased that she would search him out on their wedding morning. It was simply not done, but then again, he thought ruefully, when had she ever concerned herself about what others thought?

"To what do I owe this unexpected pleasure, my love? Could you not wait but a couple more hours to have me at your side?"

"This is important, Jerval. I did not come to trade inane jests with you."

"Ah, a serious discussion. Forgive me, but I am bound to my bath, unless, of course, you would like to join me." He saw her eyes shift down his body, as if she realized for the first time that he was naked. His weeks of celibacy began to tell as he watched her, and he was relieved the water came to his waist.

She looked quickly away from him. "It is Mary."

He gazed at her blankly. "Mary?"

"My friend, daughter of Sir Stephen. She wishes to accompany me to Camberley. I wish it also. Since Camberley is not my home, I am here to secure your permission."

He did not point out to her that Camberley would very shortly be her home as well. He smiled at her reassuringly and said, "Surely such a matter should be discussed with Sir Stephen. She is young and comely, and ripe to wed. Surely, her father—"

"You don't understand," Chandra interrupted. She drew a deep breath. "I suppose it is only fair that you know, but I beg you to tell no one else. Lord Graelam . . . raped Mary."

"Raped her?" His anger held him silent for a moment. "I do not understand . . . it was you he wanted. Why did he take the girl?"

"Neither Mary nor I would tell him where my mother and John were hidden. Without them, he could not force me to wed him. It was my fault that it happened, for had I only spoken, Mary would have been spared. I have not let her tell anyone. Her father, Sir Stephen, is not an . . . understanding man. He would come to know the truth, for Mary would have to tell him when he sought her a husband. I doubt that he would be kind to her."

He reacted immediately to her distress. "Of course she will come with us. Fret no more about it. It will be our secret."

"I—it is kind of you, Jerval."

"I can already hear the merrymaking," he said in a neutral voice, not wanting her to leave him just yet.

"Aye," she said, a reluctant smile turning up the corners of her mouth. "Sir Andrew was so drunk last night that his groans filled the hall this morning. I really must go now, Jerval. There is much for me to do."

"Although I have looked forward to this day for many weeks now, I still wish it were over. We have had no time together," He squeezed the sponge over his chest, seemingly intent on the rivulets of water that trickled to his belly. "Would you wash my back, Chandra?"

She started. It was, she knew, a task that women performed, both for their husbands and for guests. And she had many times scrubbed her father's broad back.

"You do want me sweet-smelling, do you not?" She was holding herself stiffly, and her eyes were flitting toward the door warily. "I trust," he teased her, "that you intend to be a dutiful wife," and he tossed her the sponge.

As she rubbed the soapy sponge in long strokes down his muscled back, Chandra wished that he were vilely rude toward her, or at least hunchbacked and ugly. At least then she could hate him.

"If I stand up, will you wash the rest of me?"

"Nay!" She threw the sponge at him, turned on her heel, and fled the bedchamber, his teasing laughter sounding in her ears.

Chandra stood quietly as Alice pulled the soft, saffron-tinted linen chemise over her head. " 'Tis almost lovely enough to serve as your gown, my lady," she said placidly, pleased with her chick.

"You have done well with her bridal gown," Lady Avicia said almost grudgingly to Lady Dorothy.

"Thank you, Avicia," Lady Dorothy replied, her hands fluttering over its skirt to smooth a slight wrinkle. "Hurry, Alice, it is nearly time."

"The color is odd," Julianna said. At Avicia's frown, she quickly amended, "But lovely, of course."

Alice lifted the wedding gown, fringed with magnificent ermine, over Chandra's head, and smoothed it down over her hips. It was made of two cloths sewed together, the inner of fine wool, the outer of beautiful sendal of reddish violet. "Draw in your breath, my lady," Alice said, and laced the gown so tightly that Chandra had to protest.

"Do let it out a bit," Lady Avicia instructed. "We don't want Chandra fainting from want of air during the ceremony."

Next, Alice floated the tunic of green silk over her head. It was elegant and soft to the touch, with a long train, and full sleeves that fell beyond Chandra's fingers. Her pointed shoes were made of vermilion leather and threaded with more gold embroidery. They pinched her toes.

"I shall never be able to walk in all this," Chandra said, gazing down at herself.

"Here is the girdle, my love," Lady Dorothy said. It was made of pieces of gold, each set with a good-luck stone— agate to guard against fever, sardonyx to protect against malaria. The clasp was fashioned with great sapphires.

Since the morning was bidding to be warm, Chandra carried her mantle over her arm. Like the gown, it was of silk, intricately embroidered and dyed a royal purple.

After Alice had arranged Chandra's long hair to her satisfaction, Mary stepped forward and placed a small saffron-colored veil held by a golden circlet on her head.

"You will not shame my son," Lady Avicia announced when Chandra was finally ready.

No, Chandra thought to herself, as she looked at the strange exquisite girl in her mirror, and I will not shame my father either. She straightened her shoulders and forced a smile to her lips. It was her wedding day, the only one she would ever have, and it behooved her to be gracious. She was, after all, she thought, a lady.

The castle chapel was too small to accommodate all the wedding guests, and Chandra, her father at her side, walked toward the orchard, where Father Tolbert waited to conduct the ceremony.

The servants, under Lady Dorothy's nominal direction, had raised an archway and threaded colorful flowers in the latticework. When Chandra and her father walked beneath the arch, Jerval stepped forward to join them. He wore fine brown silk stockings and a tunic of blue sendal silk that reached to his knees. His mantle, like hers, was edged with miniver. He wore a golden chaplet on his shining wheat-colored hair, set with flashing gems.

Jerval met her gaze and winked at her. She gave him a shy, answering smile.

The guests, fifty deep, formed a half circle about Father Tolbert, who was looking pompous and important, and, to Chandra's relief, clean. He nodded toward Lord Richard, who stepped from Chandra's side and turned to face the wedding guests.

He unrolled a wide parchment and real aloud the lands, servitors, and fine garments Chandra would bring to Jerval as her dowry. Next he read King Henry's greetings to the bride and groom, and his formal permission for them to wed.

Jerval reached out and clasped Chandra's hand. "If the king had refused, I would have had to abduct you," he whispered.

Father Tolbert cleared his throat portentously and called for Lady Chandra and Sir Jerval to come forward.

In but a few moments, Chandra thought wildly, I will no longer be a de Avenell of Croyland. Her breath seemed to catch in her throat. She looked helplessly toward her father, and he smiled at her, nodding his head in silent encouragement.

She scarce heard the long solemn mass of the Trinity, nor, she suspected, did Jerval. He kept shifting from one foot to the other. She wondered, a tentative smile on her lips, if his shoes pinched his toes as did hers.

At last Father Tolbert drew near the couple and pronounced his special blessing. Chandra started at his words.

"Let this woman," Father Tolbert intoned, "be amiable as Rachel, wise as Rebecca, faithful as Sarah. Let her be sober through truth, venerable through modesty, and wise through the teaching of heaven."

"By the blessed saints," Jerval whispered close to her ear, "you will be all that, my love?"

The mass ended. Father Tolbert chanted the *Agnus Dei*, then stepped back. It was the first noble ceremony he had performed since coming to Croyland, and he beamed, quite pleased with his presentation.

Lord Richard was thinking about other matters, the various gifts he would be expected to distribute among the guests, gifts that had cost him heavily. He heard the *Agnus Dei*, and brought his attention back to his daughter. She was behaving well, her bearing proud, her manner gracious. More important, she seemed to him to have accepted the inevitable. He was suddenly aware of a tensing in Lady Dorothy. He glanced up to see Chandra gazing forlornly at him, like a small frightened doe, even as Jerval, having received the kiss of peace from Father Tolbert, pressed his mouth to her cheek. She dropped her eyes as her husband embraced her.

A loud cheer went up from the wedding guests, signaling the last silent moment of the day. The jongleurs Richard had hired for the wedding puffed their cheeks against their flutes and began to dance among the laughing guests. Jerval, feeling as jubilant as their guests, pulled Chandra close to him and led the procession back to the great hall. "You are the most beautiful bride I have ever had," he said loudly, to be heard over the raucous singing of the jongleurs, and the guests. He felt her hand, clammy and warm in his, and leaned over to kiss her.

"I . . . it is over, thank God."

"Ah, no, my love, 'tis just beginning!"

The huge wedding feast was at last drawing to a close as evening neared, and Jerval felt that he never wanted to see another bite of food again. The haunch of roasted stag, the larded boar's head with herb sauce, beef, mutton, legs of pork, swan, and roasted rabbit were strewn about on the tables, now little more than meatless carcasses, or tossed to the boarhounds, who growled happily, pulling the bones through the reeds. He heard himself groan aloud when the servants staggered into the hall carrying yet more food: rabbits in gravy spiced with onion and saffron, roasted teal, woodcock, and snipe, patties filled with yolk of eggs, and cheese, cinnamon, and pork pies.

"My God," he said, crossing his hands over his belly, "we will die of gluttony!"

"That and drunkenness," Chandra said, gazing out over the guests, many of whom were already amiably drunk.

Sir Andrew raised leering eyes and shouted, "Sir Husband, how will you go about bedding your warrior bride?"

"Aye," came another shout. "Will the bride remove her armor?"

"Will the bride challenge the groom for her maidenhead?"

" 'Tis a challenge I would willingly accept," Sir Stephen said on a belch.

"It will be my pleasure, and mine alone," Jerval called back. "The rest of you lecherous goats should go take a swim in the cold sea!"

"A man's rod is his wife's dearest friend," Sir Malcolm's wife, Joanna, laughed, her voice thick with too much wine.

"How would you know, my lady?" Sir Andrew chortled. "That old man you're married to wouldn't know what to do if he discovered what he had between his legs!"

Lady Dorothy shifted uncomfortably in her chair, embarrassed by such coarseness.

"Sir Jerval knows!" Sir Malcolm roared. "He can't take his eyes off his maiden bride!"

"It's amazing that my son can still sit straight with the pain he must have in his loins!" Lord Hugh said.

" 'Twill pass, 'twill pass," Father Tolbert said, beaming, much to Lady Dorothy's chagrin.

Jerval grinned tolerantly as he listened to the ladies and men alike praising his male attributes. He leaned toward Chandra to tease her, and saw that she was sitting rigid in her chair, her face set and pale. "Do not mind them, my love," he said gently. "One expects such horseplay at a marriage feast. It means nothing."

She smelled the sweet scent of mulled wine on his breath and felt the warmth of his body as he pressed close to her. She wanted to hide away, to quash the fear that was beginning to eat at her.

"Will Lord Richard's men or Lady Dorothy's ladies lead the bride to her wedding chamber?" Sir Andrew shouted.

"And who will do the mounting? Sir Jerval, be you the stallion or the mare?"

" 'Tis no boy beneath the grand clothes, that's for certain!"

Jerval said in a loud, laughing voice, "You, Hubert, and you, Mark, see that I am blessed to have both a mare and a stallion! I will have the joy of mounting and being mounted!"

Richard rose from his great chair and banged his knife handle onto the table for quiet. "Avery," he roared, "bring in the three swine!"

Jerval's brows rose in surprise. Three filthy men, pale from their weeks in Croyland's dungeon and cowering in fear, were dragged into the great hall by Avery and Ellis and shoved to their knees before Lord Richard.

Chandra, sharing Jerval's surprise, turned to her father. He slowly drew a parchment from the full sleeve of his robe and waved it toward the men. "Listen well, knaves!" he said loudly to the bowed men before him. "For this parchment is for your master, Lord Graelam de Moreton, from our beloved king, Henry. I release you varlets to return to your lord. You will tell him that the prize he sought will ne'er be his! He will live the rest of his miserable life knowing that my daughter is another man's wife. The king herewith orders that he will pay half of all Croyland's taxes for the next full year in just retribution for his villainy." Richard thrust the parchment into one of the men's hands. "Tell your lord that the king has saved his lands from my revenge. Go now, get thee gone!"

Richard smiled down at his daughter, his eyes glistening with his gift to her.

" 'Tis well done, sir," Jerval said.

"Now," Richard shouted, " 'tis time for the dancing!"

"Aye, Chandra, come dance with me," Jerval said. "It's exercise we need, to ease our bellies of all this food."

The jongleurs grouped together and began a lively tune, their viols, guitars, gigues, dulcimers, and cymbals filling the hall with gay sounds. Chandra allowed Jerval to take her hand, and they walked to the center of the hall, where she curtsied and he bowed. The guests cheered as they touched hands and began to dance.

"Every man should have such a graceful wife!"

"Nay, it's the lusty groom I want!" Lady Joanna called out, and pulled her husband to his feet.

Chandra tripped on the train of her gown. Jerval stepped quickly forward and clutched her against his chest to steady her.

"Not here, my boy!" Lord Hugh guffawed loudly.

Chandra was awash with embarrassment. She tried to jerk away from Jerval, but he continued to hold her close. "Nay, love, we don't want to add more fuel to their sodden fires."

"Please," she choked. "I cannot bear it . . . make it stop."

"Very well, 'tis late enough." He released her and made a grand bow to the applauding company. "If anyone is still able to understand me," he shouted, "my bride and I wish to retire now."

Lady Dorothy rose with alacrity and waved frantically toward Father Tolbert, who was looking befuddled and vague.

Father Tolbert managed to stand, though he was weaving. "We will escort our bride and groom upstairs," he announced in a slurred voice, "and I will bless the nuptial couch."

"Will you be my escort, my lord?" Avicia asked in a coy voice.

Richard gallantly took her hand and followed in the weaving procession up the winding stairs to the upper apartments.

The laughing guests shoved Jerval and Chandra into her bedchamber and toward her bed, which was covered with red roses.

Father Tolbert mumbled a few words of blessing with as much dignity as he could muster, made the sign of the cross over the marriage bed, and then gave Chandra a drunken kiss on her forehead.

Lady Avicia unceremoniously prodded the gentlemen from the chamber, realizing that Lady Dorothy would likely continue to stand like a mute stick. "The bride must prepare herself for her husband. Out, all of you!"

As Lord Hugh was pushed toward the door, he called out to Jerval, "Plunge your rod deep, my boy, and plant your seed this very night!"

"Out, all of you," Lady Avicia commanded again.

Chandra gazed about her at the hovering women. "Please, I wish only Mary to attend me," she announced.

"My lady," Jerval said, and bowed deeply.

Chandra looked toward her father, saw him nod his head gently toward her and escort Lady Avicia from the chamber.

"You will be all right, Chandra?" Lady Dorothy whispered, hanging back.

Chandra stared down at her mother's pale face.

Lady Dorothy's fingers knotted about her rosary beads. "I—I have never spoken to you about a man's . . . needs, or a man's demands. Your father—"

"There is nothing I do not know," Chandra said, her voice taut.

Lady Dorothy nodded, relief in her eyes, and trailed from the bedchamber.

When Mary and Chandra were at last alone, Chandra jerked the circlet and veil from her head and shook out her hair. "It was so heavy. It was making my head ache."

"Let me help you undress, Chandra."

But I don't want to undress!

She nodded numbly and unfastened the girdle from about her waist.

"Is it fair that women must always obey?"

Mary, whose head was none too clear after three goblets of wine, stared at her, not understanding.

"Be dutiful, and not complain, like Rachel, Sarah, and all those other women Father Tolbert droned on about?"

"It is God's will, I suppose," Mary said finally, trying to gather her wits together.

"God always seems called upon when men wish to justify their actions," Chandra muttered. She jerked the soft chemise over her head.

"Chandra!" Mary shrieked. "Be careful, you will rip it! I spent days on the stitches!"

Chandra glowered at her, but laid the garment gently over the chest at the bottom of her bed, then reached for her plain woolen bedrobe.

"I think you aren't supposed to wear anything," Mary said, flushing, eyeing the old robe. "And Lady Avicia told me quite clearly that you are to be in bed when Jerval returns."

"Does she intend to come in and make certain that I've done her bidding?"

"You should have drunk more wine," Mary said, pursing her lips. "You would not be so afraid."

"I am not afraid . . . of anything!"

"Jerval is very kind," Mary continued, disregarding. "And I think he is sincerely attached to you." She paused a moment. "It is not so bad," she whispered, gulping. "Indeed, if one were with one cared about, it would perhaps be pleasant."

"How can you talk like that?" Chandra growled at her. "By God, after what Lord Graelam did to you!"

"Graelam is not Jerval, Chandra." She was struggling for more words when a loud knock came on the chamber door.

Chandra stiffened and whirled about, clutching her bedrobe over her breasts.

Jerval, attuned to his wife's skittishness, had allowed only Mark to escort him to Chandra's chamber. She had endured enough ribald jests.

"Chandra looked exquisite today," Mark said, as they stood outside Chandra's chamber. It was a roundabout preamble, a habit of Mark's that Jerval understood well. He waited for him to continue. Mark tugged on his ear. "She looked pale tonight."

"Aye, the boisterous jesting was not to her liking."

"I saw fear on her face."

"She is young, and innocent. Believe me, Mark, I am not some rutting fool who means her ill."

As Mark held himself silent, Jerval said, grinning wryly, "You of all people should trust me to do what is wise."

"Aye, I know it. I hope you will keep Julianna away from her. She is jealous."

Jerval shrugged. "Believe me, Julianna's jealousy is the last thing on my mind at this moment. Come, Mark, wish me pleasure this night."

"Aye, I wish it," Mark said.

Mary opened the door and smiled tentatively up at Jerval.

"My lady is ready for me?" he asked, his eyes and voice bright.

"Aye, my lord."

"Goodnight, Jerval," Mark said. He turned and offered his arm to Mary.

Jerval did not move until he had bolted the door after them. He smiled, pleased with himself. Chandra was his, finally.

His bare feet made no sound as he walked into her chamber.

She was not in bed, as he expected her to be, but standing with her back pressed against the far wall. In the soft light, her hair looked like spun gold, loose and curling to her waist. He knew that beneath the soft woolen robe she was naked. Her eyes stared at him, huge and questioning.

"You have not taken the roses off the bed."

She continued to stare at him as if she feared to look away from him. She shook her head, and a thick tress of hair fell over her shoulder. Her hand was fisted about the front of her robe, bunching it together tightly over her breasts.

"I will do it then," he said easily. He felt her eyes on his back as he walked to the bed and swept the roses from the coverlet.

He gazed negligently about her bedchamber. There were, he saw, few feminine touches. Her bow and quiver of arrows were leaning against the wall, her lance and sword beside them.

"Chandra?" he called gently. "Would you care for some wine?"

"Nay," she croaked.

He forced himself to turn away from her, walk to a single high-backed chair and sit down. "It has been a long day, with much merrymaking, and . . . jesting. It means nothing, you know that, save that all wish us happy."

He felt a surge of impatience with her, for she simply stared at him, mute.

"You seemed willing enough to talk to me all day. Have you nothing to say to me now?"

"I—I am tired."

"That is a beginning, I suppose. I would not hurt you, Chandra. Come here, my love, for I would hold you." When she did not move, he rose and walked slowly toward her. He heard her gasp suddenly, and looked down to see his member thrusting out from between the parted folds of his bedrobe. He grinned at her. "My desire for you is obvious. It is not an instrument of torture, Chandra."

He reached out his hand and lightly traced his fingers over her cheek. "You have a nice nose," he said. "You can look very haughty, you know, when you raise it, thus." He touched his fingers to her chin and raised her face to him.

"I do not mean to," she said.

"Mean to what, my love? Be frightened of me?"

She lowered her head to escape his probing eyes and did not answer.

"I did not know you were so shy." He closed his hands gently about her shoulders, pulled her slowly toward him, and touched his mouth to hers. He closed his eyes, not wanting her to see his desire. "You taste sweet, Chandra." He stroked her arms and could feel her trembling beneath her woolen robe, but she did not pull away from him. He laced his fingers through her silky hair and gently kneaded her neck.

"Do not fear me, Chandra," he said, his voice husky.

She felt his fingers caress the thick tresses of hair that hung over her shoulders. He kissed her again, gently, his mouth undemanding. His hand slipped inside her robe, and she felt his fingers glide over her breasts, his palms rubbing lightly over her nipples. The feel of his man's rod hard against her belly broke the hold she had on herself. She screamed in her mind for him to stop, but the sound that came from her throat was a broken sob.

Jerval released her instantly and drew back to see her face. He drew a deep breath and forced himself to slow. "You must give me a chance, my love, and yourself. A man's body is strange to you."

"Nay!" she shrieked, pulling out of his hold. "I do not want you to touch me, Jerval de Vernon! No man can!"

She saw his eyes narrow and rushed on. "It is a vow, Jerval," she cried. "A vow that is sacred before God!"

"Vow?" He drew up and stared at her blankly.

Chandra drew a deep breath and said as calmly as she could, "Aye. I swore before God that I would not let any man know me for as long as I lived at Croyland. It is a sacred vow I must not break."

"Your father said nothing about any vow to me. Come, Chandra, what nonsense is this?"

"It is not nonsense! I swore by my honor, as a maid, before God!"

He knew she was lying to him, he heard it in her shaking voice and saw it in her eyes. He was silent for a long moment, wondering what to do. He gazed about at her bedchamber, the room that belonged to the child before the woman, and realized he was the stranger here. He did not belong with her at Croyland as her husband. He forced his desire to calm. She was overwrought, and to force her would be the height of stupidity.

He said gently, trying to keep irony from his voice, "I recognize your vow, Chandra." Dammit, he had to get her away from Croyland! "We will leave for Camberley after the tourney tomorrow."

She stared at him, her victory suddenly dashed. "But we cannot! There are to be festivities for the next three days!"

"It is my wish."

He threw off his bedrobe and without looking at her again climbed into her bed. He lay naked on his back, his head pillowed on his arms, and looked up at the shadowed ceiling.

When she did not move toward him, he said sharply, "Come here, Chandra. I will honor your vow. I wish to talk to you, something that you have been reluctant to do since my return." He patted the bed beside him, and slowly, as if she expected him to leap at her, she inched toward the bed. She did not remove her bedrobe, but lay down on her back on the far side of the bed.

"Now that you are safe from me, will you talk to me?"

"What is it you wish to say, Jerval?"

He leaned over and snuffed out the lone candle. "We are married, Chandra, and will remain so until we die. You will see me every morning when you awake, eat all your meals with me, fall asleep with me at night, and put up with my snoring. We cannot continue to be strangers."

"I had not thought of it like that before," she said in a small voice.

"I know," he continued. "Your thoughts have been too filled with uncertainty and fear at leaving your home, and of this night." He turned over on his side to face her. He could make out her profile in the sliver of moonlight that shone through the small unshuttered window.

"I do not wish to become another father to you, Chandra. You are a woman grown now, and my wife. I have no wish to destroy you, to force you to become something you are not."

"You have already forced me to become a wife."

"I would that you cease harping about what is now done and will not be undone." He drew a tight rein on his temper. "Tell me, Chandra, what is it you want to do with your life?"

"I want—" She broke off abruptly, realizing that what she would have said was untrue. She did not want to spend the rest of her days at Croyland. Mary was right—the thought of being under John's thumb when he became a man was appalling. "I do not know what I want."

"At least you are finally speaking frankly to me. We will have children, you know, a quiverful, if you've the desire."

"Nay!" she cried, taken off guard. "It is . . . too soon. I have not thought about children."

"Of course you have. We discussed it before I left for Camberley. I think you will look beautiful, your belly stretched with child."

"My mother did not look beautiful! She was ill and cried, and my father ignored her!"

"I am not your father, nor, I might add, are you anything like your mother."

"I am tired," she said stiffly, turning her back to him. "I do not wish to discuss anything else with you."

"As you will," he said.

In the gray hour of dawn, Jerval gazed at his wife, curled up tightly on the edge of the bed, far away from him, still in her bedrobe. Her hair was fanned out about her head on the pillow, like a silken tangled mantle. She had awakened him with a soft moaning cry, torn from some dream.

He reached out his hand to shake her from her dream, then drew it back. If he touched her, he would not be able to stop himself. He forced himself to think of the many nights that stretched before them and turned away from her. Still, he was determined to leave Croyland as soon as possible, after the tourney, if he could arrange it. It would be churlish to leave before, for he was to ride in the tourney with Chandra's blue silk scarf knotted about his arm.

6

"YOU'LL CURSE YOURSELF, JERVAL, FOR leaving the warmth and comfort of Croyland beforetimes if those storm clouds I see to the west keep building."

Jerval slewed his head about and looked thoughtfully toward the sea. "You might be right. Let us hope the winds blow it southward."

His roan destrier, Pith, snorted as if he disliked the prospect of getting soaked, and Mark grinned. He looked over his shoulder and saw Chandra riding beside Mary near the middle of their troop, her rich fur-lined cloak spread about her, covering Wicket's rump.

"Your insistence on leaving after the tourney," Mark continued, turning back to his friend, "did make the men growl, for they were much enjoying themselves. They decided not to begrudge your getting your beautiful bride to yourself and away from Croyland."

"We stayed for a day of the festivities. I grew weary of my head throbbing with all the wine."

"Odd," Mark said, his eyes twinkling, "I never noticed you drinking much wine!"

Jerval glanced at Mark balefully and shrugged.

"All the guests' flowing wit about your husbandly prowess," Mark continued smoothly, "was none too pleasant for Chandra. Sir Andrew vowed you won the tourney so quickly because your stiff rod made riding painful."

Jerval remembered Chandra's discomfort at Sir Andrew's jest, and he growled, "The man is a fool. There was no decent competition, save for Lord Richard, and I bested him only because his destrier slipped on a clot of mud."

Mark shook his head at Jerval's foul humor. He had tried to entertain Chandra earlier and found her mood no better. It was normal enough, he supposed, for she was likely homesick.

Jerval had taken everyone by surprise, particularly Lord
Richard. Although he had explained to his father-in-law that
he wanted Chandra to see Camberley before his parents
returned, Mark knew that it wasn't precisely the truth. What
the truth was, he didn't know, and he supposed it wasn't
particularly any of his business. Lord Richard had not gainsaid his son-in-law, though his amber eyes had narrowed.

Mark was silent for several minutes, his gray eyes, out of
habit, searching the rugged hills to the east for robbers. They
traveled slowly, for the baggage mules lagged behind, weighted
down with Lady Chandra's belongings. Though a dozen men,
fully armed, accompanied them, the rich goods they carried
were a powerful temptation to the cutthroats who made their
living in the hills.

Mark heard a trilling laugh and turned in his saddle to see a
seabird winging close to Mary. She held out her hand to the
gull and laughed, a merry sound, full of pleasure. What he
wanted, he decided, was to pass the afternoon in Mary's
company. He turned his horse away and said gaily to Jerval
over his shoulder, "I will send you your bride to cure your
gloomy mood."

Jerval smiled. Indeed, now that they were away from
Croyland, there was no need to dwell on it. If he had not
been surrounded by his men, he would have been sorely
tempted to call a halt and seduce his bride in the fields, with
but her cloak for a bed. Actually, he thought, his smile
widening even more, Sir Andrew had not been far off the
mark. Jerval's frustration had made him a formidable opponent in the tourney, far more dangerous than if he had been
the ardent bridegroom waiting to return to his wife's bed.

He remembered his brief interview with Lord Richard early
that morning while they were breaking their fast. His father-
in-law had seemed hesitant to speak, but Jerval had had no
difficulty guessing his thoughts.

"I have not seen my daughter this morning," Richard had
said finally. "She is all right?"

"She is perfectly all right," Jerval said easily. He wasn't
going to admit that his bride was still a virgin. "She is with
her maids, seeing to her packing."

"Ah," Lord Richard said. There was an unasked question
in his tone.

"You need have no worry about Chandra, sir," Jerval

continued. "She is my wife now, and I promise you that I will make her content to be so."

Richard had paused, and then said gruffly, as if concluding the matter, "I would expect nothing less, Jerval."

Jerval heard the sound of Wicket's nimble hooves and swiveled in his saddle as Chandra reined in beside him.

"I have missed you, wife," he said, relishing the sound of the word on his tongue. "I much prefer your company to Mark's."

She stared stonily ahead of her, and he reached out to touch her arm. She shied away, startled.

"Though I must admit that him, at least, I don't frighten."

"I am not frightened," she said stiffly, thrusting her chin upward. "But I am homesick."

He smiled gently at her. "I know, but 'twill pass. We will visit Croyland. I am not taking you to another land."

"You jousted well in the tourney this morning," she said on a small sigh. "I was surprised that you bested my father."

He arched a brow at her. "In truth, it wasn't much of a match, save for Lord Richard. He and I were among the few men who weren't tottering drunk, and even he, I think, was suffering from too much wine."

"You did not hurt yourself?"

"I would have slit my throat had I ended up in a litter!" He added, his smile fading a bit, "Let me see your arm."

She looked at him blankly.

"I had forgotten all about the gash on your arm. Has it healed?"

"There will be no scar, if that is your worry, my lord."

"My only worry is that you have mended properly. Now, let me see your arm."

She thrust her arm at him. He pushed back her sleeve and lightly probed the newly healed flesh. "It is odd," he mused aloud, lowering his voice intimately, "but I forgot all about the wound last night."

She hunched her shoulder at him, uncomfortable with his sexual banter.

"I hope you will take more care in the future," he said, tilting his head at her. "You said you are never frightened, but I admit to being afraid when I saw the blood clotted on your arm."

"You have no reason to fear for me. I am quite capable of taking care of myself."

"Perhaps," he agreed easily.

"Wicket needs a gallop," she said stiffly, and dug her heels into her destrier's sides.

Jerval watched her velvet cloak billow out behind her as Wicket leaped forward, wondering if she was thinking about the night to come, for tonight would be their first away from Croyland.

Jerval called a halt late in the afternoon at a small protected inlet with the sea at its front and treacherous cliffs surrounding it. Only a narrow, snaking path led to the beach, an entry easily guarded by one man. He set the men about their tasks, pitching a tent for Chandra and one for Mary, unpacking the carefully wrapped food prepared for them at Croyland and gathering wood for a fire. He looked about for Chandra, only to discover that she had gone off with several of the men to collect firewood. He did not see her until the cooked meat was spitted and ready to warm over the flames.

Rolfe, one of the older men, and the weaver of tales for long nights, lolled on his blanket near the fire and at Jerval's nod, recounted the battle of Runnymede, where, according to Rolfe, his grandfather had fought side by side with the lord of Drexel to defeat the rapacious King John. It was a tale Jerval had heard since he was a young boy, and he turned his attention to Chandra. The hot fire had brought a flush to her cheeks, and the cool breeze blowing off the sea fluttered tendrils of hair about her face. Her eyes were downcast, and she looked the perfect maiden, shy, tentatively afraid of his possession, yet delicately aware of herself as his bride. He kept shifting his weight, aware of the building ache in his groin, until he could stand it no longer. At the end of Rolfe's tale, as the men were moving about to settle themselves for the night, Jerval rose, stretched lazily, and beckoned to Chandra.

"It has been a long day," he said to no one in particular. He kept his voice indifferent, wishing to spare Chandra embarrassment, for he knew all the while what was in his men's minds. "Come, Chandra, let us retire."

Chandra rose slowly and brushed sand from her gown. She saw that her hands were trembling, and whipped them into the folds of her gown. She forced her feet to move over the slight rolling dunes to the tent, kicking small pebbles aside as she walked. She heard one of the men say in a laughing undertone to one of his friends, "If Sir Jerval doesn't hurry, it will be the sand to receive his seed!"

"It is more likely that your mouth, Ranulfe, will taste the sand," Jerval tossed over his shoulder.

Chandra walked into the tent, her back to Jerval. She heard him fasten down the flap and felt the familiar rush of fear. He lit a single candle and ground the ember he had taken from the fire into the sand. He stood huge and silent, the flickering candlelight revealing the desire in his eyes.

"Well," Jerval said, mustering interest into his voice, "it's been a long day. I hope you are not too weary."

For what? she thought warily. "I am rather tired."

"We have a long night ahead of us, a lot of time for you to rest. Did you enjoy your dinner?"

"Aye, 'twas tasty."

He was silent for a long moment, unable to think of anything else inconsequential to say, and smiled at her.

"We are away from Croyland, Chandra. You are now freed of your . . . vow."

"But we just left Croyland! 'Tis been but a short time!"

"But a very long time for me." He took a confident step toward her. "Let me help you with your gown, my love."

He lifted her heavy hair and searched out the fastenings. She could hear heaviness in his breath.

She whirled about, pulling away from him, and splayed her hands against his chest. "I . . . wish to bathe! The sand . . . I feel gritty."

"You can bathe in the morning," he said, his voice hoarse. "I have spent more hours away from you than I can bear." He pulled her against him, tangling his hands in the mass of hair that fell down her back, and then caressed her face, cupping her chin upward, forcing her to look at him. "God's grace, Chandra, to be wed to you and not yet know you as my wife has made me hunger as would a starving man." His thumbs stroked the line of her jaw, and when she looked at him, his eyes seemed to devour her.

He dropped his hands to her throat and stroked her racing pulse, then fondled her soft breast. He felt her stiffen as he lightly caressed her nipples, willing them to grow taut against his fingers.

"Do not hold yourself so stiffly, love," he whispered against her closed mouth. "I will go gently with you. There will be naught but your virgin's pain, but it will be as nothing to the pleasure you will soon feel." His hands tangled again through the masses of hair at her back to the fastenings on her gown.

"Nay! Do not . . . I cannot!"

Jerval stared at her blankly.

"It is my . . . monthly flux!"

He nearly laughed, but instead stood back and crossed his arms negligently over his broad chest. "How timely that your flux should begin just when your vow ended."

She winced at the amused sarcasm in his voice, but held her gaze steady.

"Chandra, I hope that you won't insult my intelligence by denying that your virgin's vow was anything but a ploy to keep me away from you."

She looked at him helplessly, not understanding him.

He ran an impatient hand through his hair. "I would that you cease being a foolish child. You are acting as if your virginity were the most sacred possession on God's earth! It is nothing—a moment of pain and a bit of blood."

"It . . . it is not that," she whispered.

"Then what the devil is it?"

"You are a man! And men care nothing for women's feelings."

"Ah, you expect me to humiliate you, demean you. You expect me to treat you as Graelam did Mary?"

She could not prevent a shudder at his words.

"Your father's in this too. How many times have you seen him couple with serving maids, Chandra? I trust he had the good sense not to let your mother know."

"She was his wife. He did not care what she thought."

"Ah, and since you are now my wife, you expect me to rut you like a boar, then toss you aside and pursue other women."

"Aye! I don't want you to touch me, Jerval! I don't want you to treat me like that!"

"So you intend to be the mistress of Camberley, and a virgin for the next fifty years?"

To her chagrin, tears streamed from her eyes. She took a noisy gulp and dashed her hand across her eyes.

Jerval started to take a step toward her, to enfold her in his arms and comfort her, but she was shaking her head at him, sniffing convulsively, her hands spread in front of her, as if to ward him off.

"I never expected to see you, my little warrior, dissolve into tears." His voice was a mixture of impatience and irony. He drew a calming breath, for to push her further would likely make him angry and her hysterical.

"You will think about what I have said, Chandra, and if it pleases you, recognize that I do love you, and have no intention of abusing you. You have become my wife, and I expect you to face that fact and cease prating on like a foolish child. For God's sake, go to bed!"

He turned on his heel, jerked open the tent flap, and stalked away.

Mark was lying on his back, his arms pillowing his head, staring toward the dark cliffside. He saw the shadow of a man moving under the quarter moon. He clamped his hand to his dagger and rose stealthily, following him in a crouch toward the cliff. He found Jerval there, standing motionless, his huge hands clenched at his sides. Mark backed away from him, without being seen, and walked quietly back to the edge of the smoldering fire. He stepped over the loudly snoring Lambert, caught Rolfe's puzzled look, and lay down, drawing his blanket over him.

Though there was little food left for their second day, and the men awaited Jerval's order to halt for the day's hunt, Jerval pushed onward until the sun was near to setting over the sea.

"The men's stomachs will be growling tonight," Mark said, hoping for some response from his silent friend. "They cannot eat jugs of wine and a cask of ale."

It was as if Jerval had just become aware of his surroundings. He sighed and pulled Pith to a halt. "You are right, the men should not go hungry. There is still enough daylight for hunting. See to it, will you, Mark?"

"Aye," Mark said, and wheeled his palfrey about.

Jerval did not join his men around the campfire until his belly growled at the smell of roasting rabbit. He took his share, ate mechanically until his hunger eased, and tossed the meated bones to the hovering seabirds.

Chandra ate quickly and excused herself in a small restrained voice, dragging a startled Mary with her.

Lambert cocked an eye toward Jerval. "Methinks," he said aloud to the grouped men about the campfire, "that Sir Bridegroom is in need of some invigoration."

"Not a bad idea from such an empty-headed lout," Jerval said, grinning.

Rolfe guffawed loudly and thrust a jug of wine into Jerval's hand. "Wine, Jerval, is good both to get things started and to make them last," he said wisely, nodding his shaggy head. "You left your bride so quickly last night we feared that you had indeed lost your seed in the sand."

"It does not do to leave a poor lady wife all alone because a husband spends himself too quickly!" Lambert chortled.

"Methinks your wit flows from jealousy," Jerval said. He tipped the jug back and drank deeply.

"Drink up, Jerval," Mark said, "and forget these idiots! We haven't finished celebrating your wedding, and Lord knows, you pushed us long and hard today." He reached over and tipped the jug higher into Jerval's mouth until rivulets of sweet wine ran down his chin.

"We wouldn't expect," Rolfe said, wagging a fat thumb in Jerval's direction, "your warrior bride to be as understanding as other ladies would be! It's hours of a stiff rod she needs!"

Lambert nodded sagely. "Aye, she must be ridden just as she rides that hulking beast of hers."

"You ignorant bastards know about as much of the lady's needs as does her horse," Jerval muttered, but he stretched his long legs toward the fire and swallowed from the jug before he handed it to Rolfe.

"The bridegroom is starting to slur his words," Rolfe said, taking a swig from the jug himself.

"Lady Chandra was quiet today," Lambert said.

"Aye," Ranulfe grinned, "as if she were disappointed."

Disappointed hell, Jerval thought, and closed his ears to their guffaws.

The fire was dying when Jerval heaved himself to his feet. "I think I'll leave you half-brained philosophers," he announced.

"Don't forget the wine!" Mark laughed, and thrust a full jug into Jerval's hand.

"That," Jerval said, staring at the men with bleary eyes, "is about the only useful suggestion any of you asses has made."

He stepped carefully over the rocks and climbed atop an outjutting boulder surrounded by crashing waves. He looked back toward the campfire, and beyond to where Chandra's tent stood, apart and hidden by clumps of bracken from the eyes of the men. He saw her shadow illuminated by faint candlelight as she moved about the small space. He drew the cork from the jug of wine Mark had given him and drank deep.

The wine settled warm in his belly, and he drank on. It suddenly struck him as insanely funny that his men should be offering him advice on how to extend his endurance in his marriage bed. Liar, he cursed himself, belching aloud. His men would likely think him the biggest fool alive were they to know that his wife was still a virgin. That he, Jerval de Vernon, a man who had always enjoyed women, whose warm touch or caressing word had brought them willingly into his bed, had wed a woman who looked a ghost when he came near her! He swilled down more wine at the thought. He had laid down the law to her the previous night, reasonably, with but a hint of impatience at her foolish fear. Damn, he thought, he could not let it continue. Better to get it over with, so she would realize that nothing would change between them.

Aye, he thought foggily, it would be her pleasure to be ridden by him. He felt himself grow stiff at the thought of being astride her, his manhood impaled deep within her, and he moaned drunkenly, his voice lost in the crashing of the waves against the rocks.

He stared again toward the tent, swaying back on his heels, his wife's tent, and his, now silent and dark. A virgin's vow and now her monthly flux! Christ, it was time that she realized that becoming his wife would not bring down the world on her head. He tilted back his head and gulped down the rest of the wine, swiped his hand across his chin, and tossed the jug into the sea. He rose unsteadily to his feet, nearly falling on the slimy rocks into the foaming waves, and lurched forward. He broke into a run, skirting the camp, and staggered to a panting halt in front of the darkened tent. He would not see her face in the dark, and he wanted to. He walked back to the campfire, resolutely ignoring the men, who were grinning shamelessly up at him, and carefully juggled a glowing ember between two sticks of wood.

He pulled open the tent flap and saw her lying quiet upon her pallet, her back to him. The pale moonlight showed him the candle, and he clumsily set the ember to the wick.

The soft light pierced the darkness of her dream, and Chandra awakened, lurching toward the light. She saw her husband standing above her, his dark-blue eyes smoldering. She jerked herself upright, gathering her bedrobe about her. "What is it you want, Jerval? I have nothing more to say to you."

"I agree completely." He proffered her a drunken bow. "I, my love, have no more words to offer you either."

She scrambled to her knees. "Get out of here, Jerval! I will have nothing to do with you!"

He cocked his head at her, a wide smile on his face. He leaned over and began with drunken concentration to unfasten the cross garters on his chausses. "At least you, Chandra, have only your bedrobe on." He fumbled with the knotted string at his waist, and cursed.

"By God," she gasped, "you are drunk!"

"Aye." He grinned crookedly. "And seeing things clearly for the first time. Tonight, little lamb, you are going to cease your childish nonsense and do your duty by your husband."

She tried to hurl herself past him as he was pulling his tunic over his head, but he grabbed her and tossed her lightly back onto the pile of furs.

When he stood above her, naked, the candlelight shimmering off his bronze body, Chandra felt herself choke on fear. He did not seem angry, merely resolute, and she did not know what to do.

"You would not force me," she gasped, staring at him helplessly.

"Nay, certainly not," he said with drunken certainty. "A husband does not have to force his wife. It is her duty to accept him, whenever he wishes to have her."

"Please . . . do not, Jerval, I do not wish it!"

He dropped to his knees beside her, lurching to his side and nearly falling over her.

"You cannot," she whispered, hating the pleading in her voice. "You are drunk."

"Aye, my lady," he chuckled. "The men did not wish me to leave you so quickly this night." He began tugging at the tie on her bedrobe.

Chandra thrust her hand against his chest, trying to shove him back, but he fell forward on top of her, jerking her bedrobe open as he fell. He felt her breasts against his naked chest, and he crushed her to him, his mouth searching out hers.

"You stink!" she cried, her voice smothered against his mouth. "You are naught but a rutting, drunken pig!"

"Bear with me, Chandra. It is your duty," he said, his words slurred from the wine and from his desire.

He thrust his hand between them and pulled the bedrobe away from her. The feel of her slender body, naked against him, her smooth flesh like silk, made him groan aloud at the throbbing in his groin.

Chandra felt his manhood, huge and hot against her belly, but she could not move under his great weight. She suddenly remembered the sight of Mary, held motionless beneath Graelam, helpless and impotent against him. She cried aloud and struggled against him, but he merely moaned drunkenly against her cheek.

"If you will not find pleasure with me, Chandra, remember your marriage vows!"

She closed her burning eyes. She had sworn before God to obey her husband. She saw again the serving maid with her father, heard her moan like a maddened animal, saw her writhing beneath her father, her hips bucking upward to receive him. "I will not be like your other women! I will not be a mindless animal!"

"It is your choice," he muttered. Her face was blurring, and he shook his head against the dizzying effects of the wine. His need was a roar in his mind.

He heard her sob as he pulled her thighs apart, but the sound had no meaning to him. He felt only a fierce, drunken determination, and beyond all reason, he drove into her. Vaguely, as if from a great distance, he heard her cry out. He grunted, grasping her hips and forcing her small unwilling body to accept him. He heaved with all his might until he was seated to his hilt within her. He was consumed in his own passion, and her broken moans only stirred him to possess her. He threw back his head and yelled his release, then collapsed, a dead weight on top of her.

Jerval awoke the next morning at the sound of his men's voices. He tried to rise, but his head felt like a huge, throbbing melon. He realized suddenly where he was and called out Chandra's name. She was not in the tent. Memory of the previous night flooded painfully into his mind, and he groaned, both at his nauseating hangover and at what he had done.

"Christ," he muttered, and dragged himself from the bed of furs. He rose painfully and began to pull on his clothes. His gaze froze. There were splotches of blood on his member, and on the furs.

He hadn't forced her, he assured himself, he had merely reminded her of her wifely duty, and she had finally accepted him as her husband. But from the recesses of his mind, he remembered her sobbing, felt again her unwilling flesh as he buried himself within her. "Christ," he said again.

When he staggered out of the tent, holding his head, Mark walked to him and handed him a jug of ale.

Jerval gazed at the jug with loathing.

"Nay," Mark said, grinning at him. " 'Tis the best thing for your splitting head."

He drank, felt his stomach heave in protest, and then to his surprise, felt his lurching belly ease.

"Where is Chandra?"

"She is with Mary, helping the men to pack up."

He grunted and turned away from Mark's sympathetic eyes. He knew that the last man she would want to see was her rutting clod of a husband. "Drunken dumb fool," he cursed himself. "Witless sodden ass!" He had succumbed to a damned jug of wine, and treated her as would a mindless bull. All of his reasonable arguments on their first two nights together, all his gentle assurances that he loved her, that she should trust him, would surely ring hollow to her now. He decided he would let her be at least until he was fully in control of his wits again.

*   *   *

I have done my wifely duty, damn him, Chandra thought. He got what he wanted, and took his fill. Now let him cast me aside and search out other quarry. She gazed toward the front of the troop when she heard him laugh at something Lambert said. He was likely bragging of his prowess to the men, the drunken sot! At least he had kept his distance since he had stumbled out of the tent that morning.

She saw Mary watching her, her look puzzled. She knew she was acting sullen and angry, but for the moment, she did not care. She was too furious at Jerval for his drunken mauling of her, and for the raw pain between her thighs that made her wince with each step that Wicket took. At least she knew now what women endured with coupling. No wonder it was one of God's commandments that wives had to obey their husbands . . . surely no wife would ever willingly submit to such humiliation and pain.

She continued mulling over her bitterness throughout the long day, and gazing toward her husband, her angry eyes burning a hole in his back. Her tender flesh grew raw from the rub of the saddle, and she wondered how much farther she would have to ride that day.

"All goes well with you, my lady?" Mark said cheerfully, reining in his palfrey beside Wicket.

She forced a nod and gazed skyward at the thick swirling dark clouds. "We are in for a soaking, I think," she said.

"Aye. There is a small abbey some five miles to the northeast where Jerval will ask us shelter from the brothers. But another hour, and we'll have no more worry."

Another hour! she thought, and shifted uncomfortably in her saddle.

"You are not well, lady?"

He knows, she thought, shame bringing a flush of red to her cheeks. Jerval must have been bragging about his triumph! She tossed back her head and laughed. "You are mistaken, Sir Mark. Wicket itches for a gallop. Would you care for a race?"

Mark thought he had seen a tensing of pain about her mouth. "If it is your wish, my lady."

Fool! What a fool you are! she yelled at herself as Wicket lengthened his stride into an uneven, bouncing canter.

At last Mark shouted, "You win, my lady! Hold, else the rest will never catch up to us!"

She was smiling when he drew abreast of her, and he smiled back and reached over to clap Wicket respectfully on his sweating neck.

A loud thunderclap rent the silent afternoon and thick pellets of rain began to fall just as they reached the abbey. Chandra stared toward the low stone buildings, rising above barren rocks, bunched together with a kind of stark harmony about a narrow-spired church. A lay brother met them at the gate, his coarse woolen cowl pulled over his head, and bade them a quick welcome. He directed them to the thatched shed that was used for a stable, hurriedly excused himself to inform the abbot of their arrival, and shuffled out of the downpour.

The rain soaked through Chandra's thick cloak and quickly drenched her gown and shift. She guided Wicket to the stable, drew a taut breath, and slid off his back. She clung to his mane for a moment to steady herself.

"Let me help you, my lady."

Mark was beside her, his hand already under her arm. He called to Arnolf to take care of Wicket and led her slowly toward the abbey door. "But a few steps farther," he said softly.

She heard Jerval call to Mark and abruptly pulled away from him. "I am fine, I assure you, Mark," she said.

He gave her a puzzled look, then said quietly, "Greet the abbot, my lady, then tell him that you are weary from your journey. I will send Mary to you."

Jerval watched Chandra walk slowly away from Mark, past a dark-robed brother, and looked a question at his friend.

"Perhaps," Mark said, "Chandra drank some of the wine last night. I do not believe she feels well. You must tell her that it is no crime to be ill."

Certainly she had ignored him for the entire day, but ill? Nay, he thought, Mark saw sickness where there was only sullen fury. "I will see to her after we have spoken with the abbot," he said.

Mark wanted very much to ask why Jerval had kept away from his bride, but he could not. Another man, even a best friend, could not interfere between husband and wife.

"One of the brothers has taken your lady wife to the small house we reserve for female guests," the abbot said to Jerval, after he had made his greeting. "We will send her a tray for her dinner, for she was quite weary from her journey."

Jerval would have laughed aloud had not the gaunt-faced abbot appeared so serious. Chandra would drop from fatigue before admitting to any weakness.

"I will take her a tray, and join her in her evening devotions," Jerval said piously. At the abbot's approving nod, he left the main cloister and walked through the rain to the small stone house that was set by itself near the east gate of the abbey. He had passed the entire day turning over in his mind what he would say to her. He thought ruefully that she must be growing quite tired of hearing him insist that they must talk to each other.

When he tapped lightly on the narrow door, he heard her call out, her voice low and weary, "Go away, Mary. I am not hungry, and have no need of you."

His fingers closed over the rusted latch and he shoved the door open. Chandra stood in the middle of the small bare room clothed only in her damp shift. She jumped at the sight of him.

"Get out, Jerval," she said coldly, straightening.

"Nay," he said gently, and pushed the door closed behind him. When he took a step toward her, she stepped back, and to her chagrin, tripped over a wooden stool, crying out as she clutched wildly at the empty air and landed on her bottom against the cold stone floor.

He was at her side in an instant, pulling her to her feet.

"Are you all right?" he demanded tersely.

"Of course, and I would be the most content of women if you would but leave!"

"Not yet," he said on a sigh, and uttered the fateful words. "We must talk, Chandra."

She tossed her head disdainfully and took a confident step away from him.

He saw her wince. "You are ill. Come here, love, and tell me what's wrong."

"Leave me alone, damn you! There is nothing wrong with me!"

"Stubborn wench," he said, and pulled her into his arms. "Do you have a bellyache?"

"Nay!" she spat at him. "The only thing wrong with me is you!"

Suddenly, he remembered tearing into her unwilling flesh, and her cries of pain.

He drew a deep, steadying breath. "I hurt you," he said, his voice filled with anger at himself.

She turned her head away from him, her arms clutched about her sides. He saw that she was shivering from cold.

He knew her well enough to know that she would fight him if he sought to help her. He forced all gentleness from his voice, and said with harsh finality, "You will lie still and let me take care of you."

She whipped about and shrieked at him, "Nay, I hate you! Leave me be!"

"If you do not lie still," he continued as if she had not spoken, "I will call in several of my men, and they will hold you down. Fight me, and you will see that I mean what I say."

"You will not make me couple with you again!" she yelled at him.

"We will speak of that later," he said, his voice carefully neutral. "Now, come, Chandra, you are soaked and I will take care of you."

She saw that he would not be gainsaid, and held herself rigidly still as he pulled the straps of her shift from her shoulders. "For God's sake, Chandra, it is absurd to hide your body from me," he growled, as she tried to cover her breasts with her hands.

He pulled the shift over her hips and pressed her down onto the narrow cot. He lightly touched his hand to her thigh.

She turned her face away from him, her lips compressed in a thin bloodless line. He stared for a moment, unable to help himself, at her long slender legs, sleek and lightly muscled.

"Open your legs," he ordered, his voice cold in anger at himself for feeling desire for her now.

Slowly, she obeyed him. He leaned over her, one large hand on her thigh to hold her still, and winced at the sight of her raw, inflamed flesh. "Why did you not say anything to me?"

"Why? It was you who did it. Have you also the power to undo it?"

"You can lash out at me in a moment," he said calmly. He shook his head. "What I would have expected from you, a girl who is usually not at all stupid, would have been to call a halt and taken yourself from Wicket's back. You have managed but to make it worse with all the rubbing from the saddle.''

He rose and frowned down at her, his long fingers stroking his jaw. "At least you are not bleeding, nor is your flesh torn.'' He picked up a blanket and covered her with it.

She clutched it to her chin, staring at him balefully as he untied the string on his cloak.

"What are you doing?'' she croaked.

"I am only removing my soaked cloak,'' he said sharply. "You needn't squawk at me like an untamed falcon.''

"A falcon does not squawk, and neither do I!''

"You cannot ride,'' he continued, disregarding. " 'Twould but make you more raw.''

"Nay, you cannot mean it,'' she gasped. "I am no weak, useless female to be carried in a litter, to be made sport of by your men!''

"What the hell do my men have to do with anything?''

"You told them! They know, and they will laugh behind their hands at me!''

"Told them what?''

"That you . . . bested me!''

He stared down at her in incredulous amusement. "Bested you! Chandra, what we did was couple, though God knows I wish that I hadn't been such a drunken lout. I hurt you, and I am truly sorry for it. I am usually not so . . . clumsy.''

"At least it did not last long,'' she said furiously. "I thank God that you finished with me quickly.''

"That too I much regret.'' He paced about the small room, then returned and sat down beside her.

"What I most regret is that you felt only pain at our first coupling, and disgust at how I treated you. Nay, love, don't turn away from me. I will suffer your anger, for in truth I suppose that I much deserve it. The next time we couple—''

"Nay! I will obey no more of your lustful orders! Find another woman for your drunken pleasure, Jerval! I will have no more of you!''

"I will never again demand that you lie with me, but we will couple again, Chandra, when you are ready.''

He saw furious anger in her eyes, and rose. "I will leave

you now." He walked to the door and turned. "Mary was fetching a tray for you. You will eat something, Chandra. I will see you in the morning."

Chandra stepped out into the chill, gray morning. At least the rain had ceased during the night. She hurried toward the stables, ignoring the muddy water sloshing against her boots and the tingling discomfort between her thighs. She planned to have Wicket saddled and herself astride him before Jerval emerged from the abbey to give her orders otherwise.

"God's grace on you, Chandra," Mark called out when she entered the dim thatched stable. "Wicket does better this morning, but Jerval bound his hock loosely to keep the ointment against the swelling."

"Swelling?" She looked at him blankly.

At Mark's nod, the truth burst upon her. Damn him! It was she who was hurt, not her destrier!

Jerval strode down the abbey steps, several of his men behind him, to see his wife standing, furious, in a mud puddle.

He smiled, quite pleased with himself, and waved to her. "Good morning, my lady," he called. "I thought you would be up early this day in your concern for Wicket." Before she could think of a word to say, Jerval turned to Ranulf. "Milady's destrier will be in your charge today. Keep his pace slow, for I want no more swelling in that hock."

"What is the meaning of this, Jerval?" Chandra hissed at him. "You know very well that there is nothing wrong with Wicket!"

"Please keep your voice down, wife. I have no wish to be caught in a lie so near to God's house." He gazed down at her, wishing that he could draw her into arms and kiss away the mutinous expression on her face. "You are feeling better?" he asked quietly.

"I am quite well," she snapped.

"You will not be for long if you continue to stand in the water." He pointed down to the puddle she was standing in, and she ground her teeth and stepped quickly aside, aware for the first time that the wet was seeping into her boots.

"I will ride in no litter, Jerval, despite your elaborate trick!"

He nodded pleasantly. "Nay, now there is no need."

"Then which of your men's horses will I ride today?"

"Have you eaten?" he asked abruptly, ignoring her question.

She waved away his words, knowing that he was delaying purposefully, waiting for the yard to be filled with his men. "You will not shame me, Jerval."

The abbot approached them, cast a cursory disinterested glance at Chandra, and said to Jerval, "My lay brother, Arno, informs me, my lord, that your journey will not suffer more rain." A stiff smile appeared on his gaunt face at Jerval's dubious look. " 'Tis better than a weather cock he is. He sniffed the air but a few minutes ago, then clamped his nose closed, as is his way, before giving me his assurance."

"It is good news inded. My lady wife and I thank you for your hospitality."

"God's speed to you, my lord."

"Ah, there is Mary," Jerval said after the abbot had taken his leave of them. He strode away from Chandra, and she stood staring after him, her frustration mounting, for she had no idea of what he planned. "Damn you," she growled under her breath as he swung easily onto Pith's broad back.

She watched helplessly as the men mounted and drew the baggage mules into line. Wicket trailed after Ranulf, a long line fastened to his bridle.

"Mark," Jerval called, "help milady."

Jerval drew Pith up beside her and said in a loud voice, "Ranulf will take good care of Wicket, Chandra, and I will provide you the best substitute that I can."

Mark was beside her, his hands cupped for her foot. She saw a thick blanket folded in front of Jerval, to soften the saddle beneath her, she knew, and sent him a smoldering, defeated look.

He had cut her off, giving her no alternative, unless she wished to make a distasteful scene in front of the men. She allowed Mark to lift her upward. Jerval's hands closed about her waist and he placed her gently in front of him. She tried to bring her leg over to ride astride, but he held her firm in the crook of his arm.

"Trust me not to let you fall, Chandra." She heard the smug satisfaction in his voice and tensed. He held her possessively against his chest and wrapped her cloak about her legs.

"I do not want to ride like this . . . with you."

"Would you prefer a litter?" He expected no answer and

received none. He guided Pith to the fore of the men and waved them forward.

"It would appear that Brother Arno was right, or rather his nose," Jerval said sometime later to break the silence between them. He lifted his face to the flickering sun that broke through the scattered dark clouds. As he spoke, Pith sidestepped a mud puddle, and he tightened his arm about Chandra to hold her steady and felt the soft rising of her breasts against him. Chandra lifted her hand and pulled the hood from her head; he breathed in the lavender scent of her hair and lowered his chin to feel its softness.

"Have you nothing to say to me?" he asked.

At her continued silence, he drawled, "I had hoped for a gentle wife, but I did not intend her to be so in awe of me that her tongue would not move in her mouth."

He felt anger flow through her and smiled.

"You may as well begin speaking to me, Chandra, else you will have an uncomfortably silent life."

She drew a deep breath. "I would like to have our marriage annulled."

She felt the powerful arm holding her tighten at her words, but she continued, her voice calm and detached. "You have but to tell my father that you do not want me. Men have that right, I know. You can send me back to Croyland, and likely keep many of my dower rights in the bargain."

"One cannot annul a marriage that has been consummated, Chandra."

He spoke quietly, almost sadly. She was beginning to feel a faint tug of guilt when he added, "Perhaps, my love, you are at this moment pregnant with my child."

"That is impossible!" She twisted against him, but he kept his eyes resolutely between Pith's ears.

"Hold still. It is not at all impossible, and perhaps a babe would render you more reasonable."

"I hate you," she gasped, but it was hatred at herself for her own helplessness that welled in her throat. She burned with shame, remembering how she had, at his order, lain naked as he parted her thighs to gaze intimately at her flesh.

"You have already used me as a man uses a woman," she continued coldly. "Must I now wait until it suits your pleasure to cast me aside?"

"You have much to learn about me, Chandra," he said

quietly. He continued after a moment, his voice smooth with certainty, "Soon you will realize that I am a man of my word, and then—"

"I think I would prefer a litter," she interrupted him sharply. "At least I would not have to suffer your presence and yor glib arrogance!"

He smiled over her head. During the long afternoon, she slept, her supple body relaxed against him. He laced his fingers together under her breasts to hold her steady. He felt a fierce possessiveness.

Castle Camberley, Cumbria

What became of the friends I had
With whom I was so close
And loved so dearly?

—Rutebeuf, *La Complainte Rutebeuf*

7

CHANDRA COULD NOT REMAIN SILENT as they neared Camberley. She had never before traveled north of Croyland, and the sight of the winding lakes of Cumbria twisting between the lush forests, dotted with small islands and set against rolling mountains, made her exclaim with pleasure.

"It is so wild and lovely!" She swiveled this way and that, not wanting to miss anything, and pointed toward the mountains. "They are still covered with snow!"

"Aye, the Cumbrian Mountains. Many years the snows do not melt from their caps until well into late spring."

"I had not guessed that such beauty lay so close to Croyland."

"It is the most remarkable region of England, I think."

They cleared a gentle rise, and Chandra felt Jerval straighten in his saddle. "Look yon, Chandra, there is Camberley!"

Chandra leaned forward against his arm and shaded her eyes with her hand. They were descending into a gentle valley, and just beyond, high atop an upjutting hill, she saw the massive castle of Camberley. Its stone walls were a deep red-brown in the fading afternoon sunlight, and four majestic towers, squared, not rounded like those of Croyland, rose like mighty sentinels. Within the walls, the circular keep rose some hundred feet upward. Two hundred yards of land on three sides of Camberley was cleared to prevent any attacker from reaching the walls unseen. A small winding lake bounded the eastern side.

"It looks impregnable," she said.

"Aye," Jerval said proudly. "The last siege was in the early days of Henry's reign, when my grandfather was ill and prey to the rapacious de Audley clan. The granite rock upon which the castle is built made it impossible for them to tunnel beneath the walls. Even their war machines could not destroy the walls. They tried to starve my grandfather into surrender, but even that failed, for the harvest that year had been excellent.''

"I have never heard of the de Audleys," Chandra said.

"And you won't either. When my grandfather regained his health, he led a surprise attack upon their main fortress and killed every one of the bastards. With Henry's permission, or rather, I should say, with de Burgh's, the earl marshal's, permission, the de Audley lands were forfeited to the de Vernons, with of course a healthy payment to the king. The only price to be paid was a de Vernon wedding the last de Audley daughter. My grandfather bequeathed the lands to my father's younger brother, and 'twas he who wed Eleanor de Audley. Since that time, our only battles have been with the Scots.''

"You are as close to the Scots as Croyland is to the Welsh.''

"Aye, and they are more dangerous than the Welsh when roused. We cross swords sometimes three or four times a year, when their hunger drives them to raid our demesne farms.'' He saw that her eyes were sparkling with interest, and continued, embroidering a bit, "They scream a hoary battle cry when they attack, and move like shadows. When we fight them, we shed our armor, for it makes us too slow. They are not knights and do not fight as such.''

"I look forward to seeing them," Chandra said with great relish.

"I trust that I shall take such good care of you that you will never have to see the savages.''

They skirted a small village nestled in amid rich farmland before they climbed the narrow serpentine road that led to Camberley.

"Unlike your ancestors, mine did not name the village Camberley. It had been called Trackton long before my grandfather arrived, and he let it be. The villagers work the farmland, tend sheep and cattle, and fish in Camberley Lake.''

"How far north do Camberley lands extend?''

"Nearly to the border, thus our continual bouts with the Scots. At one time, my father thought to extend the de Vernon lands to the east, and considered a marriage alliance with Chester. Luckily," he continued, grinning, "Lord Richard arrived just in time and turned my father's eyes toward the lands in the south.''

"The squint-eyed girl?" Chandra said sourly.

"The very same," he agreed promptly, grinning over her head.

As they approached the castle, she heard welcoming shouts from the men lining the outer walls. "They cannot wait to meet my bride," Jerval said. "Look at the north tower. See the huge man hanging over the wall above the drawbridge? That is Malton, our master-at-arms. The man is the size of a bull and so strong that a hug from him could break your ribs."

The wide drawbridge flattened over a ditch bulging with dirty water, and the iron portcullis ground upward.

"Look," Chandra heard one of the men shout, "Sir Jerval carries his bride before him!"

The outer courtyard was not much different from Croyland's, Chandra saw, bustling with animals and people, and muddy from the last rainfall.

Jerval was yelling good-natured insults at his men, keeping tight rein on his horse to avoid hitting the children that ran in and out of his path, greeting them by name. Like Croyland, Camberley was a huge village, enclosed within stone walls six feet thick.

The inner bailey, closed in by lower walls that were, Chandra thought, thicker even than the outer walls, made her blink in surprise. All was orderly and clean. The ground was paved with cobblestones that slanted downward to allow the rain to run down into the outer courtyard. Low-roofed sheds were clustered about the great keep, and she sniffed the air, suddenly hungry at the smell of fresh-baked bread.

Jerval dismounted and eased her to the ground to stand beside him. There was a sea of curious faces staring at her, and out of habit as he called out names, she nodded, acknowledging the curtsies of the women and the respectful bows of the men.

She turned at the sound of Wicket's nervous whinny and pulled away from her husband's arm. He would have followed her, but his attention was claimed by his men, hungry for news.

As she approached, she heard Ranulf tell the men who

stood around Wicket, admiring his thick shoulders and broad-backed strength, "Aye, it is milady's destrier."

"God's teeth, Ranulf, no lady would mount that beast!"

Lambert gave a loud crack of laughter. "Our lady is like none you've ever known, Blanc!"

Ranulf guffawed, pointing to the bandaged hock. "Pay no attention to that—'twas a ploy on Sir Jerval's part to have his bride in his lap for most the journey home."

She felt embarrassed color flood her cheeks, but Wicket was her destrier, and he was growing more restive with all the racket. Her introduction to Camberley would not be pleasant, she knew, if Wicket were to kick in the skulls of the stable lads.

She threw back her head and said, "Thank you, Ranulf, for seeing to Wicket. I will take him into the stable, for he is jittery in these new surroundings." She led Wicket past the stable hands, nodding politely at them when they tugged respectfully at the hair on their foreheads.

Chandra spoke softly to him as she rubbed him down and covered his back with a light blanket. She did not leave him until she looked up to see Jerval standing in the low doorway, watching her silently. After she gave the man, Blanc, instructions for Wicket's care, she said in a challenging voice to her husband, "It appears that his hock has no more swelling. I have removed the bandage."

"I have cured him, in short. Doubtless he is ready to be ridden again." At her stony frown, he continued easily, "Come, Chandra, we will have supper shortly, and I would like to show you the keep first."

She followed him up the winding staircase, into the great hall, and drew to a halt, gazing around her. There were no rushes on the stone floor, and there was a sweet smell in the air, as if everything had been scrubbed with perfumed soap. The stone walls were covered with thick tapestries, and the wooden tables and chairs gleamed with wax. There were at least a dozen servants, all of them looking very industrious until they saw Jerval. There were excited murmurs, and he smiled and called them together to meet Chandra.

She greeted them pleasantly, trying to memorize all the curious faces, for these were the indoor servants, and she would be seeing them every day.

After Jerval had sent them all back to work, he said,

"Camberley servants respond quite well without being cuffed about. You can be certain that my mother's commanding voice keeps them in line."

"It smells so clean!" she blurted out. Everything seemed so orderly and proper, as if no one lived in the hall. Indeed, there was no one but servants, not even dogs bounding across the floor to greet them.

"Aye, but you'll soon accustom yourself to it. I have already introduced Mary to Alma, my old nursemaid and something of a seer, who will make her comfortable. There is a small room next to Julianna's that she may have."

Jerval turned away from her at a loud harumph at his elbow. A man of mighty girth, with a bearded pockmarked face and long coarse black hair, greeted them. "My lady," Jerval called to her after a few moments of conversation, "this is Trempe, Camberley's armorer. He is a master at his craft."

Trempe nodded respectfully at the lovely young girl before him. He had heard that Sir Jerval's new bride was something of a warrior, but this slender girl in her fur-lined cloak looked nothing like any warrior he had ever seen. "Milady," he said gruffly.

She smiled openly at him, vowing not to forget either his face or his name.

"Let me show you to our room, Chandra," Jerval said, and cupped his hand possessively under her elbow. She walked beside him up the thick, winding stone stairs to the upper floor, keeping a gracious smile on her face for the benefit of the servants who seemed to fill every cranny.

"They all want to catch a glimpse of you," Jerval said. "As at Croyland, it is difficult to find privacy here." At her silence, he inquired abruptly, "Are you feeling all right?"

"Of course," she snapped, and pushed ahead of him into the chamber. She supposed she had expected a room like her father's, nearly bare, its walls hung with weapons and its floor covered with thick reeds. It had none of these things. The room faced south, through rows of small narrow windows paned with small squares of glass, and the afternoon sunlight filled the room with reflected light. The walls were hung with flowing colorful tapestries, and between them were tapers held in twisted silver mounts. The floor was strewn with thick, brightly colored Flemish carpets. The bed was set upon a dais, not as large as her father's, but encased in beautifully embroidered covers that touched the floor. There was a high carved wooden screen set in a corner, and behind it was a large wooden tub and wooden racks that held linen and towels. She could not imagine that the king's chambers at Windsor were more magnificently furnished than this.

"This is hardly a man's room," she scoffed perversely, waving her arms at the soft luxury about her.

He shook his head ruefully. "Actually, my mother added a few more carpets and the racks, since it will also be a lady's room."

"It is not what I am used to either. I want my own room," she added, a challenge in her voice. "It can be a bare cupboard, if there is naught else."

"You will grow accustomed to this room," Jerval said, shrugging at her petulance.

"I will not share a bed with you!"

He looked for a moment as if he would remonstrate with her, but he only said with studied indifference, "Then you may sleep on the floor."

Two stout boys interrupted them, carrying buckets of steaming water. Chandra walked to the middle of the room, ignoring her husband. As Jerval spoke to the boys, she sat gingerly down in a high-backed chair and shifted her bottom on the soft velvet-covered cushion. She started suddenly when she chanced to see her reflection in the polished wooden arm. Her expression was that of a petulant, spoiled child.

The boys left, and Jerval ignored her. She sat alone and silent, watching him pull off his clothes. She looked away when he was naked, and did not raise her eyes until she heard a splash of water.

"You'll need a tub of fresh water," she heard him say. "Four days of grime have left it black. This time I won't ask you to join me."

She sniffed at his teasing, rose, and walked to one of the windows and gazed down over the orchard and gardens. There were apple trees, pear and peach trees, covered with tight buds. It was a beautiful, lush spot, though not, she thought, as lovely as Croyland.

Jerval touched his hand to her arm. "I will leave you now to bathe. Shall I send you one of the women to help you."

She shook her head, not meeting his eyes. She sniffed in

the clean scent of him, and became embarrassingly aware of her own horsy odor.

She splashed happily in the large tub, wishing that she had accepted a serving maid only when she washed her hair, no mean task without help. When the water became uncomfortably cool, she stepped out of the tub and around the side of the wooden screen, pulling a thick towel around her. she drew up, expelling an angry breath, at the sight of Jerval sitting silently in a chair, watching her.

"I thought you had left," she said, pulling the towel more securely about her. "What is it you want?"

He rose easily and handed her a small jar. "It is medicine for your—for you, an ointment." She grabbed it from his hand and stepped back. His voice dropped to an intimate caress. "Would you like me to apply it for you?"

"I would like you to leave!"

"Odd," he said, sighing, "that is what I guessed you would say. The medicine is from Alma."

"You did not tell her!"

"Nay, little one. That would have been quite a blow to my reputation." His eyes fell from her tangled wet hair, framing her face most alluringly, he thought, to the curve of her full breasts, outlined clearly against the damp towel. "I suppose now you will want me to leave you alone," he said pensively.

"Indeed," she snapped. "Now, if you please!"

"It would be my pleasure to assist you."

She turned away from him, her cheeks stained with an angry flush.

"Here, I forgot to give you the cloths."

"Where did you get these?" she grated, snatching the white strips of linen from him.

"From Alma."

"You did tell her!" she fairly shouted in her shame. "You want everyone to know that you are so huge and . . . disgusting that you hurt me!"

"You are blathering like a child," he said sharply, and turned to leave her. "Dress now. I will see you in the hall."

Chandra again regretted her stiff refusal of a servant, for it took her a good half hour just to comb through the tangles in her wet hair. She chose a soft, pale-blue silk gown and fastened a blue leather belt about her waist. She looked at herself one final time in the polished silver mirror, nodded approval at her appearance, and left the bedchamber.

There were at least fifty people seated at the trestle tables in the great hall, and a score of wenches and boys served the evening meal. All their faces were upon her as she entered, all of them openly curious.

Jerval rose and called to her. As she walked to the huge, high-backed chair beside him on the dais, he shouted over the hall, "My lady and wife, Chandra de Vernon." She started at her new name, and felt a crushing moment of homesickness. She supposed that she made a proper enough greeting before she sat beside her husband.

"Would be that you would be so gracious to your husband," he teased her.

She ignored him and stared down at the fat slice of warm bread that sat on a silver plate in front of her. A knife was beside the plate, and a strange two-pronged silver instrument.

"That, Chandra, is a fork, my mother's most recent addition to Camberley. It takes a bit of getting used to, but I think you'll appreciate its practical uses." He picked his up and speared a piece of meat with it.

"It is particularly useful with fish," he continued, watching her abortive efforts. "Here, try it on the lamprey." He wrapped his fingers about hers, guiding her hand in the proper motion.

She scooped up the flaky fish easily, and laughed in delight. "I imagine it is also useful for other purposes," she said, holding it poised threateningly over his hand.

She looked up to see Mark smiling at her encouragingly.

"I've never been able to understand what is wrong with fingers," he called, waving his fork at her.

"Nor I," Jerval laughingly agreed, "but since my mother's stay at the court, she is determined to civilize us despite ourselves."

Chandra was smiling, even when he leaned toward her. "Have some more spiced wine, Chandra. Mayhap you'll find Camberley's wine as sweet-tasting as a man."

Chandra's flush was covered by Malton, Camberley's mammoth master-at-arms, who called to them from the table just below the dais. "Sir Eustace was here, my lord. He seemed put off that he hadn't been told of your wedding." He gave a deep belly laugh. "I let him believe it was the squint-eyed heiress, my lord. He will be in a frenzy of jealousy when he sees your lady.''

"Who is he, Mark?'' Mary asked.

"Sir Eustace de Leybrun is Lady Avicia's nephew, and Jerval's cousin. He was wed to Matilda for a time—Jerval's older sister—but she died in childbed. He is not a particularly amiable fellow.''

"You are the diplomat, Sir Mark,'' Malton growled. "My lady,'' he said, addressing Chandra, "your husband will want to keep you well in sight whenever Sir Eustace visits Camberley. He's a leering braggart.''

Mark said lightly, "Now that you are wed, he will have to be content with his own lands.''

"Aye,'' Malton agreed, nodding his shaggy head toward Jerval, "with the sons you and your lady will breed, he'll never know Camberley, save as a bothersome guest.''

Chandra raised a questioning brow at her husband, surprised he would allow the men to speak thus of his kinsman, but he was smiling wryly. He, like his men, did not particularly like his cousin. He was such a lecherous ass that even the homeliest of the serving maids disliked sharing his bed when he visited Camberley. Nor did he relish the thought of Eustace meeting Chandra, or the image of Eustace gazing at her as he most assuredly would with his dark, assessing eyes, running his thick tongue over his lips as he did whenever he saw a girl that pleased him.

He said to Malton, "So Eustace has returned from the French court?''

"Aye, and he boasted that he was off to Windsor, to tell of his lordly adventures, no doubt.''

Malton shifted his eyes to Sir Jerval's beautiful wife. She was a stunning creature, and she seemed gracious, and pleasingly shy. The men had talked of little else save her manly skills, and he found himself disbelieving now, even though he had seen that huge destrier of hers. She looked so damned gentle and soft, as a lady should.

"When will Lord Hugh and Lady Avicia return?'' he asked Jerval, pulling his eyes from Lady Chandra.

"Within a week,'' Jerval said. He added blandly, "I wished my wife to accustom herself to Camberley before their return.''

Malton grinned hugely, having heard about how Jerval had kept his lovely bride on his lap for most of their journey home. He hoped the girl had gumption, for Lady Avicia was a strong-willed woman, and exacted strict obedience in all her domains.

Rolfe called out, "Mayhap those hell-raising Scots will pay us a visit before Lord Hugh returns. It was a hard winter up north, and I'll wager the heathen are hungry for our cattle."

He saw that the lady was looking at him, her lovely eyes resting upon him questioningly, and he sought to reassure her. "There's never much danger, my lady, usually a rout if we can catch the scoundrels."

"Do you ever ride after them, Malton?" Chandra asked.

"Aye, and it's better sport than a boar hunt. The Scots are good fighters, and it keeps the men from growing bored."

"And it is true that they wear no armor, that they must be chased down?"

Mark snorted behind his hand at Chandra's innocent questions, knowing full well she was likely making plans to join the men.

"Aye," Malton said kindly, "but you needn't worry, my lady. Sir Jerval and the men are more skilled fighters than any of those heathen."

"I am not worried," Malton," she said brightly. "Indeed, I—"

"We will ride out tomorrow," Jerval interrupted her, "or the next day, and you can become familiar with our lands and the terrain." She nodded and turned back to her dinner. "Actually," he amended softly to her, "I don't think you would be comfortable riding for a couple of days."

At the close of the meal, Chandra was too tired to stay with the men below stairs, and bid her goodnights with Mary.

Mary said as she and Chandra were climbing the stairs to the bedchambers, "The old woman, Alma, has been very kind to me."

Chandra did not reply for a moment, her attention caught by Jerval's deep booming laughter at something Malton had said. "Jerval told me she is something of a seer," she said finally.

"Aye, I believe 'tis true. She looked at me in the strangest way, then patted my arm and told me that I was never to worry again. How very odd, to be sure." She added happily, "What a marvelous banquet was served tonight! And with no warning at all of Sir Jerval's return. I am quite impressed with Lady Avicia's housekeeping.''

"Aye," Chandra said absently as they reached her bedchamber. The door was open and she heard tittering laughter within. She stepped inside, Mary at her heels, and saw a plump girl with thick brown braids brandishing her sword. Another girl, slighter and redheaded, was squatting beside Chandra's armor and giggling.

"Would you care to feel the flat of my sword on your dimpled bottom?" Chandra said coldly.

"Oh, milady," the plump girl gasped, whirling about and dropping the sword on the soft carpet. She dipped a quick curtsy. "I am Glenna, milady," she said pertly, "and that is Anis. We were just unpacking."

"As I saw," Chandra snapped. "In the future, you will leave my armor and my sword alone."

"They are yours, milady?" Glenna asked, her eyes round with disbelief.

Mary stepped forward. "Milady is tired and doesn't need your silly chatter. The both of you go to bed now, but attend milady in the morning."

The girls dipped another curtsy and scurried from the room. "Don't be angry with them, Chandra. You must admit that a lady with armor is not an everyday sight."

"I know, I am just tired." Chandra turned suddenly to Mary and gave her a quick hug. "I am a selfish beast, Mary. Do you feel all right? Have you been treated well thus far?"

"Of course," Mary said, her voice brusque. "Sir Mark gave me a tour of all the outbuildings. The kitchens are huge, Chandra, and the pastry chef is a marvelously rude fellow, French, you know. And the jakes are set along the outer wall. Only a southerly breeze will raise an odor. And there are so many children, all of them fat and well fed. Camberley is a rich keep." She stopped abruptly, grinning ruefully. "I am carrying on like a magpie! I'll bid you goodnight now, for Sir Jerval is likely to be coming soon."

She stared about her and said over her shoulder as she walked toward the door, "This room is lovely. You'll never shudder with cold here."

When Jerval entered his bedchamber some time later, he drew up short at the sight of Chandra curled on her side atop a carpet, a thick blanket pulled to her chin, sound asleep on the floor next to his bed. Like a damned dog, he thought impatiently. He stood over her for a moment, then leaned down and gently scooped her into his arms and carried her to the bed. The thought of being celibate with her not three feet away from him was daunting, but he would keep his word. The moment Chandra felt the soft bed beneath her back, she jerked awake. He saw uncertainty and fear in her eyes, and said patiently, "You will sleep in a bed, as you should. I will say it again, Chandra. I will not force you to couple with me again until you wish it. Go to sleep. The bed is large enough so that you needn't fear that I will roll over on you."

He paid no more attention to her, but flung himself down on the bed.

Chandra licked her lips and unconsciously tightened the belt about her bedrobe.

He said more sharply, "Must I keep giving you my word until I am blue in the face?"

She finally shook her head and turned her back to him, hugging the far side of the bed.

The evening had been sultry and calm, dark clouds hanging low in the western sky. Jerval lay awake listening to the approaching rumble of distant thunder. When the storm hit, the cold winds from the north chilled him, and he yanked the covers to his neck.

He was awakened when a bright flash of lightning momentarily lit the room. He blinked his eyes, and noticed that only one side of him was cold. Chandra was snuggled against his back, her belly pressed against his buttocks, her legs fitting the curve of his. Her cheek burrowed against his shoulder blade and her arm was flung about his waist. For a moment, he dreamed fondly of the coming of winter.

Slowly, he turned to face her, gently slipping his arm beneath her head, and pressed the length of her supple body against him. She sighed deeply in sleep, nestling herself against the hard warmth of his body. He stroked his fingers lightly through her soft hair until they reached her hips. He contented himself with holding her thus.

He awoke abruptly toward dawn at the sound of a horrified gasp. He lazily opened his eyes and found himself staring into his wife's wide eyes. He felt his manhood, turgid with desire, pressed against her belly. He felt a quivering in her body, a gentle ripple that had nothing to do with fear.

"You were cold during the night," he said, a betraying tremor in his voice, "and came to me for warmth."

"I—I am sorry," she gasped. She jerked away from him to the far side of the bed, her eyes lowered and her face scarlet.

Jerval awoke the next morning to find himself alone in his bed. He dressed quickly and strode down to the hall, where he was told by Maginn, one of his father's young pages, that milady had broken her fast early and gone he knew not where.

Jerval wolfed down warm crusty bread, drank a tankard of rich ale, and set out to find her. Surely, he thought, she would not be so foolish as to ride out on Wicket. Still, the stables were his first stop. Wicket, seeing a familiar face, nickered softly and allowed Jerval to stroke him.

"You are in need of exercise," Jerval said to the stallion as he patted his glossy nose. After assuring himself that Chandra was nowhere within the walls, he ordered Wicket saddled.

According to Dobbe, the wizened old graybeard who attended the cows, she had left through the small north gate, alone. He wondered whom she had cozened to let her leave the keep unescorted, or if she had managed to sneak out unnoticed.

He galloped Wicket alongside the lake, thinking she might have gone swimming, for the sun was warm overhead, the night storm having blown itself out. He did not find her there, and turned Wicket onto the rutted, muddy road that led to the small village of Trackton. Suddenly Wicket reared up on his hind legs and whinnied loudly. Chandra was walking along the narrow road toward them, Lord Hugh's most vicious boarhound, Hawk, prancing at her side, a knobby stick in his great mouth. For a moment, he was afraid for her. He watched, disbelieving, as she leaned down, cuffed Hawk playfully on his thick neck, pulled the stick from his mouth, and hurled it away from her. Hawk bounded off into the thicket beside the road to fetch the stick.

"Christ," Jerval muttered, "I don't believe it." No one dared to approach Hawk, save Lord Hugh, Jerval, and the dogs' keeper, Dakyns.

Chandra dropped to her knees as Hawk galloped back to

her, grinding the stick between his ferocious teeth. He dove toward her, nearly tipping her backward, dropped the stick in her lap, and licked her face with his wet tongue. She laughed brightly and threw her arms about his neck, hugging him to her. Hawk pulled back, his ears flattened to his head. Chandra whipped about, expecting to see a menacing stranger. She stared open-mouthed at Jerval astride Wicket riding slowly toward her. She clutched the hound to her, but he began to bark wildly in welcome and bounded toward Jerval.

She rose slowly, eyeing her destrier and the man on his back with cold disbelief. Her destrier had never allowed anyone on his back save her. "Stupid animal!" she muttered under her breath.

Jerval bounded from Wicket's back, gave Hawk an indifferent pat, and bore down upon her.

"What are you doing on my horse?" she demanded, drawing herself up.

"Don't you sidetrack me with pious rantings about your damned horse! Devil in hell, Chandra, I have been frantic looking for you!"

He wanted to give her a good shaking, but when he reached out to grab her shoulders, she twisted away from him. To Jerval's utter surprise, he heard Hawk growl. He whipped his head about and saw the boarhound crouched, his ears flattened and his eyes slewing from Chandra back to him.

"Shut up, Hawk!" he shouted, and the hound sat back on his haunches.

"Come with me, Chandra, before my hound attacks me. There is much I have to say to you, and not, it appears, in my dog's hearing!"

She wanted to tell him to go to the devil, but she saw the mulish set to his jaw. "Very well," she said in a dismissing voice.

Jerval swung onto Wicket's back and stretched out his hand to her. He pulled her up before him, her legs at Wicket's side.

"You traitor!" she hissed toward Wicket's twitching ears.

Jerval could not prevent a tug of amusement at her words. "It appears there are two traitors, Chandra," he said, clicking Wicket into a canter back toward Camberley. He whistled back toward Hawk and the hound lurched forward, easily keeping pace with Wicket.

"Why did you leave the safety of Camberley . . . and without telling me?"

"You were snoring and woke me up. I could not go back to sleep."

"Snoring! That is no excuse for leaving the safety of the keep!"

"Not so loud, my lord," she said sweetly, "else Hawk might take offense."

"You deserve to be beaten for this."

"This what?"

He tightened his arm about her waist suddenly, cutting off her air. He felt the soft giving of her beneath her layers of clothes, and his body leaped in desire. He dropped his arm away so suddenly that she fell backward, her legs flying up. She grabbed at his shoulder to right herself, and felt furious that he was laughing at her.

"You beast!" It galled her to be clutching as his tunic like some helpless gapseed.

"Wicket is a fine animal," he said easily as he guided the destrier into the inner bailey, "and he took to me so readily. It seems Wicket recognizes me more quickly than do you as his master."

"You will never ride him again, Jerval. I order it!"

He raised a mocking brow. "You order me? You'd best think again, milady."

"Arrogant bully," she muttered.

"Did you enjoy the storm last night?"

She stiffened, and he tweaked her ear with his fingertip. "I vow that you did. At least I am large and warm, a useful bed partner."

"That is all, Jerval!"

He pulled Wicket to a halt, and held him still as Mark raised his arms to help Chandra to the ground.

"What was she doing, Jerval?" he asked, his eyes laughing. "Shooting rabbits for our dinner?"

"She was playing with this damned dog," Jerval said, pointing to the panting hound.

"Christ's blood," Mark exclaimed in an incredulous voice.

"I think she lost track of time," Jerval added, gazing down at her. "Mayhap she was daydreaming about the coming of winter."

8

LADY AVICIA SWEPT INTO THE hall, her sweet memories of Lord Richard and his wicked compliments faded in her mind during the long bone-jolting journey back to Camberley. She was tired, impatient for a bath, and if the truth be told, itching to discover how Camberley had fared in her absence, with Chandra at the helm. She kissed her son and nodded to her daughter-in-law, all the while searching with worried eyes for signs of disorder. She soon found a collection of dust on her beautiful trestle table, and she stiffened at the sound of Glenna's raucous bleating from the solar. Obviously that lazy little slut had enjoyed herself during Avicia's absence! She ran a disdainful finger over the table surface.

"You have been at Camberley a week, Chandra," she said, holding up her dusty fingertip.

"Six days, actually," Chandra said, stiffening, astonished at such a fuss about a bit of dust.

Jerval shouted for wine and honey cakes to be brought into the hall, then turned to greet his father, leaving Chandra alone with his mother and the oddly silent Julianna. He had mentioned to her a couple of times that she should at least give the keep servants orders, but she had shrugged indifferently at such a suggestion, and he had let her be. It had been Jerval who had given the servants orders to carry on, but they were used to his mother's sharp eyes and attention to every detail, and he knew the wenches had grown lax in their duties. He decided to let Chandra fend for herself, at least for the moment.

"You look tired," he said solicitously to Lord Hugh.

"I am too old for such journeys," his father said, heaving his bulk into his great chair, "and this damned gout hasn't given me a moment's peace!"

"I daresay all the good food and wine didn't help. Did you leave Lord Richard and Lady Dorothy in good health?"

"Aye." Hugh grinned. "Even Richard looked ready for his bed by the time his vassals left. You broke his rib, Jerval, in the tourney." Hugh glanced over toward Chandra, who stood stiffly beside Avicia. "What does your lady think of her new home?"

He could practically hear his son sigh as he said, "She is at least used to every inch of Camberley, outside of the keep."

"Ah," Hugh said. "Let your mother handle that," he added comfortably.

"It is how they will handle each other that worries me," Jerval said ruefully.

He turned as he overheard his mother ask Chandra pointedly, "Have the servants treated you as they should, child? Have they done your bidding?"

Chandra shrugged. "I have not bid them to do anything in particular."

"Come, Aunt," Julianna said, slewing her brown eyes toward Jerval, "surely you do not expect a *warrior* to take interest in a lady's duties."

"Thank you, Julianna," said Chandra, her voice sweet, "for explaining things so nicely."

"Your wine, my lady," Mary said in her gentle voice. "Your honey cakes are delicious. I have wanted to ask the cook for his recipe."

"It is I who gave the varlet the recipe," Lady Avicia said, softening. She found herself staring for a moment at Mary. Odd that she had not noticed at Croyland that the girl had the look of Matilda, her sweet, biddable daughter, whose memory always brought a pang of sadness. "You are thin, Mary," she said roughly. "I hope you will be happy here at Camberley."

Lord Hugh's mouth was full at the moment, else his jaw would have dropped at his lady's gentle words.

"I am very happy, my lady," Mary assured her, a furtive smile on her lips. "Camberley is so lovely and there are so many windows . . . I feel as if I am standing in the sunlight."

"Do you also know about armor, Mary?" Julianna said in honeyed tones. "Or do you just polish Chandra's?"

Mary's sweet smile did not waver as she said to Julianna, "I have not Chandra's skill . . . more's the pity."

Chandra felt a moment of envy at Mary's ease in dismissing Julianna. Julianna's eyes hardened, and then she turned to Jerval, a dazzling smile on her lips.

"It rained for two days after you left," Julianna announced to Jerval. "I—we were sorry that you quitted Croyland."

"We also had a bit of rain here," Jerval said easily, ignoring the winsome look on his young cousin's face. He toyed briefly with the idea of flirting with Julianna, but knew that it could only hurt her, and gain him nothing at all with his wife.

"Well, it is not raining now," Avicia said. "The honey cakes seemed stale, Chandra."

"We were not expecting you," Chandra said, "and I have no particular liking for sweets."

"I trust the evening meal will be well prepared."

"I see no reason why it should not be. The servants know now that you are returned." She felt a moment of uncertainty, for the previous evening the meat had arrived at the table overcooked and the vegetables mushy.

"I am tired," Avicia announced, having decided that she had better visit the cooking sheds herself.

She was on the point of sweeping out of the hall when suddenly she heard Dakyns shouting frantically. She whipped about to see Hawk bounding into the hall, barking loudly, galloping directly at Chandra. Avicia shrieked and Julianna scurried to stand behind her aunt.

Lord Hugh thrust out his beefy hand to grab the hound, but Hawk eluded him. He grabbed at his sword as the beast dove at Chandra.

"Nay, Father," Jerval laughed, staying his hand.

Lord Hugh stood stunned as he watched his most vicious boarhound plant his paws upon Chandra's shoulders and lick her face with a wildly lapping tongue.

"What is that beast doing in here?" Avicia demanded in a voice of awful calm.

"Do not worry, Mother," Jerval said, knowing that the moment of reckoning had come. "He is here because he heard Chandra's voice." He said over his shoulder to his still gape-mouthed father, "It is all I can do to keep him out of our bedchamber. He is forever at Chandra's heels, begging for her attention."

Avicia drew herself to her full height. "None of those

disgusting beasts are to foul the keep. Get him out of here at
once or I'll have him killed.''

It was a mistake, and she knew it the moment she looked at
her husband.

"I beg your pardon," Lord Hugh said in a formidably
calm voice, staring at his wife.

Avicia splayed her hands in a helpless gesture that had,
some thirty years previously, led Hugh to the erroneous
conclusion that his bride was a soft-spoken girl who needed
his strong man's protection. She shuddered delicately. "You
promised, Hugh. The dog is fouling Chandra, and making a
nuisance of himself."

"Nay," Chandra said seriously, as she cuffed the hound
playfully. "You needn't worry for me, and he is not fouling
me, for Jerval and I bathed him but yesterday."

"He nearly ripped my arm off at the indignity," Jerval
said, "The men were laying bets who would end up the
wettest."

"God and the angels," Hugh muttered, torn between laughter and his wife's outrage. "You gave Hawk a bath?"

"He is no lady's dog," Julianna said, drawing away from
her aunt when she saw the hound was no danger to her.

Chandra frowned. "I did not want to bathe him," she said
forthrightly, disregarding Julianna, "but Jerval felt it would
make Hawk more acceptable to you. My father's hounds are
always in the keep. You, my lord, were constantly throwing
bones to Graynard during supper."

"Aye, 'tis true," Hugh said fondly, remembering the hounds'
scratchy coats rubbing against his legs. He forgot that he had
cursed the fleas.

"Hugh?" She recognized the obstinate tightening of his
jaw as he gazed away from the exuberant Hawk toward her.

"The dog is clean," he said in his most forceful voice.
"As long as Chandra is willing to keep him that way, he may
stay."

Chandra closed her arms about the hound's neck and let
him throw his great weight against her, dragging her to her
knees.

"As you will, my lord," Avicia said, tight-lipped. But not
for long, she assured herself. She remembered all too well the
pigsty Camberley had been when she first wed Hugh, for
there had been no lady in residence for several years. She

sent a darkling glance toward her daughter-in-law, vowing that Chandra was not going to undo her hard work.

"Hawk is almost human sometimes, my lady," Mary said with gentle humor. "Indeed, when Jerval scolded him to hold still for his bath, he seemed to understand. Alma gave me some powdery leaves to rub into his coat. She said it would keep all the vermin away from him."

The girl is a diplomat, Jerval thought, staring at Mary, a quality that seemed quite lost to his stubborn wife.

Lady Avicia was uncertain whether to be angry or mollified at Mary's assurances. She pulled herself up, deciding upon chilling dignity, and announced, "I am tired and will retire now." She swept from the hall, Julianna at her heels.

Dinner that evening was set only for the family, well-prepared and served without mishap, thanks to Lady Avicia's last-minute entrance, Jerval knew. He supposed, looking at his wife from the corner of his eye, that he had to give her time. Since she resolutely refused to see herself as his wife, she seemed equally determined not to involve herself with Camberley's management. He forked a piece of roast pork into his mouth. Having her close in bed each night was becoming a trial, and damnably, the weather had held warm.

His mother's well-measured words brought his head up. "There are no idle hands at Camberley, Chandra, as I'm certain you've noticed. Everyone has duties to perform, and we do not cater to slothfulness." She directed her next words to her husband. "Just this evening, I saw that slut Glenna whistling in the solar, and idling about."

Lord Hugh said between bites, "The girl has her uses, Avicia." He choked on the meat and added quickly, "Rather, she had her uses."

"What do you mean, my lord?" Chandra inquired.

"He means nothing," Jerval said.

"Tell me, Chandra," Avicia continued, wondering how her daughter-in-law could be such a dolt about such matters, "what were your duties at Croyland?"

"My duties?" she repeated, forcing her attention back to her mother-in-law. She shrugged. "I helped Crecy with the ledger accounts. Lord Richard despises numbers, and during the past year, I saw to Croyland's purchases and sales."

"You read?"

"Aye, my father wished it. Crecy taught me."

"We ladies do not involve ourselves in that sort of thing at Camberley," Lady Avicia said sternly.

"You have an honest steward then? One who can count beyond his ten fingers?"

Avicia thought of the oily Damis, whom she had distrusted ever since the day she had seen him strutting in a new fur-lined tunic in the village over a year ago. "Of course," she said, but she cast an uncertain look toward her husband.

"Actually," Jerval said, "I handle quite a bit of that now, Chandra. Damis needs the . . . supervision."

"What do you do that is appropriate for a lady?" Julianna inquired, fluttering her lashes toward Jerval.

"Chandra sings and plays the lyre beautifully," Mary said, "but surely you know that already, Julianna."

My little champion, Chandra thought, looking ruefully at Mary. She said to Lady Avicia, "My mother directed the servants in the weaving, cooking, and cleaning. I know nothing of it."

"You are saying," Avicia said, "that you spent all your days . . . and nights jobnobbing with the men then?"

"Aye," Chandra said baldly.

"You know," Lady Avicia continued carefully, "as my son's wife and the future mistress of Camberley there are many responsibilities that will be yours. There is the proper setting of the meals, clothes to be woven and mended, and the care of guests."

"Doubtless responsible servants are available to see to such things."

Jerval closed his eyes for a moment, envisioning the future at Camberley as a battleground.

Avicia drew herself up at Chandra's challenge. Jerval and his father, she added darkly to herself, had chosen a hoyden as his wife. "It is unfortunate," she said with sharp emphasis, "that there were no responsible servants at Croyland. The meals were ill prepared save for the marriage feast, the serving maids slovenly and shiftless, and the keep filthy. I could not even walk about in the bailey without having my skirts soiled." It was not precisely the truth, and Avicia struggled with her better self to be fair.

A more conciliating approach froze on her tongue when Chandra rose, flattened her palms on the table, and said angrily, "How dare you! Camberley is nothing compared to

Croyland!'' She waved her hand about her. ''All here is soft
and pretty, ill befitting a warrior's keep . . . and to have to
bathe a dog!''

''Chandra! Enough!''

She turned unwillingly at Jerval's harsh voice, angry words
still in her throat.

''It is late,'' Jerval said, rising quickly to stand beside her,
''and Chandra is tired. We will discuss all of this more
rationally in the morning. Come, Chandra.''

''I am not tired,'' Chandra said.

Jerval would not allow her to flout him, not openly. She
was standing rigid as a stick of wood, ready, as ever, to do
battle. He leaned down and whispered savagely in her ear,
''You will do as I tell you, else I will forget the promise I
made you.''

Chandra saw that he was smiling, a false smile to cover his
threat with honey. She felt his hand caressing her arm, to
make everyone think that he was seducing her with soft
words.

''No one insults Croyland,'' she hissed.

''Chandra,'' Mary said suddenly, rising. ''I have a blister
on my foot. I had forgot to ask you earlier . . . will you help
me?''

''I will take care of you, Mary,'' Lady Avicia said.

''Chandra is so good with medicines, my lady,'' Mary said
breathlessly. ''I would never want to bother you with my
stupid ailments.''

Chandra nodded quickly, unwilling to push Jerval further,
and pulled away from him. ''Come to my bedchamber now,
Mary.''

She nodded stiff goodnights and turned, her hand solidly
on Mary's arm.

''That woman is a harridan!'' she muttered as they walked
up the staircase.

''She is as much used to having her way as you are.''

''I do not want my own way. I simply want her to leave
me alone!''

Mary said sharply, much to Chandra's surprise, ''You
must not be so unyielding, Chandra! You made your husband
most uncomfortable, and 'twas unfair.''

''Jerval should mind his own business.''

''You are his business, and a little understanding on your

part would not serve you badly." She added matter-of-factly, "You are no longer at Croyland. Your husband seems most concerned about your well-being. But even he, given enough provocation, such as you managed tonight, might begin to question the freedom he has given you."

"He wouldn't dare!"

Mary sighed. "Lady Avicia is not at all like Lady Dorothy, Chandra."

"Aye, I begin to wish she spent all her time at devotions."

Mary's eyes twinkled. "But then there would be fleas and filth in the keep!"

Hubert had to squint against the early-morning sun to make out the figure riding toward him. It was Sir Jerval's wife, astride her destrier. A sword was strapped at her side and a lance tucked under her arm. Her slim legs were encased in chausses, with cross garters binding them to her, and she wore a tunic of dark-blue wool. Hubert met Malton's astonished gaze, grinned, and spat into the dirt.

Malton drew a deep breath and wheeled about. "I must see Sir Jerval." He had seen her on the archery range with Jerval and Mark during the previous week, and of course she was a familiar sight in her men's garb riding her great destrier. But that Jerval would allow her to take part in the Scots' competition he could not believe.

"Sir Jerval," he shouted, finding the young master naked to the waist, sluicing himself from a bucket of water at the well.

"Aye, Malton?" Jerval shook himself, took a towel from a giggling serving girl at his side, and rubbed it vigorously over his back.

Malton cleared his throat. "It's my lady," he blurted out. "She's mounted on that beast of hers, in the tiltyard! We are having the competition this morning. 'Tis dangerous, most unfit for a lady! Surely, you don't want—"

"Don't be a fool!" Jerval said, jerking the string tie together at the throat of his tunic. "Of course my wife will not compete." He finished dressing quickly, mounted Pith, and followed Malton to the tiltyard. Chandra had been sleeping when he had at last bid goodnight to his father the previous evening, and she had left early this morning. He had thought that she had been avoiding his mother, on her way to ride out on Wicket, with Lambert or Mark for escort. Jerval pressed his knees to Pith's sides and galloped to the far side of the tiltyard, where Chandra sat proudly astride Wicket.

"Just what the devil are you doing here, my lady?"

"I wish to behead the Scots," she said, raising her chin. "Lambert explained it to me."

"Well, you will not. Archery, wrestling, and hunting are one thing, Chandra, but this is not a game."

"I am well used to riding at straw dummies," she said stiffly, "and your course does not look at all difficult."

"I have no intention of arguing with you. If you wish, you may watch, but that is all."

She stared ahead of her, but did not argue further. He gave her one last long look, turned in his saddle, and roared to Blanc, "Prepare the Scots! We behead the whoresons! Maginn, you will keep the scores and count the seconds!"

Her eyes glittered in silent anger as he wheeled his destrier away from her. She had studied the course, with its straw figures bound upright to long poles, spaced haphazardly, their heads tilted at odd angles, her fingers fairly itching to draw her sword. She leaned forward to pat Wicket's glossy neck, guessing that success depended greatly on the destrier's skill.

As Lambert was readying himself for his run, Lord Hugh rode onto the tiltyard and pulled his palfrey to a halt beside his son. "So, Jerval," he observed, his heavy brows raised, "I see your wife is here. Does she wish to show the men how to run the course?"

"I am allowing her to watch, Father, that is all," Jerval snapped.

" 'Twould appear that I've saddled you with a hellion," Hugh said, grinning widely. "But damn, she's a beauty!"

"Aye, I know it well."

"And there's to be but one master?"

"You doubt me, Father?"

"Nay, I envy you the taming of her. Your mother believes that you give the girl too much rein, but all in good time, eh, Jerval?"

"She will bend when I wish her to."

Maginn raised his arm, then with a loud whoop sliced it through the air back to his side.

Lambert brandished his sword over his head and galloped toward the nearest straw Scot, yelling, *A Vernon! A Vernon!*

The staw head went hurtling into the air. There were thirty Scots in all, and by the time Lambert wheeled his horse about at the end of the run, fourteen had lost their heads.

"Not bad for a Cornishman!" Jerval shouted to Lambert as the men cheered.

As the *sewers* raced through the course to fasten the heads back to the bodies, Chandra inched Wicket toward the field. She watched the next three men take their run, heard Maginn call out their score and the time, and wondered why they had all avoided the center of the course, where most of the straw Scots were bunched together. It was a narrow passage, to be sure, but to win, it had to be tried.

"What is the prize for winning?" she called to her husband.

Lord Hugh guffawed loudly. "I suppose the prize would be in reverse, if a woman were to compete and win."

"I do not understand, my lord," Chandra said.

"I vow you will soon enough, girl. Your husband rarely loses this competition." Hugh, much enjoying himself, shouted to his son, "If you win, Jerval, allow me to give you your prize!"

"Come," Chandra said, her voice impatient, "stop treating me like a half-wit."

"The prize, Chandra, is a woman, any of the serving maids. The girls squeal with delight when your husband wins, for he always honors the prize." Hugh added sorrowfully, "Poor lad, now he will have to content himself with his wife."

How dare they! Those brave brawny men played at their competition, and it was a woman who had them gloating over victory!

Chandra looked from father to son, her lips in a thin line, and turned Wicket away. She called over her shoulder, "Jerval may do as he has always done!"

Lord Hugh gave a deep belly laugh. The girl was jealous, and her show of indifference amused him.

Maginn raised his arm and dropped it, but instead of Rolfe galloping toward him, it was Chandra, shouting, *A Avenell, A Avenell!* as Wicket bounded forward.

Chandra felt a surge of pleasure as her sword sliced through the first straw neck, sending its head flying upward before it landed, careening wildly on the ground. 'Tis not so difficult, she thought, smiling fiercely, and whipped Wicket toward the

center lane. Her smile quickly faded when she saw that if
Wicket held a straight path, she would have to lean as far as
she could from her saddle, her arm extended to its full length
to reach the straw Scots. Her sword swooped outward, and its
weight nearly toppled her from the saddle. She whipped her
arm back over Wicket's neck, nearly slashing her thigh, and
tossed her sword to her left hand. The time cost her dearly,
for a straw Scot to the right was nearly upon her. She twisted
about in the saddle and slashed her sword at it. It sliced
cleanly through the straw man's chest and embedded itself in
the pole. She did not release soon enough, and in the next
instant, she was flying off Wicket's back. She landed on her
bottom and rolled instantly to her side to break her fall. She
was laughing at herself as she pulled herself to her feet, for
she had foolishly judged the course much easier than it
actually was.

She was trying to pull her sword from the pole when Jerval
galloped to her side and jumped from Pith's back. She found
it difficult to face him tall and straight with her bottom
smarting so.

"Are you all right?" he shouted, jerking her about to face
him.

"Aye," she gasped. "I was a fool to take the center, but
now I am much wiser and my bottom much sorer."

When he saw that she had not been hurt, he gave free rein
to his anger. He tightened his grip painfully about her upper
arms. "How dare you disobey me?" He shook her, and she
had to lock her jaws together to keep her teeth from rattling.
She tried to jerk away from him, but he held her tight.
"Answer me, damn you!"

"Your order, my lord, was unfair," she muttered between
clenched teeth. "With a bit of practice, I could take the
course as well as any of the men."

"You will learn, wife," he said slowly, stressing each
word, "that you are not the master here, I am."

"Master!" she yelled at him. "I have no master! I am not
one of your dogs or servants!"

"Come with me, you silly brat. I have no intention of
giving the men any more of a show than we already have."

Before he could drag her to Wicket, the men surged toward
them and gathered about her. Rolfe thwacked her on the

back. "God's bones, lady, 'twas not so bad for your first time!"

Chandra grinned. "I was a fool to believe it was easy!"

"You still got four of the bastards, better than Rolfe did his first time," Hubert laughed, "but of course he was but seven years old at the time!"

"Liar!" Chandra retorted, laughing. "Next time I will be a coward like you, Lambert!"

"Aye, and you'll save yourself a bruised butt!"

Jerval saw Malton eyeing him dubiously, and he threw back his head and roared, "Back to work, all of you bleating goats, or there will be a lot of sore butts from the flat of my sword!"

When they were finally alone again, Jerval growled, "Don't think that all that jesting changes a thing. Come with me." He dragged her to Wicket, grabbed her about the waist, and tossed her into the saddle. "Follow me, Chandra, else I swear I'll thrash you!"

Malton shook his head as he watched Jerval and Chandra ride from the tiltyard and swing to the east toward the lake. "Sir Jerval's lady is in for it, I wager."

"The wench deserves it," Lord Hugh grunted. Taming the girl would be quite a chore, he thought, even for his strong-willed son. Lord, but Chandra had made him look the fool today! He hoped Jerval wouldn't beat her too badly.

Chandra followed Jerval to the small emerald lake. He dismounted and stood waiting, hands on his hips, for her to do likewise.

"How beautiful you look, my lady," he said, his eyes roving insolently over her body. The short ride had cooled his anger somewhat, but he had a store of words for her.

Chandra rubbed her hand across her forehead as she slithered off Wicket's back. "The men didn't seem to think that I did too badly," she said perversely.

As soon as her feet touched the ground, he grabbed her about the waist, fell to one knee, and upended her over his leg. He brought his hand down on her buttocks as hard as he could. She yelled curses at him and twisted frantically to free herself.

"You could have killed yourself, you stubborn little fool!" he shouted, and slammed his hand down again. He wished her bottom were bare, for the thick woolen chausses protected her.

"It had nothing to do with you!" she yelled back, her voice muffled in the grass.

"Stupid wench! You're my wife, and my responsibility!"

"I am responsible for myself, and you have no right to give me orders! Bully! Stop pounding me!"

To her surprise, he did. He rose abruptly and rolled her off his leg onto the slightly grassy incline, near the water's edge. She rose to her knees and glared at him. Her bottom, sore already from her fall on the course, was burning like scalding water, and tears were stinging in her eyes.

"Ignorant lump!" she shouted at him. "Misbegotten whoreson!"

"Such a loving, gentle wife you are, my pet. Listen to me, Chandra," he continued, his voice like iron, "and listen well. Never again will you disobey me. Your stubborn behavior toward my mother and your willful disregard for my wishes this morning were little more than the acts of a spoiled child. It is time for you to grow up. Dammit, woman, do you think any of the pages, squires, or men would ever disobey me? No, keep your mouth shut, else I'll take you over my knee again! From now on, you will meet with my mother every morning and learn those things you are expected to know. If you cooperate, I will allow you to continue on the practice field in the afternoons. Do you understand me?"

"Make your own beer!"

"Do you understand?"

"Aye," she said gruffly, and walked stiffly, favoring her right leg, to where Wicket stood grazing on the water weeds.

"Let us hope so, for your sake."

She saw that he was still standing some feet away from her. Beat her, would he, as if she were some sort of idiot child! Slowly, she mounted Wicket, inching toward Pith. She reached out suddenly and grabbed Pith's loose reins.

She yelled at him as she whipped both horses about, "A bully deserves to walk, my lord!"

She dug her heels into Wicket's sides, urging him up a steep slope to the path. Suddenly, a loud whistle rang out, and in the next instant, Pith reared back, jerking at the reins in her hand. Not again, she thought, as she toppled backward off Wicket's smooth rump. She landed on her side in the thick grass and rolled down the slope, unable to stop herself, the sound of Jerval's deep laughter ringing in her ears.

She came finally to a stop and looked up to see her husband, legs apart and arms akimbo, standing over her.

"Scurvy knave!" she yelled up at him, but he only laughed harder.

"Next time, you will know that even my horse obeys me," he said. "By all the saints, are you a mess!"

She struggled, trembling, to stand up. Her tunic was ripped and the cross garters on her right leg had come loose, leaving her chausses sagging and wrinkled like an old sack.

"Why don't you take a swim," he called to her over his shoulder. " 'Twill make you more presentable!" He jumped onto Pith's back and rode away from her without a backward glance.

It galled her so that she could think of nothing to yell after him. She pulled herself painfully to her feet and leaned over to fasten her cross garters. "Damn . . . everything!" she muttered.

"Ah, my lord, I forgot how brilliantly you played. You have plundered my poor king."

Jerval leaned back in his chair and crossed his arms over his chest. "Nay, Julianna, your attention wasn't on the game." Still, he felt warmed by her praise. He watched her slender fingers rearrange the chess pieces on the board, and raised his eyes to her face. He cocked his head in question, for there was a delicate flush on her cheeks.

Julianna met his eyes. "Aye, you are right," she whispered. "It has been so very long since we were alone." She picked up the queen and caressed the white ivory. "But you have always been my lord . . . and master in all things, Jerval."

If only, he thought, staring at Julianna, it could be Chandra who would say that to him in a soft, throaty voice. He wondered exactly what his wife did during the days, for he rarely saw her now. He did see Chandra once in the cooking shed, supposedly learning from the varlets what all the utensils were called and their uses, and he had heard her muttering one afternoon between shots at the archery targets, "Trivets, mortar and pestle, scummer, pothooks, dressing board," as if to fix the names in her mind. His clothes, he firmly suspected, were not mended by his wife, but by Mary. He pulled his attention back to Julianna and said gently, "Nay, Julianna, I am not the man who will be your lord and master, 'twill be another, and he will be lucky to have you."

He wasn't quite sure just how lucky the man would be, for just the previous evening, he had seen quite different behavior from her, evoked, doubtless, by her jealousy of Chandra. He could still hear Chandra snarling at his mother, "I hate soup! Why should I know how to make it?" And Julianna's smug remark, "Because if you don't, Jerval will beat you!"

"I have never wanted another man," Julianna said softly, her brown eyes liquid. " 'Twas you who taught me how to carry my falcon on my wrist, do you not remember?" She lightly caressed his wrist with her fingertips, and he tensed at her touch.

Jerval remembered quite well teaching a rapt young Julianna how to carry her falcon so that the motion of her palfrey would not frighten it, how to adjust its hood, and the day some six months ago when they were hunting in the woods and had released their falcons to soar upward, far above the line of trees, toward a flock of herons. It had been a warm day, and he had kissed Julianna's parted lips.

"I remember," he said, but he was no longer thinking of Julianna, but of Chandra, and his almost unbearable need for her. He had pushed himself harder and harder each day in order to sleep at night, and had suffered many buckets of icy water to ease the aching in his groin. He resolutely pulled his hand away from Julianna's fingers.

He saw the angry flash in her eyes and said in a steely voice, "You cannot want me now, Julianna. I am wed."

"To an ill-mannered little slut!"

"Chandra is a lady, Julianna. There is no need for me to tell you that, ever again."

Julianna lowered her eyes and splayed her hands before her, in a helpless gesture. " 'Tis what your mother says. Chandra refused to learn how to weave. Yesterday she threw the distaff at one of the servants and stomped out."

"Aye, I know what my mother says, without reminders." Actually, his last words from his mother, just the previous evening, had been of a very different nature. "If only you would get her with child!" Avicia had murmured. "At least it would slow her down."

He could not recall ever before having been in such agreement with his mother.

"Jerval," Julianna whispered, "she does not belong here, you know that. Let me give you the pleasure she refuses you."

Jerval rose. "Never offer yourself to anyone save the man who will be your husband, Julianna. It is late. I will see you in the morning."

As he climbed the stairs, he wondered why God, in his infinite wisdom, had made a man's need so great, and the wrong woman's nil.

9

"COME, LAD, THE ONLY ONE she's apt to slay is Julianna for her taunting words. Fret not."

Jerval, who had been gazing abstractedly toward the blossoming orchard, turned at the words of his old nurse, Alma. He supposed, a slight smile lighting his eyes, that Alma would always call him lad even when he became the lord of Camberley. "She is like a caged bird, Alma," he said, speaking his thoughts aloud, "and unhappy."

"Aye, and she is not the most civil of wives to her husband."

"What would you have me do?" he asked. "Beat her or starve her?"

"You've a wife, lad," Alma said softly, "who has not yet accepted herself as a woman."

"You fancy yourself a seer, Alma. Have you naught to say that I do not already know?"

Alma scratched the scraggly bun at the back of her neck, found the offending flea, and crushed it thoughtfully between her thumb and forefinger. "I have been pondering, lad. You are wondering if the girl will ever change, if there is naught but fear of you inside her, fear that will keep her away from you always."

"Enough of your chatter, Alma," Jerval said, his voice impatient. "Say what you will say and be done with it."

"Your wedding night was a debacle, lad, and I'm surprised that you, such a splendid lover, played the fool!" She shrugged, ignoring his flush of anger. "I don't know if it matters. I doubt it is you who have put the fear in her eyes when your eyes hold desire."

"How the devil do you know that?"

She grinned cunningly. "Mary, the little angel, has told me much about your wife. There is much fear in your lady, fear that even she does not understand. And, of course, she chafes 'neath your hand, easy though you have been. I have decided to help you, lad.''

"No one can help," he snapped, "least of all a foolish old woman with the trappings of a witch!''

"You are a warrior, lad, not a sniveling fool, and you give up too easily." She paused a moment to spit over her shoulder, then reached a gnarled hand inside her pocket and withdrew a small flask." This contains a goodly portion of opium, a drug that comes from the East, and a bit of man-drake.''

"What does all this have to do with anything?''

"Patience, lad, patience." She gently shook the flask back and forth. "Opium dampens fears and doubts, by far better even than good drink, and without the splitting head the next morning.''

Alma held up the flask to him.

"You see, lad, if you gave your wife the opium, it would not make her feel passion, it would simply make her more . . . receptive. It does no harm and its effects last but a night.''

"But if the woman feels naught but hatred for a man, what difference would it make?''

"It wouldn't. 'Tis no magic potion.''

Jerval shook himself, aghast that he was even listening to such drivel. "This is crazy, Alma. I cannot give my wife some vile heathen drug!''

"Why not?" she said imperturbably. "You would know once and for all if your proud warrior wife is cold as ice in winter or holds a fire within.''

"She is cold; her fear of men has made her so. Why she wishes to act like a man, when she despises them for animals, I do not know. But I do know that your precious drug would do naught.''

Alma shrugged. "Are you afraid to discover the truth, lad?''

Jerval stared away from her, remembering the morning after the cold night of the storm when Chandra had awakened in his arms, trembling against him, until her fear made her flee from him.

"I am a fool for even considering this," he said, more to himself than to his old nurse.

"If you give it to her, and you seduce her, she will remember everything the next day."

"A husband does not need some evil drug to master his wife."

"Lady Chandra is no ordinary wife, lad. But if that is your will . . ." She thrust the flask back into her pocket.

"It will not harm her in any way?"

Alma shook her head. "Nay. You pour it into her wine. It is tasteless and begins to take effect within fifteen minutes." She cackled mirthlessly at his uncertainty. "Make certain, lad, that it is not her monthly flux!"

"I will think about it," Jerval said, and stretched out his hand. She placed the small flask into his palm and closed his fingers over it. "Aye," she said, "you will think about it."

"Where is Chandra?" Jerval asked his mother over his midday meal.

"How would I know?" Avicia said shortly. "The morning is over."

Lord Hugh set his fork firmly down on the table. "Do you know, she had the impertinence to tell me that I was too soft! Told me that her father hadn't a pound of extra flesh on him and that I should be out exercising with the men to keep myself fit."

"Chandra is no politician, Father, you know that," Jerval said, stifling a laugh. "It just might be that she is right!"

"Jerval! That little fiend had no right to speak to your father that way! He cannot help that he suffers from the gout!"

"Chandra is not a fiend, Mother, merely outspoken." Jerval leaned toward his father and poked his thumb to his expanding stomach. "Come out this afternoon and practice at swords with the men. You are a master, and they could learn from you. If you shed a bit of flesh, none of the men, including your son, could best you."

Lord Hugh seemed to ponder his son's words. "I think I will," He said finally. "I could show you young fools a bit of the old ways."

"Hugh! Your daughter-in-law insulted you!"

"Leave be, wife," he said, rising. "Jerval will bring the girl around. Come, Jerval, it grows late."

Jerval winked toward his mother. "Do not worry. I will see that he does not overstrain himself."

It was a happy, albeit very sore man who sat at the supper table that evening. Malton praised him between every bite, and the practice was discussed until Lady Avicia thought she would scream with vexation. Mark watched with astonishment when Lord Hugh refused a honeyed sweetmeat, and it was only Mary's baleful eyes upon him that made him keep a still tongue in his mouth.

Jerval leaned over toward Chandra and said warmly, "I missed you this afternoon, as did the men."

"I was swimming at the lake. It was so very warm."

She looked at him warily, expecting him to chide her, but his smile did not leave his lips. "You have eaten little. Here, try a bite of heron. 'Tis well prepared."

She swallowed the morsel and found it quite tasty. "Thank you," she said. She saw that her husband was regarding her kindly, a warm glint in his eyes, and allowed herself to relax a bit.

"I like your gown. The blue matches your eyes."

She blinked, surprised. " 'Tis old; you have seen it many times before."

"I have seen you often too, Chandra, but I am continually reminded how beautiful you are."

Her fingers clutched about her wine goblet. "Why are you being so nice?"

Because I have every intention of seducing you tonight. He said softly so only she could hear, "I love you, and you are my wife. I do not like the strife between us."

She sighed. "Fifty years is a long time."

"Aye, and the time should be sweet as mulled wine, not sour like vinegar."

She stared at him thoughtfully and sipped her wine.

"Would you like to play chess with me this evening?"

"We have not played since Croyland."

"I have been practicing. Perhaps this time I can give you a good game."

She said, a small smile playing about her mouth, "I hope you have not been practicing too much. You won at least half our matches before."

At the close of the meal, Jerval told Chandra that he would meet her shortly in their bedchamber. He left the keep and stood for a time outside, watching the quarter moon as scattered dark clouds spun past it. He pulled the small flask from his belt and stared down at it. Some minutes later, he strode up to their bedchamber, carrying the chess table under his arm. Chandra was polishing her shield when he entered, and smiled when she looked up at him.

"Are you ready for our competition?" he asked.

"Talk and more talk, Sir Knight!"

While Chandra arranged the pieces on the board, Jerval turned to pour each of them a glass of wine. He paused only briefly before he stirred the potion into her goblet.

"I will take the black pieces, since I have been practicing."

" 'Tis gallant of you," she said, and took a sip of her wine.

He toasted her with his wine goblet and drank deeply, watching her.

After some several moves between them, he asked, "Do you not like the wine?"

"Aye," she said absently, studying the board, and obligingly downed the rest of the wine in her goblet.

He took his time making his next move, gazing at her beneath hooded eyes, waiting to see some change in her. She replied quickly, placing her bishop on the black square in front of her queen.

Chandra sat back in her chair. She felt a strange warmth curling inside her, a languorous feeling that made her want to stretch, though not in fatigue. She shook her head and gazed down a moment at her empty wine goblet. Perhaps she had drunk the sweet wine too quickly. The strange warmth, now a gentle pulsing in her belly, made her shift in her chair. She looked at her husband and saw his eyes flicker momentarily on her face before he lowered his head and studied the placement of the chess pieces. She found herself staring at him as his long fingers closed about his knight and placed it before his bishop's pawn.

To her surprise, she said softly, "Nay, Jerval, 'tis not a wise move."

He looked up, a slow smile spreading over his face. She found that she could not look away from him. The warmth in her belly was fanning throughout her body, and her flesh tingled. She felt very aware of herself and him at that moment, but there was no fear or anger in her thoughts, only an easing throughout her body and mind that made her want to yawn and talk all at the same time.

"Do you remember the days at Croyland?"

"Aye. I miss wrestling with you, and all the gritty sand that made me itch for a day after."

"Everything was . . . different then."

"You mean until the afternoon at the lake?"

She nodded, but there was no anger in her eyes. "I suppose so."

"I wish you had told me you wished to swim today."

"After what your mother said, I did not think you wanted to be with me."

"On occasion you are wrong in your assumptions, Chandra."

"I hate the infernal sewing. I kept pricking my finger."

"Let me see." He held out his hand to her, and to his surprise and pleasure, she turned her right hand palm up and showed him the pad of her middle finger. It was covered with tiny pin pricks.

"I am sorry," he said, and slowly, he pulled her hand to his lips and kissed her finger gently.

He looked up to see her staring at him wide-eyed, but she made no move to pull her hand away.

She blinked, shaking her head, and brought her hand back to her lap. She tried to concentrate on the chess pieces. "It is not a wise move," she repeated blankly.

"Why is it not a wise move?" she heard him say, his voice sounding distant, and yet he was close to her, but the width of the chessboard away.

Her mouth seemed oddly dry, and she licked her lips, not the way she would usually lick her lips, she thought vaguely, for her tongue moved slowly as if enjoying the feel of her own mouth.

Jerval could not seem to tear his gaze away from her pink tongue as it caressed her lower lip. He saw her thick lashes blink as if she were awakening from a dream. Her eyes appeared wide and dark in the candlelight, her cheeks slightly flushed. His gaze fell to her breasts, heaving slightly against the soft material of her gown.

"Why is it not a wise move?" he repeated, no other words coming to his mind. She reached out her hand and closed her fingers over the knight, lightly stroking the cold ivory. "I—I do not know," she said at last.

He must not frighten her, he thought. "Perhaps," he said, closing his fingers lightly over hers, "the knight would be better placed here." Together, they lifted the ivory piece and set it on another square. He turned her palm inward and felt the roughness of her skin, callused from practice with a sword.

She watched his fingers moving over her hand, strong and bluntly squared, yet warm and gentle. She drew back suddenly in her chair. "I—I do not know what is the matter with me," she gasped, aware that his eyes were probing her face.

"Perhaps you are no longer so distrusting of me."

"I probably should be," she said sharply, shaking her head at herself. Her lips seemed so dry, and she passed her tongue over them again.

Suddenly she said, her head cocked to one side, "I did not want my father to look at you and regret that he had but me instead." She fell silent, a slight frown puckering her brow, wondering vaguely why the words had slipped so easily from her mouth.

"You had nothing to prove to me. I had but to see you that first night, your clothes askew, the gold circlet falling over your brow, your eyes bright with victory and welcome for me. I think that I began to love you then."

"I did not want your love," she whispered, tearing away from the intense gaze of his eyes. His look was unsettling, and she squirmed in her chair, for the warmth in her belly was fast becoming a churning, almost painful sensation.

"It was given freely, and you will always have it. Do you think you could forgive the pain I caused you . . . and the fear?"

She pictured his body, familiar to her now, for he had no modesty before her, as she had seen him that night in their tent. His hugeness, the rippling muscles that banded his chest and belly, and his swelled manhood, hated and alien to her then.

"I have no fear of you now," she said. She leaned toward him, then caught herself, but she did not move away. "I like your smell," she whispered, a frown puckering her forehead. "Very sweet, yet like a man." She felt his fingers touch her face, lightly, tracing over her skin, and she closed her eyes, arching closer to him and his fingers, her senses so sharpened that she could not think, only feel. When he pulled back her hair and his fingertip teased along her ear she blinked. "That is only my ear," she said foolishly. "I do not understand why it should make me feel so very odd."

He released her ear, and she frowned again, not at herself, but at him for taking away his fingers. Slowly, Jerval rose and moved the chess table from between them. He sat back down in his chair, making no move toward her.

"Come here, Chandra," she heard him say in that beguiling, distant voice. She saw him pat his thighs, and did not question her body as she rose, walked to him, and sat on his lap.

He did not touch her, and she cocked her head at him. "Why do you want me in your lap?"

"So I can see if you are as beautiful close to me as afar."

"And am I?" It was so odd, but she could not seem to keep the breathlessness out of her voice, and she was being foolish, saying things that did not seem part of her. And his eyes were so beautiful to her, the deep blue darted with flecks of amber, fringed with his thick dark lashes. It occurred to her that Jerval did not look at all like her father. "I had not realized," she muttered, reaching out her hand to touch his face as he had hers, "that your eyes were such a deep blue." He grinned. "And your teeth are so white. You did not answer me, Jervel."

"Aye?" He had no idea what her question had been.

"Am I as beautiful close to you?"

"You are exquisite." He pressed his hand lightly against her back and pushed her toward him. He barely touched her lips, still afraid that she would leap off his lap and scurry away from him in fear. Go easy, he told himself. The drug was easing her, but he had no intention of rushing her. He gently eased her back, and saw her eyes go wide with mute surprise, then flicker as if she were suddenly wary of him. He dropped his hands, balancing her on his thighs. "It is a warm night," he said easily.

"Aye," she whispered, her hands clasped tightly in her lap. She turned toward him suddenly, her eyes dimmed, and her voice ragged. "I—I do not understand this night! I never wanted you to touch me before, yet now—" She shook her head to clear the gentle misty veil that curled about her thoughts.

"And now?" he asked her gently.

She shrugged, helplessly. "I do not know anymore."

"Will you trust me, Chandra?"

"I do not know what you mean, my lord."

"Will you trust me not to hurt you again . . . trust me to be your husband?"

She shuddered, yet he saw uncertainty in her eyes. He lightly caressed her lips. "Your mouth is so very soft, and warm." She closed her eyes, her lips parting slightly. He let his fingers stroke down the smooth line of her throat.

"I should not like that," she said, her voice worried, but she arched her back slightly.

He dropped his hand, and to his delight, she opened her eyes and stared at him, frowning, as if in disappointment.

"I will not push you, Chandra. You have but to tell me if you wish me to stop."

She only shook her head at him, her brow furrowing in elusive question.

He reached out his hand and gently cupped her full breast. Her heart pounded beneath his fingers, and he felt a shock of desire when she leaned forward, arching her back toward him so that he could hold her better. He slowly brushed his palm across her nipple, and drew a deep shaking breath.

"Kiss me," he commanded her gently. She leaned toward him, her lips pursed, like a virgin awaiting her first kiss.

He cupped her face between his hands and lightly touched his lips to hers, undemanding. He felt her sigh against his closed mouth, and slowly, he parted his lips and let his tongue lightly touch her lips. She leaned against him, relaxing against his arms, and he caressed her mouth with his tongue until, at last, she parted her lips to him.

She drew back when his tongue touched hers, blinking at him in surprise. He lightly kissed the tip of her nose, smiling, and his hands stroked down her back, tangling in her mass of loose hair.

"Would you do that again, Jerval?"

"Aye," he said in great seriousness, and kissed her again, thoroughly. She was passive, but he did not mind, for in all but fact she was indeed a virgin, and he the first to teach her. He felt her hands close about his shoulders, her fingers kneading him, showing him her pleasure.

His kisses became long and deep, pressing, then lightly teasing her, while his hand ventured again to cup her breast.

He would feel her start to draw away from him, then clutch at him all the harder.

He drew her to her feet and pressed the length of her against him. "Christ, you are exquisite," he said into her mouth, and she trembled, and stood on her toes to better fit herself against him. He helped her, cupping her buttocks in his hands and lifting her to press her belly against his hard manhood. He found himself cursing the layers of clothes each of them was wearing.

"Do you want me, Chandra?" he said thickly, his hands kneading her hips.

Her reply was a moan from deep in her throat. He gently clasped her arms and pulled them from about his neck. "Do not leave me," she gasped.

"I will not leave you, Chandra."

She gazed at him oddly for a moment, and to his surprise said, "I pray that you speak the truth, Jerval, for I would not want to be discarded as men do women."

There was no angry bitterness in her quiet voice, simply a plea that came from deep inside her. He had meant that he would not leave her tonight, but she had taken him to mean more, much more, and he sensed the bewilderment in her, born, he realized, from what she had seen her father do, and denied. "I love you, Chandra," he said.

"There is no reason for you to." She lowered her head to his shoulder. She clutched his arms and pressed herself against his chest, and he knew that at last her need was as great as his.

He wanted to understand her, perhaps even to make her understand herself, but he knew it must wait. He felt her fingers lightly tracing over his lips, and he gently nipped her fingertip between his teeth. He kissed her again, reveling in the sweet taste of her. When his tongue touched hers, Chandra felt her thighs go slack, though the rest of her was taut and breathless. She rubbed her body against him and tangled her fingers in his thick hair.

"Is this what passion is, Jerval?" she whispered. "Is this what you felt for me that first time in your tent?"

Nay, he thought, the night he had taken her, he had felt drunken lust. "Aye," he said only. He drew her arms forcibly away from him and pulled her gown over her head. She felt the cool air upon her flesh and had a moment of shyness.

She tentatively closed her hands over her breasts, a gentle flush covering her cheeks.

"Nay, love," he whispered to her gently. "Come, help me remove your shift."

"I am afraid."

"There is no reason to be. Keep on the shift—it doesn't matter."

"Please, kiss me again."

He did, deeply. "Would you mind if I took off my clothes?"

She shook her head mutely and let him lead her to the bed.

She sat on its edge, her legs locked tightly together, and stared at him as he swept off his clothes. His distended manhood thrust from the mat of hair at his groin, and she remembered him rearing over her, driving himself into her, making her scream. As she looked at him now, she felt only an aching need in her belly, and knew that he would ease her.

When he sat down beside her on the bed, she turned her face inward against his chest and laid her open hand lightly on his bare thigh.

"I will not hurt you. There will be no pain this time."

He kissed her and fondled her until she was languid and easy in his arms. "Your shift?"

She raised her arms and let him pull it over her head. They sat side by side on the bed, not touching, until she traced her fingertips over his chest. "You're hairy," she said, raptly studying him.

"Aye, and I thank God that you are not." He touched her back, and she blinked at him, then, with a deep sigh, pressed her breasts against his chest.

When he stretched out his full length against her, she whimpered. Jervel stroked the silken hair from her forehead and dipped his face down to seek out her mouth. He wanted still to go slowly with her, but she would not allow it. She was writhing in his arms, grinding her belly against him, and her nails dug into his arms and his back. His hands coursed over her body, and when his fingers probed the moist softness of her, she moaned and he thought she would reach her climax before he even entered her. He could feel her shuddering, her hands questing over him, not knowing where to touch him in her innocence, and he felt a shock of desire so strong he could scarce think. He stopped caressing her, and she cried out in impotent frustration. He eased her thighs apart, and she raised her hips to meet him.

"Oh God, Chandra," he gasped, staring at the delicate softness of her, and drove into her. He was engulfed in the small warmth of her, and he was throbbing, so beyond himself that he feared to move within her. He bent down to capture her mouth, and jagged moans broke from her throat. He pulled back from her, then thrust again deep within her, crushing her against him. He let himself go, and he flowed into her, his seed bursting from his body, and he lost himself in her.

He was aware that her harsh breathing was quieting, and shook his head, trying to clear his wits. He had possessed her completely, made her a part of him, but he feared that with her passion now slaked, she would break away from him again. He tried to shift his body so that he could see her face, and to his great delight, she dug her hands into his back, holding him down.

"Please do not leave me," she whispered, turning her face against his cheek. "I would feel empty and alone, and I could not bear it."

"I will remain within you as long as I am able," he said, raising himself on his elbows and grinning into her dazed eyes. "Did I please my lady wife?" He kissed the tip of her nose.

"So this is what passion is like. It is a hunger so great . . ." She fell silent, unable to tell him what she felt, for her thoughts lay softly tangled, without substance.

"Aye, my little innocent. You are a woman now, Chandra, my woman."

"You are leaving me," she whispered vaguely, clutching at him.

"The night is long, my love, and my body is not as yours." He smiled to himself as he eased off her and drew her against him. She had grown up with men, yet did not know that they must have at least a little time to revive themselves.

She nestled against him, and he thought that she slept. He ran his hands lightly down her back, splaying his fingers outward over her buttocks, gently kneading them. He felt her stir, and started at the touch of her lips softly against his chest. "You taste salty," she whispered between kisses, "and your hair tickles my mouth." She reared back when his hands left her hips, and she stared down into his face. "I would that you not stop what you were doing."

"But I would like to see if you taste as salty as I." He kissed her full on the mouth, delighting when her lips parted without hesitation. "Nay," he murmured softly, "you taste of sweet wine." He slipped his arm under her back and nuzzled his face between her breasts. She groaned softly when he suckled her nipple. She felt an awakening within her, familiar now, yet just as demanding. She wriggled against him, wanting him to show her what to do.

Jerval smiled into her glazed eyes, knowing this time their coupling would know its full sweetness before he gave her and himself release. He lightly stroked her taut pink nipple, rubbing it gently between his fingers, as he kissed her again. "You taste salty too, my wife, but I must make certain."

He eased his body away from her, and she cried out in alarm, "Nay, do not go!" She felt her flesh tingle as his tongue caressed a flaming trail over the curve of her waist down to her belly. "Sweet honey," he said, raising his head to gaze at her. When his fingers lightly entwined in the soft curls between her thighs, she drew in her breath sharply.

He laughed softly at the stunned expression on her face. He teased her, lightly kissing her smooth belly, and the softness of her inner thighs. She felt the heat of his mouth, burning her flesh, and she opened herself to him, unable to keep the cries of pleasure locked in her throat.

"I cannot bear it," she groaned. She was writhing against him, beyond herself, and he caressed her until he felt her body begin to stiffen.

"Come, my little warrior," he said, and pulled her over on top of him. She stared into his face. "I don't know what to do," she gasped.

He gently guided her hand down his belly to hold him. When she clutched at him, he winced, pried her fingers loose, and helped her to guide him into her. He drew up her legs, showing her how to straddle him, and closed his hands about her waist.

She felt him deep within her, his hands lifting her and moving her over him. When his fingers closed over her, she flung her head back, her hands splayed on his belly, and cried out in pleasure.

Jerval had thought to pace himself and her, but her climax broke his control, and he moaned deep in his throat when his own need overwhelmed him.

When she lay gasping, her body limp atop him, he straightened her slender legs over him and pulled up the covers.

He did not give in to sleep just yet, but stared up at the ceiling, trying to convince himself that the drug had simply made her at ease with him, and that he had seduced her, woven his passion around her, and made her see that her need for him had always been there. He did not know what he would do if she awoke in the morning, looked at him again with fear, and fled from him.

Jerval awoke near to dawn, his breathing labored. Chandra's arms were wrapped tightly about his neck. As he gently loosened her grip, she stirred. She raised her head from his shoulder, and he saw a sleepy question in her eyes.

"Tell me you want me, Chandra," he said against her soft mouth, but she only moaned softly, entwining her arms about his chest. They lay facing each other, and he gave himself to her. He felt such a surge of feeling when he entered her that he could have wept, wept for what he wanted, and for what had been given to him. Their coupling held no urgency, only gentle sweetness. He taught her how to move against him, and he held himself in control until she softly moaned her pleasure into his mouth.

When Jerval awoke in the bright morning, he smiled lazily as memory of the long night coursed through his mind. He reached for Chandra, but his arms closed over nothing but a crumpled knot of blankets. He cursed himself loudly for not awakening when she had. Alma had told him that she would remember everything, and now that she was free of the opium, he could not imagine what she felt.

Only Julianna was in the hall. "What a surprise, Jerval!" she cried. "I had thought you long away."

"Where is Chandra?" he asked abruptly. "Is she with Mother?"

"Nay, your mother could not find her. Glenna said she rode that horse of hers out of the bailey some time ago."

Jerval strode from the keep without a backward glance. He saddled Pith himself, too impatient to let the stable boy do it for him. He rode into the village of Trackton and searched through the dank chilly interior of the small Norman church, but she was not there, and none of the peasants had seen her.

He saw Wicket first, wandering freely about by the edge of the lake. He dismounted, not bothering to tether Pith, and set out in search of his wife. He found her sitting with her arms wrapped about her legs, high atop an outjutting rock above the water. He walked to her, his steps noiseless, and lightly touched his hand to her shoulder.

To his surprise, she did not turn to face him. He dropped to his haunches beside her. "I have been worried about you. Why did you leave me?"

She shook her head, still not looking at him. Jerval reached out his hand and gently cupped her chin, forcing her face toward him. Her eyes were swollen, and tears still trembled on her lashes.

"Please do not," he said gently, flicking a tear from her cheek.

She gave him a look of desolation, like a child who had lost all hope.

"Nay, love, everything will be all right."

She crumpled, weeping in great uncontrolled sobs that shook her slender frame, and he caught her against his chest. He whispered countless endearments, not really knowing what he said, wanting only to ease her.

She could not seem to stem the jumble of images that swept through her mind, images of her caressing her husband, clutching at him as if she would die without him. And now he must believe that he had won, that he possessed her.

It was his light kiss upon her temple that stilled her. He closed his eyes a moment, his cheek pressed against her hair, hoping that somehow she would not fling away from him.

Chandra straightened and slowly pulled away from him, not meeting his gaze. She said in a wintry voice, "You have come to take your . . . whore again, my lord?"

"You are not a whore, Chandra," he said, his voice steady. "You are my wife. A wife should feel pleasure with her husband."

"I do not want you for a husband and I do not want to feel pleasure with you."

He drew back at the flat certainty in her voice. God's grace, was there no giving, no compromise in her? He said more harshly than he intended, "I am your husband, and you cannot now deny that you felt great pleasure with me, that you wanted me.''

She shook her head slowly, back and forth, soft tendrils of hair brushing her cheeks. "I do not understand," she cried, fright and confusion in her voice. He struggled with himself to tell her of the drug, but he could not bring himself to do it. She flung her head back and for the first time gazed straight at him. "I cannot deny what I did, but I will not be your whore again!"

"My whore? Is that how you dismiss everything that happened between us last night? Do not be a fool, Chandra. Your need was as great as mine. Give over, you have lost nothing.''

She leaped to her feet, and he followed suit. She hated him at that moment, towering over her, blocking the sun from her face, knowing, aye, knowing that he was the victor. He grasped her arms in his iron hands, and she stared at him until he released her. She remembered his hands touching her, caressing her body until the heat within her flamed and she was lost, only it had not mattered, for he was with her. Then she saw her father, his golden body glistening with sweat, his member wet with the woman as he thrust into her. The woman's cries were her cries, deep, tearing moans of pleasure.

"Chandra! For God's sake!" Jerval grabbed her arms, shaking her, for her eyes were glazed and unseeing.

"Let me go!" She was panting against him. "I will not belong to you! I will not be like those women!"

He had drawn back his hand to slap her, but the blind wildness was suddenly gone from her, and she was a small broken creature, shuddering against him, wanting his strength now, yet afraid. He enfolded her in his arms, supporting her. She did not weep. "Like which women, Chandra?"

She stiffened, but he held her close, his hands gently kneading her back. She drew slowly back from him, her eyes hooded, her fear locked within her.

"Your father's women?" He knew without her telling him that it was true, but she said nothing. "Men," he began slowly, "have greater needs than do women. Sometimes they take when they should not."

"Nay," she said, her voice suddenly weary. "They wanted him, all of them. He had but to look at them . . . save my mother."

Lady Dorothy, not a woman for Lord Richard's passions, a

quiet mouse of a woman. He remembered her clacking rosary beads.

Chandra turned slightly and gazed out over the placid lake. The water was a luminous green in the afternoon sun.

She shook her head, and her movements became alert and decisive. "I am hungry," she said, "and my mouth is so dry. Your mother is likely cursing me for not attending her."

"It was the wine you drank last night," he said. "My mother will not mind."

She sighed deeply. "You have won."

"Won? I had a night of pleasure with my wife, the first, I trust, of many nights in the next fifty years. Cannot you see that you have won also?"

She shook her head at him. "Do not mock me, Jerval, with your twisting of words. What you really mean is that now you expect me to obey you in all things."

He broke into loud booming laughter, ignoring the tightness in her voice. "Had I wanted a woman to obey my every wish, believe me, Chandra, I would not have chosen you to wed." He realized that he had not quite spoken the truth. Indeed, it had not occurred to him that once married, she would flaunt him.

"Then what is it you want from me?"

"I want you to love me, to want me as a wife should her husband, to allow me to take care of you and protect you. I want you to obey me when it is a question of your safety."

She held herself tautly silent.

"You know I am right, Chandra, if you will but consider my words calmly. You must not take the freedom I allow you as a pass to do foolish things."

"You *allow* me—!"

"Aye, I am your husband, and your lord." He softened his voice. "Will you not give yourself over to me, as you did so willingly last night?"

"Nay! I did not give, you took!" She could not look at him, for she knew it was a lie. "Oh why, my lord," she cried, "did you not wed that soft-fleshed Julianna? She would have bowed to your wishes, at least before others."

"Soft-fleshed?" He caressed his fingers over her hand, just as he had done the night before. "No woman could be more soft-fleshed than are you, Chandra, save for your callused nds."

She tried to jerk away from him, and hated herself and him all the more when he would not let her go. "I have told you that I—I did not know what I was doing!"

Aye, he thought with no guilt, and I finally know the passion you possess. "But you enjoyed it nonetheless," he said aloud.

"Yes," she spat, "but 'tis a pleasure that I do not wish again! You can ease your man's needs with other women!"

"I am not your father, Chandra. I want only my wife in my bed, and now that I know your need for me is as great as mine for you, it should never again be an issue between us. Do you not remember what you whispered to me last night?"

"Nay, I said nothing to you!"

"Ah, you said many things to me, little warrior. You begged me not to leave you, for you could not bear it. You opened yourself to me, Chandra, and when I kissed you, and caressed you, you begged me not to stop."

Her hand went limp between his, and he released her. She turned her face away from him, and her loose thick hair hung in a curtain about her face, hiding her profile from him. She looked so fragile, her gown strewn about her legs, and her silky hair cascading over her shoulders, so much the soft giving woman who had slept in his arms.

"You are a woman, Chandra, my woman, and you will always remain so."

She heard husky passion in his voice and felt an answering quiver deep within her, as if a door had been opened and could not now be closed. She remembered he had said similar words to her last night when she lay replete in his arms. She felt confused and fearful, for she did not understand herself.

She spoke as calmly as the placid lake, and she forced herself to take some pride in that, for there was nothing else within her to erase the gnawing uncertainty. "Will you accept my passion in your bed as compromise?"

"I will accept your passion as . . . natural."

"I do not wish to spend my mornings with your mother."

"Does this mean," he said with a grin, "that you will come willingly to me when I desire you if I allow you to forgo your household duties?"

I will not lose myself in you again! Slowly, almost regretfully, she shook her head. "Nay. There will be no blackmail. You won once, Jerval, but never again."

"If you must make it a case of winning or losing, can you not consider that it was you who was the winner?"

She stared up at him. The bright sunlight made his thick hair gleam like burnished gold, and she felt a desire to touch him. "A woman can never win," she said.

"You are foolish, Chandra, and blind to your own needs. You are a woman, and you will learn a woman's responsibilities. I am not punishing you for refusing me despite what you may choose to believe. Croyland will need a mistress someday as well as a master, and I cannot be both. You will learn, and when you have proved your housewifely skills to me, I will reconsider." He caught her hand before she could strike him, and he tightened his grip about her slender wrist until she winced.

"You are not a man, Chandra. With but a bit more pressure, I could break your wrist."

She swallowed a cry of pain in her throat. She swung at him with her other hand, but he only laughed, pulled her arms behind her back, and held her wrists with one powerful hand. He grasped her chin and kissed her full on the mouth.

She gasped when he released her and dashed the back of her hand across her burning lips.

"Last night my mouth gave you great pleasure, wife, but I see that in the daylight you are still the stubborn hellion. Come, let us return to Camberley," he added, his voice now brusque. "There is much you still have to learn of housewifely things, I wager."

She was standing stiff, but her face was open for an instant, and he saw loneliness in her, and uncertainty. "It would help, you know," he said dryly, "if you would but learn to trust me."

Chandra brushed off her gown, squared her shoulders, and strode to Wicket, never looking back at her husband.

10

CHANDRA SNIFFED, CAUGHT THE SMELL of the jakes from a stiff south wind, and slipped back into the hall. She climbed the stairs past the family's chambers, until the steps twisted and narrowed and became finally a ladder that led to the summit of the keep. She paused on its board roof, gazing upward to the round turret that rose another twelve or so feet into the air. From atop the turret fluttered the orange banner of Camberley, embroidered with a black lion standing on his hind legs, his claws bared to all who approached him.

She turned to gaze over the lush, wild countryside to the east. Small squares of tilled land set upon sloping hills dotted the thick forests. Beyond them she saw a sparkling blue lake that wound about a tiny village of low, thatch-roofed houses. It reminded her of the sea, and the tingly salt air that left tendrils of sticky, damp hair falling over her forehead. She felt suddenly homesick, and tears stung her eyes.

"Weak fool," she muttered to herself, and quickly turned back to stare down at the castle. High above the keep, the servants who milled about below seemed small and insignificant, their chatter muted by their distance from her. But there was one below her who was neither small nor insignificant, one her eyes sought without her even being aware of it. She drew herself up, for she did not wish to think about her husband, much less see him. Images came to her mind that filled her with shame and anger, for they were of her, moaning feverishly against his broad shoulder, unaware of herself, lost in him. "Nay!" she said aloud, her hands fisted at her sides. He had possessed her, she admitted it to herself, but she would never again allow it.

To her surprise, she heard the ladder creak and saw Mary's head peep up at her.

"Careful," she called. "The ladder is rickety."

"This is like the top of a mountain," Mary said, looking about her. She turned rueful eyes to Chandra. "I saw you climbing the outside stairs, but I did not tell Lady Avicia where you were."

"What has she in store for me today?" Chandra asked wearily.

"I do not know," Mary said. She suddenly lowered her head and burst into tears.

"Oh, Mary, I am sorry," Chandra cried. "I don't mean for you to be always in the middle of our squabbles."

" 'Tis not that, Chandra," Mary gulped. "I—I had to speak to you away from the family and all the servants." She squared her slight shoulders and dashed away her tears. "I am with child, Chandra."

Chandra stared at her. "Pregnant? You are pregnant? But how do you know?"

Mary smiled weakly. "Do you know naught about being a woman? My monthly flux, it has not come, and I have sickness, particularly in the mornings."

"Graelam," she said numbly.

"There could be no other."

"But it was but one time, and you a virgin!" Even as she said the words, she felt Jerval deep within her, his seed bursting into her belly, not once, but three times. Her monthly flux—when was it due? She wiped her clammy hands on her skirt. It was not just a man's pleasure, it was his ultimate ownership, his ultimate victory.

"It seems that I am not very lucky."

"Damn men!" Chandra shouted, striking her hand against the turret tower. "They take what they want with no thought of what can come from their lust!"

"I do not know what to do," Mary said tonelessly. "The de Vernons will know soon, and they cannot allow me to stay, not a woman who will bear a bastard." Mary covered her face with her hands.

Chandra quickly took Mary in her arms and stroked her hair. "Nay, Mary, do not cry. I will think of something, you will see, I promise you."

She shook her friend's shoulders slightly. "You must not despair, and you must promise me to say not a word to anyone. Now, wipe your eyes, else my mother-in-law will

wonder why you are crying, and likely blame me for it."
Mary did as she was bid.

"Careful now," she chided Mary as she followed her
down the ladder. When they reached the solar, she forced a
smile to her lips and said, "Mary, do you know anything
about mending sheets?"

Mary smiled tremulously and nodded.

Chandra found the hall filled with angry, shouting men
when she arrived for the midday meal. "Quiet, all of you!"
Jerval shouted, and turned to Malton. "Prepare a dozen men
to ride within the hour. The Scots are but a few hours ahead
of us, and the bastards are herding cattle before them."

"Hell's fires," Lord Hugh muttered. "I cannot ride with
you, not with my damned foot swelled like a rotted melon."

"What has happened?" Chandra asked, walking quickly
forward.

Jerval met Chandra's questioning eyes, smiled, and finished giving instructions to the servants to wrap food in the
saddle pouches.

"The Scots attacked a northern demesne farm last night.
They killed three of our people, razed the farm, and made off
with the cattle. We leave shortly." He turned distracted eyes
to Lord Hugh. "There is always a next time, Father. It was
only a small raiding party from the man's report, nothing to
challenge us."

When Jerval entered their bedchamber, he found Chandra
tying the cross garters on her men's chausses, a sword strapped
at her waist, and a quiver on her shoulder.

"You have not told me how well the Scots fight with the
bow, Jerval," she said, excitement rippling in her voice.

"Quite well."

"Then we must catch them in a crossfire."

When she walked past him, he grabbed her shoulders and
jerked her about to face him. "You will go nowhere, Chandra."
He saw anger building in her eyes, and forstalled her, his
voice firm and deliberate. "My wife will not ride into danger.
You will remain safely within the keep. This time you will
not disobey me, Chandra."

"You ride into danger, and you are my husband. What, I
pray, is the difference?"

"The difference, my cocky wife, is that a man has twice

your strength and endurance. You would be no match for the Scots. Just," he added sternly, "as you are no match for me."

"I beat Arnolf in the tourney just last week!"

"Arnolf, like all the men, would give up his life before allowing you to be harmed, and I will have none of them distracted by your presence. They as well as I would be protecting you, not fighting with all their wits."

"I saved your life, or have you conveniently forgotten? You were not protecting me, Jerval, that night Graelam nearly sent his sword through your belly!"

Jerval sighed. "I have not forgotten, Chandra, but it changes naught. You will remain here."

"You are not being fair!"

"I have no more time to argue with you. I will likely see you in a couple of days." He turned on his heel, paused at the sound of her angry breathing, and said over his shoulder, "You might as well wish me Godspeed."

She was silent, and it occurred to him forcefully that he could not trust her. "Do you swear, Chandra, that you will remain at Camberley?"

He rocked back in surprise when she said softly, "Nay, I will not swear to that, Jerval."

"Very well," he said. He pulled the heavy key from the door and jerked it closed behind him. As he grated the key in the lock, he heard her running to the door, her fists pounding against it. "Let me out! Damn you, Jerval, open the door!"

"Goodbye, Chandra," he shouted to her. He met his father in the hall and pressed the key into his hand. "Release her tomorrow, after we are well away. If you would give her supper, take care."

Lord Hugh looked dubiously at his son, and nodded. "Has the girl no sense at all?" At his son's wry look, he clapped his arms about his shoulders. "God's grace, Jerval. Kill one of the jackals for me."

"Aye, Father, I will."

Julianna was waiting for him in the outer courtyard. "Take care, my lord," she said softly, her hand upon his chest. "I will pray for you."

"Where is Chandra?" Mary asked. "I saw her run from the hall. Does she ride with you?"

"She is in her room," Jerval said. "Where she will stay." He strode away to mount his destrier.

"Poor Jerval," Julianna said as they watched the men ride from the keep, "wed to such a . . ." She shuddered distastefully. "Such an unnatural creature."

"Oh hush, Julianna," Mary snapped. She turned on her heel and walked brusquely back into the keep. The truth burst upon her when she saw Lord Hugh with a huge key in his hand, speaking to an outraged Lady Avicia. Mary stared upward, wondering what Chandra was doing, locked in her bedchamber.

Chandra was busily tying the ends of the sheets together, cursing her husband with every breath she drew. Satisfied finally with her knots, she carried the bulky sheets to the window, only to discover that it would not open wide enough for her to squeeze through. She paused only a moment before shattering the costly glass with a wooden stool. She snaked the line of sheets out the window frame and watched them tumble down the stone wall of the keep. She threw down her quiver and her sword, squeezed her slender body through the narrow frame, and slithered slowly down. She passed a group of small boys watching her with large questioning eyes as she strode across the inner bailey to the stables.

She looked fondly toward Wicket, but knew that Jerval would spot him in an instant. She chose instead one of Jerval's palfreys, a roan stallion with a stout heart. When she led him from the stables, she looked about, wondering if anyone would try to stop her. She made for the cooking shed, where she found a loaf of bread, and wrapped it in the none too-clean blanket she had taken from the stable. She rode the stallion through the outer courtyard and waved jauntily to Beglie, whose duty it was this month to be porter. He waved back to her, his expression sour, and yelled something about bad weather on its way. Chandra laughed gaily, dug her heels into the palfrey's belly when he crossed the still-lowered drawbridge, and let him lengthen his stride.

Chandra settled comfortably in her saddle, her palfrey's hooves pounding rhythmically in her ears, and grinned between her horse's ears, whistling a jaunty tune. She kept a good half mile back from Jerval's men, planning to approach only when they made camp for the night. She was not foolish enough to believe herself invincible, and she would need the protection of their camp when darkness fell. She had done nothing dishonorable, she assured herself, for she had not promised her stern-faced husband to stay at Camberley, idling uselessly with the women.

Her excitement began to dim when the late-afternoon air became damp and chill as the road snaked closer toward the sea. It was odd, she thought, pulling the wool cap tighter over her hair, how slowly the time passed when one was alone. Her stomach growled, and she thought of the miserable loaf of bread that would be her evening meal, indeed, all of her meals until . . . until what? She gulped, angry with herself.

Fools act in anger, she chided herself at last. She turned in her saddle to stare back in the direction of Camberley, then slumped forward. She saw Jerval's face, grim and set, and knew that even if she returned to Camberley now, he would know that she had disobeyed him, and his anger would be nearly as great. Where is your backbone? she snarled to herself. Dammit, she would not let Jerval dictate her every action! She slapped her arms against the cold and started singing again, to her horse.

Mark turned about to let the fire warm his back and tossed the pork rind over his shoulder. "You are quiet tonight, Jerval," he said."

"Aye."

" 'Tis not the Scots you're thinking of, I wager."

Jerval raised his head and forced a smile. "I was wondering how Father would manage taking Chandra her supper. I doubt that her mood is one of sweetness."

"He'll likely send Mary, if he is wise. The girl has a soothing way about her. Even your mother treats her well, almost as if she were another daughter."

"But not, Mark, another daughter-in-law."

Mark grinned ruefully. "I shall never forget the day poor Trempe wandered into the hall looking totally bewildered with Chandra's hauberk under his arm. Your mother stared at him as if he had lost his wits, poor fellow."

"One of the links had come loose," Jerval said unnecessarily, an unwilling grin on his lips. "Chandra had very nicely asked him to repair it for her."

"Which he did, I gather, once you gave him the order.

Likely at Croyland, her word was law, even with her father's armorer. Methinks you hold the reins too loosely, Jerval.''

"You think I should have tied her up as well as locked her in her room?''

"Nay, as it is, she will likely starve herself, out of anger against you. 'Tis difficult to balance the cocky, arrogant boy with the soft, beautiful woman.''

Jerval smiled suddenly, the long passionate night he had passed with his wife still pleasurably clear in his mind. "Aye, she is soft and beautiful.''

He loves her, Mark thought, therefore his patience with her. Yet Chandra admired strength, and Mark wondered if Jerval would not more quickly gain her respect if he buckled down and beat her.

"You know," Jerval said, interrupting his thoughts, "I would not be at all surprised if Sir John is in some way in league with the Scots. 'Tis odd that they appear so suddenly, as if they were in hiding near to us.''

"Oldham keep is but five miles to the east. I have never trusted Sir John, for he is a greedy man.''

"A greedy fool, and disloyal. We will know soon, Mark. Chandra has plans of her own for Sir John.'' He broke off, a rueful grin on his face.

"What does your lady wife say?''

"That we should visit Oldham, as well as the other keeps, and introduce her to our people. It is her idea to go sniffing about to see if Sir John is up to anything.''

"A lady is more apt to be allowed to pry and ask questions. Sir John would likely fall all over himself to impress her.''

"She is upon occasion reasonable. But she will not be with us, for it could be dangerous. After we have dispatched the Scots to hell, we will ride to Oldham.''

"And catch Sir John by surprise?''

"Aye. I look forward to the meeting.''

They broke camp early the next morning, and huddled close to their horses' necks for warmth, for a cold wind was blowing in from the sea. The demesne farm was naught save smoldering ashes, and the peasants had just buried the three men slaughtered by the Scots. They did not tarry there. Jerval pushed them throughout the morning northward toward the border, over terrain that became ever more wretchedly stark and barren.

"Sir Jerval!"

Jerval reined in Pith and turned in his saddle at Blanc's shout.

"There is a man trailing us," the older man said. "Lambert spotted him but a few minutes ago."

"He is alone?"

"For the moment he is. Lambert says he looks English."

Jerval was silent for a moment. "Still, there is a chance he may be tracking us for the Scots."

"One of Sir John's men?" Malton said, reining in his horse.

"Possibly. Have Lambert hang back and keep him in sight. I have no wish for the lot of us to be ambushed. Don't let the man catch sight of Lambert."

Their horses climbed a steep rise, and Jerval raised his hand for a halt. Before them stretched a wasteland of rocky, shallow hills dotted only with splashes of green moss. Jerval swept his gaze behind them and tightened his grip on Pith's reins. The man trailing them had shortened the distance and was now riding but a mile behind them, his horse in a steady trot.

"Let us wait for the knave," he said to his men. "I wish to know what manner of fool he is."

The man rode at a steady trot through a narrow stretch of road, bounded on each side by desolate rocks. He did not see the four riders leap from behind the rocks until they formed a half circle around him. From where he sat, Jerval could hear their banshee cries as they swung their claymores in great arcs through the air.

"God's blood!" Malton cried, "Four Scots against one! At least the fellow's not in league with the villains!"

"He's a bloody fool!" Mark said.

"Follow me!" Jerval shouted. He whipped Pith about and dug his heels fiercely into his destrier's sides, back down the hill. He was yelling at the top of his lungs, as were his men, hopeful of turning the Scots' attention toward them.

"Ye wish to taste death?" a brawny Scot yelled as he rode at Chandra, his deadly claymore stretched above his head.

"Come, you whoreson!" she shrieked at him. "You will feel my sword cold in your guts!" She had no time to pull an arrow from her quiver, for the four men were closing swiftly about her.

"It's a boy, lads," one of the Scots shouted. "Look at his pretty, smooth face!"

"A little English bastard!"

"Leave him to rot and we'll take his horse!"

Chandra felt an awful fear in the pit of her stomach, nothing like what she had felt during the rough practice with swords and lances in the tiltyard. They were Scots, she thought wildly, and they seemed savage and without honor. They formed a circle around her, taunting her, waiting, she guessed, for her to lunge at one of them so that the others could slash at her back. *Get hold of yourself, Chandra!*

"Cowards!" she screamed at the man she thought was their leader, a huge man with a thick black beard and long matted hair. His eyes were as black as coals, like those of a demon Father Tolbert had shown her once in one of his books. She whipped the palfrey to face him. "Are you so afraid of one . . . man? You are naught but a worthless pack of scavengers!"

"Aiee, Alan!" one of the men spat. "Yer brave lad calls us animals!" He suddenly lashed his horse toward her, and Chandra turned to meet him. She slashed at him with her sword, and felt the blade tear into his arm. He lurched back, grabbing his arm, and she saw blood welling out between his fingers. Chandra felt her wool cap suddenly jerked from her head, and her long thick braid fell free down her back.

Jerval felt his voice catch in surprise as Pith thundered closer, for he recognized the bay palfrey. He saw the man slash out at one of the Scots, then another of them close behind him and jerk off his cap. Christ! It was Chandra! He prayed that her hair would save her life. No man, even a Scot, would want to stick his sword through a woman.

"A girl!" Alan shouted. " 'Tis naught but a girl!" He could not believe his eyes, and his men pulled their horses back, gaping at her in surprise. Alan slewed his head about to see the mounted Englishmen bearing down on them, their swords at ready.

He gazed for a moment at her lovely face, the wild fury that glittered in her eyes. He reached out his hand and grabbed her long braid, pulling her off balance. With his other hand, he brought his claymore down and severed part of the braid.

Chandra tried to pull away, but in the next instant, the huge man smashed his horse against hers, jerked her out of her saddle, and threw her face down over his thighs. Her sword went spinning from her hand and clattered to the rocky ground.

"Let's be gone, lads," he shouted, knowing they had but a few moments to escape the horsemen galloping furiously toward them. " 'Tis a marvelous prize we've won this trip!"

Chandra yelled at the top of her lungs and tried to rear up, but he smashed his hand down on her buttocks, pinning her.

"Hush, little lad," Alan said, laughing, running his fingers over her hips.

"Craven cur! Filthy knave!" she cursed him, her voice muffled against his thigh, but he only laughed harder.

"Fight the English bastards off!" Alan shouted back to his men.

Jerval rode straight toward the first of the yelling Scots, his powerful arm raised, his sword its extension. The man hacked at him, but it was quickly over. Jerval's sword plunged into the man's chest and emerged a foot from his back. He yanked his sword back and saw the man's eyes widen in astonishment as he slid off his horse and sprawled on the rocky ground.

Jerval wheeled about in his saddle, looking frantically for Chandra. In the distance he saw her thrown face down in front of one of the Scots. "Kill the rest of these bastards, then follow me!" He wheeled Pith about and dug in his heels.

"Faster, Sunnart," Chandra heard the man urge his powerful stallion. He looked over his shoulder and saw that one of the Englishmen had turned from his men and was galloping after them. "Well, lass," he said, his hand hard against the small of her back to hold her still, "it appears that one of English wants you for himself."

She knew it had to be Jerval, and took hope. "It is my husband, and he will kill you!" she gasped, scarcely able to breathe against the wrenching pain in her ribs from the horse's bucking gallop.

"Yer proud husband has a bit of a distance to cover to

catch us! Already his beast is tiring. My Sunnart will get us to safety. You will bring me a fine ransom, my little lad!''

Chandra could see nothing, for the dust the stallion kicked up was clogging her nostrils and burning her eyes. Her plan had gone dreadfully awry. This was not the way it was supposed to be! She closed her eyes against the dust, and prayed for Jerval to catch them.

"An insistent man, yer husband," Alan snarled. "He doesn't know the eastern forest—that will slow him."

Chandra tried to wrench herself free. She felt the point of a dagger pressing through her clothes, its razor tip nipping the flesh of her side. "Hold still, wench, else yer husband will find a dead wife in a ditch!"

She lay like a sack of potatoes, afraid even to breathe. They must have gained the forest, for she could hear the crunch of leaves and branches beneath Sunnart's hooves. A branch slashed her face, and she cried out, and pressed her face downward against his thigh to protect herself.

"There'll be time enough later for that," Alan laughed. "But it's pleased I am to see ye so interested! Yer tired of yer cold English husband?"

Jerval pulled Pith, winded and sweating, to a halt, and waited for his men. He knew he would not find the Scotsman in the forest; he needed Hubert to track him. Christ, he thought, cold with fear for her, he should have tied her down. He steeled himself against the sight of her flung face down before the Scot.

Lambert shouted, "We killed the three bastards! No sign of the cattle!"

"Where is milady?" Malton cried.

"The Scot has her still," Jerval said, his voice harshly calm. "He rode like the devil into the forest." He sent half of his men to scatter into the forest, and the rest, himself at their fore, skirted the trees toward the sea.

"Hubert," he called out once they were beyond the trees, "I doubt the Scot would try to hide in the forest. You must find his horse's tracks."

They slowed their horses to a walk, and Hubert circled his palfrey about, searching the rocky ground. "Aye," he shouted sometime later. "You were right, Jerval, the bastard is staying close to the cliffs. I know the ways of such as he."

"We must catch up to them before dark," Jerval growled, and all the men knew what he was thinking.

"He's carrying Chandra, Jerval," Mark said, seeing the tense set of his friend's jaw. " 'Twill slow him."

Alan Durwald reined in his exhausted stallion and slewed his head back. A gentle rise blocked his view, but he could see no clouds of dust from pursuing horses. "Well, my cheeky little lady," he said, letting his fingers once more caress her buttocks and laughing at his own joke, "it appears that yer husband has at last given up. But another hour, and it will be dark. And then, wench, we can take our . . . rest. I do hope yer husband will still want to pay yer ransom when I'm done with ye."

You will kill me first, Chandra thought, shuddering. She tried to pull herself upward, but he grabbed her hair, wrapping it painfully about his hand, and pressed her face down again. She saw the crimson of the sun setting over the sea. Please, she prayed silently, trying to swallow her tears.

Alan Durwald clicked Sunnart forward toward the next rise, swiveling about in his saddle again to look back at the rutted path behind them. Chandra felt him tense, and then he cursed, a torrent of Scottish oaths that she did not understand. She felt a surge of hope when he whipped Sunnart into a mad gallop.

Suddenly, Sunnart stumbled, and his great body heaved with effort, throwing Chandra up against the man's chest. She gave a howl of fury and mashed her fist into his belly as the stallion reared. He grunted harshly in pain, and Chandra threw herself sideways, breaking free of his arm.

Her joy was short-lived. She hurtled to the rocky ground, the impact jarring the breath from her, and she rolled head over heels down a sharp incline. Jagged rocks tore through her clothes, and then her head struck something hard.

She came to her senses, a dizzying pain pounding in her head, and looked up into her husband's set face. "Did you catch him?"

Jerval hoisted her to her feet, his fingers probing her head.

"I thought it more to the point to see if you were all right," he said. He believed he could forgive her anything if only she was unhurt.

"I am but sore," she muttered, shaking her head to clear the dizziness. "You must ride after him!"

"Shut up," he said coldly, and released her. "You will likely have a headache from the lump growing on your temple, but 'tis no more than you deserve." He took a step back from her, knowing that if he touched her again, he would thrash her.

She saw that he was furious. The numbing fear still clung to her, and she tried desperately not to let him see it. "His horse stumbled and I escaped him. And I did slice up one of the Scots for you." She turned vague eyes in the direction Alan Durwald had ridden. "We must hurry, Jerval, before he gets too far ahead of us."

Jerval stared down at her, angry cords straining in his neck. She was speaking as if naught untoward had happened, her voice jaunty and unconcerned. That she could have been so stupid and willful as to have followed them, and now care not one whit about what could have happened to her, indeed, brag about her wounding one of the Scots, left him nearly incoherent with rage. He drew a deep breath, still not approaching her. "Do you have any idea what would have happened to you if I had not seen the Scots surround you?"

"The Scots surprised me, and he was fast," she said steadily, trying not to sound frightened. "But I escaped him." She could not look at him. She wanted only to go home.

"You damned little fool!" he shouted. "If I had not seen you, you would have been taken!"

"I was taken!" She could still feel Alan Durwald's fingers splayed on her buttocks. "Thank you," she mumbled, looking away, "for coming after me."

"You are so very sure of yourself, I probably should have let you fend for yourself! Christ, you know what he intended, don't you? He would have raped you, and then if he had not killed you, you would have been hauled across the border and held for ransom! It might have been good riddance!"

It was the truth, but his last words stung her deep. She thrust up her chin. "If you hadn't locked me away in my bedchamber," she growled, "it would not have happened."

Jerval could not help himself. He strode to her, grabbed her shoulders, and shook her. Her hair, hacked off by Alan Durwald's sword, had become unbraided and swirled about her face and shoulders. It only served to increase his rage. He grabbed a handful of her hair and waved it in her face. "By God," he hissed, "I will have no more of your disobedience!" He released her suddenly at the sound of his men approaching, and shoved her away from him.

Lambert shouted, "He escaped us, Jerval! He knows every hiding place in this desolate land. We haven't a chance of finding him now."

Mark swung off his horse, his eyes dark with worry. "Are you all right, Chandra?"

"She is herself," Jerval said between clenched teeth. He strode to his destrier and leaped into the saddle.

"Can we not try to catch him, Jerval?" Chandra cried after him. She hurried to mount the palfrey one of the men was leading.

Jerval felt himself choke. "We return to Camberley," he said finally, his voice so harsh that Mark jumped.

"But, my lord, surely in the morning—"

"Enough!" Jerval roared at the hapless Malton.

Chandra heard Hubert snarl, "Damned fool girl . . . Jerval should have left her to the Scot!"

Hubert's words hurt her, and she quickly saw that the other men agreed with him. She understood their anger, for she had ruined their sport. She clicked the palfrey forward and reined in by her husband, hoping to reason with him.

Jerval saw her from the corner of his eye, but did not turn to face her. "Just how did you get out of my bedchamber?"

"I knotted sheets and climbed out the window."

A muscle jumped in his jaw. "Did it not occur to you that my parents would be frantic when they found you gone?"

"I would have left a note, but there was no parchment."

"I do not believe that you had any such notion. You are far too selfish to think about anyone save yourself and what you want."

"I did not promise, Jerval," she said stiffly. "I repeat, if you had not ordered me about like a bully, and locked me up, none of this would have happened."

He slewed his body about in the saddle, flung out his hand, and grabbed her arm in a painful grip. "I am certain, my lady, that the men would cheer were I to drag you off your . . . my palfrey this moment and beat you to an inch of your life."

She wrenched her arm free. "You would not! My father—"

"Your damned father should have beaten you, but you never disobeyed him, did you?"

"He would never have locked me away like some useless scrap. He, unlike you and other men, was reasonable."

"You do not know the meaning of the word." He jabbed his boots into his destrier's sides and galloped away from her.

When they halted to make camp, she found herself alone, for the men as well as her husband ignored her, all save Mark. She was pulling the burned rabbit meat away from the bone when he sat cross-legged beside her.

"Don't you start," she snapped.

Mark grinned. "Nay," he said cheerfully. "You are neither my wife nor my responsibility."

She sucked her fingers, for the meat was painfully hot. "It was not my choice to be any man's responsibility . . . or wife."

"That is a pity," he said, staring into the fire. "I think I recognized the leader of those Scots. If I was not mistaken, his name is Alan Durwald, a renegade and now a worthless robber."

"I think you are right. I heard one of the men call him Alan." She touched her hand to her hair. "I wonder why he chopped part of my braid. What do you mean, a renegade?"

"Durwald was in line for a rich estate in Galloway, but King Alexander would not back his claim and gave it instead to his cousin. You see, Durwald would not swear fealty to him, and caused him a sleepless night or two. Unfortunately, the trouble is now ours. He's a wily devil, never wreaking enough damage to gain the attention of King Henry or King Alexander. He's like a bothersome hornet."

Chandra realized that Mark was talking to ease her mind, and she supposed that she was grateful to him for it. She looked across the campfire at Jerval. He was gazing at her, his face drawn in harsh lines. "I am going to sleep," she said, and rose. "Goodnight, Mark."

Jerval wrapped his blanket about him and eased his tired body down near to his wife. The fire was nearly out, but from the dim shadows cast by the glowing embers, he could see clotted blood over a cut near her jaw. He cursed softly and turned away from her.

*   *   *

They were a few miles north of Camberley the next afternoon when Jerval turned in his saddle and waved his hand toward Chandra, who was riding by herself at the rear of the troop.

"Aye?" Her voice was wary as she reined in the palfrey next to him.

"I wish to talk to you, Chandra," he said, keeping his eyes for the moment on the rutted road ahead.

It was the first time he had spoken to her that day. Perhaps, she thought hopefully, he wanted to make peace.

"I have thought about what to do with you the entire day," he said finally.

"Do with me!" she gasped.

"You will hold your tongue," he said quite calmly. "I gave you all the freedom you had at Croyland, until you broke trust with me. Even then, I allowed you your manly trappings. But now, I will make no more excuses for you. You will not interrupt me, and will listen carefully, or I can assure you that all hell will break loose once we are home."

"Your home, not mine," she muttered under her breath.

He ignored her words. "I have done all that I can to change your feelings for me. Indeed, I have even taught you a woman's pleasure, much to your panting delight, I might add."

He saw a flush of anger spread over her cheeks. "Nay," he continued sharply, "keep your viper's tongue in your mouth! This last example of your thoughtlessness, your childishness, has shown me clearly that you have not a pittance of sense, or maturity, and no regard for my wishes."

The palfrey snorted as Chandra's hands yanked convulsively on his reins. "I do not have to suffer more of your insults!" She jerked the palfrey about, but Jerval whipped out his hand and tore the reins from her.

"My dear wife, you will suffer whatever I choose to mete out to you. I am your husband, your master, and it is time that you learned your place, once and for all." He forced an expressionless voice. "You will no more practice with the men, nor will you again wear your men's garb. You will spend all of your time learning from my mother the things ladies should know. Never again will you set yourself against me, or I will deal with you as befits disobedient, ill-tempered wives."

"I will listen to no more of this, Jerval!"

"Just look at you," he growled. "Your face is filthy, your hair hanging down your back like a tangled bird's nest, and your clothing—"

"Allow me to remind you, husband," she snarled back at him, "that all the same applies to you, save that you have a dirty, scratchy growth of beard on your face to hide the dirt!"

She pulled her arm free of him, and before he could stop her, she kicked the palfrey's belly, and he leaped forward into a wild gallop. Jerval held tightly to Pith's reins. He had said most of what he had planned to.

Jerval saw Chandra within sight of Camberley, sitting rigidly upon the palfrey's back as the horse nibbled at the thin grass beside the rutted road. He would have grinned had he been able, for he realized that she had not had the courage to enter the keep without him.

He merely nodded to her, and she guided the palfrey beside him, not looking at him. There were shouts from the men lining the outer walls, and as he expected, his parents were awaiting them in the inner bailey. He could hear his father's sigh of relief upon seeing Chandra. There were two spots of angry color on his mother's cheeks.

Chandra slithered slowly off her palfrey's back. She heard her mother-in-law call her name, but kept her head down and walked quickly to where her husband stood.

"Jerval, thank the Virgin you have brought her back safely!" Lady Avicia cried.

"By the saints, we did not know what she would do!" Lord Hugh said.

"I know," Jerval said. "Let us go within and I will tell you everything."

Once in the hall, Lord Hugh, who had used the time to calm his anger at his daughter-in-law, asked before his wife could begin her ranting. "What of the Scots, Jerval?"

"We killed three of them—they were a rear guard on this side of the border. I suspect that they were waiting for us and would have attacked if our force had been smaller, likely at night. As it was, the others escaped, the stolen cattle with them. Unfortunately," he said, unable to keep his eyes from flickering over his silent wife, "their leader, Alan Durwald, escaped us."

"Your hair! What happened to your hair!"

Lady Avicia was staring at the tangles that tumbled only midway down Chandra's back.

Chandra tried to shrug indifferently, but it cost her dearly. "One of the Scots chopped off my braid," she managed to say finally, her voice none too steady.

Lady Avicia's eyes bulged. "You were in the fighting?" She turned to her son, not waiting for an answer from Chandra. "You told me you would not allow it!"

"That is true," Jerval said. "As you likely know, Mother, Chandra smashed the glass in my bedchamber and climbed down knotted sheets."

"It was my window!" Lord Hugh wailed, reminded of his fury at finding his precious glass shattered. "You should be beaten soundly, Chandra!"

"You are filthy," Julianna said, shuddering in distaste.

"Oh hush, Julianna," Mary muttered. "Chandra is all right, that is all that matters." But her gentle eyes were narrowed with worry upon Chandra's face. She sensed that her friend had pushed her husband too far this time, though he had said nothing as yet.

"This nonsense must stop," Lady Avicia said. "I will no longer allow a silly, stubborn—"

Jerval held up a staying hand. "Chandra and I will bathe off our dirt now," he said. "Mother, nothing more need be said." At his dismissing tone, Lady Avicia stiffened, but the harsh expression on her son's face stilled her tongue.

Jerval bathed first, watching his wife pace silently about their bedchamber. When he stepped out of the tub, she averted her eyes. He toweled himself off, and said calmly over his shoulder, "After you have bathed, you will dress in your most ladylike clothing. You might as well begin now to accustom yourself to the role of a woman."

"I will wear what I like!" Chandra spat, whirling on him.

He nodded pleasantly. "Of course, but your choice will no longer include men's garb. Not until such time as I give you permission."

"You cannot mean what you said, Jerval," she said in a more conciliating tone.

"Aye, all of it." He looked toward the glassless window. "If you are industrious enough, I might consider it payment for breaking the glass, though I doubt that my father will. Did you ever bother to consider that Camberley is the only keep in the north of England that has glass?''

"A keep has no need of glassed windows."

"I know, 'tis soft, and unbefitting a warrior's castle." Jerval paused a moment in his dressing and studied her flushed face. "As I said, you will now learn all the responsibilities of a . . . great lady. If I am pleased with your progress, and your cooperation, I will allow you to ride, practice your archery, and hunt again. But you will do none of these things without my permission.'' He added in a deadly soft voice, "Believe me this time, wife, you would not like the alternative.''

She did believe him, and her shoulders slumped. "I hate you," she muttered.

"I do believe you, Chandra," he said coldly, his jaw tightening. "There is no need for you to remind me constantly."

He turned at the entrance of two servants carrying fresh water for the bath. "I will see you at supper,'' he said, and left her.

He returned some ten minutes later, saw that Chandra had pulled the screen in front of the tub, and walked noiselessly to the wooden chest at the foot of the bed that held her clothing. As he piled her tunics, surcoats, and chausses over his arm, he wondered why he was bothering, for in truth, he would gladly have beaten her if she had dared to flout him.

When she appeared some two hours later in the hall, Mary at her side, he allowed a cold smile. Her thick hair was still damp and flowed loose down her back in soft waves. Her gown he recognized as one she had worn at Croyland, soft pink silk, its long loose sleeves lined with bands of miniver. The cut on her cheek ruined the effect.

He had spoken privately to his parents and told them the details of what had happened, preferring them to hear it from him rather than from the men. He had also told them what he now expected from his wife. "She will do as she's told now," he said, aware that his mother's brows were raised incredulously. "Don't be too rough on her, Mother," he added gruffly.

"After what she has done, you still defend her?" Lady Avicia sputtered.

He drew a deep breath. "I suppose that someone must, though I do admit that it is difficult. Do the minstrels not sing that a man is forever a fool to a beautiful woman?''

"A man should have obedience from his wife, for that is her duty before God."

He cut her off with a laugh. "Just as you always obey Father? Do not mint two coins, Mother, one for you and another for Chandra."

"Aye, Avicia," Lord Hugh agreed.

"Believe me, Mother, Chandra's days of disobedience are over."

The evening meal, luckily, passed without any unpleasant incident, likely because Chandra kept her mouth shut, Jerval thought. It surprised him, though he said nothing, that Chandra, for the first time since he had met her, looked uncertain and subdued. She said not a word to him, which, upon consideration, was not unexpected. Never, he thought, a brooding frown on his brow, had he envisioned his married life would be so damned unpleasant.

11

AT DAWN THE NEXT MORNING, Jerval and two dozen men set out from Camberley for Oldham. Jerval cast one last look over his shoulder at the huge towers, shrouded in early fog.

"She will come about, Jerval."

Jerval turned back in his saddle to face Mark, a sardonic smile on his lips. "It seems you are privy to all of it. From Mary?"

"Aye, a bit of it, and, of course, Lady Avicia was mumbling under her breath quite a bit last night."

Jerval shrugged and turned the subject. "If Sir John is in league with Alan Durwald, he will show us his true colors soon enough. Though it is difficult to credit the fool with enough nerve to turn against us."

"Nor is Oldham keep well fortified. We could take it in a week, if he tried to break his oath of fealty. Do we stop at Penrith?"

Jerval shook his head. "Nay, I wish to see what Sir John is about, then return to Camberley."

Mark smiled. "Ah, back to the heart of the storm."

"At least the thunder has ceased for the moment."

"Do you know, Jerval, I believe she was truly frightened, despite her cockiness afterward."

"If she was, I was too angry to notice."

They reached Oldham the following afternoon. It was a small keep that sat on a flat stretch of ground on the northeast perimeter of the de Vernon lands, its thick stone outer walls its only defense. Jerval searched the walls for signs of resistance, almost disappointed when he saw none. He was itching for a good fight, as much as were his men. He called a halt and rode forward to the edge of the moat.

"Lower the drawbridge!" he shouted to a gray-bearded

man who peered at them over the wall. "I am Jerval de Vernon, and I will see Sir John!"

The old man scratched his head and disappeared. Some ten minutes passed before Jerval recognized Sir John atop the wall. "Forgive the fool, my lord!" Sir John shouted. "But a moment, I beg you!"

The drawbridge was lowered slowly, its winches groaning, and Jerval wondered if they had ever been oiled. He gave Malton orders to scout all the outbuildings for signs of the Scots once they were within, and their troop filed into the bailey. Sir John stood awaiting them, surrounded by his ill-kempt men and even filthier servants. Jerval had not seen Sir John in over a year, and time, he saw, hadn't improved him. The heavy-jowled man was dressed richly, in a long robe of red velvet, his fat sausage fingers beringed, and he looked like royalty among beggars. Beside him stood a thin scrap of a woman, as ill-kempt as the servants. It took Jerval a moment to recognize that she was Lady Alice, Sir John's wife.

"Welcome, welcome, Sir Jerval," Sir John said, rubbing his hands together as Jerval dismounted and strode toward him. "Come to the hall, my lord."

"I give you fair greeting, my lady," Jerval said politely to Lady Alice.

Sir John grunted, his eyes narrowing on his wife's face as she whispered greetings to Jerval. "Have wine brought to the hall for our guests, Alice."

Jerval nodded to Malton, then turned and followed Sir John into the keep, Mark at his side.

He was appalled at the stench. The reeds strewn over the stone floor of the hall were befouled. When his boots crunched over some bones, the remains of a supper, a rat scurried out, darting between his feet.

Sir John spread his hands in front of him, seeing the look of disgust on Jerval's face. "Last winter was hard, my lord, and many of the sheep died. As for the serfs, they are lazy louts, and the crops not what I expected."

Jerval schooled himself and nodded pleasantly toward Sir John, thinking that he did not appear to have suffered at all. "And the Scots? Have you lost stock to them?"

Sir John answered quickly, "Aye, my lord, the dirty mongrels! My men can never catch them."

Sir John's wife leaned over Jerval's shoulder to pour wine into a tarnished silver goblet. She slipped and some of the wine splashed onto his surcoat.

"Clumsy bitch!" Sir John roared at her. Before Jerval could assure the poor woman that no harm was done, Sir John struck her and sent her sprawling onto the filthy reeds.

"Women!" Sir John spat. "They are such clodpated creatures! And this one cannot even give me a son!"

"Leave her be," Jerval said evenly. " 'Twas an accident, and no cause to strike her."

Sir John gazed balefully toward the cringing woman. "I hear that you have taken a wife, my lord," he said, his voice falsely confiding. "I wager she is not a silly sheep like this one."

Jerval cut him off, his voice still calm. "My wife would cut your throat, Sir John, were she here with me."

Sir John looked startled, then he laughed. "Ah, a fine joke, my lord."

Jerval rose abruptly to his feet. "I will see your accounts now, Sir John. Your payment to the de Vernons this year was not according to your pledge."

"As I said, Sir Jerval, the crops did not yield much." Sir John's pale eyes fell, and Jerval saw a muscle twitch in his heavy jaw. "I did not expect you, my lord, and I fear that my steward, a rascally fellow I dismissed from Oldham just last week, was cheating me."

Sir John felt the stirring of fear in his belly. The huge young lord standing before him, his face implacable, was not at Oldham simply to break his journey and be on his way in the morning. He wondered angrily who had betrayed him to the de Vernons. He would have to be wily to save himself, let alone make this arrogant de Vernon pay for his interference. If only Durwald were here—the Scot would not miss the chance to kill an English knight. Aye, he thought, he could get Sir Jerval comfortably in bed with his own mistress, Dora. He could trust the little slut to amuse Sir Jerval until Alan and his men were fetched and let in through the hidden postern in the east wall. The young giant had brought but a dozen men-at-arms with him, and surprised in their sleep, they could all be killed, and the lot of them could be removed from Oldham, and the blame as well.

"Nonetheless," Jerval said, his voice cold as steel, "I will see the accounts."

"Certainly, my lord," Sir John said. He gazed toward the unshuttered windows and said brightly, "It grows dark. Perhaps you would like to wait until tomorrow. Tonight after you have eaten, I will send you a lovely morsel to while away the long night."

To Mark's surprise, Jerval said in the voice of an eager young man, "An excellent suggestion, Sir John."

"Aye, my lord," Sir John said. "A young man must ease his needs."

Mark waited until he and Jerval had been shown to the one private chamber above the hall by a furtive serving maid before he opened his mouth to protest. Jerval shook his head and placed his fingertip to his lips until the girl had slipped from the room. He remained silent as he gazed about at the oddly bare chamber. There was but one stool and an old chest against the end of the bed, and the bed itself, though large and comfortable, was covered with worn, tattered blankets.

Jerval said thoughtfully, " 'Tis too bare and poor, as if someone had stripped the chamber of its trappings. Did you notice the rings on Sir John's fingers, Mark?"

Mark nodded slowly, and a smile spread over his face.

"I wonder," Jerval continued, thoughtful still, "where his lady wife sleeps."

Rough tables were pressed together to accommodate Jerval, Mark, Malton, and three of their men. Lady Alice was nowhere to be seen. The girl, Dora, was seated next to Jerval. She had been hastily bathed, but there was still dirt under her fingernails, Jerval saw. She was not uncomely, and very young. There was a smug, assessing look in her dark eyes, and he grinned to himself. The supper was surprisingly well prepared, and Jerval was careful to eat and drink only what Sir John did.

Jerval smiled at Dora and deliberately cupped his hand over her full breast. "More wine, my lord?" she whispered, wriggling closer to him.

"Aye," he said, though he had no intention of drinking the heady brew.

"I have another girl for you, Sir Mark," Sir John said as

the meal progressed. "You need have no fear that you will spend the night alone."

Jerval sent his host a lustful grin and said in a slurred voice, "Send her to the chamber, Sir John. We will enjoy the both of them."

Sir John could scarce keep his glee to himself. Young men had mighty appetites, and it was serving him well.

The other girl was not as winsome as Dora, yet she appeared eager enough. She too, Jerval saw, had been hastily bathed. He bid Sir John a drunken goodnight and allowed Dora to take his hand and pull him with her up the stairs.

Jerval's expression did not change when they entered the bedchamber. "Take off your clothes, girls," he said, leaning his back against the closed door. "Mark, shall we draw lots to see who takes them first?"

"And you, my lord?" Dora said pertly. "Will you not allow me to help you remove your surcoat?"

"In a moment, Dora."

Jerval watched dispassionately as the girls wriggled out of their kirtles and shifts. When they stood naked, their young bodies white in the light of the one torch, Jerval walked forward and stroked his chin, as if assessing their charms. Dora grabbed his hand and guided it to her breast.

"I will make you forget everything, my lord," Dora whispered, her hand stroking down his belly. Jerval lightly shoved her away before she could discover that his body showed no signs of desire.

"Hand me your shift, Dora." The girl cocked her head in question but did as she was told. Jerval ripped it into strips, paying no heed to Dora's gasp of surprise.

"I suggest," Jerval said coldly, "that both of you keep your mouths shut."

When both girls were bound and gagged, Jerval and Mark carried them to the bed and covered them with blankets.

"Now, my friend," Jerval said with some satisfaction, "we wait."

Chandra jabbed a needle into Jerval's burgundy velvet surcoat.

"Nay, Chandra," Mary said gently. "You must be careful, else you'll make a greater rent in the fabric."

"I don't care! One of those silly girls could do this."

Mary whispered a thankful prayer that Lady Avicia had left Chandra with her and not chosen to oversee the mending herself.

"Perhaps, but it is your responsibility to care for your lord's clothing." To Mary's consternation, a tear slid from Chandra's eye and fell down her cheek.

"To be a wife is no shame, Chandra," she said gently. "Just think, when you have learned all the housewifely skills, you will know more than any man or woman." At Chandra's stiff silence, she added sharply, "I do try to understand you, Chandra, but sometimes, you make me feel such vexation!" She turned her face away and said in a choked voice, "At least you are safely wed, and your husband is . . . a fine man!"

Chandra dropped the needle and swiped her palm over her tear-stained cheek. "I have not forgotten you, Mary. You will not live in dishonor, I swear it."

"I know you will do what you can, Chandra." But time was growing short. Just this morning she had barely missed being ill in front of Lady Avicia. "You are not stupid, Chandra," she said suddenly, "and I cannot believe that you would prefer spending your days locked in your bedchamber. You have no choice in the matter now, and I beg you to accept it. I am so tired of all the fighting!"

Chandra looked at her friend, stunned. "I do not mean to be so . . . disagreeable," she said at last in a small voice.

"I know. Right now you are fighting with your pride. You must know that Sir Jerval will ease his hold once you prove to him that you can be reasonable."

"I know I should not have followed him to fight the Scots. It is just that he angered me so!" She raised tired eyes to Mary's face. "What do I have if I let him take my pride?"

"You have more than any woman could want," Mary said tartly.

Chandra suddenly grimaced. She raised her finger to lick off the drop of blood from the needle prick.

Alan Durwald stroked the thick tress of hair that was braided about his wrist, and was satisfied. Jerval de Vernon, the man who had killed three of his men, would die by his hand tonight, and his lady would be left without a husband to protect her.

It was late enough now, and the young lord was likely snoring after slaking his lust. He motioned his three men up the narrow stairs of the keep, and paused to listen outside the oak door to the bedchamber. All was quiet, as it should be. He quietly pressed the latch and swung the door open, his fingers tight about the bone handle of his dagger. He saw the outline of two figures in bed through the darkness, and motioned for his men to enter. They stepped toward the bed, their swords and knives at ready.

Suddenly, the silence was rent by a bloodcurdling yell, and he saw the glint of a sword slicing toward David. "It's a trap!" Alan shouted.

Jerval slashed his sword into the man's belly, then jerked it out. "Take that one, Mark," he shouted, and leaped aside as Alan Durwald swung his claymore high above his head and brought it down in a vicious blow.

"De Vernon," he rasped, as the huge man lunged toward him.

"Aye, you cowardly scum!" Jerval brought his sword down, and he felt Durwald's arm weaken under the blow.

Jerval heard a low gurgling sound, and felt a cold chill touch him. "Behind you, Jerval!" Mark shouted. He wheeled about, saw the man running toward him, and flung his knife. It sliced into the man's neck, and blood spurted from his throat.

"English bastard!" Alan Durwald shouted as he saw Geordie fall forward in a pool of his own blood. He fought with all his strength, but de Vernon would not weaken. He heard another man fall, and knew with certainty that he was now alone against two men.

"He is mine, Mark!" Jerval yelled.

Alan Durwald felt a blade pierce his shoulder, and he gasped in agony, falling back. His claymore flew from his fingers, and he sank to his knees. He felt de Vernon's boot strike his belly, and he fell to his back. He felt De Vernon's heel dig into his chest, and saw his enemy lean over to jerk the dagger from his shoulder. With a scream of pain and fury, he clutched his dagger and flung it upward. De Vernon twisted away, and Alan Durwald felt a sudden blinding pain in his chest. Then he felt no more.

"Light the torch, Mark."

When the chamber was flooded with light, Jerval stared down at Alan Durwald.

"He is dead?"

"Aye, he is dead."

Jerval rose. "Sir John," he said, "will not look well hanging from the gibbet at Camberley."

Jerval rode into the inner bailey at Camberley with Sir John and his wife, Lady Alice, beside him, and some half-dozen men-at-arms at his back. He had left Mark, Malton, and the rest of Camberley's men at Oldham to restore some kind of order to the keep.

Sir John faced his overlord in the great hall, and knew by the implacable look on Lord Hugh's face that he was lost. He listened in silence while Sir Jerval recounted the events at Oldham.

"The Scot leader, Alan Durwald, is dead," Jerval finished. "Our northern border should be peaceful for a time."

"The Scot threatened me, my lord," Sir John said, seeing a glimmer of hope. "He stole my sheep and bribed my men! I had no choice but to obey him. He said he would kill me and my poor wife if I did not do what he said." He waved a fat hand toward his hapless wife, who stood trembling with fear, her eyes upon her feet. Stupid bitch, he thought with impotent anger, could she not at least plead for him?

Chandra broke the silence. "You wear valuable rings on your fingers, Sir John, yet I look at your lady wife and see that she wears a tattered gown. And the bruise beside her mouth, Sir John, does not become her. 'Twould appear that you have not protected her well from harm."

Chandra did not notice her father-in-law glowering at her, for she was watching Sir John's face turn a mottled red.

Sir John gaped at the girl. That she was even allowed in the men's presence had shocked him. But that she would speak to him in that calm, sarcastic tone angered him beyond reason.

"She is a stupid cow," he spat, "and is barren!"

"Chandra," Lord Hugh began abruptly, only to fall silent when Jerval interrupted him.

"My wife speaks true, Father. Sir John is a man without honor, and his treachery speaks clearly. I think the money from the sale of all his rings will provide his wife enough to live comfortably. She bears no blame in this, I am certain.''

He looked toward Lady Alice, and was surprised to see the haunted look gone from her eyes, and her thin shoulders drawn back. "Chandra, will you see that Lady Alice is made comfortable?''

Chandra met his steady gaze, then smiled at Lady Alice. "Of course, my lord,'' she said, and led the woman from the hall.

"You are swayed by foolish women, Lord Hugh!''

Sir John saw only a blur of movement. Jerval's fist smashed against his jaw, and he dropped where he stood. "I have wanted to do that since the moment I first saw him,'' Jerval said, rubbing his knuckles. "To see his fat body swinging from a gibbet will please me even more.''

Lady Alice, Chandra discovered, was the eldest of four daughters of an impoverished knight from the south of England, near Rye. She was shocked to learn that Lady Alice was but twenty-eight years old, for she was so bowed and thin, her hair as scraggly as Alma's. There was a look of hopeless suffering etched into her pale face. "But why did you wed Sir John?'' she asked as she herself helped bathe Lady Alice.

Lady Alice winced slightly as the washcloth touched her bruised ribs. "Not everyone can be so lucky as you, Lady Chandra,'' she said quietly, without rancor. "Sir Jerval is not only an extremely handsome young man, he is also kind, an unlikely quality in a husband.''

Chandra felt color rush to her cheeks, but held her tongue.

"Sir John is—was—a mean, greedy man,'' Lady Alice continued, no emotion in her voice, "and my father, poor man, had four girls to contend with. Ten years ago, I suppose that Sir John looked at my meager dowry as sufficient, but of course it did not last long.''

Mary helped stitch up one of Chandra's gowns to fit Lady Alice, who was some inches shorter. Chandra presented her proudly at supper the evening after Sir John's hanging, an event that Lady Alice appeared oblivious of, and placed her in her own chair.

"You are such a kind child,'' Lady Alice said softly to her, "but is it wise to bring me to sup with the family?''

"You are a guest, Alice, and I am not a child. You are but

some years older than I, and soon, after you have added some pounds, you will look even younger.''

Lady Alice smiled. "You are as kind as Sir Jerval."

Jerval greeted Lady Alice, his eyes twinkling at Chandra, for he had heard her words. He was surprised at the change in Lady Alice, though he hadn't an idea what they were going to do with Sir John's widow.

Lady Avicia inclined her head politely and offered Alice a huge helping of roast lamb. "A man will not want you again unless you fill out my daughter-in-law's gown."

"Perhaps," Chandra said, "Lady Alice does not want another husband. Her first was a beast." She continued, gazing at Jerval, "Do you know what Sir John's jewels will bring?"

"Sufficient for her dowry," Lord Hugh said, seeing for the first time the soft loveliness of Lady Alice's brown eyes. What a hag the woman had been but this afternoon! He had thought her as old as her dissipated husband.

"Chandra's gown is not a becoming color for you, Lady Alice," Julianna said. "I have a pink wool that you may have."

Chandra stared at Julianna, so surprised that she did not at first hear the small sob that escaped Alice's throat.

"You are all so very kind," she said.

"You cannot eat if you are crying," Lady Avicia said sternly, and the widow meekly swallowed her tears and the lamb.

After supper, Chandra fidgeted about in her bedchamber, waiting for her husband. She had finally left Lady Alice in Mary's capable hands.

"You will wear out Mother's new carpets," Jerval said as he came into the room.

"I must talk to you," she said, not mincing matters.

"And I to you," Jerval replied. "I believe this is yours, Chandra." He pulled a foot-long plaited rope of golden hair from his tunic and tossed it to her. She caught it handily and stared at the dusty hair.

"He was wearing it as a bracelet around his wrist—like a gallant knight with his lady's colors."

Chandra shrugged. "You needn't glower, Jerval. You look like your father. What is this to me?"

Jerval strode to her and caught her shoulders in his iron

hands. "Durwald was a vicious animal. Had he escaped with you, there would have been no ransom, he would have kept you, and likely ploughed you until you cowered in fear from him."

"Like poor Alice?" she spat, trying to twist out of his hold. "God, what you men do to women! Did you see her, the bruises, the cuts? She is only twenty-eight years old!" She was trembling, so angry that the words spilled out. "And like Mary? Pregnant, abused by a damned man! And none of it her fault, just like Alice!"

Jerval released her abruptly. "By the Virgin," he said softly. "The child is Graelam de Moreton's?"

"Of course! It took but one of you men to take his pleasure, and she is the victim . . . she is the one shamed!"

Damnation, he thought, counting back in his mind, the girl was over three months gone with child. Damnation, he cursed again. He said abruptly, "You can cease your ranting. I will take care of the matter."

"What are you going to do?" she called after him, but he closed the bedchamber door and was gone.

12

JERVAL STRODE ABOUT THE HALL at Oldham, sniffing as he went, and stopped before a grinning Mark. "You have done wonders. It has not even been a week, and the place smells habitable."

"If you lean down, you'll catch a whiff of sweet rosemary and marjoram on the new water reeds. There is not a rat or a bone left! Come and eat now. The cook, bless the fellow, has kept us alive with good, hearty meals."

Jerval joined Mark and six of his men at the trestle tables. He speared a piece of roasted beef on his knife and held it up, his eyes a laughing question toward Mark.

"Eat, Sir Jerval," Malton laughed. " 'Tis good, just as Mark assured you."

"Take care with your knife," Mark said, "for the table is newly polished. And you'll notice that the servants are reasonably clean, no mean feat, I assure you, except"—he winked to Jerval—"for Dora." He lowered his voice as Dora sidled past Jerval, her eyes provocative and teasing. "You must know that I let Dora make herself a new shift, to replace the one we so rudely took from her. If you wish it, I think she would likely enjoy thanking you for it tonight."

Jerval smiled, but shook his head.

"Oldham will never be a rich holding," Mark said as he dipped a crust of bread into the beef gravy, "but with proper management, it will be an asset to the de Vernons. The peasants are still shaking their heads in disbelief that Sir John is at last resting in hell where he belongs."

Malton looked up from his trencher of beef. "What a lot of wretched scraps they are! Hubert gave an order to the cattle herder, and the poor fellow nearly kissed his hand."

" 'Tis my gentle manner," Hubert said. "Poor devils!"

"The men-at-arms?" Jerval asked.

214

Malton grinned. "We've been less than gentle with those louts, but they'll come about, or have the hide whipped off their miserable backs."

"Will there be enough food to feed the keep and the peasants for the winter?" Jerval asked.

"Nay," Mark said. He added with a wry grin, "I'm sorely tempted to ride out at night and relieve our neighbors of some of their excess crops. Unfortunately, they know of Sir John's demise, so we couldn't blame the bastard. I would hate to leave Oldham knowing that the poor fools will starve if something isn't done."

"Sir John bled them dry," Malton said.

"Well, Sir John is now bled dry himself," Jerval said. He paused a moment, balancing his supper knife on two fingers. "Oldham needs a master who will not cheat its people, and who will rebuild its defenses. It would appear that I have no choice in the matter." He gave a soulful sigh. "Sir Mark of Oldham. I like the sound of it. What do you think, Malton?"

"It does have a certain grandeur," Malton said, laughing heartily at the stunned look on Mark's face.

"Will you, Sir Mark, swear fealty to your overlord as vassal of Oldham?"

A cheer went up from the half-dozen de Vernon men at the long trestle table, and Mark, who could scarce believe his ears, did not have to reply until the noise died down. A flush of pleasure flooded his face, and when he found his voice, it was strong and clear. "I swear upon my honor and my life." The word "vassal" sounded in Mark's ears. He could have well understood if he had been appointed castellan of Oldham, but now he was the master of Oldham, and no longer a landless knight in the service of another. When Jerval asked to speak to him privately later that evening, Mark was still beaming a wide grin at his good fortune.

"I have a favor to ask of you, Mark."

"I would hesitate to cut off my arm," Mark said, "but anything else . . ."

"Oldham will need a mistress, and if you have no strong objection to the lady, I would offer you Mary."

Mark's expression became serious. In one evening he had become the master of a keep and now, it appeared, a husband as well. Mary, a sweet child, comely and gentle.

"Do you dislike the girl?"

Mark hastened to reassure him. "Nay, it is just very sudden. I had not thought of marriage." He shrugged ruefully. "You bow my shoulders with responsibilities, Jerval. Mary," he said, trying out her name with a new voice. "She is an innocent babe."

"Not that precisely. Have you wondered why she accompanied Chandra to Camberley?"

"She and Chandra grew up together, and, of course, it is expected that a new bride will have a companion of her own class."

Jerval said calmly, "It is that and more. Mary was raped by Graelam de Moreton, and she is pregnant, three months gone."

"My God," Mark whispered. "That poor child!" He shook his head over the vagaries of fate. "I am to be the father to Graelam's child," he said slowly. "God grant that it is not a boy."

"Lord Hugh dispatched a messenger to Mary's father before I left, to gain his permission. I haven't the faintest idea of her portion. It should enable you to buy what you need to provision the keep properly, I trust. If it doesn't . . ." Jerval shrugged and smiled. "Well, in any case, the de Vernons will be adding a bit."

Mark smiled wryly. "I suppose that I am to have dallied with Mary, and am doing the honorable thing by her."

"Aye, you will doubtless be cast as the lecher, particularly by my mother, when Mary's belly becomes nicely rounded in the next couple of months." The two men rose, and Jerval placed his hands on Mark's shoulders. "I thank you, Mark, as will Chandra. She has been frantic with worry, I think."

"Have you told Mary?"

Jerval looked at him, surprised. "Nay, of course not. She will doubtless be overcome by her good fortune." He added, his eyes twinkling, "I could not tell her. What if you had not wished to become master of Oldham? I could not foist a landless lout on her! You must marry the girl quickly. Do you feel that you can safely leave Oldham in Malton's hands until you can return with your bride?"

"Of course."

"I will leave Malton and a half-dozen men under your command until you are able to recruit more men from Penrith and Carlisle. Malton hopes the Scots will test him while he is here, so he can give them a taste of the new master's strength."

Jerval and Mark found Lord Hugh in the great hall at Camberley, his gouty foot raised on a stool. He was waving a rolled parchment at them when they entered.

"At last you have returned!" Lady Avicia cried, giving her son a welcoming hug. She shot a look of disgust toward her grinning husband. "He will not tell us what he has got there."

"I have been savoring it until Jerval returned and everyone was together for the telling," Lord Hugh said with smug satisfaction.

"You may stop your infernal savoring now!" Lady Avicia snapped.

"Aye, sir, what is it?" Chandra asked, drawing closer, Lady Alice at her side.

Hugh drew himself up and boomed in a prideful voice, " 'Tis a letter from King Henry. Prince Edward and Princess Eleanor are touring the lake region on their way to Scotland, and will be our guests." He sat back and beamed, watching the myriad expressions about him.

"When, Father?"

"Next week."

"Next week!" Lady Avicia repeated, her wimple flapping. "Bu the Virgin, Hugh! I must have a new gown! And the preparations!"

"How wonderful," Mary said to Mark, who had walked to stand beside her. "It is such an honor."

"Wonderful indeed," Mark agreed, smiling down at her.

" 'Twill be good to see Edward again," Jerval said. "You will like Edward's ready wit, Chandra, and Eleanor's gentle grace." He frowned suddenly at the old gown his wife was wearing. "I trust you have something fitting to wear."

"One does not greet the prince and princess in the clothes one wears to weave, Jerval." Though her tone was sharp, he heard excitement in her voice.

"The king writes that Eustace will be accompanying them," Lord Hugh said. "It appears he has been hanging about Windsor since his return from France."

"I wonder what Eustace was up to in France," Jerval said

to no one in particular. "Louis, after all, has already left for the Holy Land."

"Perhaps," Hugh said thoughtfully, "the prince has more reason for visiting the lake region than just to tour his lands."

A gleam of understanding lit Jerval's eyes before they flickered briefly on Mark's face. "I have more good news for all of you," he said. "Sir Mark has sworn fealty to the de Vernons and will be the master of Oldham. We are honored at his decision."

Mark was clapped soundly on his back amid much clapping and shouting. He saw that Lady Alice was smiling shyly toward him, and said, "Much has happened, and quickly, my lady. If it is your desire, Oldham will be your home for so long as you wish it."

"Nay, Sir Mark," Lady Alice said softly, "but I thank you for your kindness. I have no wish ever to return there. The peasants deserve a fair master. I am pleased."

Lady Avicia said brightly, "Well, I, for one, think Alice will do quite nicely here at Camberley."

"My lady?" Lord Hugh inquired gently.

"It would please me above all things, my lord."

" 'Tis settled then," Avicia said.

"It seems, Mother, that you will have much to do in the way of preparations . . . and not just for Edward's visit."

Avicia, who had just begun making lists in her mind, bent a sharp eye to her son at his words. "Whatever do you mean, Jerval?"

Jerval studied Mary's gentle face for a moment, then winked at Mark. "I, like my father, believe I will savor the telling until this evening."

"You are both disagreeable!" Lady Avicia said. "Come, Julianna, Alice, let us see what the varlets are serving these tight-mouthed gentlemen for dinner."

"He did naught but *inform* you?" Chandra said.

Mary's happy smile did not dim. "Not exactly," she said. "Jerval was most polished and gentle in his speech."

"I should never have trusted him! When he blithely *informed* me that he would see to everything, I should have insisted that he tell me what he was planning."

"But Chandra," Mary said, truly puzzled, "what does it matter that he did not tell you? After all, he had first to gain

Sir Mark's agreement. Mark will be a fine husband, and he is too kind ever to reproach me about the child. I am more pleased than I can tell you."

"But you were given no choice, Mary. How can you be pleased that Jerval simply decided that you would wed Mark, without even asking what you thought of him?"

"It would have been my father's duty to find me a husband," Mary said reasonably, "and I am thankful that Jerval took it upon himself. What more could I ask? I will have a gentle lord, be mistress of his keep, and bear his children. Mark knows that I will try to make him a good wife. It is more than I ever could have wished for."

At Chandra's sigh, Mary said with some pique, "Would you prefer that I bear a bastard in shame?"

"Of course not. 'Tis just—"

"I think, Chandra, 'tis just that Jerval did not ask your opinion. But surely you cannot disagree with the outcome. After all, what meaning would life have if one did not marry and have babes, and live together, and share joy and sadness? Such loneliness there would be without a family."

"Like the Maid of Brittany," Chandra said absently, "locked away at the king's pleasure, alone until she died."

"Exactly." Mary beamed.

"I—I am happy for you, Mary, if it is what you wish."

"I wish for nothing more." She laid a light hand on Chandra's arm. "Nor should you, Chandra."

Chandra said, suddenly brisk, "We have little time to prepare your bridal clothes. And the prince is coming!"

"Ah, Lady Avicia is already bustling about! She must wonder why we are to wed so quickly, but she has said nothing of it to me. She is most kind to me, and I fear I have done little to deserve it."

"Nonsense, you are an angel, and Mark the luckiest man alive."

" 'Tis true," Mary teased, smiling impishly. "Even he does not know that yet!"

Three days later, Chandra, her husband beside her, waved one last time to Mary from atop the outer wall.

"Mother packed the baggage mules so high, I was beginning to wonder if we would have anything left at Camberley."

"Mary seems happy," Chandra said without turning to face him, a forlorn catch in her voice.

"I trust so." He saw that she was straining to see Mary, now but a blur in the distance. "You will miss her. Perhaps we can visit them soon."

"Aye," Chandra said. "I should like that."

"I shall miss her too," he said. "She is quite skilled with a needle," he added blandly.

She glared at him, but said only, "I wish they could have stayed to see the prince and the princess."

Jerval grinned down at her. "Mark, like me, wished to have his bride alone with him as quickly as possible."

"He could have bedded her here!" she said, and presented him with an embarrassed back.

"Aye, she had made no vow. I asked her."

"You—you did not!"

"Nay, I did not." She turned to face him, taut with embarrassment, and he tried to smile. He knew that she was remembering the long night they had shared together, or perhaps their wedding night when she had cowered away from him, her lie hovering stark between them. He wanted to chide her again about her foolish fear, remind her that her world had not tumbled down around her ears when she had at last discovered pleasure with him, but she was regarding him coldly, her chin raised defiantly. "Actually," he said aloud, wondering at his patience, "there was so much to be done at Oldham, Mark could spare no more time. I do not believe that in the next couple of days you will have much time to miss Mary."

Jerval was proved right, for Chandra, like everyone else at Camberley, was caught up in the excitement and bustle of preparation for the coming of the prince and princess. Under Lady Avicia's sharp eye, the tapestries were taken down and beaten free of dust; the featherdown mattresses were hauled from the keep and aired for two days, leaving everyone to sleep wrapped in blankets on the floor. Even the jakes did not suffer from lack of Lady Avicia's attention; she saw to it that even with a south wind, there was no odor to offend the nose. Weaving and sewing went on far into the night, and the serving wenches were fitted with new kirtles of green wool. The lavers were polished until they sparkled enough to show

the prince and princess their reflections while they washed
their hands. The accumulated ashes were swept from the
huge hearth and the cavernous fireplace scrubbed. It was only
when Lord Hugh saw several boys dangling from tall ladders
trying to clean the crossbeams in the hall ceiling that he threw
up his hands, crying enough. Hawk, with Lord Hugh's
agreement, was kept from the keep, and Chandra, who spent
most of her waking hours directing servants and weeding the
garden herself, for Lady Avicia was certain that Princess
Eleanor would wish to inspect the tiered vegetable plots, was
too weary from all the work to complain much.

"I wonder which of us will have to wash the cattle," was
all she said.

It was Jerval, in fact, who directed the cleaning of the
barracks and stables, for in Lady Avicia's cleanly mind, the
prince's men would surely tell him if they found filth. Although the men grumbled, they too were infected with the
growing excitement, for royalty had not visited Camberley in
over twenty years, when King Henry had once deigned to
pass the night there. The rotted hay was swept from the
stables and burned in the bailey.

"Offal!" Lady Avicia announced as she toured the stables.
"There will be no stench to offend the princess's delicate
nose!"

Meals were meager the several days before the prince's
arrival, and the smells from the cooking sheds made everyone's
mouth water. Lady Avicia had even sent for a pastry chef
form Carlisle, and the little man, his scrawny frame wrapped
in a huge white linen apron, had quickly spread terror among
the rest of the cooks, until, under his snapping orders, piles
of pastries and breads filled the larders.

Everyone but Lady Avicia was delighted when Anselm,
high in the north tower, sounded three loud blasts on his
hunting horn. At the sound of the horn, even the smallest
child in the keep lined up beside his mother, his hands
reverently clasped in front of him, awaiting the royal review.

Chandra wished she were in the tower with Anselm to
witness the prince's vast retinue, but her silk gown was new,
as were her soft leather shoes, and she was left to wait at
Jerval's side in the inner bailey. He was dressed, she was
certain, as finely as the prince must be. His fair hair fell
shining and thick in loose waves at his neck. His surcoat of

vivid dark-blue velvet fell to his ankles, its full fur-lined sleeves wide and loose over his large hands.

"I do hope," Jerval said to her, "that the prince has bathed in the last week, else my mother will likely have him tossed in the well."

Chandra did not reply, for the inner bailey was suddenly a blaze of deep purple and crimson. Edward and Eleanor, dressed in rich velvet shot with gold thread, rode at the fore of their retinue, astride two matched, glossy white stallions.

"She is beautiful!" Chandra said, her eyes on the exquisite woman who rode beside the prince, her black hair held in a net of gold, her gloved hands, covered with sparkling pearls, lightly holding her reins.

"Aye," Jerval agreed. "If you think me tall, Chandra, wait until your neck creaks looking up at the prince."

Prince Edward leaped gracefully from his destrier and tossed the reins to one of the gape-mouthed stable boys. He was as magnificent as his princess, Chandra thought, tall, taller even than Jerval, broad-shouldered, and slim-hipped. He was not, she thought objectively, as handsome as Jerval, but his features were strong, and his light-blue eyes seemed to take in everything and everyone about him. His hair was a pale yellow and hung to his shoulders.

There was a babble of voices until Lord Hugh stepped proudly forward. "God's grace on you, sire," he boomed, and bowed deeply to the prince, and then to Princess Eleanor. "And on you, my lady."

Chandra saw Prince Edward meet Jerval's eyes, his lips parted in a wolfish grin. "Lord Hugh and Lady Avicia," he said easily, taking Hugh's hand in a sign of friendship.

"We are delighted to visit Camberley, Lord Hugh," Eleanor said in a particularly sweet voice. "We thank you for your hospitality."

"It's even more of a giant you've become, sire!" Jerval laughed, clasping the prince's hand in his.

" 'Tis good to see you again, Sir Jerval." Edward wrapped his arms about Jerval's shoulders. "You're not precisely a dwarf yourself! Eleanor," Edward called to his wife, "I beg you not to fall in love with this impossible man. 'Tis fickle he is, so I've been told. And he's but a boy, a good five years less of ripening."

"After seeing naught but your face for so many years, and

watching you grow old, I vow I will look my fill," Eleanor said impishly. "It has been too long, Jerval," she said, laying her hand lightly on his velvet sleeve.

"Far too long, my lady," Jerval said, bowing. "Sire, my lady, this is my wife."

"What?" Edward mocked. "You have finally tied yourself to one woman?" The laughter left Edward's blue eyes when he looked down at Chandra. The girl curtsying before him was a magnificent creature. Golden hair rippled down her back, hair that made his hands itch to touch it, and when she straightened and looked up at him, full face without shyness, he said, "Who are you, my lady? Surely such a lovely girl would not pass unheard of to me, even at Windsor."

"I am Chandra de Avenell," she said in her clear voice. "My father, Lord Richard, is one of your marcher barons, his castle known as Croyland."

"Sir Jerval is a lucky man," Princess Eleanor said, smiling. "Come, my lord, have we not heard tell of Chandra de Avenell?"

"My daughter-in-law," Lady Avicia said unexpectedly, "has long been known for her beauty."

"Do you not remember, my lord?" Eleanor continued to her husband. "Your father approved their marriage not long ago."

"Aye, indeed," Edward said slowly. "I remember you well now, my lady. Lord Graelam de Moreton, as I recall, approached my uncle about wedding you." He turned to Jerval, a wicked gleam in his eyes. "You beat out a fine warrior, Jerval, and stole yourself a prize!"

It was on the tip of Chandra's tongue to inform the prince that it was Graelam who had nearly done the stealing, but Eleanor said suddenly, "A French minstrel, Henri, I believe, visited the court last year. He sang about you, your beauty and your warrior deeds."

"Warrior!" Edward exlaimed, and gave a great belly laugh.

"She is now more a wife," Jerval said smoothly, and took Chandra's tense hand in his. "As for Graelam de Moreton, that, sire, is a long story!"

"My niece, sire, Julianna," Hugh said, "and my lady wife have prepared refreshments for you within."

After the prince and princess were swept into the hall by Lord Hugh, Jerval turned to give orders for the prince's retinue. "Lord," he said under his breath, "with this mass of soldiers and all the princess's women, there won't be a free inch of space either within the keep or without!"

"Well, cousin, you must be grateful that the prince is happily wed."

Jerval drew up at Eustace's deep voice. "You keep high company, Eustace." His eyes turned to his wife. "Chandra, this is Eustace de Leybrun. He was my sister Matilda's husband."

Chandra nodded politely at the dark man, sensing the dislike in Jerval's voice. He was dressed nearly as richly as the prince, his thick velvet cloak covering a surcoat of burgundy, its wide sleeves lined with miniver. He was not of Jerval's height, but he was built like a bull, his neck thick and corded, and she could see that beneath his noble clothes, his body was hard with muscle, save for his oddly spindly legs. She guessed him to be about thirty, or perhaps older, for there were lines etched about his dark eyes and his wide mouth.

"Welcome to Camberley, sir. I understand you have been in France."

"Aye, my lady," Eustace said. "Had I known that my little cousin was wedding himself to such as you, I would have returned and relieved him of his bride." His glance swept toward Jerval. "I saw de Moreton, you know, cousin. He was surly, his manners more abrupt than usual. I had no idea that it was you who was the cause of his black humor. He said nothing to me, of course, but his squire became loose in his tongue with drink, and talked of his master's defeat at Croyland by a warrior robed as a priest, and of his shoulder wound at the soft hands of a gently bred lady. 'Twas you, I presume, cousin." At Jerval's stiff nod, Eustace turned to Chandra and said in a soft voice, "So the victor won the prize, my lady. It is seldom that an heiress has claim to such beauty, and skill with a dagger. You are a prize to be treasured."

Chandra had listened to him in silence. She disliked his oily tone, his references to Graelam de Moreton, and his taunting, fulsome compliments. "Your compliments, Sir Eustace," she said sweetly, "are bright as the sun. I hope"—she gazed toward the setting sun—"that they do not fade as quickly."

"Well met, my lady," Eustace said. "What is this about your gentle wife being a warrior, Jerval, and hurling daggers at the greatest fighters of our land?" Eustace continued, looking over at her.

"Go assist my mother," Jerval said, and gave Chandra a light shove. She willingly obeyed him.

"My wife, Eustace," he said evenly, watching Chandra gracefully mount the staircase to the hall, "is many things. But most important, she is now a de Vernon."

"Do not, I beg you, Jerval, challenge me for admiring your wife's beauty. I see that you are surrounded by beauty. The fair Julianna has grown quite comely. I trust," Eustace drawled, "that she is still a virgin?"

Jerval ignored his words and said, "You have a new neighbor at Oldham. Sir Mark is now master there." He saw the tightening in Eustace's jaw, and smiled.

"How generous you are toward a landless knight," Eustace sneered.

"The de Vernon lands need proper protection from the Scots," Jerval said smoothly, "and Sir Mark's loyalty to the de Vernons and his honor cannot be questioned."

Eustace shrugged "From what I heard, Sir John kept a tight hold on Oldham. Did he have the misfortune to look lustfully at your wife?"

"Nay, he had the misfortune of believing he could help the Scots slay me through treachery. We hanged the greedy fool."

"A pity," Eustace said obliquely.

"You will see Lady Alice, his widow. She has much changed since we freed her of her bastard husband. Let us go within. Doubtless you would like to refresh yourself."

"What lovely carpets," Jerval heard Princess Eleanor say to his mother as they entered the hall.

Lady Avicia beamed. "This one is from Castile, my lady, your homeland."

"I have rarely seen such beauty," Eleanor continued, fingering one of the tapestries, seeing Lady Avicia's interest.

"How long do you stay at Camberley, sire?" Lord Hugh asked.

Edward tossed down the rest of his wine before saying with a disarming grin, "Actually, Lord Hugh, our trip north is for two purposes, the first being to travel to Scotland to celebrate my aunt's birthday. If it pleases you, we would be your guests for two days. My wife much enjoys the lake region, and it is always a pleasure to see my father's faithful barons."

"And your other reason?" Jerval asked, having a good idea what was in Edward's mind.

"Do not press me, Jerval," Edward complained. "I plan to get you roaring drunk, then gain your agreement!"

"That will be a sight worth seeing," Jerval retorted. "I could always outdrink you. You'll be snoring and sodden in your chair and likely forget what it is you're after."

"Unkind!"

"But very true, my lord," Eleanor said. "At least," she said to the company, "he is always sweet and regretful the next morning."

"What about during the night?" Edward teased his wife.

"That is a lovely gown, Lady Chandra," Eleanor said deliberately, frowning at her husband, "and I much like your unusual name."

"My mother-in-law made the pattern. As for my name, it was my father's choice and creation."

It was on the tip of Edward's tongue to say that he would just as soon see Jerval's lady without the lovely gown, but he knew it would have to wait. He would tell Eleanor, watch her pout, even as her dark eyes danced, and catch her small fists before lifting her into bed.

He said instead, "Lord Richard, your father, is one of my father's favorite men, and he has done well against the Welsh. But even castles such as Croyland are not enough to contain them."

"You are right, sire," Chandra said. "But because of the Welsh, life at Croyland was never dull."

"Now," Eleanor said, smiling, "I fear you will hear my lord's future plans."

Edward sat forward in his chair, needing no more encouragement, and rubbed his large hands together. "Aye. Someday I will build castles along the border, mighty fortresses that will hold even Llewelyn. Englishmen will need have no fear that they will awake with their throats cut."

"An unlikely event," Jerval said, and Edward leaned forward to cuff him on the shoulder. Edward, who forgot little, turned to Chandra and asked, "You find life dull at Camberley, my lady?"

Chandra felt a flush creep over her cheeks. "It has not been so since we heard of your coming, sire."

"She misses her armor," Julianna said without thinking.

Edward's brow shot up. "What is this, Jerval? You have another warrior at Camberley, yet you do not use her skills?"

"My wife," Jerval said calmly, sensing Chandra stiffen at Edward's teasing words, "is enlarging her skills, sire. My mother is teaching her the duties of a chatelaine."

"Aye, 'tis not an easy job," Eleanor said, gazing briefly at Chandra. The girl did not seem to be at her ease, though Eleanor did not understand why. She rose. "I am tired," she announced. "Lady Chandra, will you show me to our chamber?"

"My lord," Eleanor said gently as she walked beside Chandra up the stairs, "much enjoys to tease. You must merely smile at him and agree with all he says. He means no harm—it is merely his way." She paused only a moment to nod charmingly at the wide-eyed servants who appeared, it seemed, from every corner of the keep.

"I have always considered myself the luckiest of women to be married to a man like Edward," she continued. "I was wed to him as a child, and have loved him since he was but a cocky young lad. You, I think, are similarly lucky. Your husband, like mine, is a fiercely proud man, but honorable in his dealings with men, and, I am sure, gentle with his women."

Chandra was aware of Eleanor's eyes upon her, gently questioning, and she flushed. No, Jerval had not dealt gently with her save that night he had caressed her until her body had trembled for him. She shook her head, suppressing the memory. "Jerval," she said finally, "is like most men, I suppose."

"What a lovely chamber," Eleanor said easily, wondering what was amiss between Chandra and her husband. She dismissed three of her women who were fluttering about, and turned again to Chandra. "I have a blue gown, the color of your eyes, I think. It does not look well on a blackamoor like me." She leaned over and pulled out an exquisite blue silk gown, its flaring sleeves embroidered with small birds in gold and silver thread. "You see, it makes me look quite sallow, but on you—"

"Oh nay, my lady, I could not, 'tis beautiful, and truly the color becomes you."

"Hush," Eleanor said. "You and I are of a size, except that your waist is tiny. Nonetheless, a belt will solve that problem." She held the gown up in front of Chandra and said crisply, "My lord will, of course, tease you unmercifully, but you must simply disregard him."

"The prince, my lady," Chandra said wryly, "is not a man easily dismissed."

The trestle tables groaned under the weight of the food Lady Avicia provided that evening. Silver plates held the trenchers of bread, set amid pastries filled with chicken, venison, salmon, and eel. The mixed aroma of onions, garlic, carrots, artichokes, peas, and potatoes wafted through the hall, filled with over a hundred people, some of them eating on the stone floors, Avicia having wisely rolled up the carpets to prevent them from being soiled.

"A royal feast!" Edward exclaimed as servants carried in huge platters of roasted stag, cut into quarters, crisped, and larded. He watched, rubbing his hands in anticipation, as one of the cooks poured a hot, steaming pepper sauce over the stag.

"And such a wealth of vegetables, Lady Avicia!" Eleanor said.

"The vegetables are from Camberley's own gardens," Lady Avicia said proudly.

Prince Edward, true to Eleanor's prediction, said loudly, "A toast to your lovely wife, Jerval! She is too thin, but I wager a quiverful of babes will soon fill out that gown!"

"One can but try, sire," Jerval said easily.

"I imagine 'tis a nightly chore," Eustace called out.

"Would be that all chores were so enjoyable!" came a shout.

"Everything is remarkably tasty, Lady Avicia," Eleanor said, seeing Chandra flush in embarrassment at the men's jests. "It is seldom that we are so well feted on our travels."

As if on cue, Lady Avicia's pastry chef ushered in three servants who were carrying an enormous platter. Lord Hugh, grinning widely, stepped forward, eyed the huge pastry, and slashed it open with his dagger. A score of black birds fluttered out, and flew wildly about the hall, amid the men's shouts and the ladies' cries. Eventually, they winged to the crossbeams and to safety.

"However will you get the birds out of here?" Eleanor asked.

"The servants will shoo them out in the morning," Lady Avicia said, flushed with the success of her surprise.

When he was sated with food and wine, Edward sat back in his chair with a satisfied groan.

"Do you wish more wine, sire?" Lord Hugh asked.

"Perhaps," Jerval said blandly, "Prince Edward will finally tell us his real reason for his visit to Camberley."

Edward grinned at him.

"You know, Jerval, why I am here. I want you to come with me to Tunis, to join King Louis, and fight the heathen in Outremer."

"The Holy Land," Jerval explained quietly to Chandra.

"A crusade," she breathed.

"Aye, my lady," Edward said. "I have taken my vow before God, as have many others. It is a holy cause and we will not fail. We must leave soon, before winter sets in and makes travel impossible. Join me, Jerval, and bring as many men as Camberley can spare."

"How many men does Louis command?" Lord Hugh asked.

"Well over ten thousand. Although our numbers will not be so impressive, together we can crush the Saracens."

"I have heard it said," Jerval said, "that the Saracen sultan, Baibars, commands an army in the hundreds of thousands."

"Aye, 'tis true, but I am convinced, as is King Louis, that our cause will bring the other kings of Christendom to our aid."

"King Louis failed miserably in his first effort," Lord Hugh said sharply. "Captured, ransomed, and released back to France, weak and old before his time."

Eleanor said quietly, "But, my lord, his spirit inspires the most profound loyalty and admiration in Christendom, and fear in its enemies. The Saracens fear us, and our God."

" 'Twill be a costly and arduous venture," Jerval said.

"Aye," Edward agreed, sitting forward. "But think of the glory and honor we will gain in serving God by ridding the Holy Land of the heathen."

"It is a request that I must not answer quickly," Jerval said quietly, closing his hand over Edward's arm.

The talk continued, but Chandra was not listening. She had

never been out of England; indeed, the Scottish border was the farthest she had ever traveled from Croyland. She remembered her father telling her of the mighty Templars, a fierce military order, as skilled in the art of finance as in that of fighting, and of the Saracens, who were threatening the very existence of the Kingdom of Jerusalem. If only she were a man, a knight! To be free to join Prince Edward!

She was pulled from her thoughts by Lord Hugh, who said in a voice fuzzy with wine, "My daughter-in-law is talented, sire. Would you care to hear her perform?"

The talk of the crusade was over. Chandra gazed briefly at Jerval and saw his brow furrowed in thought.

Edward called out, "Aye, let Chandra play and sing, and then I can retire to my bed to dream about her."

"You have eaten so much, my lord," Eleanor said severely, "I wager it is nightmares you'll have!"

Chandra's lyre was fetched and she settled it on her lap, running her fingers lightly over the strings. She sang of King Richard and his final battle with the great Saladin, a song she herself had written. Her eyes sparkled as the notes rose to a crescendo at Richard's victory, then fell muted and sad at the treachery that imprisoned him, far away from England, in the dark dungeons of Leopold of Austria. There was silence for a brief moment when she had finished, then Edward leaned forward in his chair and said, his voice low and serious, "My great-uncle taught the heathen that the Christian God would not be denied, that our Lord makes us strong and brave in battle. I thank you for your tribute."

"Thank you, sire," Chandra said, moved by his words.

"Would that you were part of my retinue, my lady. I vow my knights would willingly die for you."

"I need no defenders, sire," Chandra said, meeting Edward's eyes.

Eustace laughed. "Ah, sire, she is a warrior, do you not remember?"

Edward's bright-blue eyes glittered. "Tell me, then, my lady, what other talents do you possess?"

"I joust, though I do not have a man's strength." She smiled brightly. "And, sire, I should not be surprised if I could best you on the archery range."

Edward looked taken aback, then he threw back his head and gave way to booming laughter.

"A soft, delicate girl best me?" Edward wiped his eyes on his sleeve. "You have much wit, my lady."

"I was not jesting, sire," Chandra said.

"Chandra!"

She twisted about to see her husband's face, his eyes narrowed with anger. She tensed, lowering her eyes to her slippers. She had not meant to flout him.

Jerval rose abruptly to his feet, his hand closing tightly about Chandra's arm. "My wife is tired, my lord."

"And you, my lord," Eleanor said severely to her husband, "have drunk too much wine."

Chandra saw a sea of perturbed faces, and she slowly rose from her chair to stand beside her husband. It is not fair, she thought, tears of anger and frustration stinging her eyes.

"Nay," Edward said, his eyes resting with laughter on Chandra's face. He rose and slowly pulled a heavy emerald ring from his finger. "If you, my lady, can indeed beat me, the ring is yours. And will you, Jerval, give your colors to your wife so she may wear them on her sleeve?"

Chandra heard a gasp from Lady Avicia.

"You will have to accept me in my wife's stead, sire," he said harshly. "My wife has drunk too much to know what she is saying." His fingers tightened over her wrist. "Tell him that it is so, Chandra."

"Indeed, sire," she said, her voice taut, "it is so."

Eleanor tugged on Edward's sleeve, and he leaned down to hear her softly spoken words. When he straightened, he said, "Perhaps, then, my lady, we can speak again on the morrow."

"You bloody, stubborn wench," Jerval growled at her. "Do you delight in making me look foolish, Chandra?"

He had drawn her outside the keep, for there was no privacy within. The moon was a sliver in the night sky, and below in the bailey, Chandra could hear the loud voices of the prince's men mixing with those of Camberley.

"I did not mean to make anyone look foolish, nor did I mean to make you angry, or to flout you!"

"Then why did you do it?"

She rubbed the wrist he had held so tightly. "I . . . it . . . slipped out. I meant no harm. Are you afraid that I could best the prince?"

He stared at her, then thundered, "Do you think it gives

me joy to have my wife bragging like a bloody man? Christ, do you never think?''

''I was not bragging. What is wrong with my pitting my skills against the prince, or anyone else for that matter?''

Jerval turned abruptly away from her, his fists clenched at his sides. ''You will never change, Chandra. I was a fool to believe that you would. At least you have made my decision easier.''

''What decision?''

He did not turn, but gazed upward toward the heavens. ''There is little reason for me to remain at Camberley. I am going to the Holy Land with Edward.''

13

TO AVICIA'S DELIGHT, ELEANOR TOURED even the newly weeded garden the next day. Chandra had supposed that the future queen of England would not involve herself with looms, cooking, or vegetables, but she discovered that Eleanor was not only sincerely interested, she was appallingly knowledgeable.

"Lady Chandra," Eleanor said when Lady Avicia had excused herself to see to the evening meal, "I have heard of your beautiful destrier. Would you show him to me?" She raised her voice a bit and added, "Just the two of us."

As they walked to the stables, Eleanor grinned impishly. "My ladies are so very . . . attentive! At Windsor, it is ever the same—always so many people about."

"I know," Chandra said. "Sometimes it is difficult even to visit the jakes alone."

Eleanor praised Wicket and stroked his glossy mane. "Sir Jerval," she said carefully, "told my lord this morning that he wishes to accompany him on the crusade. You know," she continued, "I, as well as other wives, will be part of the retinue."

She could picture Edward shaking his head and calling her a meddler, and it was true, she supposed. "My lord," she had said against his shoulder late the previous night, "if Sir Jerval leaves his lady in England, it could be several years before they are together again. By that time, they would be strangers. You saw the tension between them."

"So you want the girl with you?" Edward had said, nuzzling her cheek with his chin. "I get the impression that her beautiful hide covers a stubborn streak." He had added, "I would, though, like to see her on the archery range."

"Nay, my love, leave be." She had added on a giggle, "If she is indeed a warrior of sorts, she can help to protect me in Outremer."

Chandra stared for a long moment at Eleanor. "I would give everything I possess to go with you."

" 'Twill not be easy, Chandra. So many make it out to be a romantic adventure, but I have been told by those knights who have been to Jerusalem that it is wretchedly hot, the people filled with disease, and the battles cruel and bloody. It is dangerous, for all of us."

"I do not care," Chandra said. A shadow darkened her eyes, and she said in a forlorn voice, "I think that my husband will not wish it."

"Sir Jerval, once my lord has spoken to him, will agree to your coming." She shrugged her elegant shoulders. "Now that it is all settled, I must tell that you that we will leave shortly to meet King Louis in Tunis. First, of course, you and Sir Jerval will come to Windsor to take the cross and discuss preparations."

"I thank you with all my heart, my lady."

Eleanor cocked her head to one side. "Could you really best Prince Edward in archery?"

Chandra's dimple deepened. "I am quite good, you know."

"Aye, I imagined it to be so. Now, Chandra, I shall speak to Lady Avicia, and tell her the good news."

Chandra stood quietly in the dim-lit stable after Eleanor had left her, stroking Wicket's shining mane.

"Well, my lady," a silky voice sounded behind her, "at last I have you to myself."

Chandra turned slowly to face Eustace. "I bid you good day, Sir Eustace," she said coolly. "Is there something you require?"

Eustace smiled widely. "It is but the start of a good day, my lady," he said in a caressing voice. "Nay, Chandra, do not leave. I have been watching you, and I have seen you blush prettily at my gaze. I know what you have been asking me with your lovely eyes."

He took a purposeful step toward her, and Chandra answered him quickly, "If you were talented enough to read messages in my eyes, Sir Eustace," she said, "you would know that they regard you only as my husband's kinsman."

"On no, my lady," Eustace said confidently. "I see you regard your proud husband coldly, but I doubt not that you spread your lovely thighs for him in his bed. Trust me to give you more pleasure than he can."

For a moment, Chandra was stunned at his words. She had little experience with lecherous men, and was at first disbelieving that her calm dismissal had not convinced him. She shrugged her shoulders and said in an indifferent voice, "If I wanted a man, Sir Eustace, I fear you would be one of the last in my mind."

His face turned a mottled red. "You teasing little whore," he growled at her. "You brag about your warrior skills, and all the while what you want is a man to toss up your gowns."

Chandra felt anger surge through her at his insult. "Really, Sir Eustace, you are in the stables. The pigsty is beyond the cooking sheds."

She saw that his hands were fisted at his sides, and quickly walked toward the stable door. She heard him move after her, and paused a moment, refusing to let him see her fear. "Do not forget, Sir Eustace, that you are at Camberley. If Jerval would not kill you for your insolence to me, rest assured that I would."

"You are the insolent one, my lady," she heard him hiss angrily behind her, "and you may be certain that you will regret it." She broke into a run, stopping only when she reached the keep. She realized she was trembling.

"You will not have to be near me," Chandra said to Jerval in a clipped voice. "Indeed, you will not have to speak to me, if it is your wish."

"That is not the point!" He ran his hand through his hair, muttering curses against Edward. Christ, he had finally made up his mind to leave England, and to leave Chandra. He had lain awake throughout the night, listening to her gentle breathing, knowing that he would ache for the sight of her once he had left, yet knowing his attempts to reconcile her to him had failed miserably. Now he would have to bear her company, and bear her coldness toward him.

"I am prepared to be useful to you, Jerval," he heard her say in a surprisingly conciliating voice. "I will mend your clothes, see that your armor is not rusted, cook—"

"I am taking Lambert to see to my arms. Aye, and the first battle, I will have to tie you down to keep you safe!"

"I—I swear upon my honor that I will never seek to fight with you."

"Women have no honor!"

She stiffened. "I have never lied to you, Jerval, never."

"No, I suppose you have not," he admitted. "It would appear that I have little choice in the matter in any case. Why do you wish it, Chandra? I cannot believe that you wish for my company any more than I do for yours."

"I want to see other lands, other peoples. If I do not go with you, I will never see anything but the north of England all of my life."

"And you are willing even to put up with your husband to get what you want?"

She turned away, not answering him. "I must go now, Jerval. Your mother and father are not yet reconciled to our both going. I beg you to speak to them. There is so much to be done before we leave for Windsor."

The journey to Windsor would occupy the better part of four days, Chandra was told. Although Lord Hugh sent a dozen men-at-arms to protect them on their journey to Windsor, Chandra was the only woman in the troop, a circumstance that left her much to herself. She found the hours in the saddle restful after the two weeks of frantic preparation at Camberley, particularly with the weather blessedly hot and dry. She stretched in the saddle, swiveling out of habit to look back at the long line of baggage mules plodding behind the men. They had with them enough to furnish a small keep: cooking utensils, dried herbs from the garden, barrels of flour and wheat, sheets, blankets, even bars of soap. Lambert, excited and talkative, rode beside Jerval. Rolfe and Arnolf rode behind, with Eustace and his four men bringing up the rear.

Their leavetaking had been protracted. Mary and Mark had traveled from Oldham to see them off. Mary, her belly gently rounded, wiped her eyes as she hugged Chandra. "You will not be here to see my babe," she had said. "Pray, Chandra, that it will be a girl."

Never, Chandra thought, was a girl child so fervently wished for. "We will send letters, though I have no idea if they will ever reach you."

Lady Alice showed no signs of ever wanting to leave Camberley, and Lady Avicia seemed quite pleased to keep her with her. "It will be lonely, after all," Avicia had announced, "and Alice is a good girl, and quite sensible."

To Chandra's surprise, her mother-in-law suddenly embraced her, and whispered urgently, "Take care of my son, Chandra. Promise me that you will not let him be harmed." Chandra wondered how the devil she could keep such a promise, though she had solemnly vowed it. She had also written her father, her first letter to him since arriving at Camberley. When they had left, there had been no reply.

She was drawn from her thoughts when Jerval reined in beside her. "We are near to Oxford," he said, "and will be staying with Lord and Lady Huntington, at their manor house, Caxton."

"Thank you for telling me, my lord," Chandra said. "I will ensure that all our baggage is safely secured for the night."

He nodded, and turned Pith back to again join the men. It was like Jerval recently, she thought, to be polite to her, yet distant. He had spent most of his time with the men since they left Camberley, as if oblivious of her. She knew he did not wish her to be with him, that he was still smarting from Edward's interference, but she told herself again she would be no bother to him, that he would not come to dislike her more. She was relieved at his behavior, for since they had finally left Camberley, he had at least not gazed at her at night with that leashed hunger in his eyes.

She caught Eustace's dark eyes, and turned quickly away from his brooding stare. How dare he, she raged silently, be angry at her for spurning his ridiculous advances! If only he had not accompanied them to Windsor! He would be with them in the Holy Land too, she knew, but sooner or later, he would get over his wounded man's vanity. She fastened her gaze on the bright summer flowers along the side of the road and determined to admire them.

Chandra had already forgotten the thick-lipped Lord Huntington when they neared Windsor. She drew in her breath at the sight of the royal fortress, sprawled atop a gentle rise, its thick walls following the ridge of the escarpment beside the Thames. The village of Windsor lay at the base of a gentle slope below the castle.

"Look yon, Chandra," Jerval said, riding up beside her. "That is the Round Tower, the main stronghold of the castle built by King Henry II a century ago. It was built on the same spot as the original wooden structure put up by the Conqueror.

In King John's day, the castle was attacked over a period of three months, and there was serious damage done to the walls. 'Twas likely only the death of John that saved the castle.'' He smiled, and Chandra knew his excitement was as great as hers, great enough, she thought, to make him forget that she was the last person on earth he wanted with him.

"You wonder about Mother's passion for luxury. Wait until you see the king's chambers—all carpets and tapestries and beautiful furniture.'' She followed his waving hand. "You see the thick forest yon? 'Tis the favorite hunting ground for Prince Edward and the nobles who visit Windsor.''

Chandra was listening with but half an ear, her attention on the huge circular tower, its massive stone a soft brown-gold in the sunlight. As they drew nearer, she saw that the huge inner courtyard swarmed with people of all stations, mules piled high with baggage, and the king's guards, directing peasants and nobles alike. It was in this stream that they took their place. One of the guards was assigned to escort them to the Upper Ward, to the domestic apartments of the king and his family.

"It has been five years since I was here,'' Jerval said to Chandra as they made their way up the wide stone steps into the tower. The huge hall into which they were shown shimmered with rich tapestries, and their footsteps were noiseless on the thick carpets. Servants were everywhere, carrying trays covered with food and drink for the king's guests. To Chandra's pleasure, Prince Edward, Princess Eleanor at his side, came forward from an antechamber, a wide smile of welcome on his face, his hand extended. After their greetings, Jerval and Edward left Chandra and Eleanor to meet with some other nobles.

"Remember my telling you that Windsor was like a rabbit warren,'' Eleanor said, smiling. "There is not a moment's peace, or privacy, particularly now.''

Chandra felt suddenly like a dirty peasant in her travel-stained clothes, facing the resplendent Eleanor. Her gown was a pale yellow and embroidered with pearls. The wimple that framed her lovely face was of the same yellow, and studded with rubies.

"I have never seen anything like it,'' Chandra said with simple awe. "I had not imagined that any residence, even the king's, could be so grand.''

Eleanor suddenly leaned toward her and whispered in her ear like a naughty child, "I am so glad that you are here! My ladies are driving me frantic with their dithering and their complaints, except, of course, for Joanna. You will like her, I think."

Chandra did not have time to ask who Joanna was, for Eleanor was smiling at someone standing behind her. "My lord," Eleanor said, in the formal voice that Chandra would soon learn to know.

Chandra turned and found herself looking up into Graelam de Moreton's dark face.

"I know, Lord Graelam, that you had wished to make Lady Chandra your wife. However, since it was not God's will, I trust that you will greet each other as friends."

"Indeed, my lady, Lord Graelem and I met but a short time ago," Chandra said in a clear voice, "but I had little opportunity to speak to him then."

Graelam chuckled, despite himself. "You are as you were, my lady," he said.

Eleanor said suddenly, "There is Rayna waving to me— one of my children's nurses. I must see what is the matter."

To Chandra's consternation, Eleanor slipped gracefully away from them.

"If it is possible, you have grown more beautiful, Chandra."

"Your adder's tongue coated with honey does not please me, my lord."

"My lady's tongue is still thorny, I see. Yet your eyes hold fear of me. If I could, I would draw you away from all these cursed people."

" 'Twould have to be by force, Graelam."

"Aye," he said softly, "by force. Sir Jerval has quite a reputation," he said abruptly, "both as a warrior and a lover. It is still only your bed that he seeks?"

"I would have thought, my lord, that you would have learned from your . . . expensive lesson," Chandra said, her voice low and taut, "but since it appears that you have not, I would wish that you would remember where you are, and cease boring me."

He laughed, but she could sense coiled anger in him beneath his rich clothing. His long surcoat was of black velvet, the wide sleeves lined with gray ermine.

"Do you visit Windsor often?" she asked.

"The prince and I grew to manhood together, fought together, and tumbled maids together, until, of course, his marriage to the lovely Eleanor. Aye, I am here occasionally. The hunting is excellent." He paused a moment, his black brows drawing nearly together over his dark eyes. "I go with Edward on his crusade, as, I hear, do you, my lady, with your husband. You have no reason to fear me, Chandra."

"You needn't concern yourself with my wife's fears, Lord Graelam." Chandra felt Jerval's hand close over her arm like a vise. As they glared at each other, they looked like two dogs, two huge mongrels, fighting over a bone. She could not help herself, and giggled.

Jerval's hand tightened, and he pulled her back against his chest.

Prince Edward came up behind Jerval and clapped him on the shoulder. "Ah, the two of you have discovered each other," he said easily.

"My lady," Edward said smoothly to Chandra, "I think Eleanor is looking for you. Ennis," he called to a page near his elbow, "take Lady Chandra to the princess."

"I am not a bone," Chandra said quite clearly, and pulled her numb arm free of her husband's hold. "Sire," she said, inclining her head. She walked away with the page, her head high.

"I am pleased for the first time," Edward said quietly, "that my father forbids tourneys, for I would wager that I would have one fewer knight to join me in the Holy Land. Leave be, Graelam; that is my wish and my command. Lady Chandra is Jerval's wife before God, and will remain so. If you want to break bones and crush heads, there will be ample opportunity, I vow."

At the men's continued taut silence, Edward said sternly, "You will keep your jealousies to yourselves, my lords. Graelam, England abounds with lovely ladies, and many of them are here." He slapped Graelam's rigid shoulders. "Come, I will introduce you to Lord Remy's niece."

Jerval's eyes followed the darkly handsome Graelam de Moreton, as if he were alone with him in the room, though every moment someone brushed his sleeve in passing. He was not jealous, he told himself, he simply did not wish Chandra to make a spectacle of herself in the middle of the king's court. Perchance, he thought, he believed that his wife might have changed her mind about Graelam, might have gazed at him with new eyes, might have preferred him to— He made a growling sound deep in his throat, caught the winsome smile of a lovely, dark-haired lady whose sloe eyes gave him a clear invitation, and made his way with angry confidence to where the woman stood.

The great banqueting hall at Windsor was ablaze with light. The mammoth trestle tables were weighted down with baked pigs, sides of beef, pheasants, heron, and peacocks with their tail feathers standing high and colorful. Those guests of high rank, the de Vernons among them, sat on cushioned chairs and ate off plates of thick mottled silver. Chandra fingered the embroidered tablecloth and smiled, knowing that her mother-in-law would be memorizing the rich pattern to reproduce it for Camberley.

King Henry and Queen Eleanor sat in splendor upon a raised dais, Prince Edward and Princess Eleanor flanking them. Chandra looked with some disapointment upon King Henry. He was old, his hair as white as snow, but still thick. He was bent and small, and beside his son he appeared a dwarf. Queen Eleanor, to Chandra's surprise, looked rather common. Her dark hair was streaked with white, and she had at least three chins. If she eats like this every day, Chandra thought, she is fortunate that she is still able to walk.

"If I remember," Jerval said at Chandra's elbow, "you had nothing but disdain for the so-called opulence of Camberley. What say you of the king's tastes?"

"I cannot find words," Chandra replied. "There is so much of everything, and all of it is gold and silver."

"Windsor has achieved this grandeur only in the last thirty or so years. It is all Henry's doing."

"There is so much food," Chandra said on a smile, "I do not know where to begin. Indeed, just looking at all of this makes my appetite flee."

"You like pheasant," he said, and carved her a slice of breast.

Chandra began to wonder at his good humor. She remembered she had seen a handsome dark-haired woman smiling up at Jerval, her soft lips parted, her intention quite clear. She took several bites of the pheasant, finding it delicious. She asked him sweetly about his accommodations, and they passed the evening discussing the nobles who sat about the long trestle tables.

When the gluttonous supper was ended, an army of servants cleared away the remains and replaced them with huge trays of sweetmeats and more wine, rich sweet wines from Provence, Queen Eleanor's native land. The minstrels were summoned, then a troop of jongleurs imported to Windsor for the occasion from Rheims. It was late in the evening when the herald who stood behind the king tapped his ornately carved staff for quiet in the hall.

King Henry rose slowly from his chair, like the old man he was, Chandra thought, but she forgot his look of fragility when he spoke. It was a king's voice, deep, vigorous, and oddly compelling.

"We have labored long and with great singleness of purpose," he said, his voice filling the huge hall, "in God's work. We have long admired and blessed King Louis, a saintly man who has dedicated his life to the freeing of the Holy Land from the heathen paynim. I am old now, too old to join him in God's great mission." He turned to smile fleetingly down at his son. "My hopes and prayers, nay, the prayers of every pious man in Christendom, will go with you, and God in his infinite mercy and wisdom will protect you and give you the strength to cleanse the Kingdom of Jerusalem of the heathen who even now pray to their pagan gods to save them from Christ's army.

"We are all wretched creatures whose only worth lies in our humility before God. You are his soldiers. Be worthy of God's trust and the nobility of our cause."

Chandra felt a tremor of anger ripple through the crowd as Henry spoke of the atrocities committed by the Saracens in their plunder of Christian cities and castles in the Holy Land. "The paynim," he concluded, "must be destroyed. With God's grace it will be done."

There was a long moment of silence. Prince Edward rose slowly, lightly touched his hand to his father's shoulder, and spoke. "Our army for God will be small—but a thousand men will leave England's shores to undertake our great mission. Hugh of Cyprus was elected two years ago by the High Court of Acre as king of Jerusalem, but he has been a king in name only. He has been helpless against the heathen Saracens and their sultan, Baibars of Egypt, who have ravaged and plundered the Holy Land. Even Antioch herself is now rubble and ashes, her people butchered or enslaved.

"Even while we speak, Christians are fighting Christians, for they have no unity, no common bond. We will, with our beloved king of France, Louis, and his army, join together, and bring all Christians together as one. Together"—Edward raised his fisted hand—"we will crush the infidel!"

A loud cheer went up in the hall, and Chandra studied the faces of the men around the tables, men who had chosen to take the cross. She saw in their eyes something beyond a lust for battle and glory, something she had not seen before.

Prince Edward walked to the canopied high-backed chair from which the Legate Ottobuone, bowed in his heavy white-and-crimson robes, was now rising, a black-gowned priest at his side. Edward knelt before him and kissed the heavy golden cross in his aged hands.

The Legate Ottobuone gave Edward his hand to rise, and turned slowly to face the company. He had no need to preach the crusade, for he had already done so with such energy several years before that he had moved Prince Edward, Henry of Almaine, and William de Valence to take the cross publicly. He gazed solemnly now upon the men Edward had cajoled to join him, and the men who had paid enormous sums to finance the crusade. His lips moved in silent prayer, thanking God that at last the saintly Louis, so inept a soldier, would have Prince Edward with him. There would be no disaster this time, for Edward was a soldier.

He began to speak softly, intoning in Latin the blessing of God upon his apostles, and the nobles bowed their heads in prayer. Slowly, he raised the heavy golden cross with both hands before him. He nodded to the scribe who stood beside him, and as he read the names of the nobles aloud, each man rose and walked solemnly to stand before him.

Ottobuone let his voice carry to every corner of the hall. "Do you swear by almighty God to be his soldiers, to fight with honor and might, to give your lives in his keeping, to scourge the Holy Land of the pagan corruption?"

There was a low rumbling murmur among the men as they answered, "Aye, I swear before God!"

Jerval fell to his knees before Ottobuone, his head bowed. He directed his loyalty through Edward to God, whose valiant purpose was to be made possible through him. He felt the legate's heavy golden cross lie heavily on his shoulder for a moment, before it moved to Thomas de Clare, on his knees beside him. When finally he rose, his eyes met Graelam de Moreton's, and he knew that whatever Graelam's motives were, he had shared the holy moment.

"God's grace go with all of you," Ottobuone said. He made the sign of the cross, then walked upright and stately from the hall. Chandra drew a deep breath, bowing her head. She knew that she would never forget, as long as she lived, her sense of God's presence, like a living force lighting the faces of all those about her. She felt a moment of guilt, for she knew that her presence here was not inspired by God, but by her own unworthy desires.

In early August, Edward took leave of his father, who bestowed on him the cross which he had hoped himself to carry against the Saracens. He commended his children to the care of his uncle, Richard of Cornwall, a tall, darkly silent man, who looked to Chandra more kingly than did the aged Henry.

When at last they arrived at Portsmouth, Chandra saw for the first time the ship that would carry them and all their belongings to Tunis, moored with the other ships in the harbor, barges, their bellies wide to carry the horses and most of the supplies, and the huge men-of-war that would surround the fleet, filled with soldiers. She gulped and touched her hand to Jerval's sleeve.

"Have you never been on the sea?"

She shook her head. "Nay," she said. "It looks endless."

" 'Twill be a long journey," Jerval said, "but do not fear. The Legate Ottobuone would lose all credit were God to let us drown."

Their ship seemed vast to Chandra, almost one hundred feet long, Jerval told her, in the shape of the old Viking boats, its one massive sail set on the single mast at its center. The fore and stern castles rose thirty feet above the hull. Like castles on the land, Jerval explained to her, they were fitted with embrasures through which archers could shoot, with merlons to protect them. Extending from the castles was a wooden ceiling supported by posts that would provide them shelter on the long voyage. There was space for some sixty rowers lining the belly of the ship, and they, Chandra saw, would have no cover.

She was introduced to Payn de Chaworth and his wife, Joanna, who were to sail with them to Tunis, with Payn's two knights and six men-at-arms. Payn de Chaworth was a short, wiry man, older than Jerval by some ten years, a longtime friend of Richard of Cornwall's. Joanna was but two years older than Chandra, plump, dark-haired, and forever optimistic, a ready laugh on her full lips.

Fifty of Prince Edward's soldiers would journey with them on the ship, their leader a man called Orford, a seasoned veteran with a leathery face and a voice that boomed from one end of the ship to the other. Their captain was Nevin, a grizzled seaman from Normandy. Payn, Jerval, Joanna, and Chandra were settled in a small space beneath the forecastle, near the squawking chickens and kegs of fresh water. There was a wooden bucket for slops and a thick woolen curtain that provided them their only privacy.

"Well," Joanna said brightly, surveying their cramped quarters, "this is quite a change from Windsor!" She shot an impish grin toward her husband and whispered to Chandra, "My poor Payn must needs forget the making of his son, at least until we reach Tunis."

Neither would she herself have to fear Jerval's scrutiny when night fell, Chandra thought. There was nothing for her to fear, save the memories that pierced her when she least expected it. Tunis. Chandra rolled the strange-sounding name about her tongue. The city was not Christian, but even now, King Louis was converting the bey to the faith. She breathed in the salty air and stared up at the two archers high above her in the forecastle.

She heard the captain bellow orders to the rowers and watched the huge single sail belly out with wind. She felt only elation as the vast fleet drew away from the shores of England.

Outremer

Love hath so long possessed me for his own
And made his lordship so familiar.

—Dante, *La Vita Nuova*

14

"YOU HAVE A SPRINKLING OF freckles," Jerval said. He dropped to his knee beside Chandra and touched his finger to her nose.

"Aye, I look like dirty sand all over." She was sitting cross-legged on the forecastle beside Boren the archer, her elbows holding a parchment down against the stiff breeze.

"Another letter?"

She nodded. " 'Tis foolish, but at least they keep everything fresh in my mind."

She crinkled her eyes into the sun and looked up at him, fully bearded and deeply tanned. "You look like a Viking," she said. "Would you like me to trim your beard?"

"Since I can't be sweet-smelling," he grinned, shrugging, "I might as well look presentable." He sat cross-legged in front of her, drew his dagger from his belt, and pressed its bone handle into her palm.

"Payn tells me you should not spend so much of your time with the archers up here on the forecastle. He thinks you distract the rowers."

Chandra smiled, then furrowed her brow in concentration as she sheared away an uneven curl of his beard. "Those poor fellows need some distraction. If I make them forget their back-breaking job and their aching muscles, then I must be a gift from God."

"That," Jerval said with formidable severity, "is just what I told Payn. You have made the long days more bearable, Chandra."

"It is Rolfe who deserves your compliment, Jerval," she said. "Have you heard the stories he's been telling? 'Tis quite a hero you have become, my great bearded lord. The Sultan Baibars would quake if he heard how brave and fierce you are." She smoothed down his thick bronze beard and sat back on her heels to regard her handiwork. "Much better," she said. "Your dagger, my lord."

Jerval looked at the clumps of hair scattered on the deck. "Christ, I must have looked fierce indeed."

She sprawled upon her stomach beside him and propped her head in her hands. "I must agree with Joanna. I am so tired of this infernal ship, tired of my own smell—and yours—and tired of eating what the servants would not touch back home."

"Then you will like the surprise I have for you. Nevin says that we should be sighting Tunis this morning."

Chandra lurched up to her knees in excitement and crawled to the edge of the forecastle. Boren merely shook his head, smiling down at her, and stepped aside.

Chandra stared into the horizon toward a sun-bathed point of barren land, white and hazy through the shimmering waves of heat. "I do not see anything," she grumbled.

"Patience, Chandra."

"Look, Jerval," she called. "The water is like blue glass. You can see your reflection." She stared down at herself in astonishment. "I don't look like me at all. I look like a blackamoor."

Nay, Jerval thought, joining her at the railing, she looked like a dirty but happy child, but she was thin, too thin.

"If you are through admiring yourself, look yon."

She followed his pointing finger. "That, if I'm not mistaken, is Tunis," he said.

There was a growing swell of noise from the soldiers, and shouts suddenly rang out, not only from their ship, but from the man-of-war that sailed off their bow. She strained her eyes through the haze in the distance, but it was several minutes before she could be sure she saw the sprawling mass of buildings that was the city.

"Look, Jerval, at those tall towers with the odd onion-shaped domes. Whatever are they?"

"They are called minarets," Jerval said. "The Moslem religious men climb to their tops to call the people to prayer."

"Did Rolfe tell you that?" she asked suspiciously.

"Nay, I had it from Nevin."

Their ship sailed close in to the rest of the fleet as they neared the outjutting point of land. Chandra saw one of the soldiers hurl a bag of spoiled flour overboard and shout, "Food at last!"

"You'll kill the fish!" someone answered him.

"At last, indeed," she breathed. "I think," she added, scratching her arm, "that the chickens had fleas."

He saw the wild excitement in her eyes and smiled. "I for one never wish to see another hen as long as I live," he said, and pulled her to her feet. "I must join the men soon, Chandra. You will find Joanna and stay with her."

"By God," Nevin said when they were finally in sight of the harbor, "behold all the ships! With King Louis with us, we will make a fearsome sight when we sail into Acre!"

Their ship eased behind a huge man-of-war, and the rowers held to a narrow channel between the French ships. Chandra could make out scores of men waving wildly toward them from the rough wooden docks. Their ship scraped an anchor line as they neared the docks, and Nevin's fierce shouts rang out over the soldiers' cheering.

It took several hours for their ship to take its turn at the dock. Chandra fidgeted about impatiently as she waited with Joanna on the forecastle. They could see clustered buildings, low stone huts separated by narrow alleyways, rising behind the dock. From their vantage point, it seemed that all of Tunis was French soldiers, loitering about on the docks, waving and shouting toward the English ships.

"Everything looks so very strange," Joanna whispered to Chandra when they finally stepped onto the rolling dock.

"Aye," Chandra whispered back. They were flanked by a dozen soldiers, Rolfe and Lambert at their head. After weeks at sea, the noise made her ears ring, and her feet were none too steady on land. Outside their line of soldiers, she saw a knot of Moslem men ogling them, most of them short and wiry, with faces dark almost to blackness. They were dressed in baggy white wool trousers and loose shirts, their heads wrapped in thick white turbans. Their black eyes looked insolent and angry, and Chandra felt a quiver of fear. Skinny-legged children, many of them naked, darted out between their legs, yelling and pointing wildly toward her and Joanna.

"They hate us," Joanna said, shuddering. "Look, Chandra, at the women."

Chandra looked toward a small knot of women who stood hunched like a flock of black crows in an open doorway.

Unlike the men, they were covered from head to toe in black, even their faces shrouded with thin black veils.

"I feel naked compared to them," Joanna said, touching her fingers to her face.

"I wonder why they are all covered up like . . . dead people. Surely that black must be terribly hot."

"My lady," Rolfe cried, shoving the men aside to reach her. "The king is dead!"

Chandra looked at him stupidly.

"King Louis—he died over a month ago of the stomach flux! All these soldiers and ships belong to King Charles of Sicily."

Poor Edward, she thought. He had dreamed of joining with the sainted Louis on the crusade. "Who is King Charles?" was all she could think to ask.

"King Louis's youngest brother. Sir Jerval has asked me to escort you to King Charles's encampment outside the city. He said he would join you as soon as he could."

Joanna clasped her hands over her plump bosom and moaned, "What will happen to us now?"

Bathed and gowned, Chandra paced the narrow width of the tent, awaiting Jerval's return. She had sent away the Moslem slave woman after her blessed bath, a gift, Rolfe told her, from the bey. She opened the tent flap and stepped outside, hoping for a breeze from the sea, but she soon retreated within, for the sun was beating down mercilessly upon the treeless camp. For as far as she could see toward the sea, small, stiff-topped tents were being raised over the rocky terrain. English soldiers were still arriving, their belongings slung over their shoulders. Chandra could make out Edward's pavilion, larger by far than the other tents, set atop a small rise. His personal guard, some dozen soldiers dressed in his blue-and-white livery, were clearing a defensive perimeter about his pavilion.

Chandra stared at Jerval in surprise when he strode into the tent. His beard was gone and he was dressed in a long robe of white linen, hemmed with purple.

"What happened to you?"

"The bey provided all of us baths and clothing. I begin to feel human again."

"King Louis," she said. "Rolfe said he was dead."

Jerval ran a distracted hand through his thick hair. "Aye, and Edward is bowed with grief. I left him with King Charles."

"What will happen?" she asked.

He smiled, as if seeing her for the first time. "I had forgotten how you look with your hair loose. Were you also allotted a slave?"

She nodded and shook her head, feeling soft waves of hair caress her cheeks, a rueful grin on her lips, thankful to be free of the dirty braid that had hung down her back during the long weeks at sea.

"We go to a banquet at the bey's palace, in Edward's honor. The bey is anxious to be rid of us all, both English and French. We will likely leave Tunis very soon."

"Where will we go?"

"To Sicily for the winter. Edward will try to persuade King Charles to take up his brother's holy cause, though I doubt he will succeed. Charles has not admitted it, but there are rumors that he has signed a treaty with Sultan Baibars." Jerval watched her frown as she considered what he had said. He found himself staring at her for a long moment, uncertain if he should allow her to accompany him through the city to the bey's palace. He had seen few Moslem women, and those he had passed had been heavily veiled and eerily silent, their eyes downcast. He closed his hand briefly over the sword strapped at his side.

"Are you ready?" he asked abruptly.

"To leave Tunis?"

"Nay, little jester," he said, smiling, "ready for a banquet, with real food."

"Have you seen Eleanor?"

"Aye, I walked through the encampment with Edward to his pavilion." He added on a smile, "Eleanor is with child. His ship had some privacy, I gather."

"A child! How terrible for her! Is she very ill?"

Jerval cocked his head at her. "She is quite well and very happy, as is Edward. To carry and bear a child is not the end of the world, Chandra."

She flushed. "I—I did not mean to say . . . it is just that it must have been terrible for Eleanor aboard their ship. I . . . don't wish her to be ill."

"I know," he said at last, not wishing to cause her further embarrassment. "Come, it is time to leave."

Rolfe, Lambert, and Arnolf escorted them to the camp perimeter, where they were met by a turbaned man, short and black-bearded, who was to guide them through the city to the palace. He looked curiously at Chandra, but said nothing. The streets were a labyrinth of narrow, rutted paths, with low stone houses on either side, piles of garbage climbing their dusty walls. Chandra felt her belly knot at the overpowering stench.

"The peasants do not bury their dead animals," their Moslem guide said calmly. "The ground is too hard."

"The bey's palace is much more appealing," Jerval said.

They passed a group of Moslem men, smoking pipes that gave off a sickeningly sweet smell. Chandra felt their eyes raking over her. One of the men stepped toward her, smiled at her insolently, and spat. His spittle landed inches from the hem of her gown.

Jerval's hand clapped to his sword scabbard, and he growled a curse.

"Do not, my lord," the Moslem said. "You are strangers here. A woman, a Moslem woman, is not allowed to flaunt herself unveiled in the streets." He turned and said something in harsh, guttural sounds to the man who had spat at her. The man backed away, but Chandra saw contempt in his black eyes. She found that she was trembling, and she drew closer to Jerval. He closed his hand protectively over her arm.

"Place your hand here, Chandra," Eleanor said. "That's right. Do you feel the babe?"

A small foot kicked against Chandra's palm. She raised surprised eyes to Eleanor. "Does that not hurt you?"

"Nay," Eleanor laughed, "but sometimes it is difficult to sleep, with the little one so active. Edward delights in pressing his ear to my belly and telling me he can hear the babe's heartbeat. You will see, Chandra, what a wonder it is when you carry Jerval's child."

Chandra turned abruptly away and stared out over the palace grounds toward the beautiful city of Palermo below. She breathed in the sweet scent of the flowers that splashed their bright colors over the hillside.

"Even the market stalls are sweet-smelling," she said after a moment to Eleanor.

Eleanor leaned back against the soft, gold-embroidered

cushions and regarded Chandra quietly for a moment. She sensed that Chandra was bored and restless, just like the men, she thought, smiling to herself. Although King Charles was gracious and surrounded them with every luxury, Edward and the men itched to be gone from Sicily, for it was becoming clear that Charles was unwilling to accompany them to Palestine. She sighed as Chandra rose and began to pace the balcony.

"You are thin, Chandra," she said, resting her hands on her rounded belly. "And pale. Jerval is concerned for you."

"Jerval should not be surprised that I am pale, Eleanor. I have been allowed to ride out only once into the hills, and then only in the company of two dozen soldiers."

"It is for your own safety," Eleanor said reasonably. "The peasants grow more discontent by the year, I'm told, with their French masters. Even the men ride out armed. Have you spoken to Jerval? He would arrange for you be out of doors more often, if it is your wish."

Chandra hunched her shoulders irritably. "Nay, he is too busy with Payn, Henry, Roger, Thomas, and, of course, Edward."

"Men," Eleanor said, smiling, "cannot seem to be happy unless they are busy with something, and now they are fighting, or at least preparing to fight. I feel sorry for them in a way, for when they are wounded, or old, and can no longer fight, they grow bored and think themselves useless. There are few men I have known who have found the serenity that women seem to possess naturally. Most women, that is," she added on a smile. "My dear father-in-law is an exception. He much prefers directing the architects in Westminster Abbey or playing with his grandchildren."

Chandra remembered her father cursing King Henry for bleeding his subjects to the point of rebellion to fund his building, but let it pass.

"Do you know," Eleanor continued, "that I was married to my lord when I was but ten years old, and he but a young, long-legged lad? How the years have flown by! I can still remember my father, Ferdinand, soothing me, telling me about my new home and my future family, all in a language that no longer comes easily to me." She drew a blood-red hibiscus to her nose and sniffed the sweet fragrance. "I came to England as a child, and was fortunate enough to love my husband the moment I saw him. It is odd to be a wife when one is not yet even a girl, but thus it was."

Chandra cocked her head to one side. "I had not thought of it before," she said, "but even you had no choices. You were bartered for political gain. What if you had not loved Edward?"

"Then my life would be a series of events with no particular sorrows and no particular joys. But of course, even if a lady does not care for her husband, she still has her children. What if Edward had taken me into grave dislike? He had no more choice than did I, you know."

"But it is fathers, Eleanor," Chandra said sharply, "who choose their daughters' husbands, and then the husbands who rule their wives just as did their fathers. And what of all the widows in England whose husbands are scarce laid under the earth before another man comes to claim them, despite their wishes? Why should they at least not have the right of choice?"

Eleanor arched a sleek black brow. "Choice? It is only when I see a black-veiled Moslem woman, drawn back with her head bent in the shadow of her husband, that I see a woman with no choices, no freedom. She is the slave, not you or I."

"Even our own husbands can beat their wives, if they wish."

"Has Jerval ever beaten you?"

"Nay, but still he thinks himself my lord, and he is angry if I disobey him."

"That is something I have not seen." Since Camberley, she added silently to herself.

"We—we have had no reason to disagree, lately. But you know well, Eleanor, that if we do disagree, I must bend to him in all things."

"When you discover a perfect world, dear child," Eleanor said wryly, "I beg you to invite me to visit you. Edward is stronger than I just as Jerval is stronger than you, and it is to them that we must trust our safety, and the safety of our children. We, and not our husbands, are the givers of life. It is through us that life continues."

"But why must we be less than men? Why must we always live in the shadow of their wishes?"

"I have never believed myself less than my lord, nor do I

perceive that Jerval yearns for the cowering, veiled Moslem women. I have my responsibilities, my duties, just as does Edward. Together, we make a whole, and a meaningful life. Our marriage vows bind us, but it is our love and our respect for each other that give us joy. Are you so unhappy, child?''

Chandra shook her head. ''Nay, I have not been so really since we left England.''

''I think Jerval would be happy to hear it. Look yon, Jerval approaches, my lord with him.''

''My lord,'' Eleanor said, rising to greet Edward. He took her hand and pressed her back gently onto the cushions. ''Nay, my love, do not disturb our babe.'' He sank down on a cushion next to his wife and rested his hand on Eleanor's stomach, grinning with masculine pleasure. ''Jerval, when will you fill Chandra's belly? I vow she'll look nearly as beautiful as Eleanor when she is with child.''

''Such things take time, my lord,'' Jerval said evenly.

''You, my lord,'' Eleanor chided him gently, ''seem to take all the credit!''

''I would kill any other man who dared to,'' Edward said.

Chandra jumped suddenly to her feet and said to Jerval, ''Cannot we walk for a while? Along the palace walls?''

Jerval rose gracefully and looked a question at Edward.

''Aye, get you gone, Sir Jerval. Do what you will to bring the roses back into your wife's cheeks.''

As they strolled away along the marble balcony, Chandra heard Eleanor giggle. ''They are so happy, I think,'' she said.

Aye, Jerval thought, because she accepts herself and Edward. Aloud, he said, '' 'Twould seem so.''

They stopped along the balcony wall and Jerval leaned his elbows on the smooth mosaic tiles to look out over the blue Mediterranean. '' 'Tis beautiful—scarce like the winters at Camberley.''

''I have yet to spend a winter at Camberley. Is there much snow?''

''Aye. Three years ago the lake froze. We rubbed wooden planks with duck lard and held races.'' He grinned. ''You should have seen Malton. Arnolf gave him a mighty shove and he went flying over the ice, flailing his arms, screaming for God to save him.'' He turned to face her. ''When we are home, the lake will freeze again. Mayhap,'' he added on a grin, ''you might even win.''

''I am grown so soft I would likely break my neck!'' She thrust her arm toward him and pushed up her loose sleeve. ''Feel—I have scarce any muscle left.''

He closed his fingers about her upper arm and squeezed gently. ''Aye, you are soft, but it is not at all displeasing, at least to me.''

''Take care, Jerval.'' She grinned impishly up at him. ''Else I may be too weak to wield a needle or a cooking pot once we reach the Holy Land.''

''Thank God Rolfe cooks so well, else we would both starve.'' He said abruptly, ''How are you passing your days? I scarce see you.''

''I am much with women. Sometimes I grow so tired of their chatter. And the waiting.''

''Well, I am much with men and grow tired of their talk. Waiting is the same for all of us.''

''Whenever I talk of exercise to Joanna, she looks at me as if I have lost my wits. A turn about her chamber and she is ready to rest!'' She grinned suddenly, and said without thought, ''Do you know that she lies in wait for poor Payn? She wants to have a child, like Eleanor.''

''No wonder I see him smiling so much, and at nothing in particular.'' Poor Payn indeed, he thought. His own months of celibacy had been a trial to him. He awoke some nights so taut with desire that it required all his will not to pull Chandra against him and damn the consequences. But Chandra lost all her easy confidences when they were alone in their bedchamber at night, and her eyes were still frightened and wary whenever he chanced to gaze overlong at her. But she had kept her word to him. Not once since they had left England had she disdained his words, or refused to do as he bid her. He said aloud, ''You have changed since we left England.''

She did not take offense, merely grinned. ''Not once have I had to yell at serving wenches to air the beds, or oversee the making of butter.''

''It is not that, and you know it. You seem more at ease, with yourself, and with me.''

''You,'' she said hesitantly, ''have been very kind.''

''As kind as I was at Croyland before we were wed?''

Her eyes leaped to his face. Such a long time ago it

seemed, yet she knew that what he said was true. "Aye,"
she said slowly, "then and now."

"You know, Chandra, Edward is right."

"About what?" she asked quickly, relieved.

Jerval lightly touched his fingertips to the tendrils of hair
on her forehead and brushed them back. "You would look
beautiful with your belly rounded with child."

She flushed, and he felt her withdraw from him.

"Camberley must have an heir, Chandra."

"Someday," she heard herself babbling, "but not here in a
foreign land! You have told me how dreadfully hot it is in
Palestine, and how dangerous it will be. Eleanor has borne
many children . . . she is used to it!"

He forced a smile to his lips. "You could trust me to keep
you safe, just as Edward will keep Eleanor from danger."
She did not answer him, and he said after a while, "There is
really more to it than that. I cannot remain a celibate. My
body has needs that are becoming more and more difficult to
ignore. I have known no other woman's body since you
became my wife."

She was staring down at her toes, and he clasped her
shoulders until she looked up into his face.

"I desire you, Chandra, but I cannot continue to live together,
yet separate from you." He drew a deep breath, but before he
could finish what was for him a painful ultimatum, he saw
Edward and John de Vescy over her shoulder striding toward
them. He shook his head sadly.

"Edward is awaiting you, my lord," she said, her voice
high and shrill in her relief.

"Indeed you are right," Jerval said harshly. "Undoubtedly
I shall see you later, surrounded by women."

He left her standing alone, staring after him uncertainly.

A silent Sicilian woman had brought Chandra buckets of
steaming, fragrant water for her bath, and at Chandra's distracted wave, she had left her. She sat on an ornately carved
stool in her bedchamber, her legs resting over the side of the
wooden tub, soaping herself as was her custom before rinsing
herself in the clear water. She was thinking of Croyland, of
the days before her marriage, when she had competed with
Jerval in every sport she could devise. She could practically
hear his laughter mingling with hers, hear his voice teasing

her. She had felt a sense of freedom, and of belonging, with him then. Her washcloth slowed its path over her breasts as she remembered watching him riding tall and ramrod-straight in his saddle, his lance held firmly in his strong hand, his eyes bright with concentration as he galloped Pith toward Rolfe on the tiltyard. She remembered the sunlight illuminating the darker golden streaks in his hair the day he had galloped toward her on the promontory. She sighed softly and tried to shake away his words of two days before. He had said nothing of it since, and she prayed that he would not. She could not bear the uncertainty, nor the struggle she saw within him. There was so much to remember, then and now. She preferred the memories of Croyland, pure and gentle, without confusion.

Jerval opened the door of their chamber, grumbling silently at himself for his stupidity. He had forgotten a sheaf of notes Edward needed for discussions with King Charles. He drew to a halt, all thoughts of the notes gone from his mind. Chandra sat naked on a stool beside a wooden tub, her profile toward him, her back arched as she trailed a soapy cloth downward over shoulders. He watched her touch the cloth as would a gentle lover over her nipples. There was a dreamy expression on her face, one that reminded him of that long-ago night at Camberley when he had held her body until her eyes were soft with longing. She threw her head back, showing him the graceful line of her throat. She looked exquisite, her firm breasts thrusting outward, almost too heavy now for her slender frame. His eyes dropped downward to her waist, so slight that he could encircle her with his hands.

She began to hum softly to herself as she rubbed the soapy cloth downward over her belly. When she at last parted her thighs and touched herself, slowly caressing the cloth over her gentle woman's mound, he felt his swelling manhood as a nearly painful ache. At last he recognized the song she was humming, a song of love she herself had written and sung to him, in all innocence, he knew, long ago at Croyland.

His tongue lightly touched his lips as he watched the cloth retreat, leaving the soft, dark golden curls between her thighs naked to his hungry eyes. He remembered the feel of her, the honey taste of her soft flesh.

She rose slowly and leaned over to rinse the cloth in the water and wring it lazily over her body. His eyes swept down her long slender legs, sleek and smooth, endlessly beautiful legs. In that instant, she saw him. For a long, still moment, she simply stared at him, her eyes locked to his, the cloth quiet in her hand.

Jerval forgot everything except the raving desire that was consuming him. He strode to her and closed his hands about her waist, lifting her to him. At the touch of her, he moaned deep in his throat and swept her upward, pressing her against the length of him. He swept his hands over her, reveling in the feel of her, and tugged at the thick knot of hair at the back of her neck, pulling her toward him until he captured her mouth. He buried his face against her throat and breathed in the lavender scent of her slender neck.

"Dear God," he whispered hoarsely against her temple. He found her mouth again and moaned her name against her lips.

Chandra felt the fierce hardness of him against her belly, felt his fingers curving over her hips to find the softness between her thighs. She had felt only surprise at seeing him so suddenly, and when he walked toward her, she saw herself as he must have seen her, languid, her every movement inviting. She weaved him into the soft, incoherent thoughts and memories that had washed through her as she had bathed her body, and her mind and body accepted him, wanted him to touch her. She felt him bend her gently against his strong arm, felt his fingers trembling as they caressed her breast. For a long moment, she felt her body quiver at his touch.

When his hand coursed over her belly, his fingers tangling in the curling wet hair between her thighs, she caught herself, starkly aware that she could still not give herself to him, could not let herself know his possession.

"No, Jerval . . . please!"

"Aye, Chandra," he whispered harshly. "I want you, now, here."

Her words warred with her body, and came as a broken whisper from her throat. "Please, Jerval, do not do this. Please . . . do not—"

His hand stilled. "You want me, Chandra," he said softly against her mouth. "I can feel how warm and wet you are."

"It is from my bath," she babbled, twisting her head away from him. "It is the soap. It is not me!"

Suddenly, she felt him grow very still. He pulled her

tightly against him, so tightly that she could feel the pounding of his heart against her breast. She grew quiet, knowing that he was trying to gain control of himself, trying to calm his raging desire.

Jerval buried his face against her hair. I will not force her, he repeated over and over to himself. I will not see the hatred and fear in her eyes again. Slowly, he loosened his grasp and pushed her away, almost roughly. She stumbled to the tub, leaned over, and grabbed the towel, wrapping it clumsily around her.

She stared at him, standing but an arm's length away from her, his powerful body heaving. She said stupidly, "I was bathing. I thought you were with Edward and the other men. I thought I was alone."

"You were alone until I came in," he managed to say in a near-calm voice. "I had forgotten some papers."

Again, he thought, we are together, yet apart. Her pride would always keep her separate from him. She would always suffer him as her husband, but not as her lover. He felt a great weariness, and turned away from her for a moment. It pained him to see her looking at him so warily, as if he were some sort of monster bent on attacking her.

"Chandra," he said finally, still not looking at her, "do you remember our conversation? I told you that I cannot remain a celibate. I cannot continue living together, yet separate."

"Aye, I remember."

He drew a calming breath at the sound of her taut voice. He turned slowly around to face her. "The next time I see you thus, naked and open, I will take you. I will not be able to stop myself." He smiled grimly as his desire eased. "You cannot give yourself to me as your husband, can you?"

The towel slipped, and she jerked it frantically over her breasts, flushing with embarrassment. It was answer enough.

"Nay, I know that you cannot. Weave me no meaningless excuses." She started at the infinite sadness in his voice. "I will find relief, Chandra."

She stared at him, paling at his words, and the remembered feel of him warred again with the tumbling confusion in her mind. She dropped her gaze. "If that is your wish, my lord," she whispered stiffly. "I . . . please, Jerval!"

He raised his hand to stem her words. "Nay, Chandra, no

more." He looked at her sadly, then turned away and walked to the chest that held his papers. He grasped them tightly in his hand, and said, "We have so much time, yet so little. Return to your bath. There is still soap on your hips." He turned away and strode from their chamber, his arms stiff at his sides.

Chandra lay moaning on her pallet, so ill from the tossing of the sea that she prayed for oblivion. She felt a damp cloth on her forehead and forced her eyes to open. "I want to die," she said.

"Nay, little one," Jerval grinned. "Here, drink some wine."

She did as she was bid, but the wine settled uncomfortably in her stomach.

"Please leave me alone," she whispered in embarrassment. "Don't you feel anything?"

"I cannot be ill," he said. "Who would take care of you?" He settled her back onto some blankets and stroked her shoulders. "The first thing we must do when we reach Acre—other than fight the Saracens—is fatten you up, Chandra."

"You must hate me to speak of food!" she moaned, and doubled over, drawing her knees to her chest.

He rose and looked down at her clammy face, a worried frown furrowing his brow. "I must leave you with Joanna, and don my armor."

"Why?" she asked, suddenly frightened.

"The watch has sighted Acre, and it is under attack by the Saracens," he said quietly. "Our timing could not be better. King Hugh must be within the city walls."

She tried to rise, but he gently pushed her down. "Joanna," he called, "see that she stays quiet."

"Please take care," Chandra whispered.

"You may be certain that I shall," he said.

Chandra cursed softly to herself when Jerval had left her. She had been so excited when they had finally set sail for Acre with the thousand men in Prince Edward's army. Now that it was in sight, she could not even rise to see it. She closed her eyes, remembering how Edward had slowly risen to his feet in King Charles's magnificent banquet hall and kicked the soft pillows upon which he had sat away from him.

"Here me, all of you," he had said in a voice filled with passion. "King Charles has told us why we should not journey to the Holy Land. Now I will tell you that I made an oath before God. If my life is to be forfeit for keeping my holy vow, so be it." He had thrown out his arms, embracing the entire company. "Do what your consciences dictate. I pledge before God that I will go to Acre to fight the paynim if naught but my groom be with me!"

Payn de Chaworth had jumped to his feet and shouted, "You, sire, your groom, and I!"

Soon all were shouting, and Edward, flushed with pleasure, had clasped each of his nobles in his arms, tears in his eyes.

Chandra opened her eyes.

"You will feel better soon," Joanna said. "We are in the calmer waters of the harbor."

"I want to see Acre," Chandra said and pulled herself to her feet.

"Chandra, I promised Jerval to keep you quiet!"

"How can you look so healthy?" Chandra gritted at the plump Joanna. "I will not fall overboard, though I am tempted to end my misery. Are you coming with me?"

"Aye, I would see that Payn is all right."

From a ladder on the forecastle, Chandra looked toward the walled city of Acre. It was the largest city she had ever seen, its long white seaward wall towering over the water, seemingly impenetrable. There was smoke rising above the white stone walls that hugged the dock, and the acrid smell of fire. She saw Jerval in his glistening silver armor, the de Vernon lion emblazoned across the breast of his blue surcoat, standing at the fore of his men, poised to jump ashore when they reached land. Their ship scraped against the wooden dock, and Jerval leaped ashore, soldiers swarming after him. A huge seaward gate opened to them, and he was soon lost to her sight.

She called after him, but of course he did not hear her. The seaward gate opened several more times as groups of soldiers ran to it from the docking ships, and then there was an almost eerie quiet. She could hear only muted shouting, and the sound of the waves slapping against the ships that lolled near the dock. Chandra watched the stormclouds over the city turn a deep crimson when the sun fell into the sea. She turned to see Joanna on her knees, praying, she thought, for Payn's safety. There was no messenger to tell them what was happening.

She awoke that evening to see her husband staring down at her, his blue surcoat splattered with blood. "Are you all right?" she croaked.

"Much better than you, I vow," Jerval said. "What in God's name are you doing up here on the forecastle?" He shook his head, expecting no sensible answer, and turned to the knight beside him. "Sir Elvan, Chandra, a Templar, and a physician. He is here to help you." A tall, leather-faced man in full armor stood beside him, a huge red cross stitched on his white surcoat.

"I am sorry," she moaned, clutching her belly. "You must not waste your time with me."

She felt his hand upon her forehead.

"What of the wounded? What has happened?"

"The Saracens fled," Jerval said, "and Acre is once again safe. We lost only a few men. Now, shut your mouth, little one."

Sir Elvan mixed a white powder in a wooden mug of wine. "Drink this," he said gently, holding the mug to her lips. "When you awaken, the cramps will be gone and you can hear all about what happened."

"You swear you are not harmed?" she asked after she had downed the liquid. She heard him laugh.

"Nay, Chandra, but my surcoat is ripped."

"I suppose you want me to mend it," she muttered.

15

EUSTACE WAS HOT, THOUGH NOT so infernally hot as he had
been in full armor. He followed a silent olive-skinned slave
into the cool interior of Ali ad-Din's private chamber. He
drew up at the sight of the merchant, black-eyed, heavily
bearded, his huge belly held in place by a wide gold-threaded
sash, and felt a tug of envy. His long robe was of cool
light-yellow silk, richly embroidered and studded with gems.
He wore stiff brocade slippers with the same oddly pointed
toes the other local men of wealth wore, they too crusted with
gems. Ali ad-Din was rich, a member of the High Court of
Acre, and as Eustace's eyes swept across the opulent chamber
and the dark-skinned slaves, he wished he owned but a
portion of his wealth.

Ali ad-Din sighed to himself, softly cursing the early arrival of Sir Eustace de Leybrun. He had hoped to see Princess
Eleanor's milk-white skin stretched over her belly as she
stepped into his bathing pool, but she had not removed the
silk robe his women had provided her. The golden-haired girl
with her, though beautiful, her full breasts with their rosy-
capped tips undeniably enticing, was a bit too thin for his
tastes. He had given only a cursory glance at the plump,
dark-haired girl, pretty enough, but of little interest compared
to the full-bellied princess.

Although Ali ad-Din was nominally Christian, he proffered
Eustace the Moslem greeting, touching his forehead with his
beringed fingers. "Ah, Sir Eustace," he said, his voice softly
welcoming. He walked away from the veil-covered wall where
he had been standing when Eustace entered the room. "You
have come to remove your beautiful English princess and her
ladies from my humble house?"

Eustace nodded, and at Ali ad-Din's graceful wave of his

hand, sank down on a pile of soft pillows that surrounded a low sandalwood table inlaid with ivory.

A slave girl poured him a goblet of sweet red Cypriot wine and held a huge fruit-filled bowl toward him. He selected several sticky soft dates, a delicacy that seemed to be everyday fare in Palestine.

"I hope your noble Prince Edward and his mighty lords are in good health?"

Eustace had grown used to the roundabout questioning, a disconcerting trait of all the heathen in the Holy Land, be they Christian or Moslem. "Aye," he said only, savoring the sweet dates.

Ali thought Sir Eustace as boorish an oaf as most of the arrogant nobles who had traveled with the English prince, but the smile never left his full lips. He continued in his soft voice, "I fear that you must rest awhile in my company, Sir Eustace, for the beautiful ladies have not yet finished their bath."

"I will wait," Eustace said, chewing on another date. "The prince has commanded that the ladies be escorted at all times, as you know." He added the words Edward had bade him to speak. "The prince does, of course, treasure your kindness in offering your house for the ladies' comfort."

"It is an honor," Ali said, his black eyes hooded. He prided himself as a judge of a man's character, and Sir Eustace's envious glances had not been lost to him. He suspected that Sir Eustace was not a religious fool like the English prince, nor, he thought, did he seem capable of the almost blind loyalty of Lord Payn de Chaworth and Sir Jerval de Vernon, the two English nobles whose wives were at this very moment enjoying his bathing room with the child-swelled Princess Eleanor. The man would make himself sick if he continued to eat the sweet dates. Ali silently clicked his fingers together toward the boy slave. The bowl of fruit was removed and Eustace's goblet was filled with more wine.

"It is a pity that the saintly King Louis did not succeed," Ali said. "But he was a sick old man, and Tunis such an infested rat hole. The Saracens believed, of course, that Acre would be an easy plum to pick now that the new French king, Philip, and King Charles of Sicily have made peace with the Sultan Baibars. All of Acre, my lord, is grateful to you English nobles for your defiant bravery."

Eustace's belly felt warmed by the sweet wine. They had indeed saved a beautiful city, one of the few Christian fortresses left in Palestine. The Venetians and Genoese had garnered great wealth here, and the Sultan Baibars's lust for the city was understandable. But Christ, to pit one thousand men against Baibars's vast armies! Even Edward had not understood why the Saracens had fled the besieged city, for the sultan commanded ten times their numbers.

"You seem to have weathered the siege well."

Ali shrugged. "A merchant, even a humble one as myself, must arrange his affairs so that he will survive, no matter the outcome." He added on a smile, "Since I am neither Genoese nor Venetian, I have not had to concern myself with their bickering, and have been able to trade with both of them."

"You have many slaves," Eustace said, as a lithe young girl clothed only in a filmy silk robe stepped toward them.

Ali's mouth split into a wide smile over his white teeth. "And many beautiful women, my friend," he said. "Several of my slave girls are with your English ladies now, attending them at their bath."

"The prince," Eustace said, "is grateful for your offer of a banquet tonight. He has grown tired of the rations."

"It is not unexpected," Ali agreed pleasantly. "My humble house is his to command. I understand that he thinks to leave Acre soon."

Eustace looked up quickly, surprised that the merchant knew of the prince's plans. He had cursed Edward under his breath when he had learned they were to leave even the nominal comforts of Acre to scout the blistering inland.

"I am not certain," Eustace said.

"No matter," Ali said agreeably, waving his beringed hand toward the slave girl. She silently stood next to Eustace, her olive features expressionless. When Eustace raised his face, his eyes fell upon the supple flesh of her bare belly. "Her name is Loka," Ali said smoothly. "She is only thirteen years old, but skilled in the art of men's pleasure. Perhaps tonight, after the banquet, you would wish to enjoy her gifts."

"Aye, perhaps," Eustace said.

"She has never before seen such as you, madame," Beri said. "She says that you are golden everywhere, even between your thighs."

Joanna de Chaworth held her sides with laughter, but
Chandra felt herself flush at the slave girl who was on her
knees before her, a soapy sponge poised in her hand.

"I wish that you would be quiet," Chandra said, frowning
toward Joanna and wishing the girl would stand up again. She
still hadn't shaken the sense of embarrassment she felt at
being naked around the women, and the slave girls seemed to
delight in looking at her and touching her. "I think I am
clean now, Beri. I would like to swim in the pool."

Beri said a few swift phrases to the girl. She rinsed the
sponge free of soap and poured warm, perfumed water from a
pottery jug gently over Chandra's soapy body. Chandra
stretched, her arms clasped above her head, and flung back
her mane of wet hair.

"You must try that, Joanna," Chandra said when she was
rinsed. She smiled at Beri and slipped beneath the surface of
the cool water of the pool, enjoying the absolute stillness.
When her lungs cried out for air, she flipped onto her back
and floated, her hair fanning out about her head. She cocked
an eye open and raised her head from the water at Joanna's
shriek of laughter as the soft sponge caressed her body.
Chandra wondered, looking at Joanna, how the girl could
remain so round. She was still too thin, Jerval kept reminding
her, but at least she was fit again. She had seen the Templar
physician, Sir Elvan, but once since they had settled in their
sprawling tent encampment just beyond St. Anthony's Gate,
outside the walls of Acre. He had treated her kindly, gently
kneading her belly and nodding his approval to Jerval.

She felt a hand on her shoulder, and emerged from the
watery silence to hear Joanna say, a seductive grin on her
face, "If only Payn would but take a few moments from his
infernal plotting and join me in this pool! I vow he would
soon have the son he so desperately wants."

"I think you should have a daughter, Joanna. She would
laugh and make everyone happy."

"Chandra," Joanna exclaimed with mock severity, "Payn
has worked so very hard, he deserves a son first. Do you not
think Sir Jerval would enjoy himself with you in this pool,
floating and whatever else in the water?"

Chandra dropped her eyes and felt color staining her cheeks,
as she remembered her bath in Sicily. She had felt so languid,
lazily dreaming, enjoying the touch of the soapy cloth on her

body. And Jerval had watched her and wanted her, had held her so tightly that she felt the pounding of his heart against her breast. She shook her head, blotting out the unwanted memories.

"You are a dreadful tease, Joanna," Eleanor said, rousing herself from her comfortable stupor. "As you can see," she continued, a twinkle in her lovely dark eyes as she patted her swelled belly, "one does not need such opulent surroundings to breed a babe."

Joanna sighed dolefully. "Payn is always telling me that the prince requires all of his waking hours, and thus he has little time for me." She wrinkled her pert nose. "But of course Prince Edward and Sir Jerval are younger than my poor Payn, and must have more stamina." She raised a wet strand of her hair from the water and sniffed it. "Perhaps this marvelous perfume will make him less tired tonight."

"You are silly, Joanna," Eleanor said, smiling, and leaned back against the cushions, closing her eyes again.

As one of the slave girls toweled her dry, Chandra raised her eyes to see Beri gazing at her, a thoughtful expression on her lovely face. Chandra smiled, cocking her head in question. Beri motioned Chandra to lie on her stomach atop a cushioned table. "The girls will rub a soothing oil into your skin. It will protect your beauty from the fierceness of the sun."

Chandra felt a warm liquid run down to the small of her back before gentle hands caressed her, rubbing the oil into her flesh. She felt light-headed, and so relaxed that she could not keep her eyes open.

"You are very beautiful," Beri said, "and golden everywhere." A slight smile indented the corners of her mouth. "I had thought you would be ugly, perhaps lumpy and fat."

"Why did you believe I would be ugly, Beri?"

Beri paused a moment, then smiled sadly. "You are lucky in many ways, my lady. You are a noble lady, a great lord's wife, and have the choice to do whatever you wish. I am a slave, and but do my master's bidding. My mother was also a slave. An Armenian merchant sold me to Ali ad-Din when I was thirteen years old."

Beri turned away and calmly directed a slave girl to fetch another jar of perfumed oil.

"My master," Beri said, her eyes downcast, "has taken a great liking to your husband, Sir Jerval. He took my master's side before the High Court against a Genoese merchant who wanted to strip him of his trade route to the Mongols. The Genoese are dirt,'' she added in a serious voice, ''and so greedy that they would give Acre itself to the Sultan Baibars if they could fatten their purses by it.''

''Aye,'' Chandra said. ''My husband told me of it, though he said that Ali ad-Din would have won his case anyway.''

''Your husband is a very handsome man,'' Beri said matter-of-factly. ''There is another, an English noble whose name I cannot pronounce. He has such intense eyes, and they burn deep when he looks at me.''

Chandra searched her mind, and said dubiously, ''You do not mean Sir Eustace de Leybrun?''

''Never that one! He is outside with my master, waiting for you to finish with your bath.''

Chandra reviewed the nobles in Prince Edward's retinue. She said quietly, not looking up, ''You mean Graelam de Moreton.''

Beri nodded happily. ''Am I right about him? Do you know him well?''

''I know him,'' Chandra said grimly. ''He is ruthless, and I, Beri, do not like him.''

''Men should be ruthless,'' Beri said with great seriousness. ''It makes them more desirable.''

''Come, Chandra,'' Joanna said playfully, lowering her towel. ''It is my turn to be oiled down.''

Chandra obligingly rolled off the table and rose. She pulled the towel from about her hair and shook it out free. ''It will take an hour to dry,'' she said. She turned to see Beri gazing after her, her expression puzzled.

The banquet was held in the tent-covered inner courtyard of Ali ad-Din's palace. The air was redolent with fragrant incense, and the oil lamps burned softly, casting gentle shadows on the rich silk and brocade furnishings. Chandra was gowned in a pale-blue silk robe, and her hair hung to her waist in rippling waves, held back from her forehead with a band of twisted gold. There was no breeze blowing off the Mediterranean this night, and Chandra felt her gown sticking to her back. The aging archbishop of Liège, Tedaldo Visconti, looked at her approvingly, and she found herself wondering if it was her soul or her person that pleased him.

Chandra greeted Sir Elvan warmly. "I have never seen a sword scabbard studded with precious stones," she told him.

"A physician receives many gifts in payment for his services," he said.

"Don't believe him, Chandra," Jerval said. "He is more than a physician. He is a Templar, and he shows equal skill in commerce."

"I have heard it said that you do not always agree with another military order, the Hospitalers."

"And you find that strange, Lady Chandra. 'Tis true, and the reasons for our disagreements precede my birth. If we take one side of an issue, you can be certain that the Hospitalers will take the other."

"As Christians," Chandra said, ignoring Jerval's frown, "we should all fight on the same side."

To Jerval's relief, Sir Elvan merely smiled. "Nothing, my lady, is ever so simple, I fear."

Chandra took her place beside her husband on the soft, down-filled pillows. Small sandalwood dining tables were set close together across the courtyard, a red-robed slave standing beside each of them. Along a long table at the far end of the courtyard, Prince Edward and Princess Eleanor sat with Ali ad-Din and King Hugh of Cyprus and Jerusalem. Although Edward wore a pleasant smile, he had a distracted air about him that seemed to Chandra to be shared by all of his nobles present tonight.

She heard Roger de Clifford say to Jerval, "It seems that King Hugh has arranged a farewell banquet for himself tonight, Jerval. He cannot afford to remain here much longer, else he might lose Cyprus to his greedy barons."

Chandra took a bite of the roasted lamb, and turned toward Jerval when he said, "You are right, Roger. Now that the powerful Ibelins and the barons have sent word they are willing to serve only in defense of Cyprus, there is little reason for him to stay. Edward, at least, took it well. Though King Hugh had promised us men to defeat the Saracens, in truth, their numbers would not have added much."

Chandra said, "I can scarce believe that a king has so little control over his kingdom. Methinks King Hugh should muzzle the Ibelins."

Roger de Clifford blinked in surprise. "I did not think you ladies had any interest in or knowledge of the matter."

"Why would you think that, Sir Roger?" she asked baldly.

Jerval bit his lips so as not to grin at Sir Roger's discomfiture, and quickly intervened. "Where did you hear of our problems with the Cypriot barons, Chandra?"

"From Ali ad-Din. I asked him why King Hugh was here with so few men."

"I fear that the Mongols are our last hope," Payn de Chaworth said. He asked Roger de Clifford, "Has Edward heard aught from the Ilkan Abaga?"

"Abaga's Mongol army is now fighting in Turkestan, as you know. I have heard that he has agreed to send what aid he could, but we know not when."

"What chance have a thousand men," Eustace muttered, "against the damned Sultan Baibars? Only the Mongols can drive him back for good into Egypt, and they give us nothing but promises."

"Do not forget," Graelam de Moreton called out, "that the Venetians, our Christian brothers, are busily supplying Baibars with all the timber and metal he needs for his armaments. And the Genoese supply them the slaves to build their weapons."

"Do you know that when Edward reproved the merchants," Payn de Chaworth said, his brow knit in an angry frown, "they simply showed him their licenses from the High Court at Acre? It is all nonsense. By God, I would drive them all into the sea!"

Joanna de Chaworth, her full lips pursed, interrupted the grim conversation. "I cannot get used to these white grains called sugar!" she said gaily. She held up a sweetmeat made of dates and lemons, sticky with the sweet substance, for her husband's inspection. "I still cannot believe, my lord, that it will replace honey, as you keep telling me."

Payn smiled indulgently. "It is one of Palestine's main trade goods to the West, Joanna." He clasped his hand over his wife's arm when he saw she would continue to chatter if given the chance.

Chandra turned to her husband, a frown puckering her brow. "What do you think will happen if Abaga does not send us aid?"

Jerval found himself wondering if she ever had a frivolous thought in her head, but he said seriously enough, "I agree with Payn and Eustace. There will be little that we can do against Baibars.''

The rich meal and heavy wine did not lighten the men's mood, and when Ali ad-Din called for the dancers, Jerval, Payn, and Roger de Clifford left the table to join the prince.

To Chandra's discomfort, Graelam de Moreton eased himself down beside her. She had seen little of him since they had left England. In Sicily, if rumor was correct, he had amused himself by indulging freely in the women offered to the English nobles by King Charles. She eyed him warily and watched him smile widely at her.

"Do you enjoy the music, my lady?"

"It is music, I suppose," Chandra said coldly, the clacking cymbals and the tinkling bells sounding oddly to her ears. "Do you not wish to join the prince . . . and my husband?"

"Aye," he said easily, still smiling, "in a moment. Is not the girl in the red veils Beri, Ali ad-Din's slave?"

She nodded, wishing he would just go away. "It is a pity that such a lovely, soft-spoken girl must be a slave."

The smile faded from Graelam's face. She does not know, he thought, and he was irritated at her ignorance. He shrugged his shoulders and held out his silver goblet for more wine.

"Doubtless even Beri has some amusement in her life," he said.

Chandra stiffened at his intimate tone. "I have seen what amusements you promise for women, Lord Graelam. But of course, you look upon women, slaves or free, as naught but instruments for your pleasure, do you not?"

"Instruments or vessels, my lady?" He grinned more widely, and watched her gaze toward Jerval. "You still fear me, I see."

"I do not fear you, my lord. I was merely thinking of Mary, the young girl you forced at Croyland."

Graelam raised a black brow. "I am likely the only man the girl will ever enjoy. Is it possible you now regret my losing you?"

"My only regret is not being more accurate with my dagger, Graelam. Your conceit is boundless."

"Aye, your dagger, Chandra. My shoulder was raw for weeks, and each time I flexed my shoulder, I thought of you. Then, of course, when my men returned with your noble father's message, I found myself a bit angered." He shrugged his broad shoulders. "You consider it all ancient history, do you not, Chandra?"

"I consider it all best forgotten, my lord."

"But sometimes memory is long, Chandra, very long." He was silent a moment, looking again toward the swaying Beri. "I think you are too trusting, my lady. And this is a treacherous land that twists men's souls."

"Do you threaten me again, Lord Graelam?"

"I? It is an interesting question, but one that is much too simple."

Chandra said quickly, "I own to some surprise that a man such as you would forgo your pleasures to fight in the Holy Land for a holy cause."

Graelam winced at her words and said roughly, "We are a pitiful lot. If you would know the truth, my lady, my motive for being here is not quite as noble as it could be."

"You wish for glory," she said.

"Glory?" He raised an incredulous brow. "Your father did you a great disservice, my lady. Be thankful your husband did not allow you in the fighting for this wretched city. In that, at least, I must admire him. You imagined the glory of our victory from a distance. I felt flies crawling over my face. The heat was so intense that I felt baked beneath my armor, and I was blinded by my own sweat. There is no glory in this hellhole, Chandra. Edward's noble cause is doomed; you have but to listen to know that. There is nothing in this miserable land save disease and death and treachery. Look yon at Ali ad-Din, our fawning host. He is as treacherous and ruthless as any of Baibars's emirs, as dishonorable as the damned Venetians, and he licks Edward's boots only to ensure his own safety. Do not blind yourself with the myth of glory, Chandra."

"You speak so fluently of treachery, my lord."

"I will not remind you of it again, Chandra."

She waved away his words, hating herself for the quiver of fear that raised gooseflesh on her arms. "Surely discovering that for myself would be better than the pain of boredom in my woman's gowns."

"You will never discover a man's truths, despite your unwomanly ways. You have no real understanding of either honor or treachery. You will spend your days knowing only a man's protection."

"I need no man's protection, Lord Graelam."

He laughed. "Your memory is blessedly short, Chandra." He shrugged, but his voice became serious. "Think on what I have said, though I imagine that your proud husband has told you much the same things."

"Nay, Jerval said nothing of the fighting when we arrived at Acre. I only watched from our ship in the harbor."

"But you saw his surcoat—'twas covered with blood."

"Aye, I saw it," she said. She rose quickly. "Princess Eleanor is waving to me, my lord. I must attend her now."

Graelam watched her walk gracefully toward the princess, his eyes narrowed thoughtfully on her back.

Edward gazed about the faces of the nobles inside his pavilion and loosed the tie of his tunic. It was near to midnight, for Ali ad-Din's banquet had lingered long.

"King Hugh is leaving shortly to return to Cyprus," he said.

"Not that it much matters," Jerval said. He met the tired eyes of John de Vescy, a former supporter of Simon de Montfort and now a loyal friend and counselor to the future king of England, and saw him nod his head.

"Christ, 'tis so infernally hot," Payn de Chaworth said.

Edward felt as though he were drowning in his own sweat, but he disregarded Payn's plaint, and said in a musing voice, "I understand that the Sultan Baibars considers us a sufficient threat to hold in his steel claws, at least for the moment." He suddenly slammed his fisted hand against his open palm. "If only Abaga will fulfill his promise! Without the Mongols, we are powerless against Baibars."

John de Vescy gave Edward a tired smile. "Abaga must first see to his own lands, sire. His army is, as you know, fighting in Turkestan. We must be patient."

"Nay," Edward said, rising. "I will not sit idly here in Acre watching the bloody Genoese and Venetians trade all the wealth of Palestine to the damned Saracens!"

"My lord," Jerval said. "We came to Palestine to reconquer the cities and castles captured by Baibars. I suggest that we do just that, beginning with Nazareth. By God, it is our Christ's city and it is in heathen hands."

Edward's eyes gleamed with sudden decision, and his fine chiseled features hardened with purpose. He walked to stand beside Jerval, towering even taller than he, his head brushing against the top of the pavilion. His generous mouth widened into a pleased smile. "Sir Jerval is in the right. With God's aid, we will succeed in this venture. Gather the men and provision them for the march to Nazareth. We leave in the morning."

Jerval did not return until very late. Chandra felt his cool hand upon her cheek, and she smiled at him through sleep-blurred eyes.

"Is something wrong?" she asked.

"Nay. We leave for Nazareth in the morning. 'Twas decided tonight."

She clutched his hand suddenly. "You will be careful, my lord."

He grinned. "You give me the order, my lady, I must obey you. Sleep now. I will wake you at first light."

16

THE DUST KICKED UP FROM the rutted road by the horses' hooves was a hazy white in the morning sun. Chandra craned her neck westward for a glimpse of the Mediterranean, but they were too far inland to make it out. Nothing grew here save an occasional yellowish shrub. Even the hearty olive trees, gnarled and bent, lay a mile or so to the west, still within the sight of the sea, across a barrier of dunes and craggy rocks.

Although Chandra's head and most of her face were covered with thin white gauze, she felt gritty sand fill her nostrils each time she breathed. She, Eleanor, and several of her ladies were on their way to Nazareth to join Edward and his army. They were well protected, surrounded by a hundred soldiers, Payn de Chaworth at their head. Eleanor rode in a covered litter, her only concession to her pregnancy. She had been as excited as Chandra to leave the confines of Acre, prayers of thanksgiving on her lips for the Christian victory.

Chandra clicked her nimble-footed bay mare to the fore of the troop, to search out Arnolf. Instead, it was Payn who reined in beside her. He wore a white linen surcoat over his armor, his only defense against the baking sun, and his head and face, like hers, were covered with swaths of white cloth.

"I was trying to find Arnolf," she said, smiling at him. "You look tired, Payn."

"Nary a bit," Payn said, looking back briefly toward Joanna, who rode next to Eleanor's litter. "I wager you want to hear all about the battle."

She heard amusement in his voice and turned in her saddle to see his eyes crinkled above the line of cloth. "Certainly more than that we won, and God be praised," she said tartly.

Before he spoke, Payn once again twisted in his saddle to check the troops behind them. Their party formed a wide phalanx, the ladies in the middle, surrounded on all sides by Edward's men.

"My Joanna would likely prefer spending this day in the cool bathing room at Ali ad-Din's residence."

"It is dreadfully hot," Chandra said, wiping gritty sand from her forehead as she spoke. "I do not know how you can bear your armor."

"One adjusts. My squire can no longer remove the stench of my own sweat from the mail." Payn cocked a sandy brow at her and saw her excitement. She leaned toward him as he said, "Edward's spies told us the Saracen garrison at Nazareth had grown lax, especially at night. We were able to form in a semicircle twenty men deep about the walls before dawn. You are probably picturing the thick walls of Acre, but Nazareth was besieged by the Saracens several years ago, and they had not bothered to rebuild. Our Lord's city is a filthy, devastated place, its wealth long ago seized, and the Saracens had little heart to defend it. We lost few men breaching the walls. But the heathens did not want to leave us any gain. Instead of fighting us, they butchered Nazarenes as they fled through the streets. I did not see much, for Edward sent me back to fetch the ladies, but what I did see was not a pretty sight."

"War is never pretty," Chandra said.

Payn looked at her askance, knowing that she was mouthing words without knowing their meaning. There had been no devastation in Acre, and she still had no concept of what armies could do to a people caught in their midst. "Perhaps your father raised you to picture war as the battles of gallant knights, riding in honor," he said. "It is not the heroic Roland, my lady, dying with dignity, a prayer to God on his lips. War in the Holy Land against the Saracens is a hell most men would give their souls to forget."

Chandra's first impression of Nazareth in the distance was a peaceful one. The city was set upon a rise, and to Chandra's surprise, there were lush date trees and palm trees surrounding it.

"Nazareth was built," Payn said, "as a trading center. There is water, and once the city was as beautiful as Acre, so I'm told."

As they drew nearer, she saw that the city was like a giant ravaged carcass, its dirty brown stone walls in ruin. There was a pungent odor in the air, a nauseating smell that made her stomach wrench. She looked a question toward Payn.

" 'Tis the stench of the dead and dying," he said. "It was here before we arrived. As I told you, the Saracens killed and maimed as many people as they could, believing, I suppose, that we would take whomever they left as slaves."

Their horses picked their way through the rubble in the narrow streets. Children in pitiful rags stood huddled in doorways, staring at them with dull eyes. They were too weak for the Saracens to bother with, Payn told her matter-of-factly.

"But they are only children!" she cried.

"That is why they still live. The Saracens knew they would die before they could be sold as slaves."

She saw bedraggled women, their stomachs bloated with hunger, tending to men whose cries of pain rent the air. Her mare snorted and sidestepped a pool of blood. A man's body, covered with a rag, lay alone at its center, blackened by the ferocious hot sun. She gagged, unable to help herself.

"How can this be our victory, Payn?"

He shrugged, weary and saddened. "It is worse than I imagined. You, Joanna, and the other ladies will stay with Eleanor," he said, pointing to a small stone house that lay ahead of them beneath the collapsed northern wall of the city. "That is Edward's headquarters."

Chandra followed Eleanor into the bare, derelict interior of the house. Wounded English soldiers lay on blankets along its walls. "Where is Jerval?" she asked Lambert, who was kneeling over a wounded soldier.

He raised his once happy boyish face to her, and she drew back at the haunted look in his eyes. "He will return," Lambert said in a weary voice.

She saw Graelam holding a gourd of water to the pinched lips of one of his squires, the look on his face one of fury mingled with despair. His eyes met hers briefly, and for the first time, it was Graelam who looked away.

Chandra stayed close to the women, praying for the sun to set on the misery. She heard Edward say to Eleanor, "If I had known that it would be so wretched, I would not have sent for you. We lost few men. But the people! God, the people."

Eleanor's face was pale, her dark eyes dimmed with the

suffering she had seen. "It is beyond anything I could have imagined," she said.

"You will stay within. I do not want you outside."

Chandra helped Eleanor and her ladies prepare a small chamber in the back of the house for them, but she could not remain with them, hidden away. She stood in the doorway of Edward's headquarters, awaiting Jerval. When he finally strode toward her, his surcoat drenched with sweat, she saw that he was carrying a small girl in his arms, one of her legs wrapped in the bloody hem of his surcoat. He nodded at her, and she felt suddenly like an outcast, her body clean and whole, her belly filled with food. He looked unutterably weary. She felt tears start to her eyes when the child looked at her, for she did not utter a sound or a groan, and her dark eyes were glazed with shock.

"I saw a Saracen hack at her leg," Jerval said blankly, the first words he spoke. "He simply leaned low off his horse's back and slashed his scimitar. I killed him, of course, but it was too late for the child."

She remembered her glib words to Graelam the night of Ali ad-Din's banquet, and her confident words to Payn that war was not pretty. "I am sorry," she said, but her words meant nothing in the face of the horror that surrounded them, and she knew it.

She watched him lay the child tenderly down upon a blanket and force some water between her pinched lips. Her small head lolled to one side. He rose and looked about the wall at the English soldiers.

"You are all right?" she asked him.

"Nay," he said, "I am not all right, but I am alive and healthy, which is more than I can say for these poor wretches." He shook his head, as if to block out the chaos outside the house. "I wish that you had not come."

"Is there nothing we can do?"

He ran his fingers through his matted hair. "Aye, many of the people are starving. I am taking some men to give them what food we can."

"I would go with you, Jerval."

She saw that he would refuse, and quickly added, "If I must be here, do not deny me a useful task, Jerval."

He seemed to struggle with himself for a moment, then

shrugged. "Very well, but you will stay with me. I do not know if there is still danger. Help us gather the food."

It was late afternoon when they left the English quarters, and the sun still blazed overhead, making the stench almost unbearable. She would have given away all the bread she carried to the men and women huddled close by Edward's headquarters had Jerval not stopped her, his voice grim. "Nay, there is much need. You must dole it out, else you'll have nothing to eat later."

"I do not care," she said, but she heeded him and followed him through the labyrinth of rubble in the narrow streets. They saw women crouched down in the piles of waste, burrowing for food or clothing.

"The Saracens took pride, I think, in beggaring the Nazarenes," Jerval said wearily. He turned to see Chandra leaning over a ragged woman in the doorway of a small house. She was shaking her, begging her to take a hunk of bread. Her voice rose, almost angrily, when the woman did not raise her head.

He felt a stab of impotent pain, and touched his hand to Chandra's shoulder. "She is dead, Chandra. Come, there is nothing you can do for her."

Chandra raised angry eyes to his face. "Nay!" she cried. "She is not dead, merely sleeping!"

He saw that she could not accept it, and forcibly drew her to her feet. He said to one of the soldiers, "Tell the men that there is another for the funeral pyre.

"Come," he said, forcing her away. "There are living who need our food."

She said not another word throughout the rest of the afternoon, even when they passed one of the burning funeral pyres. When they had no more food, she raised glazed eyes to Jerval's face. "What are we to do?"

"Nothing. I am sorry, Chandra," he said quietly. He drew her against him for a moment to block out the squalor around them.

He led her back to Edward's headquarters as evening fell. Chandra passed by the wounded English soldiers and fell to her knees by the small girl. Her dark eyes stared. She was dead.

Geoffrey Parker, one of Edward's surgeons, knelt down beside her. "The child had no chance," he said.

Chandra heard Jerval give a low growl in his throat behind her. She watched him lift the small child in his arms and carry her from the house. She rose to accompany him, wishing there were something she could say to him, but he strode away from her as if she were not there.

"She is beyond pain," Geoffrey Parker said, touching his hand to her arm.

"He is taking her to be burned," Chandra whispered.

"Aye. Come, my lady. If you wish it, I could use your help with our wounded."

She looked up sometime later to see Jerval strapping on his helmet. She jerked to her feet, filled with sudden fear. "What are you doing? Where are you going?"

"There are reports of Saracens outside the walls. Stay here and do not worry. I will be back soon." He left her without another word, Lambert at his side.

Joanna de Chaworth handed her a piece of bread. "Here, Chandra, you must eat something. Eleanor sent me to fetch you. She wants you to rest now."

Chandra looked at the bread, held out to her as the dead woman would have seen it. "Nay," she whispered. "I have no wish for food."

When the wounded men were tended, Chandra walked to the doorway and sank down, waiting again for Jerval to return. The night air was cool upon her face. Over the housetops beyond, she could see black smoke billowing upward from the funeral pyres.

"Lady Chandra!"

She looked up to see Lambert running toward her.

"It's my lord," he cried, clutching at her arm. "He has been wounded! The Saracens came upon us from the rocks."

Geoffrey Parker, Edward's physician, jumped to his feet and hurried to the door. For an instant, Chandra could not move. She could bear no more suffering, no more death. Oh God, please, not Jerval!

"My lady!" Geoffrey shouted to her. "Prepare a place for him, quickly!"

"God's teeth!" she heard Jerval bellow, pain deep in his throat. "Do not tear my flesh from my bones!" He was carried through the door by Payn, Rolfe, and two men-at-arms.

"Do not worry," Payn de Chaworth said, casting her a

quick glance over his shoulder. "The wound is not deep, but the blood has congealed and stuck to his shirt."

Chandra could only nod. She smoothed down a bed of blankets, and Jerval was lowered, cursing, onto his back.

"God, Payn," he growled, "would be that you were not such a clumsy oaf!"

"Aye, and you not such a noble lout!"

Chandra fell to her knees beside him. "You told me you would be all right," she said, her voice accusing.

He smiled up at her through the gnawing pain in his side. "The wound is not deep."

"My lady," Geoffrey Parker said, waving her away. She watched as Lambert and Payn unstrapped his armor and stripped off his bloody clothes. Geoffrey probed at his torn flesh. "I am relieved, Sir Jerval," he said. " 'Tis but a needle and thread I'll need for you."

Edward leaned over Jerval, shaking his head in grim humor. "What have you to say, Sir Knight? I send you forth to dispatch the heathen, and it is you who are on your back."

"I will survive, sire," Jerval said.

"The blood is clotted," Chandra said. "I will bathe him."

Geoffrey saw shock in her eyes, and nodded. It was better to let her care for her husband. "Aye," he said aloud, "you bathe the wound, then call me."

Jerval looked up at her and smiled. "I am not going to die, Chandra, even though you were not at my side to protect me."

"I do not know how you can laugh about it," she said angrily. She stared down at his naked body, at the dried blood clotted over his right side and streaking down his leg. "Damn you, you could have been killed!"

He winced from the pain in his side.

"Jerval, you must have something for the pain!"

"Do you care so much for my pain?"

"You cared for me when I was so vilely ill aboard the ship," she said in a more controlled voice. "Now I will care for you."

Jerval felt the jabbing pain draw at his senses and closed his eyes. He could still see the wild-eyed Saracen, hear his curdling yell as he swooped down from his horse's back, his curved blade but inches from Payn's neck. Jerval's sword had slashed deep into the man's leg, so deep that its tip had wounded the horse beneath him. The beast had snorted in pain and fallen on the man, crushing him beneath its massive body. He had pulled off his helmet to rub the burning sweat from his eyes, and it was then that two Saracens had come at him. He had thrown his helmet at one of them, but the other had reached his side with the tip of his scimitar. He had been unlucky, for their force had far outnumbered the Saracen band. He felt Chandra's hand lightly touch his shoulder, and he opened his eyes.

"Drink this, Jerval. 'Twill ease the pain."

Lambert helped him to rise from the blankets enough to drink from the goblet. The liquid was sweet and cool, and almost immediately, Jerval felt a soothing warmth pervade his mind. When the pain lessened, he opened his eyes to see Chandra, a bowl of water and a cloth in her hand.

"Thank God," he said, grinning crookedly, "that Geoffrey will stitch me up. I know that you hate all needlework. You would doubtless skewer me."

"Please do not jest," she said in a whisper. He stared up at her, but he said nothing as she dropped to her knees beside him. "I must bathe the wound. I will try not to hurt you more than I must."

She found that she had to scrub at the jagged flesh to cleanse away the clotted blood. She felt his muscles tense beneath her hand, and stilled.

"I am sorry, Jerval, but it must be done."

"Aye, Chandra, I know." He closed his eyes again and clenched his teeth. He felt her hand rest momentarily on his thigh, and said softly, "Forgive my nakedness, Chandra, and my foul odor. I smell like stinking death."

"I will bathe you when I am through," he heard her say, her words sounding strangely distant from him.

When Geoffrey had finished stitching his flesh, he rose and said gently, "You did well, my lady. Sir Jerval is young and strong. He will be fit within the week. You may bathe him now, if you wish."

She sponged him with warm soapy water. He cracked open his eyes and smiled hazily up at her. "Ah, that feels good," he said. Her hand stroked down his chest to his belly, and he felt her hesitate.

"I cannot attack you, wife," he said dryly. "Do with me what you will."

" 'Twas not my thought," she said. She looked up, her face drawn and strained, as Payn de Chaworth strode into the room. "How are you, Jerval?" he asked.

"Alive, I believe."

"Excellent." He peered closely at Jerval's side. "Whenever you look at that scar," he said, "you'll be reminded of me."

"A pleasure I could do without," Jerval grunted.

To Jerval's surprise, Chandra would not leave his side. She chatted with him aimlessly, or simply sat in silence, staring at him.

"Chandra," he said finally, "you need to walk about and get some fresh air."

"Nay! There is no fresh air, not anywhere!"

"I have to relieve myself, and I would prefer Lambert to help me."

She left him for but a minute, but upon her return, he was surrounded by Edward, Payn, and John de Vescy. She sank down in a corner, listening to them speak quietly of their losses and what was to be done for the Nazarenes.

When she awoke the next morning, Jerval was sitting up, eating a hunk of bread and drinking ale. She wiped the sleep from her eyes. "You look better," she said.

He leaned back a moment, gazing at her from beneath half-closed eyelids. "I have never seen you so frightened," he said after a moment, "save after you were taken by Alan Durwald. I did not realize it then, for you were full of cocky bravado, but you were terrified."

"Aye, I was scared. But it was not like . . . this."

"No, nothing is like this," he said, and handed her a piece of bread. "I dreamed last night of Camberley, the lakes, and the Cumbrian Mountains. I think I would gladly give a year off my life to be back there now, with you, even to hear my mother complaining about your throwing the distaff at her."

Se stared at him, not smiling as he had intended at his joking words. "Why, Jerval?"

"Why what, Chandra?"

She waved her arm about her. "Did you know that it would be like this?"

"Aye, for I have fought before, Chandra."

"Then why did you agree to come with Edward, if you knew that war was ever thus, and that you could be killed?"

He looked away from her a moment, weighing his words.

"One wonders why God, in his infinite mercy, wishes his followers to win battles in his name, if this is the outcome. We have spoken many times, Chandra, about a woman's responsibilities, and a man's. It is my duty to keep all that I hold dear safe against my enemies. It does not mean that I am less enraged than you by the waste of it. But my duty forbids me to turn away and leave other men to fight and possibly die, in my stead."

His eyes narrowed suddenly in pain, and he shifted his position.

She was at his side in a moment. "Please," she whispered, "hold still. Shall I fetch Geoffrey?"

"Nay, little one. Send Payn to me."

They rode out of the city two days later, the wounded English either tied to their horses or drawn by them on litters at the center of the phalanx of troops. Chandra rode next to Jerval, cursing his pride. He should not have refused a litter. She knew that he felt pain, but he was in his armor again, and in his saddle. Edward had done what he could for the Christians, but beyond providing all the food he could spare and leaving two of his physicians behind with a hundred soldiers, there was little he could do.

Chandra looked up and saw Eleanor ease her palfrey next to the prince's destrier. She had given up her litter to a wounded soldier. She extended her hand and laid it gently upon her husband's mailed arm. It was an offer of comfort, a sign of love and trust. Chandra saw Edward close his hand over hers. They rode, touching, for some minutes, speaking quietly to each other.

"I hope that Eleanor and her babe will not suffer from this," she said.

Jerval did not answer her. She turned to him and saw his mighty shoulders slumped forward, and his head bowed in sleep.

Acre now seemed like the most comfortable haven in the world. At least there, Jerval could rest on a cot, protected from the scorching sun. The thought that he could easily have been killed still haunted her. Tentatively, as she had seen Eleanor do, she stretched out her hand and lightly touched his mailed arm.

"My lord," she said quietly.

"I shall survive, Chandra. The wound is naught."

"Is it so unmanly to admit that you feel pain?" she snapped at his dismissing tone.

He grinned at her. "Nay, Chandra, but you did pull me from a pleasant dream."

The column narrowed as they rode through the Neva Pass, a barren grotto with jagged boulders jutting from its walls around them like armless sentinels. Beyond the pass, she knew, the dusty road veered toward the coast.

Suddenly the air was rent by yells that seemed to come from everywhere as they echoed off the surrounding rocks. Chandra scarce had time to pull in her frightened mare before the screaming Saracens jumped from their crevices, their scimitars whirling over their heads.

"Go to the women!" Jerval shouted at her, and slapped his mailed hand on her palfrey's rump. Her palfrey jumped forward toward a small clearing where Edward's personal guard were forming a circle three men deep around Eleanor and the other women. The English horses were careening into each other, snorting in trapped fear. Dimly, she heard Edward shouting orders even as a screaming Saracen broke through the raging throng toward him. Edward's sword dipped gracefully downward.

She looked toward Jerval, fear for him clotted in her throat. He was cut off from the men, hacking his sword methodically at three bearded Saracens around him. John de Vescy yelled at her to keep close to the women. But she saw her husband's face, grim with determination. She knew the strength of his arm, and saw that he was weakening. He would be killed! "Jerval!" she yelled at him, but he did not hear her. She remembered her promise to him, and knew that she could not keep it. She would not let him die! She gritted her teeth, reached beneath her robe, and pulled her hunting knife from its leather sheath. She dug her heels into her palfrey's side and sent him galloping toward her husband. A wild-eyed Saracen lunged toward her, his curved sword arched high above his head. She hurled her knife, and it pierced the man's chest. He seemed to choke on his cry. She kicked her horse forward and jumped from her saddle to wrench the sword from the man's hand as he lay on the rocks.

She hurtled her horse again toward Jerval, the screams of wounded men filling her ears. She was frightened, so fright-

ened that she could scarce breathe. She flung the heavy
scimitar from her left to her right hand, and slashed out with
it as she had been taught on the tiltyard. She saw a surprised
look on a beardless face, a boy's face, who stared up at her
blankly until his blood spurted from his mouth. She screamed
his agony for him, feeling his death as if it were her own. She
felt a sharp pain in her right arm, and saw her own blood
oozing from her flesh. She looked at her arm stupidly, knowing that his blade could just as easily have entered her breast.
She felt beads of sweat sting her eyes, and dashed her hand
across her face.

"Chandra!"

She heard Jerval's shout, and whipped her horse forward.
He was at her side in the next instant, hugging his destrier
close to her horse's head. He was trying to protect her, she
thought wildly, pushing her behind him toward the rocks. She
saw blood at his side and knew that his wound had opened.
She would not allow him to die for her.

"*A Vernon,*" she yelled, and broke away from him, bringing her horse's rump around to protect his flank. She heard an
unearthly shriek and whipped her horse about to see a Saracen
leap from an outjutting rock toward Graelam de Moreton's
back.

Graelam jerked about to see Chandra's sword slicing into
the screaming man's belly. For an instant, he was frozen into
stunned silence. Then a faint smile touched his lips, and his
eyes met Jerval's. Jerval turned away from his gaze to meet
two Saracens who were bearing down on him. He jerked back
on his destrier's reins, and the mighty horse reared back,
striking the neck of one of the Saracen's mounts. The Saracen
went flying, and the other had little chance against Jerval's
sword. Jerval looked through a blur of sweat to see Chandra,
still astride her horse, next to John de Vescy, who had fallen
to the ground. She was protecting de Vescy, who was struggling to his feet, only to fall back as his wounded leg
collapsed beneath him.

A shout of victory tore from Jerval's throat. The Saracens
were fleeing over the jagged rocks, or riding on horseback
like the devil himself back toward the boiling desert. The
time had seemed endless, but only fifteen minutes had passed
from the beginning of the assault to its end. The English

troops were yelling obscenities and curses at the fleeing
Saracens, and curdling cries of victory.

Jerval dismounted painfully from his destrier. Chandra was
leaning over John de Vescy, probing at the gaping tear in his
leg. John de Vescy was looking up at her with a surprised,
crooked smile, and then fell on his back, senseless. Chandra
ripped off the turban that now hung loose down her back and
wrapped it tightly about his thigh to staunch the flow of
blood.

Jerval knelt down beside her, not speaking until he was
certain that the gaping wound had stopped bleeding. He
raised his face and found that she was staring at him, relief,
and something else he could not fathom, in her eyes.

"Your side," she croaked. "Are you all right?"

"Aye." He saw the blood streaking down her arm, and felt
himself go cold. "You are hurt," he said, his voice sounding
so harsh that Chandra jumped.

" 'Tis nothing, really." She attempted a weak smile. "We
beat them off."

Sudden memory of the battle rose in her mind. She rose
shakily to her feet and stumbled away from Jerval toward a
narrow crevice in one of the jagged rocks. Nauseating bile
rose in her throat, and she fell to her knees. Convulsive
spasms racked her body, doubling her over. She felt his
hands on her shoulders, steadying her.

"Here, Chandra, drink this." She accepted the water skin
from Jerval, and forced herself to swallow the cool water.
"Please forgive me. I do not know what is the matter with
me." She tried to rise, but her legs would not hold her
weight. She felt his arms about her, and she leaned back
against him.

She heard herself babbling, her throat dry with horror.
"We are so fragile . . . our lives so easily snuffed out in but
an instant with the twist of a hand!" She turned about on her
knees to face him. "By God, it was a vision of hell! To know
that you are about to die . . . to become nothing in but a
moment! And to kill, to rob another of life! Dear God, he
was but a boy, and I killed him!"

Jerval fell to his knees and gathered her shaking body into
his arms. "He did what he had to. You fought for the first
time with the specter of death at your shoulder." As he spoke

the words, she felt him stiffen. "You could have been killed playing the gallant hero for me!"

She looked up at him wildly. "I could not bear it if you had fallen and I had done nothing!"

"But I could not have borne the cost had you been killed, never! Was it your damned honor or something else?" He calmed his anger, born of his fear for her. "You saved de Moreton's life and probably de Vescy's. I must thank you."

Jerval looked up at Graelam de Moreton.

"See to de Vescy," Jerval said, tightening his hold about Chandra's shoulders. He could hear John de Vescy cursing at the top of his lungs at one of the physicians who was probing at his leg.

He looked down at Chandra. She was tugging at his arms. "Please, your side. I must change your bandage."

"Your arm first, Chandra." He ripped away the sleeve of her gown, and drew a relieved breath. He bandaged the gash as best he could.

"Is Eleanor safe?" she managed in a thin voice.

"Do not worry. She was well protected, surrounded by at least fifty men."

She looked up at him, wanting to speak, wanting to beg him never again to place himself into danger, but she knew she could not. It was his duty to fight. She said gruffly, "I have no desire to be a widow, Jerval."

His eyes flew to her face at the raw passion in her voice, but she had turned away from him, pressing her cheek against his shoulder.

"And I, Chandra, have no desire to be a widower," he said, his voice harsh. "You will stay safe with me until we are once again back in Acre."

She sat on the ground beside the unconscious John de Vescy while the English buried their dead. The hovering birds were but waiting, she thought, for them to be on their way, leaving the bodies of the Saracens.

She saw a large shadow from the corner of her eye, and gazed up to see Graelam de Moreton towering over her.

She said nothing, and he dropped to his haunches beside her. He simply gazed at her for a long moment, his hands fisted against his thighs.

"Why did you save my life?" he growled at her.

She looked at him full face and said honestly, "At first I

did not realize it was you, my lord. You were simply an English knight who would die if I did nothing.'' She drew a deep breath, shaking her head. ''But it made no difference. No matter what has happened, or what you have done, I could not let them kill you.''

''Your arm,'' he said, his tone almost as harsh as Jerval's had been.

'' 'Tis nothing,'' she said.

John de Vescy groaned and twisted sharply. Graelam helped her ease him onto his back and straighten his wounded leg.

She felt his hand touch hers, and her eyes flew to his face.

''You will hear no more veiled threats from me, Chandra,'' he said quietly. He patted her hand and looked off into the distance. ''I had intended to take you, and I know that I meant you harm. I hated you almost as much as your father after the humiliation I suffered through Jerval and the king's order.'' He sighed deeply and looked back at her, a grim smile on his lips. ''You have robbed me of my revenge, Chandra.''

He rose suddenly, the shadow of his huge body blocking out the sun. ''Your husband is returning. I bid you goodbye, my lady.'' He turned and strode away from her to his destrier.

Chandra stared after him until she heard John de Vescy moan softly. She laid her hand gently on his chest, and he opened his eyes and stared up at her. He said, pain rumbling in his throat, ''I thank you, my lady, for protecting my wretched skin. I had heard you could fight, of course, but I did not believe that it could be true. Sir Jerval must admire you greatly.''

She raised her head, a bitter smile on her lips. Mayhap he did, she thought, despite his anger at her for fighting, but she found little pleasure in the notion. She felt free of herself for the first time in her life, free from the bonds of a meaningless pride. She heard wild cursing. It was Eustace, howling, as a physician stitched up a gash in his cheek.

''He is carrying on like a damned woman,'' John de Vescy growled. He was on the point of apologizing for his loose tongue when Chandra laughed beside him.

17

"YOU LOOK AS IF YOU swallowed a prune," Joanna said to Chandra.

"Nay, I was just wishing we had word from Haifa. It has been nearly a week without news."

Eleanor, arranged comfortably on thick soft cushions in Ali ad-Din's bathing room, said easily, "They will send word soon, Chandra. There is little to fear. My lord told me before they left that the Saracens had only a loose hold on the city, and would likely flee at the sight of our army."

The slave girl who had been soaping Chandra rose at a word from Beri, and poured a jug of warm, perfumed water over her. Chandra sighed with pleasure, and slithered into the cool bathing pool. As was her habit, she floated in the water, listening to the giggling Joanna and the chattering slave girls. When she opened her eyes, she saw Beri staring down at her, an odd assessing look in her dark eyes. She stood up, pulled her blanket of thick wet hair over her shoulder, and twisted out the water.

Beri handed her a towel. "Come," she said. "This time I have a very special perfumed oil for you."

"Will it remove this ugly scar?" Chandra asked, looking at the jagged ridge of flesh on her arm.

"Nay, but 'twill make men wild to be near you."

Chandra gave her a twisted smile. " 'Tis not something I wish."

"Perhaps you should," Beri said.

Chandra stretched out on her stomach and felt the warm oil trickle down her back until a slave girl began to rub it lightly into her flesh. She turned her face toward Beri. "Why did you say that?"

Beri shrugged. "I told you once that I did not understand.

You are beautiful, your body glows with health, and you are not at all ill-tempered.''

"You have never seen me angry, Beri.''

"You are proud, that is different, and perhaps that is what I do not understand. Sir Jerval will also have a scar, just as do you.'' Her gentle fingers lightly probed at the raised flesh on her arm.

Chandra felt her words sear through her mind. She reared up on her elbows, only to have the slave girl gently press her back down.

"What do you know of Sir Jerval's scar?'' Her voice sounded taut and harsh in her ears.

"I told you once that my master, Ali ad-Din, wished to repay your husband for his assistance against the Genoese.'' She cocked her head to one side, her eyes liquid with gentle question. "I am his payment to Sir Jerval.''

"I—I do not know what you mean,'' Chandra said, but she did know.

"You are lucky,'' Beri said, and smiled sadly. "You have a noble husband, and a kind one. And, I suppose, I am lucky too, for he is the only man to possess me other than my master. He gives me great pleasure.'' She shrugged again, and said with stoic calm, "But he will leave soon, you his wife with him, and I will stay here and do as my master bids me.''

Memory of Sicily flamed in her mind, memory of Jerval telling her of his need, and she had not disagreed. But that was just talk! She stared at Beri's slender, smooth olive flesh and her gentle-featured face, and could find no words. She raised her head and looked blindly toward Eleanor, who was sitting up talking to the splashing Joanna. A desolate rage burned within her.

She heard herself say, "Is he gentle with you, Beri?''

Beri smiled wistfully as she brought her attention back to Chandra. "Aye, even though his hunger for me is many times great.'' Her gaze flickered toward Eleanor. "I have heard it said that the handsome prince has refused all such offerings, even though his lady is filled with child. She is beautiful, but not as are you.''

"Do you not mind that you must accept him?''

"It would not matter if I minded or not,'' Beri said, surprise in her eyes. A smile again curved up her full lips,

lips that Chandra knew had roved over her husband's body, giving him pleasure that she had denied him. "I only hope that my master does not take a liking to other nobles of Prince Edward's army, for I would be too tired to see to my duties during the day."

"Chandra? Did you not hear me? There is a message just delivered. We have taken Haifa, and our husbands are all safe!"

Chandra gazed blankly toward Eleanor, who was waving a letter a slave girl had given her. "Thank God," she said. She rose from the table, and allowed a slave girl to help her dress.

"Stay awhile, Chandra," Eleanor said, after she had dismissed the other ladies and the slaves from the pavilion.

Eleanor gazed at her, her graceful brows drawn together. "I have seen you praying every day at St. Andrew's Church since our men left. God in his infinite mercy must have heeded your pleas. The army will return perchance tomorrow. Does that not please you?"

"Aye, of course," she said. But she was numb with a pain she could not define. It gnawed at her, giving her no peace.

"That is more than you have said all evening. Come, Chandra, what troubles you?"

Chandra dug her fingernails into her palm. "Nothing troubles me, Eleanor."

"Are you upset because you could not accompany Sir Jerval to Haifa?"

"He could have been killed," she said, sudden anger blazing in her voice. "Had I not been with him during the Saracen's attack at the Neva Pass, I would not have known how close I was to becoming a widow!" She turned wild eyes to Eleanor. "Damn him! He was angry with me because I fought to protect him!"

"Nay, he was angry because you could have been killed. Men such as Sir Jerval and my lord think it their first duty to protect the women they love." As Chandra continued rigidly silent, Eleanor said gently, "Would you still, Chandra, after all you have seen, have women ride into battle? Then what would you expect our men to do? Put their great strength to use at the looms, overseeing the servants at their tasks? By the Virgin, Chandra, the only useful function men would have would be to spend occasional nights with us, and plant their seed in our wombs.''

He plants his seed in Beri's womb! ''Nay, you do not understand, Eleanor,'' she whispered brokenly. ''I do not want that.''

Eleanor smiled. ''Good,'' she said briskly, her hands lightly folded over her huge belly. ''At last you perceive some value in our husbands.'' She saw Chandra stiffen, and added sternly, ''I know something of the conflict between you and Graelam de Moreton. Even you, Chandra, would have been taken against your will had it not been for Jerval.''

''I know it well, Eleanor.''

''Then, child, why are you crying?''

Chandra gulped, but her tears fell unchecked down her cheeks. ''Jerval couples with Beri!''

Eleanor started in surprise. She had known for some time, for Edward had told her. When she had protested, he had told her to mind her own affairs, and leave be. So Chandra had just discovered the fact. Eleanor was pleased that she was so distressed. It boded well.

''You are jealous,'' she said.

Chandra shook her head vehemently. ''Nay!'' she cried, then covered her face in her hands. ''I want to die!''

Eleanor paused a long moment in thought. ''Men are selfish creatures,'' she said at last, ''and they justify themselves by saying that their needs are great. Sir Jerval has broken faith with you, before God. He has betrayed you.''

Chandra's head whipped up. ''But he is not selfish . . . and he has not broken faith. 'Twas I who forced him to another woman!''

''Now why would you do that?'' Eleanor asked, her expression puzzled. ''What woman would turn away Sir Jerval? Surely you are wrong, Chandra. Surely it is as I said. Your husband is not the honorable man I believed him to be. Perchance you should continue keeping him at a distance, letting him take his lustful pleasures elsewhere.''

''It is too late in any case,'' Chandra said dully.

''Nonsense.''

''Nay, 'tis true. My father forced me to wed him, and I was afraid.''

''Afraid of what?''

"Afraid of coupling, and being the weaker, afraid that he would own me."

"Do you believe that I am owned, that I am useless?"

"Of course not. . . . 'Tis different with you, with Edward."

Eleanor laughed. "You are foolish, Chandra, but I begin to see that you do not believe your litany." She leaned forward and patted her hand. "To love someone is always frightening. But if I did not trust Edward with my life and my happiness, I should not wish to continue. Do you not understand, Chandra? Your husband's happiness lies equally in your hands."

"But I do not know what to do!" Chandra wailed. "He no longer wants me, for I have driven him away."

"Thus his anger when you could have been harmed," Eleanor said dryly. "Of course, that is not what he told Edward. He praised you, as did John de Vescy. But he will always fear for you, and demand to protect you, for you are a woman, and there is no changing that."

"I do not know how to be a woman."

"I think you have a day to think about it before Sir Jerval returns. You are not still a virgin, are you?"

Chandra flushed, and shook her head. "The passion I felt for him was . . . frightening, but it has been so very long."

"Men, I think, need very little encouragement," Eleanor said, "once they understand what is expected of them."

"Do you really believe so?"

Such innocence, Eleanor thought. Aloud, she said firmly, "Aye, I think you will find that Sir Jerval is not at all dull-witted."

While Chandra was pacing restlessly about their tent waiting for Jerval, Eleanor was recounting to Edward her conversation with Chandra, giggling at the unexpected treat Jerval most assuredly had in store for him. "Good lord," Edward said, grinning wickedly, "would that we could be flies on the tent flap to watch!"

"I am returned, hale and hearty, Chandra."

She whirled about to see Jerval stride into the tent. She only stared at him.

"You are surprised that I am clean? And out of my armor?"

"You are all right?" she managed. "Your side did not pain you?"

"Aye, I am fit again." He stopped abruptly, staring at her. "You look pale. What is the matter?"

She looked uncomfortably away. "Why, nothing, my lord. Have you yet eaten?"

He nodded and turned to pour himself a goblet of wine, but he wondered at her appearance. Her eyes were too bright, as if she were feverish, and she was wearing her hair loose in flowing soft waves to her waist, not in its usual severe braid. "Edward has asked us to come to their pavilion later."

"I—I would prefer to remain here."

"I see," he said, not understanding at all.

"I would like to play a game of chess," Chandra said, pleased with her inspiration.

"You would? It has been so long." He looked at her curiously. "Are you certain you are all right?"

"Of course! Let me get the table!"

As she arranged the pieces on the table between them, he said thoughtfully, "Edward wishes to go to Cyprus. He still hopes to be the peacemaker between King Hugh and his barons. With their aid, there is a chance that Hugh could retain some portion of his kingdom here."

"Would you go with Edward?"

He started, for there was a forlorn catch in her voice. "Likely," he said cautiously.

"Oh," she said. She moved a white pawn forward and raised her goblet, sipping the sweet wine, searching for something beguiling to say.

Jerval looked down at the chessboard, and said, "You had a bad time with your monthly flux two weeks ago. Are you certain that you are well now?"

She felt color stain her cheeks. "How do you know of that?"

He shrugged. "One of Eleanor's slave girls told me. She does not think that you should ride so vigorously when it is near your time. Indeed, she scolded me."

"I will be more careful in the future, my lord."

He looked up at her. "My lord? You are formal tonight, Chandra." He held her eyes for a moment, still wondering at her. It was very unlike her that she had not asked him anything about the battle at Haifa.

"I do not mean to be formal, Jerval," she said.

He moved his pawn to face hers.

She gazed down stupidly at the pieces, unable to concentrate. She moved a knight at random, then a bishop. In five more moves, she had lost her queen.

"You seem to have forgotten more than I have, Chandra," Jerval said, grinning at her.

"I—my mind is on other things." She blurted out, "You smell nice."

He cocked his head at her. "I bathed before, I told you."

"Would you care for more wine, Jerval? 'Tis quite cool and calms the senses."

"I like my senses just as they are," he said, arching a thick brow at her. "Do you dislike the thought of defeat so much, Chandra?"

"What defeat?"

"I think I was speaking of our chess game."

"Your hair is long. I—I like the way it curls at your neck."

Jerval sat back against his chair and crossed his arms over his broad chest. "Why?" he asked her.

At his bald question, she jumped. "I thought to . . . compliment you."

"Then allow me to return the favor, my lady. Your gown is lovely, as is your hair."

"You are being kind," she muttered, "but you needn't be so now, if you don't wish it."

"Chandra, you are making no sense."

"I mean that you needn't do or . . . say anything you do not wish to."

"Christ," he said. "It rained today, so I know you have not been too long in the sun. You must know that I will say and do just what I wish."

She could not meet his eyes. Everything was going awry. She felt helpless tears sting her eyes, and shook her head.

"Were you too much alone while I was gone?" He rose and held out his hand to her. "Come, we will go visit Edward and Eleanor."

"Nay!"

"What? Chandra, you are crying. Whatever is the matter?"

"I am not crying! I am angry!"

He cupped his fingers under her chin and forced her to look up at him. He was taken aback at the look of frustration in her eyes, and something else that held him silent.

"You are supposed to understand," she grated at him, "but you do not! I do not know what to do!" She looked down at her toes.

His eyes fell to her breasts, heaving against the thin material of her gown. Slowly, he drew her into his arms. "I understand now," he said gently, kissing her soft hair, "and I know what to do. You have been trying to seduce me, have you not?"

"Aye, Jerval, but I am wretchedly bad at it."

"Kiss me, Chandra, and you will succeed."

She raised her face and pursed her lips together, her eyes closed. He grinned, and lightly touched his fingertips to her mouth.

"You had but to tell me, my lady, without resorting to a chess game." He stroked his hands down her back, tangling his fingers in her thick hair. He kissed her, lightly probing her mouth, and she parted her lips to him. He felt a tightening in his loins, and lifted her against him, pressing his manhood against her soft belly. He held himself in rigid control, for she was offering herself freely to him, and it was a gift and a pleasure to be savored.

She clutched at his shoulders and felt the power of him, felt the urgency of his need for her. For an instant, she was afraid, but his mouth was gentle, his hands lightly stroking, and she relaxed against him. She rubbed herself against his body, remembering the scalding sensations he had given her so long ago, the convulsing passion that had imprisoned her, then freed her.

His hand cupped her breast, then slowly coursed downward, his fingers splaying over her. Jerval forced himself to calm, and released her. She cried out softly, deep in her throat, her arms still on his shoulders.

"Our clothes, Chandra," he said. To his delight, she tore at the fastenings on her gown. He followed suit, a curse of frustration on his lips when the string on his chausses knotted.

"Do you still want me, Chandra?" he asked when she stood naked, gazing wide-eyed upon his manhood.

"Aye," she whispered. "I think so."

"I will help you decide," he said. He drew her against him, and smiled when she arched her body against him, mewling softly. "Lie beside me," he said, his voice an almost painful whisper.

She nodded, no words in her mind. They lay facing each other, and for a moment, he feared to touch her. He stared into her eyes, smoky and vague. Beautiful eyes, a deep blue, shimmering like the sea at dawn.

"Why do you stare at me?" She was suddenly afraid that he was pulling himself away from her. "Do you not want me?"

He clasped her hand and gently guided it down his belly. When her slender fingers closed over him, he smiled. "How can you think I do not want you?" He kissed the tip of her nose, and watched her eyes widen when he rubbed his palm lightly over her nipples.

She touched her fingers to his face and pressed herself toward him, wanting to feel all of him against her. She wrapped her arms about his back, and explored the bands of muscle beneath his smooth, warm flesh. The image of Beri touching him came to her, but she resolutely shut it out.

She still held him, and her fingers were light and delicate, her touch an innocent and exquisite torment. "Chandra," he groaned, and firmly pulled her hand away. "You will make me shame myself."

She wondered vaguely at her power until his fingers pressed downward from her belly, and he found her.

"Move against me," he said softly, nuzzling her throat.

She started to tell him that she did not know how, but she pressed her hips upward, clumsily at first, then in a steady rhythm. She groaned at the aching need she felt, and stared at him in wonder.

He pulled her trembling body tight against him, and slowly his fingers eased their caressing, and slipped easily inside her.

"Does that please you?" he whispered, and she moaned against the pulse in his throat.

He pressed her onto her back, and stared down at her delicate womanness, her curling golden hair, damp with her desire. She opened herself to him, and when he guided himself into her, she thrust her hips upward, and cried out.

Jerval eased himself deep within her moist softness, his eyes upon her face. When he felt her slender thighs hugging his sides, her body open and yielding to him, he could not contain himself, and plunged wildly into her. She tensed beneath him, and he heard her cry out. He covered her lips with his, and moaned his release into her mouth.

She was whispering love words to him, and clutching his back, holding him down on top of her. For many moments, his mind was a vague blur, raw sensation warring with thought. He could feel her pounding heart against his chest, the giving softness of her breasts and belly. He shook his head, clearing away his passion, and balanced himself over her on his elbows to stare down into her face.

"Did I hurt you?" he asked foolishly.

She smiled, a smug smile, replete and satisfied. "You are terribly big. I am filled with you." She puffed out her cheeks. "Did I hurt you?"

"Aye," he said softly. Her eyes dimmed in sudden fear, and he kissed her. "Little fool," he whispered into her mouth. "You drove me frantic and nearly killed me with pleasure."

"I—I feel so good," she said, her hands closing about his arms.

"As do I." He paused a moment. "Did you mean all those things you were whispering to me?"

"You would not believe me if I said nay."

He felt himself slipping away from her. He closed his arms beneath her back, and rolled her over onto her side against him. He felt her soft cheek against his shoulder, and gently smoothed her hair away from her face.

"This is the first time you have ever wanted me," he said.

"Nay, you know that is not true. I wanted you desperately that night at Camberley, and in Sicily when you found me in my bath. I had forced myself to forget until you caressed me and kissed me." He was silent, and she raised herself on her elbow and looked down into his face. "Why did you say that?"

He cursed softly to himself. "Because it is true, at least about Camberley." He raised his hand and curled thick tresses of her hair about his fingers. "I suppose I owe you the truth about that now."

"You have always been honest with me."

He drew a deep breath. "That night, long ago, when you were frantic with passion, 'twas I who made you so."

"Indeed, that is true."

"I gave you a drug that lulled your fears. I felt I had to

know if your fears were so great that you could feel no pleasure with me. I reproached myself the next day, for you were so frightened, of yourself, and of me.''

"I thought I was a whore." She sighed deeply. "There was, and is, such passion that it is that which frightens me.''

"There should be naught to frighten you. I remember telling you—''

"Nay, shouting at me.''

He grinned. "Aye, shouting at you that a wife should know pleasure with her husband. It helps, you know, when there are . . . disagreements between them.''

He felt her fingers lightly brush down his belly and tangle in the thick bush of hair at his groin. He cocked an eyebrow at her. "I gather you forgive me?''

"I want to ensure that there is enough intimacy between us so that we will not disagree for at least a week.''

He kissed her parted lips, and let his hands caress her breasts. "I see that you are not indifferent to me," he mocked softly.

"I have never been indifferent to you, Jerval," she whispered.

He drew a deep breath, knowing the words had to be spoken. "Why, my love?" he asked her quietly.

When she raised soft, liquid eyes to his face, he knew she understood. "There was naught else I could do," she said. "I could no longer bear to be alone, locked within myself." She lowered her face, rubbing her chin against his shoulder. "So many things have happened, and I have known such fear for you. I thought I would die when you were wounded at Nazareth.''

"And, of course, there was Eleanor," he said. At her startled look, he added quietly, "I am not blind, Chandra.''

"Aye," she said, " Eleanor is wise in her love." *And Beri*. "Will you still love me if we continue to disagree?''

"Inevitably." He looked at the scar on her arm. "There will be some things I cannot change, Chandra, some things that you will have to accept.''

"Because you are a man.''

"Aye, because I am a man, and life, even at Camberley, is so damned uncertain.''

"But I was not useless during the Saracen attack. I did save Graelam and help John de Vescy.''

"That is true. I suppose I sound like a fool, and if John heard me, he'd likely call me an ungrateful dog, but perhaps the next time it would be your life to be forfeit. Never could I bear that cost, never."

"So it must always be I who waits in fear?"

"Believe me," he said, grinning, "our fear will be equal." He released her arm and laid the flat of his hand in the hollow of her smooth belly. "When you carry my child, it is his safety that must be your only concern."

"I am to be the giver of life, and you its protector."

His eyes lightened with amusement. "Those sound like some philosopher's words."

"Nay, they are Eleanor's."

"Can you say them, and mean it?"

"If by doing so I am not less than you."

"Ah," he said, "we are back to obedience." He paused, laughter rumbling deep in his chest. "Aye, we will likely have great fights and make the servants cower in fright. But there will be love between us, and respect. If you will agree to that, then all else will work itself out."

She grinned at him impishly. "If I agree with you, my lord husband, how will you seal our . . . coming together?"

His tongue trailing over her flat stomach was his answer. He reveled in the silken feel of her smooth flesh. He heard her moan softly, and felt her fingers tangling in his hair. He raised his head to look at her while his hands followed the path of his tongue over her belly, not quite touching her where her need was greatest.

"Jerval," she said on a groan. When his mouth closed over her, she pressed herself against him, unable to help herself. Jerval heard her wild, breathless cries, and felt her nails dig into his shoulders. He lifted himself and raised her hips in his large hands, gazing at her for a moment before he drove deep into her willing flesh. He fitted himself tightly against her, pounding his belly against hers, until she cried out, and her legs tensed about his sides. He intensified her moment of pleasure, then, with a gasp, seated himself deep within her, and gave himself his release.

Chandra's passion had been so great that for many moments, she could do nothing but breathe raspy breaths. She felt absurdly happy, and snuggled her face into the hollow of his throat.

He kissed her forehead and nuzzled at her ear until she obeyed his silent command to raise her lips. He caressed her mouth lightly, undemanding.

"I must rest a moment, my lord," she said, giggling into his mouth, a sweet lassitude pervading her mind and her body, "else I will be hoarse in the morning from the joy you give me."

"For a while, perhaps," he said, tracing his tongue over the curve of her ear.

"You will not leave me?"

"I doubt if I could leave you even if the damned Saracens besieged Acre." He let his hand glide over her belly and tangled his fingers in the silky hair between her thighs.

"You are sticky with my seed," he said, bemused. His fingers lightly stroked her soft woman's flesh, and he laughed softly when he felt her wriggle against him.

"Not as yet, my love," he said. He rolled over onto his back and drew her against his side.

"I love you, Jerval," she whispered, the simple words spilling easily from her mouth. For an instant, she tasted the fear of vulnerability.

"It took you long enough to realize it," he said, tightening his arms about her. "You will not now forget, will you?"

"Nay, never. You know once I make up my mind, I am most stubborn."

"I am more stubborn than you, Chandra. I have loved you since I saw you standing in the great hall of Croyland." He paused a moment as his fingers lightly probed the raised scar on her arm. "I have sometimes believed myself a witless fool, but I am a de Vernon. There has been too much between us . . . and not enough."

"I would that it change," she said simply.

"It has."

There were no more words between them, and they slept within minutes, Chandra sprawled beside him, her hand curled upon his chest.

Chandra awoke to find that she was alone. She sat up, staring about their tent. She clasped her arms about her knees, shivering.

"What is this, my lady? I leave you curled up asleep like

an innocent babe, and return to see you huddled over and trembling.''

Chandra jerked up her head at the sound of his voice, and for several moments she did nothing but stare at him. ''I—I thought you had left me,'' she stammered.

''I had to relieve myself.''

Jerval stood silently, watching her. Her golden hair was tousled about her face, falling over her shoulders and down her back. Her full breasts, a creamy white, contrasted alluringly with her tanned face. She seemed suddenly to become aware that the cover came only to her slender waist. To his delight, she blushed.

He sat down on the side of the bed. She did not move, simply gazed at him wide-eyed, her cheeks still flushed. He gently pressed her onto her back, pulled the cover from her waist, and let his gaze wander over her slender body. He touched his hand lightly over her belly, and felt her tense.

''You are beautiful, wife,'' he said.

''Nay, my lord,'' she whispered, '' 'tis you who are that.''

He leaned down and lightly touched his lips to her golden curls.

''You wish to possess me again, Chandra?''

''Will I always feel this way when you touch and caress me?'' she managed. She curved her body to fit him as he pulled her into his arms.

He kissed her temple. ''Aye, always, even when we are old.''

''In fifty years,'' she mused aloud, smiling.

He loved her gently, slowly awakening her, relishing the incredible warmth of her giving flesh. He watched her face in the moment of her pleasure, and knew himself possessed.

When she lay at her ease beside him, her breathing calm, he carefully pulled away from her and stretched his arms above his head. He could not recall when he had felt so alert, yet so relaxed. He turned his head slightly to look at her. Her expression was thoughtful.

''Are you still pondering what I said, and your agreement?''

''Nay, I am thinking about . . . you.''

''If you were thinking only about me, there would be a smug smile on your face.''

''You know me too well, Jerval. I—I was thinking about my father.''

He was relieved that it was she who brought it up. He said carefully, "Do you still believe that I am like him?"

She smiled faintly, but her eyes were clouded. "I am not certain," she said slowly. "I suppose I want you to reassure me that you are like him only in . . . the good ways."

"And if I tell you that I am not?"

"I should not like it, and should probably want to die."

He brought his arms from behind his head and turned on his side, balancing himself above her on his elbow. "I am no saint," he said quietly. He saw a flash of pain in her vivid eyes, and wondered if she knew about Beri. He said softly, "My love, I could never leave our bed if I knew that you were waiting for me."

"Even when I am lumpy and fat and filled with child?"

"Even then," he said firmly.

There was a babble of voices outside their tent, and regretfully, he kissed her, and rose. He stood, staring down at her, a smile hovering about his mouth. "I find you strangely bereft of modesty now, Chandra."

She stretched languidly, and he felt a leap of desire. "I believe I shall consider your words, my lord, while I watch you dress."

18

JERVAL ROLLED OVER AND DREW Chandra against him in the early dawn. "Nay, my lord," she whispered, "you must let me go. Joanna is waiting without for me. Eleanor's pains have begun."

Jerval shook away the sleep and sat up. "I will go with you. Edward is likely pacing a ditch in the ground."

"And what will you brave warriors do, my husband? 'Tis Eleanor who works now."

Jerval stretched and pulled his tunic over his head. "I shall clap him on the back for being such a virile bull."

Chandra left her husband with Edward outside the pavilion surrounded by his nobles, and joined Joanna at Eleanor's bedside. Her other ladies were fluttering about, but Eleanor, smiling and calm, bade her welcome.

"I have told Edward to keep Geoffrey away from me until the poor man has at least broken his fast," she said. "It is early yet." She winced, catching her lower lip between her teeth, and Chandra gasped. " 'Tis nothing, child," she said.

Chandra braided her long hair to keep it from tangling about her face. She was beginning to believe that there was not so much to birthing a babe when Eleanor suddenly groaned, and gasped, "Bring in Geoffrey Parker now. You, Chandra, take Joanna with you and leave the pavilion."

"Nay, Eleanor," Chandra protested. "Our place is here with you!"

"Neither of you has given birth as yet. You will come back to me when it is over."

Chandra turned pale and glanced back nervously when she heard a cry from within the pavilion.

"What is Geoffrey doing?"

Edward's thick blond hair stood in spikes about his head,

308

but at her words, he grinned. "Nay, Chandra, 'tis the babe, not poor Geoffrey."

"Where is Jerval? He told me he would help you pace a ditch."

"And Payn?" Joanna asked.

"I sent them away. They were driving me distracted. Christ, they were worse than Eleanor's women."

"I hope Payn still wishes his son," Joanna said.

Eleanor's pain lasted but another hour. Edward, his eyes gleaming with pleasure and relief at the sound of a thready infant's wail, rushed into the pavilion, Chandra and Joanna at his heels.

Chandra, her face glowing, returned to their tent, calling out to Jerval before she even raised the flap, "Jerval! Eleanor has given birth to a daughter, and she is beautiful! She is not at all wrinkled and ugly, and do you know what she will be named?"

Jerval quickly swallowed the roasted beef, and rose, smiling at her excitement. "What is the fair princess's name?"

"Joan of Acre."

" 'Tis fitting," he said. "Thank God it is over." He sat back down, and Chandra dimpled at his rumpled hair. "You are as bad as Edward," she said, "and the child is not yours."

"Come sit on my lap," he said, "and give me succor. 'Tis been a trying morning."

"Ah, my great, brave warrior," she murmured. She sat on his thighs and nuzzled her face against his throat.

"Edward is so happy," she said. "He kept kissing Eleanor—in front of me—and telling her how much he loved her. Then he would gaze at his daughter and smile like an idiot. Would you like to see her now?"

"Come lie with me first, Chandra," he said abruptly.

"It is the middle of the day!" She tried to look shocked, but she succeeded only in giggling.

"It is always you who have your way," he said, his warm breath upon her mouth. "When you moan in your passion, I am your slave."

"You are no one's slave, my husband." She smiled dolefully. "I have no experience other than you, but I think that you would feel less than a man if I do not share your

pleasure. And that, my husband, is because you want to be
my conqueror.''

He was nuzzling her neck, lightly nipping at her smooth
flesh. He raised his face, cocking his head to one side.
''Mayhap,'' he said, grinning lustfully down at her. He pressed
hard against her, molding her supple body to his.

''Do you feel conquered?'' he asked her later when he saw
passion glazing her eyes.

''How can you expect me to talk, much less make sense?''
she gasped.

He laughed and turned onto his back, bringing her on top
of him. ''So I am to be your conqueror, Jerval?'' she said
huskily when she straddled him.

He could not long contain himself, and pressed back his
head, moaning deep in his throat. He closed his hands about
her waist and pressed her down upon him.

''I have heard it said,'' he said softly, ''if I stay within you
like this, it is likely you will soon become like Eleanor.''

To his utter delight, Chandra wriggled her hips, drawing
him deeper.

''I am eighteen now,'' she said.

''An old woman.'' He wrapped her hair about his hand and
pulled her face down to him.

Edward sat alone in his tent, wearing only his tunic, having
rid himself of his hellishly hot armor, wondering what the
devil was keeping al-Hamil, an emissary from a local chieftain who had made a truce with the Christian knights. He was
impatient to join Eleanor and their babe, Joan, and the fly
that kept hovering about his forehead did not improve his
temper.

He heard conversation outside his tent, but did not rise. He
looked up as the flap was raised, and nodded welcome to
al-Hamil, a large man for a Saracen, nearly as tall as Edward,
with black bushy eyebrows that nearly met across his forehead.
Al-Hamil stepped inside the tent, and bowed low to Edward.

''Sire,'' he said softly, walking slowly forward.

''What have you to say to me today, al-Hamil?'' Edward
asked. He waved him toward a stool, and turned slightly to
reach for a goblet of wine. He saw a shadow of swift movement
from the corner of his eye. He flung the goblet of wine
toward the Saracen and threw himself sideways even before

he saw the gleaming dagger descending. He felt a prick of pain in his upper arm, and with a growl of rage, he lunged at the Saracen, his iron fingers gripping the wrist that still held tight to the dagger.

"Christian dog!" al-Hamil cried, spitting into Edward's face. "It is too late for you, for the dagger has pierced your flesh!"

Edward felt the Saracen's arm weakening beneath his fingers, and slowly, he turned the dagger toward al-Hamil. Before the Saracen could wrench away from him, Edward brought up his knee and thrust it brutally into his belly. Al-Hamil bellowed in pain, staggered, and fell to his knees. He saw the dagger's vicious point aimed at his throat.

"Allah!" he screamed.

Edward locked his arm behind the Saracen's neck, and with a final surge of strength, drove the dagger into al-Hamil's chest. The Saracen gazed up at the prince and smiled, even as his blood trickled from his mouth. He slumped backward, his eyes, now sightless, locked on Edward's face.

Edward jumped back, his chest heaving. He saw his guards flooding into the tent, staring at him in shocked silence. He wanted to speak to them, but he felt a wave of nausea close over him. *It is but a prick in the arm,* he thought as he crumpled to the floor.

Jerval, Chandra on his heels, burst into the crowded tent to see Edward's two physicians leaning over him, probing at the swelling flesh of his upper arm. Eleanor stood at the foot of his cot, keening softly, tears streaming from her eyes.

Jerval, angry at the babbling disorder, shoved the bewildered soldiers from the tent. "For God's sake," he shouted at them, "keep everyone out!"

"The dagger was poisoned," Payn said, "and the damned physicians are but wringing their hands!"

Edward slowly opened his eyes. He felt a numbing chill radiate from the wound in his arm. He looked up at Geoffrey Parker. "Is there nothing you can do?"

"Sire, it is a heathen poison, a poison that we do not understand. We have cleaned the wound." He turned his eyes away from Edward's gray face. "We can do naught save sew the flesh together, and pray to God."

Jerval turned to Roger de Clifford. "Send a man to fetch

the Templar physician, Sir Elvan. If it is a heathen poison, he may know what to do.''

Eleanor raised her eyes at Geoffrey's words. For an instant, she looked about her blankly, at the hovering nobles standing impotently about, at the drawn faces of the two physicians.

"Poison,'' she whispered. There was a bluish tinge about her husband's lips, and he was trembling uncontrollably. Her eyes fell to the still-swelling gash in his arm. Edward gave a low moan, and his head fell back against the cushions.

"Nay!'' Eleanor cried. "He will not die!'' She rushed from the foot of the cot and shoved Geoffrey roughly out of the way.

"My lady, please!'' Geoffrey pleaded. "You must leave! There is nothing you can do!''

"I will not let him die! Get out of my way, all of you!'' She fell to her knees beside Edward and lowered her mouth to the gaping wound. She spat the blood and the venom from her mouth, and sucked again at the wound until she could draw no more blood or poison from it. Slowly, she fell back on her knees, and bowed her head in prayer.

There was stunned silence, until Chandra slipped away from Jerval and eased down to her knees beside Eleanor. "My lady,'' she said gently, lightly touching Eleanor's white sleeve, "you have done all you can for your husband. Come away with me now.'' She looked up, a flush of anger coloring her cheeks. The physicians had begun to argue with each other in hushed whispers.

"Likely kill our lord,'' she heard one of them say. "And to bring in a Templar physician!''

Eleanor seemed oblivious of them. "Nay, Chandra, I cannot leave my lord.'' She shuddered, wiping her hand across her mouth. "I tasted the poison . . . it was awful, like decaying flesh.''

Chandra quickly poured her a goblet of wine. "Here, Eleanor, you must wash out your mouth.''

Jerval and Payn shoved aside the bickering physicians. Chandra helped Eleanor to her feet, and they watched silently as Jerval vigorously rubbed Edward's arms and legs.

"By all the saints!'' Payn cried softly. "He should not remain unconscious so long!''

Eleanor sat beside her husband and lightly slapped his face.

"My lord," she whispered. "Please, my lord, open your eyes."

Edward's fair lashes fluttered. He heard Eleanor's voice from afar, vague and distant, and he was suddenly frightened that she needed him. He heard her voice again, closer now, and with a great effort, forced his eyes to open. He felt light-headed, and the wound in his arm was a raging pain, so great that he clamped his lower lip between his teeth to keep from crying out. When he focused his gaze, it was not Eleanor he saw above him, but the dark-seamed face of Sir Elvan, the Templar physician.

"Hold still, sire."

Sir Elvan nodded to Jerval and Payn. They sat on either side of Edward and held him firmly.

Edward scarce felt the knife plunging into his flesh. He heard Eleanor sobbing softly. He wanted to soothe her, but no words seemed to come to his mouth. A fiery liquid followed the path of the knife, and Edward lunged upward with a cry of agony.

"Payn, hold him!" Jerval shouted. It required all their strength to keep Edward down as Sir Elvan opened the wound still wider and poured more of the dark liquid into it.

Sir Elvan slowly straightened. "The poison should have bubbled up from the wound," he said. "It may have worked so rapidly that my remedy will have no effect."

Jerval smiled toward Eleanor. "I believe, Sir Elvan, that there is no poison because the Princess sucked it from the wound."

Sir Elvan's expression did not change. He looked at Eleanor, still sobbing, her black hair straggling about her pale face.

"My lady," he said softly, "it is likely that you have saved your husband's life."

Edward heard his words, and gazed up vaguely into his wife's face. She was smiling.

"I am so blasted weak! Damn, but this is ridiculous!"

"And ill-tempered, and impatient to be well again," Jerval said, standing over him. "At least you are no longer worried about making out your will."

"You make my neck sore, Jerval. Sit down."

Jerval complied. "Eleanor is suckling her babe and will return to you soon." Jerval smiled suddenly, his white teeth gleaming. "Now, Edward, both you and I owe our miserable lives to our wives."

"Aye," Edward said. "It is a strange and daunting thought." His fair brows lowered. "Why did you not stop her? The poison could have killed her."

"It did not occur to me to stop her. Indeed, I believe if anyone had tried, she would have killed him."

" 'Tis likely true," Edward said, and smiled. "She has been like a clucking mother hen, just as Chandra was when you were wounded at Nazareth." He shook his head. "Geoffrey Parker now meets with Sir Elvan daily, to learn from him. At least he will return to England with something."

Jerval looked at Edward steadily, saddened at his bitterness.

Edward laid his head back against the pillow and closed his eyes. "I wonder what would have happened had King Louis not died. He would have added another ten thousand men to our cause."

"As pious and well-meaning as Louis was," Jerval said quietly, "he still fancied himself a leader of men—"

"Which he was."

"Not in battle. It would have been you to lead our armies in battle, Edward, not Louis. I wonder, after seeing all the bickering among Christians here, if all would have gone as we hoped."

"I remember so clearly feeling that God himself laid the cross of his holy cause upon me," Edward said slowly, "that I was to be the instrument of his hand, to free his land of the Saracens. Even after hearing of Louis's death, I still believed that I was chosen to take Palestine."

"It was the thought and belief in all our minds."

What in God's name am I to do? Edward cried silently, the pain of his spirit making his wound as nothing. "God knows we have tried," he said aloud, "but with a thousand men, we have achieved so little. Sometimes I feel the hideous desire to pray to God to rain destruction upon all the sanctimonious Christians who have refused to leave their comforts and come to our aid."

"The Holy Land is thousands of miles from most of Christendom, sire. It no longer holds the promise of great wealth, or even the promise of freedom of God's people. I have wondered if we were right to ask the ilkan of Persia to send his Mongol armies into Syria to stave off the Saracens.

The Mongol hordes are heathen themselves, just as the Saracens.''

"Aye, but if the Christians would not help us, I saw no other choice. When I think of King Hugh's miserable barons, snug and safe on Cyprus, I want to kill the lot of them. And King Charles of Sicily! He is a ruthless, ambitious man, our Charles. He watches like a giant hawk, waiting to see whether he can bring himself greater wealth and more land. He schemes only for control of all the trade routes in the Mediterranean.'' There was a bitter glint in Edward's eyes. "Perhaps he will succeed. I begin to believe that God has forsaken His land. We came with such hopes, like children who look only to God for succor.''

"Acre would have fallen had we not come, Edward.''

Edward said quietly, "Acre will fall, Jerval. 'Tis but a matter of time. I find myself with most unchristian thoughts. When Acre does fall, the damned Venetians and Genoese will know the death their greed has brought them. I have pleaded until I am hoarse, but it does no good. They are bent upon destroying each other, and Palestine is the bone they are fighting over.''

Jerval was silent, knowing well that even Edward's near death had brought only mendacious letters of concern from Christians in the Holy Land. There was nothing more, never anything more. Duty to God and to Edward was a grave cross to carry.

"I have given it much thought,'' Edward continued quietly. "What I sought to accomplish was a child's dream. I see clearly now that all we can hope for is a temporary halt to the Sultan Baibars's craze for the rest of Palestine. I have heard it said that Baibars fears me.'' He laughed, bitterly. "Why, I cannot imagine. He probably believes that confronting me would bring the rest of Christendom to my aid. He seeks a treaty, Jerval.''

Jerval sucked in his breath. "I did not know, sire.''

"Nay, I have told no one. I think he grew restive at my delay and took a chance that the rulers of Christendom would simply mourn my death with pious prayers, as they did King Louis's. Had I been gracious enough to succumb to the assassin's dagger, he would have had what he sought quickly enough, though even he has sent me his profound regrets that the Syrian assassin could have done such a dishonorable deed.''

Jerval muttered, ''The damned whoreson. God that I could stick my sword through his miserable belly.''

''Save your anger, my friend. If I guess aright, he is even now taking advantage of my weakness to gather an army to attack us. It is sound strategy, I must admit. I need you to lead our troops, Jerval. I have no wish to be forced to negotiate a treaty with Baibars without an army.''

''John de Vescy has men scouting to the north. We will know soon enough if and where the Saracens are gathering.'' Jerval turned questioning eyes toward Edward. ''You have decided upon the treaty with Baibars, then?''

''Aye, I have decided. Our failure will be a grave disappointment to my father.''

''You have accomplished more than your great-uncle, Richard,'' Jerval said.

''My great-uncle was driven by the lust for adventure and battle. I was driven by God.'' He added wearily, ''It seems that neither is enough.''

19

DAMARIC WATCHED THE LADY CHANDRA as she paced outside her tent, awaiting news of the battle. He had not liked being assigned as her personal guard so that Lambert could join the battle. He wished she would at least go back into her tent, so he could find some shade and return to his dice without the sun beating down on his head.

They both started at the pounding of horse's hooves. Damaric moved closer to Lady Chandra, saw that it was Sir Eustace de Leybrun, and eased again.

"Eustace," Chandra greeted him, her voice neutral.

"Chandra, I must speak to you."

She felt a lurching fear at the intenseness of his tone. "What is it, Eustace? Come, tell me, what has happened?"

Before he answered her, Eustace's gaze flickered toward Damaric. "Something has happened to Jerval!" Chandra nearly shrieked at him.

He nodded his head, not meeting her frantic eyes. "He has been wounded, Chandra, badly, and sent me to fetch you. I have already sent the physicians ahead, for the fighting is over. Quickly, get something to cover your head. The ride will be hard. We must hurry."

Chandra stumbled away to do his bidding. When she emerged from the tent, she saw Damaric standing by her horse. He tossed her into the saddle and jumped astride his own destrier.

"Damaric will help me protect you," Eustace said shortly. He brought his mailed hand down upon her palfrey's rump, and the mare broke into a gallop.

"He will be all right," she whispered to herself. "I will be in time." In time to see him die, her mind answered her. She dug her heels into her palfrey's sides, and lowered her head close to her mare's neck.

They rode north toward Caesarea, keeping the inland sea

but a mile to their west. They had ridden but half an hour when she heard Damaric call out behind them, "Sir Eustace! The fighting was to the north. We are headed east!" Chandra looked to her left, for she had not noticed they had lost sight of the sea.

Eustace drew in his destrier and waited for Damaric to rein in beside him. Chandra turned her mare, frowning. She saw Damaric slide to the ground from his horse's back. Eustace, a grim smile on his lips, was rubbing his blood off a dagger. She stared at him in shock, and then at Damaric, sprawled dead upon his back.

"What have you done?" she screamed at him.

He grabbed her palfrey's reins and pulled her in.

"My God, you killed him! Why?"

"So you have finally come out of your daze, Chandra. Well, no matter now—we will soon be far from Acre." He sent a quick gaze toward Damaric. "There will be no one to say that happened to you, save me."

"Jerval!" she shrieked at him.

"Your precious husband is well."

She weaved in her saddle with relief. "But what is it you mean, Eustace? Dear God, what are you saying?"

He laughed harshly and sat back in his saddle. "I will have to tell Jerval that his stubborn wife insisted upon joining him, and that Damaric and I, fearing for your safety, rode with you to protect you. How sad that we were attacked by Saracens, and only I will be alive to tell of it."

She cursed herself as a fool for not strapping her dagger to her thigh. She squared her shoulders and demanded, "What do you want, Eustace?"

"My dear Chandra, you and I are going to the camp of al-Afdal, one of Sultan Baibars's chieftains. He heard of you from one of the Saracen soldiers who escaped from the Neva Pass. The man described a beautiful creature who fought like a man, all white-skinned, with golden hair. Al-Afdal gained a fortune from the looting of Antioch, and he is quite willing to share it with me, once I give you to him."

"You are braying like an ass on a dunghill," she said coldly. "You are a fool."

Eustace raised his hand to strike her, but drew it back. "Nay, I will not mark you. Your new master would not like it."

Chandra dug her heels into her palfrey's sides, but Eustace

held fast to the reins. "That was your one try, Chandra, and your last. I know all your tricks, so you needn't waste your time trying them on me."

She spat at him, full in the face. He stared at her for a moment, wiping her spittle from his cheek, before he smashed his mailed fist into her ribs. She doubled over in pain, and heard him say softly, "I told you only that I would not mark your face, Chandra."

"You will not succeed, Eustace," she panted, trying to recover her breath. "Jerval will not believe you. He will kill you."

"Did you not listen, my lady? The direction your captors lie will, unfortunately, be miles from where I lead your husband."

"Why, Eustace? Why do you do this? Have you no honor?" She stared at him, still disbelieving, even with Damaric dead at her feet.

He gave a crack of rude laughter. "Riches, my lady, riches. And the joy of knowing that you will part your white thighs for your heathen master the rest of your life, or until you lose your beauty and he tosses you away."

She gazed at him, unable to believe that he still carried hatred of her for her refusal of him so long ago at Camberley. "Let me go, Eustace. Your treachery will gain you naught."

"Enough talk, Chandra. I wish to be farther away from Acre. You will ride with me, else you will feel my dagger in your breast." He brought his hand down again on her palfrey's rump and forced her to a gallop beside him.

They rode due east, and the ground turned hilly and brittle beneath the horses' hooves. It seemed like hours to Chandra before Eustace jerked on her palfrey's reins and pulled his destrier to a halt. "We will take our . . . rest here, my lady." His eyes scanned the surrounding countryside, and turned back to her.

Graelam rode toward Acre to give Edward word of his own victory, in the company of one of his men-at-arms and his squire. Edward would be quite pleased with the outcome of the battle. They had attacked the ill-prepared Saracens as they themselves gathered for a final blow after the attempted assassination of Edward, and had scattered them easily.

Graelam stretched his tired bones in his saddle, and looked

Catherine Coulter

inland, away from the sun-reddened sea. He saw a riderless horse cantering toward them, and frowned, recognizing the stallion as Damaric's. For a long moment, he held his destrier still, his dark brows lowered. He knew that Jerval had ordered Chandra never to leave the camp without a guard. Without another thought, he ran the horse down and reined him in. He saw a drop of blood on the saddle.

"Christ," he muttered under his breath. What in God's name had happened? He turned to his men. "We ride east until we find Damaric."

It was Albert, Graelam's squire, who spotted Damaric's body on a flat stretch of ground, his legs covered with sand by the desert wind. There was a clean stab wound in his throat, and his sword was sheathed. Graelam raised his lifeless arm. It was not yet stiff in death.

"Albert, ride back to Sir Jerval. Tell him that we found Lady Chandra's guard murdered." Graelam studied the ground for several moments. "There are two horses riding to the east. Tell Sir Jerval that we will follow and will leave a trail for him. Quickly, man!"

Graelam swung onto his destrier's back, wondering why in God's name Chandra could not be like the other ladies and remain safe in the camp until her husband's return. Had she been so impetuous as to demand that Damaric accompany her to the battle site? Perhaps Jerval's proud lady had not been at fault. He smiled faintly at this thought as he dug his heels into his horse's belly. He owed her his life, and it displeased him to owe his life to a woman, even the fierce maiden warrior of Croyland. Perhaps he could repay his debt.

"Off your horse, my lady," Eustace said. "We wait here."

Chandra did not move. "You are mad, Eustace," she said.

He laughed. "Not mad, my lady, never mad." His eyes swept over her. "Besides the riches I will have, I will also have the memory of your lovely body, a very lovely body that you once denied me. Since you are not a virgin, it makes little difference how many men plow you before you become al-Afdal's sole property."

"I will see you in hell first!" She drove her fist into his jaw. More from surprise than from pain, Eustace reared back and dropped her palfrey's reins. Chandra scooped them up, and with a wild cry she sent her horse into a frenzied gallop.

Eustace's powerful destrier quickly overtook her, his shadow huge and black against the moonlit rocks. She gave a cry of fury when his thick arm closed about her waist and lifted her off her palfrey's back. She felt herself strangling in his grip for want of air, and fell against him.

Eustace pulled his destrier up and flung her to the rocky ground. She looked up to see him jerking up his surcoat and ripping at the string of his chausses. Eustace was grunting as he tugged at a knot in the string. He looked down at her, sprawled before him, her gown torn and riding up her legs. "I begin to see why Jerval does not want to leave your bed." He tossed her his mantle. "Spread your lovely body upon it."

Chandra rolled to her side away from him and jumped to her feet. She grabbed the mantle and flung it over his head. She heard him curse as she rushed over the ground toward her palfrey. Jagged points of stone cut into her slippers, but she did not slow. She heard him still cursing loudly, close behind her now, and she gave a cry of anger and whirled about to face him, knowing that she could not outrun him. She kicked at his groin when he reached her, but her gown held firm above her knee, and her foot landed against his armored thigh. Eustace grunted in pain, but closed his arms around her and flung her backward.

"Now, you little hellcat," he growled, his voice a mixture of pain and lust, "you will know a man!"

Chandra writhed beneath him, trying to throw him off balance, but he was like a bull, crushing her into the cold stones. She felt his hand ripping her gown, and she screamed at him, cursing him. His hand was upon her bare thigh, squeezing her flesh.

"Nay!" she screamed, flinging her head from side to side in her fear. She could feel the cold night air against her naked skin, and his rasping breath dinned in her ears. She reared up in one final surge of strength and struck at his face.

Chandra heard low, angry voices. She raised her head, painfully. She saw about a dozen desert-garbed Saracens, some still on their horses, and several standing near to her. She heard Eustace growling angrily, "You have no right to interfere, you damned heathen! I was told I could enjoy her before she became al-Afdal's whore!"

She raised herself to her elbows. The Saracen who ap-

peared to be their leader was speaking quietly. "The bargain
was made, Sir Eustace, but you will not take the English girl
here, on the rocky ground, and give her bleeding and cut to
my master." Munza breathed a sigh of relief. If his master's
physician found seed in the girl's body, his life would be
worth less than an old slave's. He turned and looked down at
her. All she could see was a dark face, framed in a white
cloth turban. "Ah, she is awake."

He dropped to his knees beside her. She did not move
when he touched his fingers to her jaw. She thought she saw
a glint of pity in his black eyes. "Do you have pain?"

She shook her head.

The Saracen said over his shoulder to Eustace, "You will
pray to your Christian god that you have not scarred her."

"She fought me, Munza," Eustace snarled. "She is a little
bitch, and wants taming!"

"Cover yourself," the Saracen said coldly, his eyes dropping to Eustace's open chausses. "It will be for my master to
say what is to be done with her." His black eyes flickered
over her, thoroughly assessing. "She is more beautiful than I
believed possible. Al-Afdal will be pleased. It is a pity she is
not a virgin."

Chandra raised her hand to clutch at his sleeve. "Do not do
this," she said. "You must return me to Acre and my
husband. You will be greatly rewarded, I promise you."

He shook off her hand and rose. "Can you stand?"

She nodded, knowing there was no hope with him. Slowly,
she forced her knees to lock and hold her weight. "Here,"
the Saracen said, and threw her a mantle to cover her ragged
gown.

She wrapped it about her thankfully. At least her body was
no longer open to these men's eyes.

"When can I have her?" she heard Eustace demand, frustrated anger in his voice.

Munza shrugged. "When my master accepts her, your
bargain will be sealed. Come, al-Afdal awaits."

Chandra was helped to her feet and set upon her horse.
There was no more talk among them, only the sound of the
horses' hooves pounding over the rocky ground. They were
riding to higher ground, and the night air became colder. She
thought of Jerval, wondering if he yet knew that she was
gone, wondering what he would do. She felt tears sting her

eyes, tears of grief for what could have been, tears for what she had found so briefly, and lost. She knew she would still have to suffer Eustace's body; the Saracen had agreed it was part of the bargain. Then he would take his money and return to Acre, full of feigned anger and grief at her capture. And she would be left, like Ali's slave girl, Beri, for the rest of her years as a man's whore. New tears welled up in her eyes, tears of self-pity. She would kill herself, aye, she would kill herself, before she would let Eustace or any of the Saracens touch her. But her vow of suicide curdled like sour milk in her belly. She did not want to die, at least by her own hand. It was a coward's vow, and by Christ, she would not be a coward.

Graelam and his man-at-arms drew up in the shadow of a huge rock at the sight of a ghostly white-garbed band of Saracens. Chandra was riding in their midst, Eustace with their leader at their fore. Graelam gripped his soldier's arm. "We can do naught against a dozen Saracens. Ride back and bring Sir Jerval and his men. You will have no difficulty tracking us. I will follow to see where they take her."

As he rode through the night, keeping well out of sight of the Saracens, Graelam smiled grimly, picturing his huge hands choking the life out of Eustace.

The mountainous terrain gave way to a barren plain of low sand hills pressed among scattered rocks and boulders. Chandra looked up as she shifted wearily in the saddle and saw lights in the distance. As they grew nearer, she could make out a cluster of palm and date trees, and the outline of tents set between them. They formed a small village at the edge of the plain, its back pressed against the mountains. Horses whinnied and groups of armed men shouted in welcome. They rode past a pool of clear water with women kneeling beside it, filling goatskin jugs. Thoughts of escape dimmed in her mind at the sight of so many people.

The Saracens drew to a halt before a huge, many-domed tent, and their leader jumped down from his horse and threw the reins to a boy standing beside its entrance.

"Come inside, Sir Eustace," Munza said in his lilting accent. "My master will want to see you."

Eustace dismounted and swaggered toward the huge tent.

He turned as Munza helped Chandra off her palfrey, and said, "It is just as well. I will enjoy her more once she is bathed and readied."

Munza said nothing, though his lips tightened. He grasped Chandra's arm and forced her to walk beside him to the tent. He stopped her a moment in the light, and studied her face. "There is a slight bruise, that is all. My master will be pleased."

Chandra gazed at him coldly. "Your master will be pleased for only a short time. Then he will be dead."

Munza drew back, and then frowned at her. He was not a tall man, and the English girl's cold eyes bored into his. He knew that the Christian women were not like Moslem women. But still it shocked him that she could speak so brazenly, and stare at him with such contempt. "You will learn how to behave, my lady," he said. "Else my master will flay the white skin from your beautiful body."

"Another brave man," she mused aloud, pleased with the disdainful hauteur in her voice. "Take me to this marvelously brave master so that I may gaze upon his noble face."

Munza seemed suddenly worried. "A slave does not look into her master's eyes unless he wishes it. Remember my words, my lady, else you will not live to say more."

Chandra forced herself to shrug indifferently. She pulled the mantle about her torn robe and walked, stiff-backed, beside Munza, into the tent.

She blinked her eyes rapidly, adjusting to the blazing resin torches that lit the interior of the tent. It was an immense structure, its floor covered with thick carpets, slashed with vivid reds and golds. Fat, brightly embroidered pillows were piled beside small circular tables, delicately carved in sandalwood. Flowing, translucent veils of cloth separated the tent into chambers, and it was toward a large central chamber that Munza led Chandra. She was aware of silent dark-skinned women, their faces covered with thin veils, who briefly raised their downcast eyes at her. They were dressed as slaves, with flowing tops of light material fitted snug beneath their breasts, leaving their skin bare to the waist, and long, full skirts, fastened at their waists by a thin band of colored leather. She could see the line of their naked legs through the shimmering cloth. Dark, bearded men stared at her openly, undressing her with their eyes. She forced herself not to shudder.

She began to feel as if she were walking through a gauntlet designed to humiliate her. At last, Munza drew apart a golden veil that hung from the roof of the tent to its floor, and shoved her forward. She stood silent for a long moment, and drew in her breath. She could not believe that such riches could be gathered in a tent, set in a barren desert. There was gold everywhere: goblets that glistened upon the low tables, chests that were bound with intricately carved gold bands, and even thick pillows embroidered with gold thread. The light was not so bright here, and its softness added to the opulence of the room. Munza grasped her arm and pulled her forward.

"Bow to my master, al-Afdal," he hissed close to her ear.

"I will see him in hell first," she said coldly, loud enough to reach the man sprawled at his ease on the far side of the chamber. She threw her head back and stared insolently at the man. His dress was different from that of the desert-garbed Saracens. He wore a short jacket, without sleeves, fastened across his wide chest by golden chains. His trousers, like his jacket, were of pristine white wool, full at the thighs, and bound by a wide golden belt at his waist. When her eyes traveled to his face, she was surprised to see a young man, with a beard curving to a sharp point at his chin. He was not ill-looking, but his black eyes were coldly assessing. She saw thick black hair on his chest curling about the golden chains, and shuddered.

"This is Lady Chandra de Vernon," Eustace said in a loud confident voice, stepping forward. "She gave me a bit of trouble, but I barely marred her beauty."

"Come here," al-Afdal said. He raised a heavily jeweled hand toward her. He did not answer Eustace or even acknowledge his presence.

Chandra jerked her arm free of Munza and strode forward. She drew to a halt some three feet before al-Afdal and crossed her hands negligently over her breasts. "So, you are the jackal who bribed this weak fool"—she paused a moment, and cocked her head contemptuously toward Eustace—"to bring me here."

"You little bitch!" Eustace roared and took an angry step toward her.

"Quiet, my friend," al-Afdal said softly. He rose grace-fully to his feet, and Chandra was taken aback at his size. In her experience, Saracens were small men, wiry and slight of stature. "I believe I told you to come here, Chan-dra." She started at the still-gentle tone of his voice. He spoke her name as two distinct words.

She shrugged and stepped forward, aware of a sigh of relief from Munza. "Are you so desperate that you must steal women? So ugly and ill-formed that you cannot persuade women to come to you without force?"

He moved so quickly and gracefully that Chandra scarce had time to draw back. He dropped her mantle at her feet onto the carpet.

"I see that you did fight Sir Eustace," he said in that same soft voice. He turned his dark eyes to Munza. "Did the English knight take her?"

Munza shook his head quickly. "Nay, master, but he would have had I not stopped him."

"She is no virgin," Eustace growled. "What does it mat-ter how many men plow her belly?" Al-Afdal did not reply, and Eustace continued, emboldened, "I would prefer to have her once she is bathed. Then I will take my leave of you, with the gold you promised me."

Al-Afdal nodded slowly. "As you wish, Sir Eustace." He raised his hand toward a group of women who had entered silently. One of them, a girl with skin and flowing hair as black as ebony, stepped forward, her eyes upon al-Afdal's pointed slippers. Even they, Chandra noticed, were braided with gold and studded with gems.

"Calla," he said to the girl, "take Chan-dra to the baths, then return to me. I wish to be present when the physician examines her." He said to Chandra, "Do as you are bid, else I will have my men hold you down. Do you understand?"

Chandra nodded slowly.

"Calla," he continued, "speaks your tongue. She will give your instructions to the other slaves."

Again Chandra nodded. She knew that she must learn the extent of her confines before she could act. She quickly lowered her eyes, afraid that al-Afdal would guess her thoughts, so keen was his gaze.

Al-Afdal watched her as she followed Calla from the chamber. She was proud, he thought, proud and untamed and exquisite, like a white-petaled rose. He remembered that his father had once purchased a young girl from Persia, a fiercely proud girl, and he had crushed her spirit, and the beauty of her pride. He turned back to the English knight, his dark eyes hooded. Perhaps he would not give the English girl to Eustace as he had planned. She wore her pride like a maidenhead, and he wanted that prize for himself when he plundered her belly.

Chandra followed Calla into a smaller room at the far end of the tent, with several of al-Afdal's men close behind them. It was not unlike Ali ad-Din's bathing room, save there was no sunken pool and no mosaic tile covering the floor. A large brass tub, shaped like a hollowed-out lemon, was set in its center, and women were filling it with steaming, fragrant water.

"Please to undress now," Calla said.

Chandra looked quickly about her, but there were only women. As she shrugged out of her torn clothes, she gazed more carefully about the chamber. It was an inner room that did not touch the perimeter of the tent. The roof dipped down in scallops between slender wooden supports. She wondered what would happen if she managed to pull down one of the wooden poles. A bit of a commotion, perhaps, she thought, but that was all. She laid her clothing on a low, linen-covered table that she guessed was used to oil the bathers after their bath.

"Calla," she said suddenly, turning to the ebony black girl. "I am here against my will. I do not belong here. Please, you must help me."

Calla's great liquid brown eyes stared silently into Chandra's pale face. She said softly, "I know who you are, but there is naught I can do about it. My master seems to think you some kind of . . . goddess."

Chandra snorted disdainfully. "Goddess! That is ridiculous. I am but a woman, like you, Calla, and I have a husband, an English noble, who will miss me."

"You are prideful," Calla said softly, slowly shaking her head, "but you must take care. Al-Afdal is not a patient man. No one dares to gainsay his will, and especially not a slave."

Chandra said nothing more, and stepped into the tub, unaware that Calla was studying her body, her huge sad eyes hooded.

She allowed herself to be bathed by the silent women. Like

Ali's slaves, some of the girls were scarce into womanhood, their young breasts barely molded into roundness. She lay back and closed her eyes, trying to think what she was to do. *I will not let him touch me, him or Eustace, no matter what happens*. Her silent vow made her strangely calm. Much to Calla's surprise, she fell asleep in the swirling hot water.

Chandra started awake, feeling refreshed, and she smiled up into Calla's astonished face. At least her fatigue was gone from her. She felt strong and alert.

Calla motioned her to lie on the linen-covered table. Chandra lay on her back, staring up at the tent top, and did not bother to look at Calla until she heard her say in her soft voice, "Do not move. I do not wish to cut you."

Chandra started up, balancing herself on her elbows. She saw that Calla held a thin razor in her hand.

"What are you doing?" she yelled, scooting back.

Calla's eyes traveled down Chandra's belly to the nest of damp golden curls between her thighs. "My master does not like woman's hair," she said.

"Your master can go to hell!" Chandra gritted, and in a quick movement, she swung her legs over the table and grabbed Calla's arm at the elbow. "Get that thing away from me."

There was no fear in the girl's brown eyes. She shrugged, and Chandra released her. "You are not like the rest of us . . . perhaps the master will not notice."

Chandra watched her place the razor on a pile of linen towels and take some colorful gossamer cloth from the arms of another slave girl. "Let me dress you now. The master, as I said, is not a patient man."

Chandra did not resist. She had no intention of being naked in front of any of these heathen. The veils that covered her breasts were a pale lavender, as soft to the touch as moth's wings. Calla fastened the material together beneath her breasts with a golden clip. She stepped into a floor-length skirt much like the one Calla wore, and let Calla tighten it in folds at her waist with a leather belt. She noticed that Calla was barefooted. She sat docilely while several slave girls, under Calla's direction, combed out her wet hair.

"Don't you want to shave it off?" she said dryly.

"You show no fear. I do not know what the master will think."

"Mayhap he will be intelligent enough to release me." She heard Calla sigh softly.

They fastened her damp hair back from her forehead with a gem-covered strip of stiff golden cloth.

"You are very beautiful," Calla said finally. "I will fetch the physician and my master now."

"Why a physician?" Chandra called sharply after Calla's retreating figure.

Calla did not reply, and Chandra was left to stand among the whispering girls. She walked about the small enclosure, as if with great indifference. The girls watched her for a while, then resumed their duties. She stood next to the pile of linen towels, inching her hand toward the razor. Her fingers were hovering above the ivory handle when the veiled curtains parted suddenly and al-Afdal entered. She whipped her hand away and turned to face him.

She felt his eyes upon her, studying her, she thought, as if she were a prized bit of horseflesh. He lowered his head a moment and listened to Calla's softly spoken words, words that Chandra could not hear.

She saw his dark eyes flash and one of his hands clench into a fist, the huge ruby ring he wore on his middle finger gleaming in the soft light. She noticed a man standing behind him, tall and painfully thin, dressed in a white turban and a full white robe that covered him from his throat to his toes. His eyes reminded Chandra of a lizard's, small and never calm. Like his master, he wore a full beard that was trimmed to a sharp point at his chin.

Al-Afdal's anger grew as he watched Chandra. Even from where he stood, he could see purple bruises on the English girl's bare ribs. A man did not need to harm a soft-fleshed woman, unless he wanted to, of course. And Calla had said that there were other bruises on her body, and cuts on her arms and legs. He began to doubt Munza's assurances that he had saved the girl from being ravished by the English knight. He strode over to where she stood, staring at him proudly, her golden head thrown back, a disdainful look in her sky-colored eyes.

He waved his hand back toward the physician. "You will remove your clothes. I wish my physician to examine you."

He saw her stiffen and could practically see the words of refusal forming in her mind. He continued patiently, "If you do not, I will have the clothes ripped from your body, and there will be no more for you. A woman without clothes is a more malleable creature."

"If you meant me to be naked, then why did you give me clothes in the first place? If you would call these . . . veils, clothes!"

A smile twisted his full mouth. "My little Calla dressed you because she feared my wrath. She tells me that you refused to have your woman's mound shaved."

Chandra felt a flush of embarrassment course over her cheeks. "You will not touch me, you miserable jackal!"

She saw his dark face flush, but he only shrugged. "We will see, Chan-dra."

"No, we will not see!" she yelled at him. "It is your hair that is disgusting—why do you not shave off that black chest? You have the look of a matted animal!"

She heard Calla gasp and saw the slave girl recoil from the corner of her eye, but al-Afdal did not move. She saw his cold black eyes narrow in rage, and she stiffened her shoulders. If she was to die, she could not die cowering like a slave.

"Help her do my bidding," he said finally to the slave girls, his voice cold as the air of the desert night. In an instant they had surrounded her, and were unclasping the fasteners and unwinding the soft material that covered her. Chandra tried to keep the agony of shame from showing in her eyes when she at last stood naked before al-Afdal.

"Lie down," he said shortly, his eyes firm on her face.

She did as she was bid, holding her body stiff, like a wooden puppet. She tried to cover herself with her hands, and turned her head away, her eyes closed.

She jumped when she felt fingers, light and probing against her bruised ribs. She turned her face and stared up at the physician's impassive countenance. He was speaking quietly to al-Afdal as his fingers roved over her. Her arm was raised and examined, then lowered back to her side. They spoke quietly again, words she didn't understand.

The physician left her side, and al-Afdal strode forward to stand beside her. "The physician finds you fit, Chan-dra." His eyes roved down her body, and he gave a crack of laughter. "I will not demand that you be shaved—indeed, the golden hair against the white flesh is pleasing." She jerked away at the touch of his hand.

"Do not fear me, Chan-dra," he said softly. "You have but to please me and your life will be contented."

"Fear you!" she spat at him. "You are nothing but a crowing little rooster, a heathen above other heathens, atop his dunghill!"

"I cannot allow you to continue insulting me. You will keep your mouth shut, else I will have your tongue removed."

"Then my eyes will tell you what you are to me. What will you do then—blind me?"

His jaw worked in convulsive anger, and she held herself stiffly, forgetting for the moment that she was naked, and awaited for him to strike her.

Al-Afdal turned away from her a moment, and said abruptly to the physician, "You will examine her belly, to see if there is a man's seed within her."

Chandra grabbed at the embroidered linen cloth that covered the table and pulled it around her. "No more," she hissed. "I am not a slave, nor am I your possession. I will not allow this!"

Before al-Afdal could raise his arm to strike her, his patience at an end, Chandra lunged toward the pile of towels and grabbed the ivory-handled razor. "Now let us see what a brave man you are, al-Afdal!"

Al-Afdal took a step toward her, for a moment so angered that he forgot the reports of the Saracen soldiers that the English girl was a fighter, swift and deadly. He was drawn up suddenly by an unearthly shriek of pain from outside the chamber. He whirled about, his dagger unsheathed, to see a huge English knight lunge into the chamber, his sword flailing over his head, three of al-Afdal's men swarming behind him.

"Graelam!"

Graelam took in her long flowing hair, the white cloth that was wrapped about her, and the glinting razor clutched in her hand. "Get behind me, Chandra," he yelled. "Cut through the tent! There is but a women's chamber beyond!"

For an instant, she believed that the entire English army would follow him. But there was no one, only more of al-Afdal's men. She whirled about and slashed her razor out at one of the Saracens as he passed her.

Al-Afdal heard his man yell out, and whipped about to see him fall to his knees, clutching his shoulder, and Chandra's razor red with his blood. One of his men tossed him a curved scimitar, and he caught it handily, only to see that Chandra had grabbed the sword of the man she had wounded. The small chamber was fast filling with his men, rushing toward them. If the fighting continued, she would be killed, and likely a half-dozen of his men with her.

He came to a quick decision. "Surround him!" he shouted, raising his scimitar toward Graelam. "And keep away from the girl. I will kill the man who draws her blood!"

Graelam knew that he would die, and he cursed himself for being a noble ass and a fool to believe that he alone could save her. Only his heavy broadsword was holding back the men who surged toward him, and their number grew with every moment. He felt the flat side of a scimitar strike the back of his legs, and he went hurtling to the floor onto his back. He saw a black-eyed Saracen above him, his scimitar raised in an awful arc, and a prayer came to his lips as he prepared himself to die.

"Do not kill him!" Al-Afdal's voice cut through the din. The man above Graelam stiffened, his scimitar poised to strike downward. Even as Graelam tried to push himself up, another pointed blade touched the flesh of his throat.

"Chan-dra!" Al-Afdal shouted. "Throw down the scimitar, else the English knight will die!"

Her scimitar was poised to strike down at a Saracen's blade when she heard al-Afdal's words. She saw Graelam upon his back, some five men pinioning him. She gave a cry of fury and defeat, and drew back, panting.

"Drop the scimitar!"

She saw al-Afdal's black eyes boring into hers, and slowly, she let the scimitar slip from her hand. One of the men, dazed with a blow she had given him, lunged toward her before al-Afdal could stop him. He looked on in horror and then in utter surprise.

Chandra jumped to the side, the cloth that covered her pulling from her body, and tripped the man as he lunged past her. She grabbed his wrist and brought her foot down on his elbow. In the next instant the man lay on his back, clutching his broken arm. Her foot was poised to crash into the man's ribs when she heard al-Afdal shout at her again to back away.

She looked toward Graelam, unaware for the moment that she was naked, and let her shoulders slump forward.

Al-Afdal grabbed the fallen cloth and threw it over her. She clutched the material to her and took a stumbling step away from him.

"Do not kill him," she whispered, still panting so that she could barely speak.

"Is he your husband?"

She shook her head mutely.

"A brave man," al-Afdal said, "but stupid to believe that he alone could save you." He saw the bleak look in her eyes, and pivoted about. "Well, Englishman," he continued, "it appears that Sir Eustace was not so careful as he thought." He motioned to his men, and they pulled Graelam to his feet.

"Chandra," Graelam said, "I am sorry."

Chandra turned furious eyes toward al-Afdal. "You will not kill him," she said.

"No," al-Afdal said thoughtfully, staring at her. "I have other plans for your brave knight."

He saw Munza standing in the entrance. "Was the Englishman alone?" he barked.

Munza nodded. "He must have seen Sir Eustace and the English girl and followed them, master."

"Post more guards. I think we would be wise to leave for Montfort soon."

Montfort. The once Frankish castle captured by the Saracens. It would be impenetrable. Chandra chewed at her lower lip frantically, but the truth was inescapable. Once inside the fortress, all of Edward's army could not rescue her.

Graelam's arms were bound and he was dragged from the chamber. Al-Afdal looked a moment toward the slave girls still cowering against the walls, the physician beside them, then back to Chandra, a slight smile curving his wide mouth.

"Calla, dress her and bring her to me." He touched his hand to Chandra's bare arm. She did not flinch, but stood rigid. "You will, of course, do as you are told now, Chan-dra."

He nodded toward the physician, and in the next moment, Chandra was once again alone with the slave girls. The women seemed afraid to come near her. She shrugged out of the cloth and said sharply, "Bring me clothing."

20

CHANDRA FOLLOWED CALLA THROUGH THE tented corridors to the chamber where al-Afdal waited. She looked about anxiously for Graelam, but he was not there. Eustace stood next to al-Afdal, who lay sprawled on soft cushions, much in the same pose she had first seen him, a golden wine goblet in his hand. She felt numb with uncertainty. Was Graelam dead? And if not, what was al-Afdal up to, that Graelam would not be here?

"Come here, Chan-dra."

She walked stiffly toward him, the shimmering fabric of her skirt clinging about her legs.

"Is she not exquisite, Sir Eustace?"

Eustace took in the gem-studded clasp at her waist and followed the movement of her thighs through the translucent veils. Her hair, now dry, flowed down her back in deep waves.

"I suppose you would like to take her now, as we agreed."

Eustace felt a bulge of lust beneath his chausses. "Aye," he said, his voice thick, "and then I will take my leave of you."

"Would you care to take her here, in front of my men? They have never seen an Englishman rut a woman."

"She will fight me," Eustace said. "She must be tied down."

To Eustace's surprise, al-Afdal threw back his turbaned head and laughed. "Yes, she would fight you. She would also likely unman you before you thrust yourself into her belly. But, my friend, I don't want her . . . bruised. See what you already did?" Al-Afdal rose gracefully to his feet and walked to Chandra's side. He did not touch her, only pointed to the dark purplish bruises over her ribs.

"Perhaps," he said thoughtfully, turning back to Eustace,

"Chan-dra needs a man to fight for her." He watched, a half-formed smile on his lips, as Eustace glanced contemptuously about at his men.

"Give me a sword. I will fight him."

Al-Afdal glanced at her face and saw that she was perfectly serious. "I cannot risk that you would be harmed, Chan-dra."

Eustace started forward, suspicious now of the Saracen chieftain's intentions. "Just give me my gold, and I will leave. I do not want her."

Al-Afdal stroked the point of his beard thoughtfully. Eustace felt a shiver of fear.

"Is it not a practice among you English," al-Afdal said, "to provide a champion for the weaker?"

Chandra felt the blood rush to her temples. Al-Afdal had Graelam, and it would be he to fight Eustace. Did Eustace not know anything of Graelam?

Eustace's hand clapped about his sword, and he slowly backed away.

"Do not be so anxious to leave, my friend," al-Afdal said softly. "I have another English knight for you to meet." He nodded toward Munza, and Graelam was shoved into the chamber, flanked by four of al-Afdal's men, his arms bound tightly behind his back.

"De Moreton!" Eustace cried.

"Aye, you filthy bastard!" Graelam snarled at him.

Al-Afdal returned to his seat of cushions. "I will make you a bargain, Sir Eustace," he said. "If you can defeat Lord Graelam, you will leave here with your gold."

Eustace ran his tongue over his lips, held silent by fear.

"If Lord Graelam defeats him, will we be allowed to leave?"

Al-Afdal smiled toward Chandra. "Not you, Chan-dra, but your noble Graelam will be free."

"Release me," Graelam said hoarsely. "I will carve his gullet from his throat." He did not trust al-Afdal to free him if he killed Eustace, but at the moment, he did not care. He turned his hooded dark eyes toward Chandra, and saw that she was gazing at him sorrowfully, her eyes glistening with tears. He smiled at her, nodded almost imperceptibly, his gaze warm and comforting.

"Clear the chamber," al-Afdal said. "I do not wish my possessions hacked to bits. Come stand beside me, Chandra.'' He held out his beringed hand toward her, and she had no choice but to obey him.

"May God be with you, Graelam," she whispered as she passed him. "I—I thank you."

Eustace saw the bloody gash in Graelam's arm and ceased to sputter about al-Afdal's trickery. It was his sword arm, and Eustace knew that he must be weakened. He drew his sword, ran the tip of his thumb along its sharp edge, and threw a glittering smile at Graelam. "Aye," he said, gloating at him, "you have lusted after her, have you not? You will die in your lust, Graelam, and the little bitch will spend the rest of her days serving the heathen paynim."

Graelam did not answer him. He concentrated on his memories of Eustace in battle, as his hands were unbound. He knew that Eustace thought that his wounded right arm would do him in. His sword was placed in his right hand, and he left it there. Nay, he thought, let the fool believe he will have an easy time of it. He flexed his arm, and grimaced. Eustace slashed his sword before him, his mouth set grimly, his eyes alight with the victory he knew would be his.

"Well, Chan-dra," al-Afdal said, closing his hand about her wrist, "I do not need to ask you whom you favor, do I?"

She kept her eyes steadily upon Graelam, not deigning to reply to him. Her heart was pounding in her breast. "Be careful, Graelam!" she wanted to shout, but the words emerged from her throat in a hoarse whisper, like gritty sand.

Al-Afdal raised his arm, and brought it down swiftly. "Now, my noble English knights!"

With a loud roar, Eustace lunged toward Graelam, his sword high above his head. In the instant Eustace's sword arced downward in a blur of silver, Graelam tossed his sword to his left hand. The clash of ringing steel jarred the silence of the tent.

Al-Afdal watched calmly as Graelam and Eustace joined swords, hacking at each other. They moved slowly, their armor restricting their freedom, and he saw that it was a test of strength between them. His men would have dashed in and out, whirling about to avoid the crunching blows, relying on their quickness rather than a grueling contest of might. Both men were soon panting heavily, their brows beaded with sweat.

Eustace suddenly disengaged and took several jerking steps

backward. He saw Graelam holding his sword easily in his left hand, and cursed aloud.

"You will rest soon enough, coward!" Graelam shouted at him. "Come to me, you scum!" But Graelam did not wait. Like a raging bull, he rushed toward Eustace, his sword flailing before him, cutting a wide path of control.

As he neared, Eustace kicked his leg out and smashed it against Graelam's thigh. Chandra cried out as Graelam fought to retain his balance, but his foot caught on a fringed edge of the carpet, and he hurtled onto his back. Eustace lunged toward him, his sword raised high. He gripped it in both hands to send it downward to Graelam's chest with all his might.

Graelam saw Eustace's gloating face above him. He did not have time to twist out of the sword's path, for his armor was like a coffin of dead weight, making him slow and clumsy. He saw the blur of silver steel, and heard Chandra moan softly in her throat. Dear Christ, he thought, his mind strangely detached, to die because of a kick in the leg and a clumsy fall on a carpet.

The instant was like an eternity of time. Eustace opened his mouth to shout his victory, but the words never emerged. He heard an odd hissing sound, and a soft thud. Eustace raised his eyes in astonishment, his sword slipping from his grasp. Graelam awkwardly jerked himself onto his side, just as Eustace, a thin-bladed knife in his throat, fell heavily to the floor.

Graelam heaved himself up. He gazed stupefied toward al-Afdal, then at Eustace, who lay dead, his blood welling from his pinioned throat.

"You killed him," he croaked, staggering to his feet.

"Yes, my friend," al-Afdal said easily. He nodded to Munza. "Bring me my knife."

Chandra swayed toward al-Afdal, and felt his hand, the one that had hurled the deadly dagger, close about her wrist, steadying her. She looked up at him stupidly. "Why?" she whispered helplessly.

He did not immediately answer her. "Take Lord Graelam to your tent, Munza, and guard him well. Give him food and drink, and a girl, if it pleases him."

Graelam shook his head, still disbelieving that he was alive, and the heathen Saracen had saved his life. He gazed at

Chandra, but he had no chance to speak to her before he was prodded from the chamber.

"Sit down, Chan-dra. You do not look well."

"Why did you spare Graelam?"

He gave her a long, considering look, his fingers lightly stroking his bearded jaw. "It is really quite simple. You hated Eustace and are grateful to the other man, Graelam, for trying to save you. It would do me no good were Graelam to die. While I have him, I have his life to give you, and you will obey me because you will not want me to kill him as you watch."

Al-Afdal saw understanding fill her eyes before her thick lashes swept down to her cheeks. "Come with me now, my proud captive, for I would enjoy your body and the touch of your soft mouth upon mine." He saw her stiffen, and added, his voice softer still, "You will never deny me or fight me now, Chan-dra, for if you do, my dagger will pierce Graelam's throat, and your brave knight will die because of your stubborn woman's pride."

She forced herself to look up into his face, and recoiled from the gleam of male assurance in his black eyes. "I hate you," she whispered with hopeless calm. "Believe me, I will always hate you."

He shrugged, his eyes indifferent. She did not realize that her words had filled him with silent anger. To punish her, he sent for the physician to accompany them. He would humiliate her, make her realize that he could do with her what he wished. He took her arm and led her through a curtained doorway.

Chandra drew up, staring about her. She had believed the larger chamber was his own, but it was not. Luxury she would not have imagined greeted her eyes. Vivid colors of gold and crimson, and the smell of incense, strangely sweet, filled the chamber. Slender tapers were set in golden-branched holders about the chamber, filling it with soft, shadowy light. There were no furnishings save for a small sandalwood table that stood on delicately carved legs beside a wide bed of flat cushions covered with animal furs. A brass brazier was set beside it, filled with glowing coals for warmth.

Al-Afdal stood watching her. "You are unused to such beauty," he said. "I do not relish returning to Montfort. The Frankish castles are drafty, and all my wealth cannot disguise

their ugliness." He smiled thinly. "But until I know that
Prince Edward and all his men, including your husband, have
been pushed into the sea, it is there we shall stay." He
looked about him with negligent pride. "Tonight, we will
enjoy these comforts."

He looked beyond her and raised a beckoning hand. Chandra
turned about to see the gaunt-faced, silent physician behind
them. She felt a shudder of shame course through her. She
wanted to plead with him not to make her endure this, but she
knew that he would only gloat more were she to beg.

"Take off your clothes and lie upon your back."

Jerval, her mind cried helplessly. Could Graelam not have
said anything, merely followed her here alone? Her fingers
moved clumsily over the golden clasp beneath her breasts.
She felt a tear fall from her eyes and spill down her cheek.
The clasp came loose, and slowly, she loosed the soft drapes
of cloth that covered her breasts.

Al-Afdal felt desire flame in his loins at the sight of her
white breasts, full and soft, their rosy nipples smooth against
her silken flesh. His fingers itched to caress her, to make her
smooth nipples tauten at his touch.

Chandra's hands hovered about the gemmed clasp at her
waist. She felt a numbing dread. Would Jerval still want her
if she was taken by this Saracen? Perhaps death would be her
only salvation, her only escape from al-Afdal. The clasp fell
open. She knew that his eyes were studying her, and she felt
herself quiver in agonized shame as the soft material fell from
her hips to the thick carpet at her feet. She turned away,
unaware that the sight of her white back and full hips gave
al-Afdal as much pleasure as her breasts and belly, and
walked with a hesitant step to the cushioned bed.

She closed her eyes tightly for a long moment, praying she
would not become a quivering, pleading woman, and forced
herself to ease down upon her back, her thighs locked together.

She heard al-Afdal say to the physician, "Quickly, examine her, and be gone." There was an urgency in his voice,
and she knew that he wanted to take her, and quickly. She
felt a hand touch her thigh, and she shuddered. Because she
could not bear to hear his humiliating order, she parted her
legs.

The physician's hands were delicate and curiously gentle as
he probed at her. When his thin finger, slippery with some

kind of ointment, slipped inside her, she felt a crimson veil of shame fall over her. She stiffened, drawing upward, when she felt him deep within her, and al-Afdal pressed his hands on her shoulders to hold her still. When the physician's hand was gone from her, she forced her eyes to open. He was standing over her, but his eyes were upon al-Afdal. He said quietly, "She has been with no man in the past day. The Englishman, Eustace, did not take her."

"She is healthy, without blemish?"

"She is healthy."

"I want many sons from her."

The physician bowed. "She is narrow, but will bear as many sons as you wish."

Al-Afdal waved his hand in dismissal, and the physician bowed again, and backed out of the chamber.

"Are you hungry, Chan-dra?"

She shook her head, and reached for the fur cover. He stilled her hand. "Nay, I wish to look at you."

Al-Afdal stood over her, his eyes on her body as he stripped off his clothes.

"Look at me, Chan-dra," he said, his voice taut with his lust. "I want you to gaze full measure at your new master. I want you to imagine the magnificent sons you will bear me."

"I want you to think only of my hatred for you," she said dully. She let her eyes rove with studied insolence down the hard length of his body. His dark body was lean and wiry, yet hard with bands of sinew and muscle. She felt a wave of revulsion at the black matted hair that covered him. Her eyes fell to his turgid member. "My hatred," she said, "and my pity, for you are scarce a man, I see."

Her taunt, ridiculous in truth, made him tense with fury. She saw that she had angered him, and smiled cruelly. "Must I also lie to you, as I am certain your other women do, and tell you how very magnificent you are?"

No woman had ever in his life scorned his manhood. His first impulse was to beat her until she cried for mercy, and vowed to him that she had lied. He saw the hard coldness in her eyes, and knew that beating her would not have the result he wished. No, he would thrust himself into her soft body until she was raw from him, until he saw tears of pain fill her eyes.

"Open your legs," he spat at her. "Now!"

She struggled against him as he clutched at her thighs and jerked them savagely apart. With a growl of fury, he reared over her and smashed the flat of his palm against her cheek.

The dizzying pain snapped her eyes open, and for an instant, she stared at his mottled, angry face. She forgot his threat to kill Graelam, indeed, forgot everything except her rage. "Filthy savage!" she shrieked at him. She kicked at him with all her strength, and landed her foot squarely in his naked belly. He was thrown off balance, and fell heavily onto his back to the carpet. She picked up the small table, and before he could fling up his hands to protect himself, she crashed it blindly against the side of his head. She was raising the table to strike him again when her mind suddenly cleared, and she stared down at him. He was moaning softly, his eyes closed. There was a gash at his temple, and blood was oozing down the side of his face. Suddenly, he lunged upward, and struck her jaw with his fist, flinging her backward. As she weaved dizzily from the blow, she saw him try to rise, clutching his face, and then fall back, sprawling naked upon his back.

She grabbed at the empty air to save herself, and as she fell, she struck the coal-filled brazier. She heard a soft hiss as the flame-red coals rolled over the silken cushions.

Chandra struggled to her knees, shaking her head to clear her mind, and rubbed her burning eyes. Murky gray smoke swirled about her, and licking flames were curling up behind the cushioned bed, climbing the thin veils to the roof of the tent. She staggered dizzily to her feet and looked down at the Saracen chieftain. Suddenly one of the wooden supports gave way, bringing a flaming cloud of azure material with it. She watched in horror as it crashed down over him.

The heat and smoke were choking her, and she whipped about. She grabbed the thick embroidered cloth that had fallen from the small table, clutched it about her, and lunged toward the veiled entrance of the chamber.

The roaring flames blazed over her head, spreading across the roof with amazing speed. She crouched over in the dense smoke, pressing the edge of the cloth against her face, and struggled forward. She heard women screaming, saw shadows of men running toward the entrance. She dashed past two of al-Afdal's soldiers, but they paid her no heed. They were rushing back to his chamber, intent upon saving their master.

She fell forward onto her knees in the cool night. For a moment, she could not move as her tortured lungs gulped in the clean night air. Even outside the crumbling tent, she could feel the raging heat reaching out toward her. She struggled to her feet and looked wildly about her. Frenzied horses were screaming at the towering flames, and Saracen men and women ran past her, intent upon saving themselves and their belongings.

She had to find Graelam. She looked back at the blazing tent, but remembered that al-Afdal had ordered him taken to Munza's tent. The flames were leaping from the tent roof, orange embers and burning swatches of cloth falling onto the smaller tents around it.

"Graelam!" She screamed out his name as she rushed from one tent to another until her voice was a hoarse whisper. Saracen men slammed into her, but paid her no attention. She pulled back the flap of an outer tent and rushed inside, Graelam's name on her lips. She found him there, struggling frantically against the bonds that held his arms and legs.

He saw her, a white apparition with billowing golden hair, and a strange laugh broke from his throat. "By Christ's blood, Chandra, I should have known that it would be you to bring the heathen to their knees."

She dropped to her knees beside him and quickly unfastened the knots on the rope that bound him. When his arms were free, he worked at the knots at his ankles.

He jumped to his feet, then stood a moment, staring down at her. "Thank you," he said. "Now, I do not wish to join the devil in a heathen camp."

"The horses," she gasped, "they are behind this tent!"

They both whirled about at a cry of rage. Munza stood in the entrance, his eyes burning red from the flames, his scimitar raised. "You!" he spat at her. "You have killed my master!" Hatred for her flowed through him, and an anguished craze for revenge. He lunged forward, readying his scimitar to strike her.

Graelam flung Chandra out of the way. She lurched to her feet, grabbing a clay pot that lay on the earthen floor.

"No!" she screamed, bringing Munza's eyes toward her. She flung the pot at his chest. As Munza stumbled backward, Graelam lunged at him, crashing his mighty fist against the side of his head. The scimitar went flying from his hand and he slumped to the ground.

"Graelam!" she yelled, pulling frantically at his arm. For a moment, his mind was locked against her and he smashed his fist again against the Saracen's face.

"The tent is on fire!"

Graelam smelled the bitter smoke and tore himself away from the Saracen. He grabbed the scimitar, and together, he and Chandra rushed from the flaming tent.

The horses had broken free, and were galloping from the camp through the masses of men and women. Chandra saw a man with his clothes aflame, running in blind frenzy and pain. Graelam jerked her back as a maddened stallion galloped in front of them, flinging clots of dirt in their faces. He tried to clear his mind of the raging spectacle about them, and plan their escape. He grabbed Chandra's hand and pulled her with him toward the cliffs, away from the people and the trampling horses.

Jerval felt a numbing band of pain in his chest. His eyes followed Payn's shout and pointing finger.

The dark sky was cast in orange. "It is the Saracen camp," he heard himself croak.

"By Christ, we are too late!"

Jerval did not hear Roger de Clifford's voice. He kicked his spurs into his destrier's side and pushed him across the plain toward the eerie orange glow in the sky. He heard Payn's shouts behind him, a battle cry to the fifty men that followed.

They thundered into the camp, their swords ready to strike, but the Saracens fled away from them, leaving whatever they could not carry.

Jerval drew his destrier to a halt in the center of the camp, his eyes burning from the acrid smoke, straining to find Chandra. He saw the huge tent, collapsed on itself. "Jesus, no!" he prayed, and spurred his horse toward it.

He drew up at a roaring shout." Jerval!"

It was not Graelam that held Jerval's frantic eyes, but the sight of a girl wrapped in white, golden hair swirling about her face, clutched close to Graelam.

Jerval yelled over his shoulder as he pointed toward Chandra and Graelam, "Stay close to me, then fan out!"

Graelam saw a crazed horse veering toward them. He slammed Chandra against the cliff, covering her body with his. He splayed his hands on either side of her, flattening her against the rocks to protect her. He felt her heart pounding against his breast.

"If we are to die, Chandra," he said, pressing his cheek against her temple, "I would that we not meet our maker as enemies."

"You risked your life for me, Graelam. That alone must make me forgive your . . . ruthlessness at Croyland."

To Chandra's numb surprise, Graelam laughed. "It has come to me, my lady, that had I succeeded in claiming you then, we would have likely killed each other. You are not a restful woman, Chandra." She felt his shrug against her. "Jerval has won you at last, has he not?"

"Aye," she said, choking down a sob. "But you mistake it, Graelam. It is I who have finally won him."

He held her pressed tightly against him, closing out the din of noise about them. Chandra struggled to look beyond him. He heard her say in a strangely calm voice, "Jerval is here. We will be all right now."

He whipped about to see Jerval and a dozen men forming a barrier around them. "Aye, Chandra," he said, shaking his head in disbelieving relief, "we are safe now." He stepped back, allowing Chandra to see what was happening. She did not move, even now that the danger was past, merely stared toward her husband as he shouted orders and rode toward them.

"Chandra?"

"My lord," she whispered. She seemed to shudder, then with a cry, she rushed toward him. Jerval caught her in his arms.

He looked over her head at Graelam, who stood silently, watching.

To his surprise, Graelam smiled. "Your wife and I," he said, "are very relieved to see you."

Jerval nuzzled Chandra's head with his chin. "Are you glad to see me, wife?"

He was again held in surprise when she looked up at him, her face streaked with black soot, and burst into tears. He tightened his arms about her back, and felt the cloth that covered her begin to slip.

"I cannot have you naked, love," he whispered into her sooty hair. He forced himself to release her for a moment, pulled off his mantle, and wrapped it about her. She hiccupped as she tried to swallow her tears, and he laughed, a deep rich sound, filled with relief.

"Come, Chandra, there will be no fighting here tonight. Let us go home." He lifted her into his arms and set her upon his destrier. He turned back to Graelam, and said softly, "You have saved what I hold dearest on this earth. I thank you, my lord."

Graelam grinned, and gave Jerval a self-mocking bow. "Even though you see her crying now, like a weak woman, my hide would be naught but fodder for the desert if not for her. It galls me, but it is she who has saved me twice."

"My sword is sheathed, Graelam de Moreton."

"And mine also, Jerval de Vernon."

The two men grinned when Chandra said loudly, her voice indignant, "I am not a weak woman!"

"You can be weak or strong," Jerval called to her, "just so long as you are alive." He turned back to Graelam. "Let us get out of this place. I wish to come no closer to hell."

"Aye," Graelam said, "but the devil of this hell died in his own flames this night."

21

CHANDRA STOOD BESIDE JERVAL AT the harbor mole, a thick breakwater of sandstone, watching their provisions being hauled aboard their ships. The sun was like a bright white ball overhead, and the day, as always, was unmercifully hot.

"You do not look very happy," he said.

"I am afraid I will be ill again."

"Nay, not this time. The sea is calm." He reached inside his tunic and drew out a small parchment square. "Sir Elvan gave me some medicine for you, just in case."

Chandra smiled at Sir Elvan's thoughtfulness. "I think he is the one I will miss. He is a kind man."

"He accompanied Edward, with, of course, his own physicians in tow, to Caesarea for the signing of the treaty."

"I saw Edward this morning. He seems to have thrown off his depression, and is looking stronger."

"Edward has realized that the treaty is not so meaningless an accomplishment." He suddenly pulled her to him and gave her a great hug. "Do not," he whispered fiercely, "ever again get yourself abducted. I found a gray hair in my head this morning, doubtless there from worry."

"I swear," she said, nuzzling her cheek against his shoulder. "I know of no other Alan Durwalds to take me by force from Camberley."

He held her silently, then gave a tug on her long braid to make her look up at him. "If Mary's letter is to be believed, you, my love, will not even have anyone to fight with. Mother, it seems, has grown positively benign under Lady Alice's influence."

"Give her one day with me," Chandra said, laughing.

"Perhaps by the time we reach Camberley, your belly will not be so flat. Your carrying my heir would make her more than pleasant toward you."

346

"But there will be no privacy aboard our ship!"

"I spoke to Payn. Poor Payn, I suppose I should say. We will have sufficient privacy so you should not forget the pleasures of lying with your husband. Payn will have the same courtesy." He saw that she was embarrassed, and said in a soft, teasing voice, "Do not worry, my love, that anyone will hear you moaning. I will clamp my hand over your mouth."

She flushed, and he grinned widely. "Jerval," she said suddenly, "I do not know how I will . . . that is, what will happen to me when we are home again?"

"I will bully you and love you," he said promptly.

"Nay, do not jest. Our life has been so different here."

"When you are not heavy with child, we will doubtless argue about what is proper for you and what isn't." He saw that she was still frowning, and added quietly, "I believe that at least you and I have learned that we can disagree, and not rant at each other. You may be certain, Chandra, that our children all will know that my wife saved my worthless hide in the Holy Land."

She smiled, but briefly. "I never wish to look upon blood and death again," she said quietly. "I shall never forget the horror of it, and my fear for you."

It was on the tip of his tongue to tell her how pleased he was that she had finally come to her senses, but he was wiser with her now. Nor did he tell her that he loved to fight, if his opponents were soldiers, and not innocent women and children. Aloud, he said only, "Always fear for me, Chandra. It will make me all the more careful."

"I think I shall become a great diplomat, so that I can keep you safe with me."

"Unfortunately, greed is a vice few men escape. I will fight, you know, to keep what is ours."

She appeared to accept his words. "Speaking of greed, have you decided what we will say about Eustace?"

"That he died honorably. There is no reason to let his treachery be known. Julianna will not be too saddened, I vow, though my father will have to find her another likely husband, if he hasn't already."

"How can she ever really be happy, my lord? She wanted you, after all."

"How do you know she didn't have me?" he said coolly.

But it was not Julianna's face that rose in her mind, it was Beri's. "If ever you touch another woman, Jerval," she said, her laughing voice tinged with bitter memory, "I shall do something terrible to you." She added, throwing back her head, "And I shall not look at Graelam de Moreton with anything save gratitude."

He knew her too well to do anything save laugh. "Mary, thank God, gave birth to a girl," he said. He shook his head and said ruefully, "Graelam will be the only noble to leave Palestine with great wealth. Al-Afdal's treasure trove, what remained from the fire, was an unbelievable find."

"You accepted the jewels he offered you?"

"Aye, and the rubies will adorn your white neck."

"Look yon, Jerval," Chandra said, pointing toward the open seaward gates of Acre.

"The Christians of the city are gathering to bid us farewell."

It was probably the only time, Chandra thought, that Templars had stood next to Hospitalers in temporary truce, and Genoese next to Venetians. Now, thanks to Edward, they would have ten years to bicker and fight among themselves, without threat from the Saracens. A resigned King Hugh had bid them goodbye a week before and returned to Cyprus to continue the endless arguments with his barons.

She saw John de Vescy limp aboard his ship, Roger de Clifford at his side. Jerval laced his fingers through hers. "Lambert is waving to us, Chandra. It is time to leave."

She gazed one last time toward Acre. She saw a veiled woman atop the wall, her hand raised. Beri, she wondered, though she could not be certain. Aye, she thought, smiling sadly to herself, I am the lucky one. I am free.

Chandra turned to see Eleanor smiling at her, the babe, Joan, in her arms.

"You will take care, Chandra," Eleanor said softly. "It will be some time before I see you again. As you know, my lord has no wish to return to England immediately. We are to see more of the world."

"I will write to you, Eleanor."

"I pray that you will. My lord's heart is heavy, and I will need happy news to cheer him."

"I trust that I will have only happy news to tell you," Chandra said, smiling toward her husband. She hugged Eleanor, touched her fingertip lightly beneath the baby's dimpled chin, and straightened.

"I am glad, Chandra," Eleanor said, "that you and he at last found your way, together."

"I assure you, Eleanor, that I will not let him tread any other way."

"Chandra," Jerval called.

She threw her arms around him when she reached him, and hugged him fiercely.

"What is this, wife?" Jerval murmured in her ear. "Are you so hungry for me that you must needs attack me in the light of day before every Christian in Acre?"

"Nay," she whispered against his throat, "I am merely showing everyone that you are mine. I have won you."

"I have been trying to tell you that for the longest time, my lady. Do you not remember my telling you that the de Vernons are a stubborn lot?"

"Aye, I remember," she said.

He took her hand and tugged her forward. "Let us go home, Chandra, to England and to Camberley."

About the Author

When best-selling Regency and historical romance writer Catherine Coulter is not at work on her latest novel, set in mid-nineteenth-century Victorian England, Rome, and New York, she spends her time sailing, playing the piano, or enjoying San Francisco with her husband, Anton.

Catherine Coulter is the author of another historical novel, *Devil's Embrace*, as well as several Regency romances—*The Autumn Countess, The Rebel Bride, Lord Deverill's Heir, Lord Harry's Folly, The Generous Earl, An Honorable Offer, An Intimate Deception*—available in Signet editions.

Great Reading from SIGNET

*Prices slightly higher in Canada

**Buy them at your local
bookstore or use coupon
on next page for ordering.**

Fabulous Fiction from SIGNET